We hope you enjoy this book. Please return or renew it by the due date.

You can renew it at www.norfolk.gov.uk/libraries or by using our free library app.

Otherwise you can phone 0344 800 8020 - please have your library card and PIN ready.

You can sign up for email reminders too.

# ALSO BY ALEXANDRA BELL

**Frozen Charlotte**
*Frozen Charlotte*
*Charlotte Says*

**Lex Trent**
*Lex Trent Versus the Gods*
*Lex Trent Fighting with Fire*

**The Polar Bear Explorers' Club series**
*The Polar Bear Explorers' Club*
*Explorers of Witch Mountain*
*Explorers of Black Ice Bridge*
*The Ocean Squid Explorers' Club*

*The Ninth Circle*
*Jasmyn*
*The Haunting*
*Music and Malice in Hurricane Town*
*A Most Peculiar Toy Factory*

# THE
# WINTER
# GARDEN

## ALEXANDRA BELL

1 3 5 7 9 10 8 6 4 2

Del Rey
20 Vauxhall Bridge Road
London SW1V 2SA

Del Rey is part of the Penguin Random House group of companies whose
addresses can be found at global.penguinrandomhouse.com.

First published in the UK by Del Rey in 2021

www.penguin.co.uk

A CIP catalogue record for this book is available from the British Library.

HB ISBN 9781529100822
TP ISBN 9781529100839

Typeset in 12/16.5 pt Dante MT Pro
by Integra Software Services Pvt. Ltd, Pondicherry

Printed and bound in Great Britain by Clays Ltd, Elcograf S.p.A.

The authorised representative in the EEA is Penguin Random House
Ireland, Morrison Chambers, 32 Nassau Street, Dublin D02 YH68.

Penguin Random House is committed to a sustainable future for
our business, our readers and our planet. This book is made from
Forest Stewardship Council® certified paper.

*For my cousin, Hayley Switzer-Willrich.*

*Becoming mothers in 2020 may have had its challenges, but we weathered the storm with our beautiful little boys.*

# PROLOGUE

They say gardens are good for the soul, and the magical Winter Garden most of all. You'll never find it in one place for long. It goes where it is needed, appearing from nothing and vanishing just as quickly. Some days you might spot it high in the mountains of Nepal; on others it will materialise in the mists of Mongolia. During the summer it may choose to settle for a spell in the rolling green fields of England, or shrink down for the winter to squeeze into the inside of a teacup.

The garden is a place of wonder and magic in a world that often has so little of both. Full of strange birds and impossible flowers, mushrooms that dance with you and trees that whisper secrets, frog music and frosted fairies in their finest fur coats.

Nobody knows how it came to be – only that it belongs to the elusive Spider Queen, about whom almost as little is known as about the garden itself. She decides where the garden should go and who should be invited to see it. By all accounts she has an affinity for the lost and the lonely, the misfits and the misunderstood, the broken and the bereft, the heartsore and the hurting.

Certainly those who claim to have seen the garden say that it appeared to them in their darkest, bleakest moments, when they were most in need of its soft lights and scented delights, its compassion and kindness for all lost souls. Beatrice Anne Sitwell was eight years old the first time she discovered the garden. Or, more accurately, when it discovered her. It was already a day to remember, because it was the day her mother died.

'Do you understand what I'm telling you, Beatrice?' her father had said that morning in the parlour. The circles beneath his eyes looked like bruises, the smallest sound made him wince, as if he were the one who was ill, and he gazed through her with raw, unseeing eyes. 'Your mother is at the end,' he went on. 'She wishes to see you. To say goodbye.'

Beatrice did not understand, not truly, but thanks to her recent operation, she could not utter a word and so the questions piled up in a smouldering heap at the end of her useless tongue. *The end of what?*

She wished she could simply remain in the parlour, playing with her mother's key collection. Beatrice loved the keys. Some were larger than the palm of her hand, whilst others were tiny enough to open a fairy door. They were made of brass, and silver, and iron, and gold. Her mother had said she liked to imagine there was a story that went with each key, and that the key itself still knew what that was, even if everyone else had long since forgotten.

Instead, a maid was summoned and Beatrice was hurried away so quickly she did not even have time to replace the silver key she'd last been playing with. She slipped it into her pocket unnoticed. She was taken upstairs to have her hair combed, her hands cleaned and her dress brushed free of wrinkles. For some reason, it seemed to be important that she look her best before being presented to her mother.

After months of not being allowed anywhere near the sickroom, it felt fearsomely strange to be ushered over the threshold into the moist, sticky sickliness of its walls. Beatrice gripped the key in her pocket as a sort of talisman. The curtains were drawn and the windows tightly closed, so as not to allow in any harmful sunlight or fresh air. Beatrice suddenly longed to be outside, hunting for mushrooms. It was a pulsing hot day, and the smell within the room was dreadful. It reminded her of the time her nanny had shown her the sticky black stem-bleeds upon a majestic old oak's trunk and told her it meant the tree was rotting from the inside out. Knowing that Beatrice had a fascination for plants and animals, her nanny probably thought she would find this interesting, but instead Beatrice had wept at the news, and grieved for the tree as it slowly declined.

'Go on,' her father said now, giving her a little push. 'She's waiting for you.'

Beatrice walked slowly towards the four-poster bed, which had all its curtains drawn. Her indoor shoes seemed to creak too loudly on the floorboards and the room appeared to stretch and stretch ahead of her, so that it took an eternity to reach the bed.

By the time she arrived, she'd forgotten her injured tongue and tried to say her mother's name, but only a hoarse rasp came out.

'Do not try to talk,' her father said from the shadows behind her. 'Your mother knows you are incapable.'

Beatrice wondered how she was supposed to say goodbye when she could not speak and might never do so again. It made her heart ache to think that speech could be a power forever consigned to her past. She had so many questions about the world – and if she couldn't ask them, then how would she ever learn its many secrets? Yet, in spite of the circumstances, she longed to see her mother. It had been so long since she'd been permitted to visit. And even if she could not talk, at least she would be able to feel the warmth of her mother's hand and the reassuring squeeze of her fingers. She could bury her face in her shoulder and breathe in the scent of her *Otto of Roses* perfume.

Her hand trembled with yearning as she reached out to draw back the drape. It slid aside on clanging rings – only to reveal an imposter in her mother's place. The skeletal woman with waxy skin propped up against the pillows was not Beatrice's lovely mama. The sinew stood out in her neck, and the bones showed through her skin, and her eyes were chasms that led somewhere dreadful.

Beatrice jerked back and looked to her father for an explanation as to who this stranger might be, but he was staring at the floor rather than at her. Her hand squeezed so tightly around the key in her pocket that it was in danger of piercing her skin.

'It's all right, Beatrice,' the woman said.

Beatrice flinched. It was her mother's voice, and yet how could it be coming from this wraith, this absolute nightmare of a person?

'Come here, Beatrice.' The imposter reached out her claw.

The truth was too dreadful to accept and Beatrice took a step back, shaking her head.

'Oh, please, darling.' Her mother's face crumpled, like a paper doll abandoned in the rain. 'Please . . .'

Beatrice turned on her heel and fled the room. She ducked her father's outstretched hand but couldn't avoid her mother's cry of grief. It only spurred her on faster. She ran along the corridor, down the staircase, through another hallway and out into the freedom of the garden. She ran and ran, and kept on running until she reached her favourite oak tree and climbed up high into its branches where she wouldn't be found, even if anyone came looking for her.

Nobody did. She stayed there by herself for hours, with nothing to do except listen to the birds singing, count the leaves on the nearby branches or gaze down at the bright-yellow spread of *Exidia glandulosa* – witches' butter fungus – flourishing on a piece of rotting log below.

She wished she had brought her notebook. She could have jotted down notes and drawings and ideas for the garden then. When her mother was well again, they were going to design and build it together. It would be a special place, just for the two of them, full of the most beautiful climbing roses and blooming chrysanthemums and fragrant lilies. Beatrice hoped it might also have magical things in it like fairies, and her mother had said that if they made it pretty enough and welcoming enough, then they would surely come.

Beatrice loved to draw and had started sketching ideas for it already, but with her notebook back at the house, she had only the key from her mother's collection to play with. She tried to imagine it was a magic key that might take her far away from her home and into a world where people did not get ill and die.

Finally she tired of the game and slipped the key back into her pocket. She wished that her father would come looking for her, that he would spot her up in the tree and speak gently to her from below, perhaps persuade her to come down so that he could wrap his arms around her and they could comfort one another. He had never done anything of the kind before, but she still hoped. Her mother was the only person who ever embraced her, and Beatrice knew, deep down, that this would not happen ever again. She shivered, despite the heat of the day.

An hour later someone finally came, but it wasn't Lord Sitwell. Beatrice heard the rustling of leaves and the creaking of branches and looked down to see a dark-haired boy climbing nimbly up the tree. James Sheppard was a couple of years older than her and spent even more time outdoors than she did. His father was Half Moon House's head gardener, and James was due to become his apprentice very soon. Beatrice's nanny had explained that this meant they were not allowed to be friends, because one did not become friends with servants. And yet Beatrice liked James because he loved plants and animals as much as she did. He did not chastise Beatrice for being too strange, or too quiet, or getting the game wrong, or saying awkward things, as her cousins so often seemed to do. It didn't appear to matter to him that she was not like other children.

Before the operation on her tongue, James had been the one person Beatrice could speak to without stammering. Of course the first time she had ever spoken to him she had stammered as badly as usual and had braced herself, waiting for his sneers and ridicule, but they never came. He simply waited patiently for her to get out whatever she was trying to say, and then responded normally, as if the stammer was nothing remarkable at all. Pretty quickly Beatrice had ceased to do so in front of him altogether, unless there was someone else around.

'Hello, Beatrice,' he said now, as he dragged himself up to her level.

She offered no reply, but James didn't seem to mind as he wedged himself into the small gap beside her on the branch. He was a gangly shape, all knobbly knees and elbows. His skin was browned by the sun, since he had no nanny to be forever wrestling him into a sunhat or compelling him to stay within the shelter of the shadows.

They sat together in silence for a while before James said, 'I'm sorry about your mama.'

Beatrice shrugged.

'It's all right if you don't want to talk about it,' he said. 'Once your tongue heals, I mean. I wouldn't, either. But if you ever do, then I'm here.'

It never seemed to occur to James that Beatrice's tongue might never heal. Whenever she felt the cold fear that she might never utter another word again, James's confidence that she would certainly recover made her feel just a little better.

'Look,' he said. 'I thought you might like to see this.'

He reached into his pocket and carefully drew out a small, pearly white snail. Beatrice's nanny didn't care for snails, but James thought they were more interesting than butterflies. He had told her that there were over a hundred different types in the United Kingdom alone, and more than forty thousand in the world. He intended to see every single one for himself one day.

'I haven't found this sort in the garden before,' he said, carefully setting it down on a branch between them.

Beatrice hadn't, either, and was pleased that he had come to show her. Her pleasure didn't always show on her solemn face, though, and a moment later James said quietly, 'I thought maybe you might like some company, but it's all right if you don't – just nod your head and I'll go.'

Beatrice glanced at him. His brown eyes were the colour of chestnuts and normally held a look of mischief, but today they seemed serious and a little sad. The bare skin of his arm was warm where it brushed against her. His presence took some of the weight off the ache in her chest, so she shook her head and patted the tree, trying to indicate that she wanted him to stay.

'Right you are,' James said, leaning back against the trunk and crossing one booted foot over the other.

They sat together quietly for a while, watching the snail make its slow journey towards a leaf. Eventually the minutes turned into hours. James was not made for sitting still and fidgeted beside her, but he didn't leave. Beatrice later wondered whether he would have stayed in the tree all night if she'd done so.

Finally, though, the light powdered into dusk and she needed to use the bathroom so badly that she knew she had no choice but to return to the house. She tapped

James on the shoulder and pointed at the ground to indicate she was going down. He scrambled to help her, which she appreciated as her legs had gone to sleep. Soon they both stood beneath the tree, whereupon James dropped to one knee to retie a loose shoelace.

'When my mama died,' he said, without looking up, 'the adults were always saying that it would get easier.'

Beatrice knew that James's mother was dead, but he never talked about her and she was surprised to hear him do so now.

'That was a while ago,' he went on. 'And it's still . . . well, I miss her. And I hate that she's not here. I feel like there's a big central piece that's been ripped out of me. I think the grown-ups lie to try to make you feel better, but it isn't true. It doesn't get easier. But you do get stronger. And that's . . . well. It's something.'

Beatrice nodded. She was grateful to him for telling the truth, and for staying with her. She wished she could remain in the garden with James and the snails forever, but it was time to return to the house and the reality of whatever had happened there over the last few hours. Beatrice knew it would be nothing good. So she raised her hand in goodbye and made her way back across the grounds. The flowers were closing up their petals for the evening and the purple sky became a vast ballroom for the bats.

As soon as she stepped inside, Beatrice knew that her mother was dead. The house was loud with the echoing silence of dozens of stopped clocks, and every mirror was covered or turned to face the walls. After using the bathroom, she tried to slip away to her bedroom, but the servants must have been told to keep watch for her because she was soon summoned to her father's study.

'I am ashamed to call you my daughter today, Beatrice,' he said in a voice as cold and hard as iron. 'Refusing to say goodbye to your own mother. You wicked child! Because of you, she left this earth broken-hearted. I hope you are pleased with yourself.'

Beatrice did not think it could be possible to feel more wretched. She suspected her wickedness had torn right through her soul, ripping her neatly in half – the final page of a story that no longer made sense and could never be finished.

'She wrote a letter for you.' Her father held out an envelope with Beatrice's name written on it in her mother's elegant handwriting. 'Although why she should waste her final effort doing so, I cannot for the life of me fathom. Take it. And get out of my sight.'

Beatrice reluctantly took the letter, and the paper felt somehow hot beneath her fingers. Her father dismissed her into the care of a maid, who escorted her upstairs to change into one of the itchy new mourning gowns that had been waiting in the wardrobe for several months. How Beatrice loathed the sight of them. The letter was even worse. Beatrice felt suddenly furious with her mother.

If she had wanted to tell her something, then she should not have died.

Once the maid had gone, Beatrice seized the letter, then ran down to the parlour to fetch her mother's box of keys. Clutching them both close, she went out to the little wishing well in the grounds. It was dark by now, but Beatrice knew the way perfectly. She and her mother had come here often and it had always felt like a special place.

She emptied the keys into the well, listening to them clink and clang as they knocked against the mossed bricks all the way down. Then she looked at the letter still clutched in her hand and threw it in after the keys, as forcefully as she could. Tears filled her eyes as she watched it drift slowly down into the darkness, where she knew it would be swallowed up by the chilled water and would slowly disintegrate. Her heart overflowed with a miserable sense of grim satisfaction at the idea that she had punished her mother somehow.

She trudged back to the house to find that the servants had finished preparing it for mourning and had retreated to their other world below stairs – that boisterous, comforting place, full of busyness and chatter and squabbling and laughter. It was quite forbidden to Beatrice. For reasons she did not completely understand, her realm must forever be the chilly, lonely grandeur of the upstairs rooms – like a cursed princess continually doomed to her frozen tower.

Her nanny had recently returned home for a family emergency and so Beatrice was left quite alone. All of a sudden she found herself frightened by the strange, heavy silence that hung over the house like an angel's broken wing. She was frightened of the room where her mother's body lay. She was frightened she would go to hell for refusing to say goodbye to her. She was frightened that nothing would ever be the same again.

She went up to the day-nursery where her motley collection of pets waited. Her nanny did not approve of them at all, and Beatrice wondered with despair whether she would be allowed to keep them now that her mother was gone. There were three tame mice, a rabbit and a hedgehog with an injured foot – the only friends she had in the world, except for James.

Beatrice longed to talk to her animals, but her swollen tongue ached and ached inside her mouth. When she tried to whisper comforting words to the hedgehog, clots of blood dribbled out from between her lips. So she remained silent, and the rest of the house seemed to forget all about her until later that evening, when a maid brought up a dinner tray. They'd overlooked her ruined tongue, and the fact that she could only eat mashed food or soup, so Beatrice let the meal go cold upon its plate. Eventually she went to the night-nursery and lay in her petticoats upon the bed, trying to remain completely still in the hot, sticky August air. She was bone-tired but sleep wouldn't come, eluding her as stubbornly as a sly-faced fox.

Her mind was ablaze with the worry that perhaps the servants might have missed one of the mirrors in the house and that her mother's spirit would get trapped behind the glass. The thought of it appalled her beyond all reason. What a cold, strange world of nightmares it must be on the other side of a mirror, doomed to stare back forever at the life that had been taken from you. Certainly no place for her mother, with her beautiful gowns, and lustrous eyes, and joyful laugh.

She had been ill for some time but, still, it did not seem possible that she could be dead. It did not seem possible that Beatrice would never see her again. It did not seem possible that her mama would not sweep into her room at any moment to embrace her, uncover the mirror, start the clock and chuckle over how foolish everyone had been. But nobody came and the house echoed with the choked silence of all those suffocating clocks.

Finally, though, Beatrice must have slept because she awoke to the ringing of chimes. She gasped, dismayed that a clock had been missed and might prevent her mama's spirit from moving on. And yet . . . as the chimes continued to ring, they seemed to be coming from outside, which made no sense – the only timepiece out there was the permanently silent sundial. Not only that, but she was sure she counted thirteen chimes.

The next moment her room filled with a powder-blue light. She sat bolt upright and stared around the nursery. It was transformed. Dozens of ice roses wound around the posts of her bed, each petal as clear and cold as glass, their thorns like crystal, their stems sparkling in a layer of frost as fine as lace. Strange flowers hung down from the ceiling, shaped like trumpets, casting a blue glow over everything, from the rocking horse in the corner to the doll's house on the shelf. Leaves and branches crowded the open nursery window, which was barred for safety, but the trees still managed to poke their fingers of twig through the gaps.

Some snow had blown in too. Beatrice saw it piled up in drifts in the corners of the room, despite the roasting heat of the day and the fact that everyone complained almost constantly about how it was one of the longest, hottest summers they could remember.

But there the snow and the ice roses were, twinkling and sparkling in the soft, pine-scented light. Beatrice scrambled to the edge of the bed and touched a rose, felt the icy kiss of its petals, before hurrying over to the snow itself. It was the coldest, softest powder – perfect for snowmen and sleigh bells, frost fairs and plum puddings. The flowers filled the room with the scent of winter and fairy tales.

She raced to the window, but the leaves crowding the frame were so thick that she couldn't see properly through to the outside and could only make out the occasional flicker of lantern light beyond. She could hear the garden, though – strange songbirds calling to one another in the darkness, toads croaking, fountains splashing and perhaps even a tiger's roar.

She turned back into the room and froze. A white frog sat on her bed, holding a letter in its mouth and staring straight at her with bulging black eyes. Beatrice's nanny shrieked whenever they saw a frog in the garden, but Beatrice loved them and had always enjoyed collecting frogspawn and hatching the froglets. She'd never come across a frog like this one before, though. It almost seemed to glow in the dark. And it wore a pale golden crown.

When Beatrice looked at the envelope in its mouth, she saw her name printed there, so she slowly reached out and took hold of it with her finger and thumb. The frog released it at once and hopped away to settle itself upon her pillow.

Beatrice turned her eyes to the envelope in her hands. Her full name was written across the front in an elegant script, and the back was sealed with a purple wax crest sporting an emblem of a frog wearing a crown. Flowers entwined all the way up the back of the letter, and songbirds and spiders graced the loops of her name. Beatrice opened the envelope and a white ticket fell out into her hands:

*Dear Beatrice,*

*You are cordially invited to*
*the Winter Garden.*
*Open only at thirteen o'clock.*
*Should you care to attend, simply follow the*
*dancing mushrooms.*

*Fondest regards,*
*The Spider Queen*

Beatrice stared at the words for barely a moment before shoving the invitation inside her pocket and grabbing a coat from the wardrobe. She stuffed her feet into shoes and socks as she stumbled towards the door. She had no idea where her gloves and winter bonnet were kept, so she snatched up her mourning parasol instead.

She threw open the door of her bedroom and immediately saw a single golden mushroom glowing in the corridor beyond. Before her eyes, another one sprouted a little further down the corridor – growing up right out of the parquet floor – and then another and another. They ran all the way to the staircase, as if they were guiding her out of the house. As soon as she laid eyes on them, they began to twirl gently on the spot, like spinning tops.

Beatrice hurried down the corridor. The golden mushrooms led her to the second floor, where she took the Adam and Eve staircase to the ground level. The mushrooms suddenly uprooted themselves and danced along the floor beside her, casting golden glitters over the Sèvres vases and glinting off the rotting fruit and withered flowers of the Dutch still-life paintings upon the walls.

Finally they led Beatrice right to the Winter Smoking Room on the ground floor. She fumbled with the bolts and, at last, threw open the door and stumbled out onto the veranda. No stuffy summer air embraced her – instead, the world beyond the house was cold and crisp as a fresh-fallen autumn apple.

Beatrice took it in and gaped. All afternoon her guilt and grief had been as ravenous as twin black rats, gnawing away at her insides, but she forgot them when faced with the spectacle of the twinkling garden before her. The skeletal trees proudly wore their winter crowns and glass lanterns hung from bare branches, flickering like something from a fairy world. The air smelled of snow, and magic, and steaming cups of hot chocolate. Beatrice ran down the steps into it, her boots crunching in deep drifts of perfect white snow, her breath fogging the air before her.

It seemed as though she spent many hours exploring the magical garden, and yet when the ice clock rang for closing time there were thirteen chimes just as before, and the sky did not appear to have lightened at all. It was almost as if the garden existed in its own little pocket of time and none had passed whilst she'd been gone.

Beatrice reluctantly returned to the house with the taste of drinking chocolate melting on her tongue and her fingers sticky from sugarplums. By the time she reached her bedroom and went to the window, now empty of leaves, the Winter Garden had vanished.

She turned away and set down the tiny snowman she'd brought from the garden, placing it on her toy shelf beside the beribboned dolls and stuffed teddies. The snowman was small enough to have been built by goblins and wore a velvet top hat. Shining raisins formed his mischievous dark eyes. He had a miniature pipe in his mouth, which he continued to smoke even after Beatrice set him on the shelf, filling her room with a tobacco scent bursting with bonfires and toffee apples and cinnamon spice.

The garden had disappeared and the room seemed to be growing warmer, but her pillow still smelled faintly of frogs and frosted visions, and she fell asleep that night with a smile on her face.

By the time the maid came to wake her the next morning, the snow and ice roses were long gone, the bedroom was sticky and hot once again, and the only sign of the snowman was a damp pile of raisins, a tiny hat and a pipe that smelled faintly of toffee. But they were enough. They were a promise to Beatrice that the garden was real. She had not dreamed or imagined it; it had existed and she had been there, wrapped up in the swirling cape of its magic.

She longed to tell someone about what she had seen, but she still couldn't speak and, besides, there was no one to tell. Her father kept to his rooms when he wasn't watching over her mother's body, and the servants were too busy with their household duties.

The day passed in a vacuum. Not only was there no sound inside the house, but there was no life in it, either. Beatrice couldn't stand it and spent most of her day out in the grounds, searching for mushroom rings and trying not to think about her mama. There was no sign of James and she hoped he hadn't got into trouble with his father for the time he'd spent with her the day before. She longed to confide in him, but his apprenticeship had started and she knew he was busy weeding, raking, scything, stoking the stovehouse boilers, hoeing borders and a myriad of other tasks that had to be recorded in the Garden Day Book each evening.

When night fell, she hardly dared hope she would see the garden again, but once more she woke to thirteen chimes. They'd barely stopped echoing before she ran outside into the lantern-lit garden.

When her nanny returned the next day, she scolded Beatrice for losing her mourning parasol. Beatrice tried to explain in writing that it had been eaten by a strange tree in a magic garden, but her nanny thought she was making up stories and boxed her ears to teach her a lesson.

Beatrice visited the magic garden every night for seven evenings in a row. Each time she would see different wonders and return with some new treasure – the tooth of a tree, or a tiger's whisker, or a shining apple with black skin, dark and sweet as secrets. On the seventh night the Spider Queen tried to offer Beatrice a gift that she did not want and, without even waiting for the ice clock to chime, Beatrice practically fled back to the sanctuary of her bedroom.

On the eighth day her mother was carried from the house feet-first inside her coffin. After she had been safely laid in the ground, the servants started the clocks up once again and the mirrors were all uncovered.

Beatrice sat on her bed that night, dressed in her coat and boots, but the garden did not come. No clock chimed the thirteenth hour and her room did not fill with ice roses. When she went to the window she saw that the grounds remained unchanged – there was no luminous snow upon the summer-scorched lawn, no flicker of candlelight, no butterfly wings, no frog music, no sparkling tiger. The Winter Garden had vanished, taking its magic with it.

Beatrice took out the box hidden in her wardrobe, filled with the treasures she'd collected from the garden – all that remained to her now of its magic. She wondered whether she ought to have taken the Spider Queen's final gift after all, but no. How could she? It was the last thing she had ever wanted to see, and she was glad it had gone forever. Finally her eye fell upon the black apple. Fruit contained seeds, from which new trees would grow. Could it be that she had managed to save a small piece of the magic after all?

Her hand tightened around it as hope flared in her chest. Her mother might be gone for good, but Beatrice promised herself that, whatever it took, she would see the garden again one day.

# Part One

# CHAPTER ONE

*June 1836*

Seventeen years had passed since Beatrice last saw the magical Winter Garden. After her tongue had healed (as much as it was ever going to), she'd tried to speak of it a couple of times, but no one had ever believed her. Even the black apple trees did not convince her father, who insisted the strange seeds must have been dropped by passing birds flying in from abroad.

When Beatrice persisted with her tales, he finally sent for doctors who talked of unsound minds, female hysteria and trauma brought on by grief. The treatments seemed more like punishments, so Beatrice retracted her story, admitting that she'd made it all up for attention. Anything to make the doctors go away, to escape their penetrating gazes, pitiless and cold-eyed as reptiles. The garden would simply have to remain a treasured memory for her, one that she occasionally took out to silently marvel over, holding it as carefully as one of her beloved children's books filled with fairy tales and happy endings.

That afternoon she sat in the White Drawing Room of Raven Hall, frowning down at the blood opal on her ring finger. Her fiancé, Eustace Hamilton, Duke of Chalkley, had placed it there when he made her the envy of all her acquaintances four months ago, but still she was not accustomed to it, found its weight strange and unwelcome, like a devil's eye staring insolently back at her.

'*The bad-luck stone*,' her lady's maid had whispered, looking aghast when she first saw it. Remembering herself, the girl had quickly apologised and haltingly attempted to admire the ring, but it was the first sentiment that had been true to her heart.

Against the black silk of Beatrice's mourning gown, the stone seemed to glow redder and hotter, full of sparks and fireworks and erupting volcanoes. She knew that opals were considered unlucky by many, but this ring had been in Eustace's family for centuries, worn by generations of bejewelled, beautiful duchesses. And superstitions aside, it wasn't the ring that was the problem. It wasn't even the man. It was the proposal itself.

At twenty-five, Beatrice knew she was not like other women. Her heart did not flutter when a man placed his hand on her waist at a dance. She had never longed for any particular gentleman to glance her way. Love poems left her as cold as the mossed, marble statues in her home's manicured gardens.

She knew the role that was expected of her – the flirting with fans, the sly sideways glances, the coquettish teasing, the eyelash-fluttering. It was simply that she'd never experienced the slightest romantic interest in any person, no matter how eligible. On the contrary, how dull the men all seemed to her, with their blustering, and their posturing, and their fragile egos.

As suitors went, Eustace was as close to perfection as it was possible to be – a fact that Beatrice's aunt had pointed out to her on more than one occasion. Not only was he charming, handsome, wealthy and titled, but he treated Beatrice with perfect courtesy, and came from one of the most noble families in England. It would be hard to marry any higher without marrying an actual prince. And nobody seemed to care that Beatrice had never wanted the prince in the fairy tale, that she'd always been more enamoured with the cursed frogs and poisonous mushrooms and wicked fairies.

Since she'd been very small, it had seemed perfectly and painfully self-evident to Beatrice that a man could not possibly compare with the fascination of a mushroom. He could not distract from the joy of studying, dissecting and cataloguing the various types of fungi, or from the delight of painstakingly creating highly detailed and accurate botanical illustrations.

Beatrice enjoyed collecting interesting plants and tending to her herbarium, and the thought of putting all that aside to become a wife and mother left her itching abominably within her own skin, causing it to feel too tight, as if it had been made for another person altogether. Regret burned in her stomach, as hot and black as a lump of smouldering coal. The match was a mistake. She knew that in her bones. She'd been an unwilling participant from the start. But the marriage had been organised by her aunt and Eustace's mother, and it seemed that Beatrice was to have no say in the matter at all.

She'd tried to explain how she felt to her father when the proposal was first made, but it was hopeless. Perhaps things would have been different if her mother had still been alive. She had never minded Beatrice's lack of poise, her plain features, her social awkwardness, her stammering, her fascination with mushrooms. She had seemed to accept Beatrice for who she truly was. But her father was a different matter.

*A young woman needs a husband, Beatrice,* he'd said. *I beg you, don't be unnatural. Don't make life miserable for yourself. I want to leave this world knowing that you're taken care of.*

He'd known that he was dying, and the knowledge only seemed to make him more immovable. Still, he'd never called her unnatural before, and the memory continued to sting, white-hot as the lash of a whip. Beatrice wished she had spoken differently during that conversation – one of the last ones she'd had with her father before his death.

She ought to have insisted on making herself heard and calling the marriage off, but instead she had allowed herself to get swept along on the tide of other people's plans for her. The opal ring felt like a manacle, a brand of ownership, smoking and smouldering through all the delicate layers of her skin.

*The bad-luck stone . . .*

The door opened then, and Margaret Sullivan, the dowager duchess, walked in, carrying a book. She was dressed in an oriental teal-and-green striped gown, her chestnut hair was streaked with steely grey and she possessed a poise that Beatrice could never hope to emulate. When she'd first met the duchess, Beatrice had been struck by the thought that this was the snow queen straight from the pages of one of her childhood books, brought to life in every detail – so perfect, and beautiful, and cruel.

'Ah, Lady Beatrice,' Margaret said. 'Thank you for coming. I know you must have much to do before tomorrow.'

In truth, Beatrice had very little to do except wait. It seemed that all preparations for the wedding had been taken entirely out of her hands. She stood up to take the duchess's gloved hand. 'M-M-My p-p-p . . .'

She flushed deeply as she tried to force out the words. She could speak perfectly well when she was alone, without the slightest stammer. But panic always raced to the surface when faced with other people, and the harder she tried, the more impossible it would become.

'P-P-Pleasure!' she managed.

The duchess gazed at her, mouth pinched in an expression of disapproval.

'I have something for you,' she said. 'Do sit down.'

Beatrice reluctantly took her seat on the chaise longue and Margaret sat in the armchair across from her. The door opened again and a maid entered with a tea trolley. She laid a silver tea service out on the table between them, along with plates of dainty, frosted cakes, all dusted in crystals of sugar that looked like little shards of ice – poisoned offerings from a snow queen's banquet hall.

'I trust you don't mind the liberty, Beatrice,' the duchess said. 'But since your own dear mother is no longer with us, I thought I would ensure your ownership of this volume myself.'

She handed over the book, which felt heavy in Beatrice's hands. She rested it on her knees and looked down at the title stamped across the cover: *The Wives of England, Their Relative Duties, Domestic Influence & Social Obligations.*

'Take heed of its wisdom and you will enjoy a most satisfactory marriage,' the duchess went on, picking up a teacup. 'It is a fine volume. I've marked some of the most illuminating passages for you.'

Beatrice opened the book at random to one such page and the words blazed before her eyes:

*It is quite possible you may have more talent than your husband, with higher attainments, and you may also have been generally more admired; but*

*this has nothing whatever to do with your position
as a woman, which is, and must be, inferior to his
as a man . . .*

Beatrice's fingers itched to tear out the page and stuff it
down the duchess's throat. Instead she closed the book.
'Th-thank you, your g-grace,' she said. 'You are m-most
k-k-kind.'

Margaret waved her hand. 'It is nothing,' she said.

*You are right about that,* Beatrice thought. She knew she
was not adept at controlling her facial expressions, and
concentrated hard on keeping her face a mask as best she
could. It would not do for her lip to curl in contempt at
this moment.

The women took their tea in an atmosphere of stilted
awkwardness. Beatrice had never been alone with the
duchess before and her nerves only made her stammer
worse. Margaret had a way of looking at her as if she
could see right through to the inside of her head, and
always there was that pinched look about her mouth, as
though she found Beatrice wanting in every possible way.
The tea was too weak and milky for Beatrice's taste. The
cakes were ash in her mouth. There was not even a dog
in the room for her to pet, and it seemed to Beatrice
suddenly ridiculous for there not to be any dogs at all in
such a mansion as Raven Hall.

She wondered what would happen if she put down her
teacup and told the duchess, quite decisively, and without

a hint of a stammer, that she was calling off the engagement. She suddenly ached to declare that she would not be sucked into this house, or shackled into matrimony; that she meant to spend the rest of her days a blissfully contented spinster, accountable to nobody but herself, concerned with no one's wishes but her own. How glorious such a thing would be. How full of oxygen the world would suddenly become.

It was not the first time the thought had appeared but, on this occasion, it was accompanied by such a fierce rush of longing that Beatrice rattled her teacup in its saucer, earning her another look of reprobation from the duchess.

Since last week's conversation with her solicitor, she'd realised that her father's death had left a fortune at her fingertips. And that money changed things. It changed everything. For the first time, she could smell freedom in the air, and another life calling to her, if only she had the courage to take the plunge. And yet still she hesitated, afraid of offending people, of doing the wrong thing, of causing hurt, of making a scene, of upsetting her family, of being unnatural.

The tea was finished. Surely it was permissible to take her leave now, at last? Whenever Beatrice was forced into company, she often found herself overwhelmed with the sudden desperate urge to flee. She felt herself drowning in chit-chat and teacups, hungry to gulp down the air of solitude. A glance out of the mullioned windows showed her there was still plenty of daylight left in the summer sky. Enough to go foraging for mushrooms and take one last turn about the grounds of her home whilst they still belonged to her.

'Th-thank you for the t-tea, D-Duchess,' she said, standing up in a rustling of crêpe and bombazine.

'My dear, you can't leave yet,' the duchess said. 'Our guest hasn't arrived. That was the entire purpose of bringing you here today.'

Beatrice's skin seemed to shrink even tighter around her bones, like a pair of wet gloves.

'G-Guest?' she managed.

'A doctor. It was Eustace's idea. A surprise for you before the wedding.' The duchess glanced at the carriage clock ticking upon the mantelpiece. 'He'll be here any moment. It's a great honour that he's made time for us today. He's a specialist in his field, you know. You will be quite delighted.'

A bubble of irritation swelled larger and larger in Beatrice's chest, threatening to pop. Must people be forever telling her how she was going to feel? *You will be delighted with this, you will be grateful for that, you will be shocked, you will be bored, you will be overawed, you will not understand such complicated matters, you must do as you are told.* It was intolerable.

'W-Why would a d-d-doctor c-come here?' she asked.

'Your stammer, of course,' the duchess replied impatiently. 'Eustace has consulted various physicians and they all agree that the inability to control one's own tongue is caused by a weakness of the nerves, or of character.' Her mouth pinched in distaste once again. 'It hardly matters which. Either way, this physician has promised he can cure you. He simply requires an initial consultation to determine which course of treatment is most suitable.'

Suddenly Beatrice was a child once again, back at the London hospital her father had sent her to in the hope of having her stammering surgically corrected. She'd been made to sit with her head leaning back against the chest of an assistant, whose job it was to hold her still. Her mouth was forced wide open with a metal clamp. Her tongue was pulled so far from her mouth that she feared they would rip it out by the root. The grip of the forceps on the tip was bruising and cold, but that was far from the worst part. That came when the doctor reached into her mouth and began to cut away part of her tongue with a small, sharp surgical knife.

She recalled the agony of trying to scream whilst blood poured down her throat; the arms of the assistant were a steel vice, pinning her like a butterfly. But this time she was not a child and she would not submit to such treatment again, not for anyone.

At that moment the footman reappeared to announce the arrival of the doctor – a small, portly man with a neatly trimmed beard. Margaret rose to her feet to receive him, but Beatrice's mind was suddenly racing. She saw life unfolding before her as Eustace's wife, her tongue sliced into silence, her fortune shredded to pin-money for trinkets she did not want, and all her mushrooms and flowers and insects stolen away from her.

'Lady Sitwell,' Margaret said, leading the doctor over to her, 'I am delighted to present Dr Livingstone.'

Beatrice ignored the bow the man gave her. She carefully placed the book the duchess had given her on the chaise longue and stood up. But she did not speak to the doctor, or respond to his bow, or even glance at Margaret. With a feeling of complete calm, she simply turned her back on them both and walked towards the door.

'Where on earth are you going?' Margaret demanded behind her.

She sounded scandalised, but Beatrice didn't care. She was leaving. She walked right out of Raven Hall without another word to anybody. And as she climbed into her carriage she made a promise to herself that she would never be mistress of that dreadful house.

# CHAPTER TWO

Beatrice wrote the letter as soon as she returned home and sent a servant to deliver it to Raven Hall that evening. Eustace ought to have arrived from London by then. She'd spent some time over the composition of the message, wanting to be as polite as possible under the circumstances, whilst remaining firm and making it clear that this was no spur-of-the-moment decision:

*I am truly sorry for any hurt or embarrassment I may cause, but it seems to me that it would be the gravest folly to avoid one misfortune by committing oneself to a much larger and more permanent one.*

She enclosed the blood opal, fiercely glad to be rid of it, and promised to return all other engagement gifts in due course. It was too late to prevent the wedding guests from arriving the next day, but she promised that she and her aunt would explain matters, and that there was no need for Eustace himself to appear at Half Moon House.

Her Aunt Emily was utterly distraught when she found out what her niece had done, but it was too late to get the letter back by then. Beatrice slept well that night for the first time in months, warmed by a deep sense of contentment, an enormous glow of satisfaction at having freed herself from a horrible fate.

But her peace was short-lived. When the maid woke her with her cup of chocolate the next morning, the first thing Beatrice saw was the blood opal gleaming beside a bouquet of flowers on the walnut chiffonier. She jerked upright in bed, staring at the ring, quite unable to think how it could possibly have got there.

'The r-ring!' Beatrice began when her aunt came into the room.

'It's quite wonderful, Beatrice,' Aunt Emily said, patting her shoulder. 'Eustace sent a message first thing this morning. He says he forgives you your nerves and promises there'll be no more said about it. It was a lucky escape, to be sure, but fortunately the duke is a gentleman.'

Beatrice could not believe what she was hearing.

'B-But, Aunt, I r-really *d-don't* want to—'

'Do get out of bed, dear. The guests will be here sooner than you think and we've so much still to do.'

Beatrice tried desperately to make herself heard, but it seemed impossible. Aunt Emily refused to listen, just as Eustace had disregarded her letter, and her father before that. Her frustration made her stammer worse and worse until she could hardly speak at all. Before long, there was an army of maids pushing her this way and that, tugging at her hair and covering her face in powders.

Finally Beatrice reached for an old copy of *Curtis's Botanical Magazine*, hoping to calm herself by examining the coloured plates of newly discovered plants and the intricate sketches of seeds and leaves inside. But she only managed a few pages before she came to an article about an orchid hunter named Benjamin Smith who'd been gored to death in a bull trap in Hawaii. She frowned down at the words. Before she could read any further, Aunt Emily happened to see the headline and whipped the magazine from her hands with an expression of profound distaste.

'This really isn't suitable reading material for you at all, dear,' she said.

Angrily, Beatrice tried to demand it back, but her tongue had completely tied itself into knots and she found she could not utter a single coherent word. The morning raced by and before she had time to blink, there were guests assembled on the lawn outside, and she was wearing a sumptuous wedding dress, trimmed with elaborate flounces of Honiton lace. There was even a gauzy veil, fastened to a wreath of orange blossoms.

Her aunt and the maids cooed that she looked beautiful but Beatrice thought it quite plain that she looked utterly ridiculous. She stepped away from the mirror and crossed the room to the windows where she could look out at the guests, already taking their seats upon the croquet lawn.

Perfect June sunshine shone down on the gathering and the medieval woodland beyond the ha-ha. Beatrice saw there was an abundance of orchids, so at least one of her requests had been granted. It had become fashionable for wealthy collectors to employ orchid hunters to travel the world, and Beatrice had witnessed the most absurd scenes in London auction houses, with people paying a fortune for a single bloom. Despite the mania for them, she had always thought orchids rather dull – they could not begin to compare with the beauty and fascination of a mush-room, to say nothing of all she had seen in the Winter Garden – but after leaving the employ of Half Moon House, James Sheppard had made a name for himself as an orchid hunter, and Beatrice liked the idea of putting some business his way.

She hadn't seen him since he had handed in his notice as their head gardener seven years ago. An action she had not approved of, but it had not been her place to object. Still, she had kept abreast of his exploits in *Curtis's Magazine*. Orchid hunting was a dangerous profession

– the article she had read earlier was not the worst she had heard, by far. When they weren't feuding with one another, these men regularly met their demise through drowning, fever, wild animals, treacherous terrain, tropical diseases or local brigands.

She turned her attention to the guests. Many of them were people she'd never seen or heard of, but she knew that a couple of members of the Royal Family were expected. Eustace looked as carefree and comfortable as ever, standing with his best man. They both wore top hats and matching frock coats in a fashionable shade of claret. Eustace was tall and handsome, with his perfectly straight back, ash-blond hair and neatly trimmed beard, but Beatrice realised her hands were clenched into fists at her sides.

Her mind snagged once again on the thorny fact that, if she married Eustace, Half Moon House and everything in it would legally become his. She'd not been permitted any involvement in the marriage settlement, but she'd seen the terms when she'd gone through her father's desk after his death. Now that Beatrice was an heiress, Eustace would get everything, including the house.

*No*, she thought, with sudden conviction. *This will not happen.*

She found she was smiling without realising it.

'Don't grin like that, dear,' Aunt Emily chided. 'Remember, nature gave us lips to conceal our teeth.'

'Nature gave us lips to s-speak,' Beatrice replied. 'The wedding. Is. Cancelled.'

She was delighted that, for once, she managed to get her words out almost without stammering at all.

Aunt Emily glanced at the maids. 'Thank you, that will be all,' she said, dismissing them with a wave of her hand. 'You may take your place outside with the other guests.'

The maids filed out obediently, and Aunt Emily turned back to Beatrice.

'Now then, do sit down whilst I—'

'Don't p-pretend you d-didn't hear me, Aunt,' Beatrice cut her off. 'I w-won't marry today. Or ever.'

Emily had gone quite pale and it was impossible to tell whether it was from anger or fright. Beatrice had never spoken to her like that before; in fact she'd never done anything like this before. All her senses seemed suddenly heightened: the eyes of the peacock-feather wallpaper were shockingly blue, the scent of the orange blossoms in the bridal bouquet so intense she could taste them.

'My dear, I think the wedding excitement must be making you a little hysterical,' Aunt Emily ventured. 'Shall I fetch a sal volatile?'

'You m-may fetch Eustace so I can sp-speak to him in private.'

'I certainly will not!'

Beatrice glared at her, then gathered up big handfuls of her lacy skirts to stride from the room.

41

'If you go out that door, I shall faint!' her aunt cried at her back.

*Then fetch your own sal volatile,* Beatrice thought, with a certain vicious satisfaction as she walked into the hallway.

She made her way along the landing to the Adam and Eve staircase. It was a seventeenth-century original with elaborately carved bannisters showcasing the Garden of Eden's flora and animals. Twin statues of Adam and Eve watched from the posts as Beatrice descended in a rustle of petticoats, her long veil whispering over the polished wooden stairs behind her.

She thought of that night seventeen years ago when she had descended this very staircase as a child, clutching her mourning parasol and following the trail of dancing mushrooms. It was a night she had not thought of in some while, but the memory of it now was oddly comforting, reminding her that there was more to the world than wedding guests, marriage vows and blood opals.

When she reached the ground floor she found the house infuriatingly empty. It seemed that everyone was already assembled outside for the ceremony. She passed through the Summer Dining Room, the Billiards Room, the Winter Smoking Room, the Marble Hall, the White and Gold Music Room, the two-storey Library with its ten thousand volumes, but there was simply not a soul around.

As she strode down the long South Front viewing gallery it was impossible not to recall the many occasions she'd wandered the house as a girl, in the months after her mother had died and the Winter Garden had gone, when her father was so often absent. With the servants closeted away below stairs, it had sometimes felt like she was the last person alive in the world.

The mansion was too large for one child and she had been afraid of its endless corridors, certain there must be ghosts watching her from the shadowed alcoves. Now, on her wedding day, it felt much the same, except for the fact that the house smelled of blossoms and broken promises, and Beatrice felt alive and sure of herself for the first time.

She decided to go to the Blue Drawing Room. It faced the croquet lawn and she thought to catch Eustace's attention by waving at him from the window. But when she opened the door, she found the room already occupied. Her huge wolfhound, Wilkie, wandered over to lick her hand, and her friend Rosa Warren looked up from the long table covered with crimson cloth on which the wedding gifts had been laid out.

Beatrice had first met Rosa at her aunt's town house during the Season last year and, although she'd only known her a short time, she liked the nineteen-year-old American very much. Rosa was an heiress and a master artificer who never passed up an opportunity to flaunt her family's immense wealth, even going so far as to decorate her opera box for the Season with a constant supply of prized and exotic white orchids. Not only that, but she brimmed with confidence and automatically assumed she was the social equal of everyone she met. Beatrice had never met anyone quite like her.

At the train station last summer, a gentleman in their party had explained how it simply wasn't appropriate for Rosa to go into the buffet, since this was a male preserve. She had cheerfully told him not to be such a dolt and then marched straight in, her clockwork pug trotting at her heels, and ordered a stirrup cup. Everyone had been terribly shocked, and rather disapproving. Beatrice alone had smiled at her in quiet admiration, and from that moment the two women had formed an unlikely friendship, despite the fact that they could hardly be more different.

'Why, honey!' Rosa exclaimed now. 'What a breathtaking dress!'

'I'm the wrong b-bride to wear it,' Beatrice replied.

'Nonsense. You're a vision,' Rosa said. 'I was just finding a place for your wedding gift, but as you're here, I'll present him to you in person.'

She held out both her gloved hands. Cupped inside was an extraordinary clockwork peacock. Sensing it was being looked at, the bird immediately spread out its tail. Its frame was made of pale gold with real sapphires studded amongst the metal feathers. In places it was possible to glimpse the delicate clockwork cogs within, clicking and whirring their constant heartbeat hum. It gave a tinny shriek in greeting and Beatrice stared at it, speechless. She recognised this peacock. She had seen it before, many years ago.

Suddenly she was a child again, gazing up at the magnificent clock that marked the heart of the Winter Garden. Its design resembled the cuckoo clocks of Germany's Black Forest, except it was made entirely from ice. Intricate carvings of leaves, birds and stags' heads adorned the façade, sparkling in the frosted moonlight. A swinging pendulum ticked and tocked beneath it, counting out the minutes remaining until the garden would vanish for the day. Beatrice had grown to love that clock, for its chimes were always the first indication she had of the garden's arrival for the night. But the thing she loved most of all was the mechanical bird that called out the hours. It was no cuckoo, but a dazzling clockwork peacock.

Beatrice looked up at her friend, a sudden surge of excitement making her fingertips tingle. 'Have you s-seen it t-too?' she whispered.

'Seen what?' Rosa asked.

'The W-Winter Garden! You re-created the p-peacock from its c-clock.'

'Honey, I'm afraid I have no idea what you're talking about,' Rosa replied, looking mildly offended. 'The peacock is my own design. I don't imitate other people's work. You know that. I made you a peacock because you asked me about them once, remember? Shortly after we first met?'

Beatrice frowned as she recalled their conversation about the clockwork creatures. Rosa had been permitted to study mechanics within the family business back in Georgia, and later in New York, and was now one of the best artificers that Warren's Clockwork Creatures had. Since her arrival in England she'd received more commissions than she could accept, for everything from clockwork monkeys to songbirds. Every fashionable upper-class lady wanted one.

'You looked quite disappointed when I said I hadn't made one,' Rosa went on. 'So I thought you might like one.'

Beatrice tried to gather herself. This wasn't the moment to be thinking about the Winter Garden. And now that she looked more closely at the peacock, she could see that it did not resemble the other one as much as she'd thought after all.

'He is quite w-wonderful,' she said. 'But I regret I c-cannot accept.'

'Why in the world not?' Rosa asked.

'I'm c-c-calling it off. The w-w-wedding.' Beatrice felt annoyed that her worsening stammer betrayed her nerves. She so badly wanted to do it, but it was impossible to ignore that the consequences would be grave, especially now that the guests were all assembled outside. Eustace would be humiliated and both their reputations would suffer, although Beatrice would come off worse. There would certainly be a scandal, and endless recriminations from her family and his. It would be a truly shocking thing to do, by anyone's standards.

'Goodness.' Rosa carefully set the peacock down on the long table with the other wedding gifts. It pattered up and down, inspecting the offerings and occasionally letting out a tinny shriek of excitement. 'Whatever for?' she asked. 'I can't think you'll find anyone more eligible in the whole of England than the Duke of Chalkley.'

'I don't *w-want* someone more eligible!' Beatrice exclaimed, with renewed irritation. 'I want to be a s-s-spinster. And m-manage my own h-home. And a-affairs.'

Rosa had made no secret of her own ambitions to make a fortuitous match in England, so Beatrice suspected she might not understand this sentiment, but in fact her friend broke into a dazzling smile.

'Bravo, my dear! But how marvellous!'

'I t-tried to tell Eustace yesterday. He w-would not. Accept. My l-letter.'

'What a bounder!' Rosa exclaimed. 'Still, one can hardly blame him. I suppose he thinks if he makes it too difficult, then you'll simply give up.'

Beatrice shook her head. 'I w-won't.'

'Is there anything I can do?'

'Thank you, n-no. I m-m-must do this for m-myself.'

There were too many people on the lawn for Beatrice to hope to catch Eustace's attention and the idea of sending Rosa out on her behalf seemed cowardly. Beatrice would simply have to march confidently out there, just as her friend had gone into that buffet last summer.

'The truth is, I didn't even want a stirrup cup particularly,' Rosa had confided to her later. 'I simply wanted to prove a point to that intolerable coxcomb.'

Beatrice went out through the door, encumbered by her huge, ridiculous dress, which Rosa attempted to help her with. The moment she appeared, the string quartet started up a bridal march, the guests oohed breathlessly and her bridesmaids came rushing over to pick up the train. Her aunt also hurried to her side, having clearly tired of the fainting couch upstairs.

'Come along, Beatrice,' she said, once again pretending their earlier exchange had never happened, as she thrust the bridal bouquet at her niece and then deftly lifted the long veil over her head. 'A decorous bride is too timid to show their face in public until after they're married.'

Beatrice tried to protest, but her throat was closing up again, making her voiceless as well as faceless, and then her uncle was there, taking her arm to walk her down the aisle. Rosa had been shown to her seat and it felt like time had sped up faster than usual, racing her along with it like a tide.

As she walked ever closer to Eustace, she felt the grim weight of expectation pressing down upon her shoulders, and a trembling started in her legs, spreading throughout her body. Their assembled family and friends all gazed up at her, and their approval seemed suddenly to matter more than it should – much more than it had a few moments ago – tangling her up in multiple sticky strands of some invisible web.

She'd been so sure last night, and in the study with Rosa, but now that feeling was slipping through her fingers like water. Her palms itched with sweat inside her lace gloves and, suddenly, she doubted whether she had the strength to break her way out of this box, after all.

Then her uncle deposited her before Eustace, her aunt whisked away her flowers and the moment had arrived. She was glad of the veil, because there was a steely-cold look in Eustace's blue eyes that she'd never seen before. It was a look that made her feel small and powerless and very foolish. Half a woman, with half a mind.

Wilkie appeared from somewhere and brushed against her dress, poking his muzzle at her as he gazed up with adoring brown eyes, wagging his tail slowly back and forth.

'Who let this fellow out?' Eustace asked in his usual pleasant tone.

He extended his hand to stroke the dog's head, but was too rough with his ear, twisting it back so that Wilkie yelped and pulled away.

Eustace turned to Beatrice and reached for her hand. 'Please do not concern yourself about yesterday, my dear,' he said. 'There is nothing lost. After all, there would not have been sufficient time to cure your speech before the wedding anyway, and we have many years ahead of us. I want you to know I forgive you entirely.'

Beatrice narrowed her eyes.

*But I never asked for your forgiveness,* she thought.

Eustace smiled, making it seem as if his blond moustache moved by itself – a gesture Beatrice suddenly despised beyond all reason. She couldn't bear the thought of that moustache touching her skin. Even the feel of it through her glove was intolerable, and she had to force herself not to snatch her hand away when he pressed his mouth to the back of it.

The music stopped and the priest stepped forward, a benevolent smile on his face. Beatrice wondered what else her husband would take from her. First it would be her fortune and Half Moon House, then her stammer, and what then? Her unladylike interest in the sciences? Her love of fungi? She had been careful never to discuss such things with him during their courtship, sticking only to acceptable topics, but he could hardly fail to notice her interests once they were married and shared a home. And what about her desire to carry as few children as possible, or preferably none at all? He would not accept it; she knew that he wouldn't.

Suddenly she was back at her mother's deathbed, making the wrong choice, being a coward, taking the easy way out. It was a mistake that had haunted her ever since. Was she really so stupid that she was going to make another one just like it? One that would decide the course of her life forever? She glanced back at the house and, for just a moment, thought she saw her mother at the window of her old bedroom, looking down upon the wedding with a sad expression on her face. Of course her mother was not really there – she was only the ghost of an idea, the light reflecting strangely upon the glass – yet suddenly

Beatrice was certain that she would not have approved of Eustace, or this wedding.

*The world is a difficult place to be a woman,* she had told Beatrice more than once. *Do not allow yourself to be bullied into unhappiness.*

Beatrice had let her mother down once. She didn't intend to do so again. Her determination exploded out of her fear, bursting right through any dread she had about what people would think, what they would say, how they would judge her. They could all be damned, the lot of them.

'Stop,' she said.

The priest looked startled. Eustace had gone utterly still.

'Beatrice,' he said. The word came out very quietly. There was a warning in it and his gloved hand held hers too tightly, squeezing the bones of her fingers together, making her whole hand ache. But Beatrice was done with being obedient. She was done with being decorous. And she was done with being trapped.

She yanked her hand free and pushed back her veil to look her betrothed in the eye.

'I'm s-sorry,' she said. 'But I c-can't marry you. I won't.'

A sudden breeze picked up and a sigh ran through the knotted old branches of the bearded oaks in the woods beyond the ha-ha. It did not seem like a reproachful sound, but one of quiet approval. Beatrice felt suddenly that the house, and its gardens, and the entire estate, realised what she was doing and were glad. The windows in the Gothic façade of Half Moon House shone back at her like smiling eyes from their walls of creamy-yellow Caen stone. The towers and turrets formed a crown that pierced the perfect blue dome of sky above. It looked more beautiful to her than ever before.

*Mine*, she thought, with another rush of determination. *This is all mine, and no one is taking it from me.*

'Please,' Eustace began, 'do not distress yourself by—'

'I am *n-not* distressed.' She took a deep breath and looked up, willing him to understand. 'Please. L-Listen. I would n-not make a g-good wife. I am not m-made the r-right w-way.'

'What nonsense is this?'

She took his hand. 'I am . . .' She forced the word out like a stone, 'D-Different.'

He pulled away from her touch. Beatrice let him go and turned to face the guests. 'I am s-sorry. But th-this wedding. Is c-cancelled. There are r-refreshments in the M-M-Marble Hall. H-Help yourselves. And then, p-please, leave my h-house.'

There was a moment of absolute silence. Beatrice clearly saw Rosa seated a few rows down, both hands pressed to her mouth, her eyes shining with delight. All the other guests were staring at her, mouths agape, their expressions ranging from disgust, to fascination, to anger. The dowager duchess had turned an interesting shade of puce.

'So be it,' Eustace finally said. And then strode from the scene without another word.

Beatrice knew she had just done something unthinkable and that there would be grave consequences. Irreparable damage to her reputation. Concerns about the very stability of her mind, in all likelihood. People would say that not only was she a nervous weakling who couldn't control her tongue, but that she suffered from female hysteria too. And yet, as she watched the duke go, she had space for only one emotion – and that was relief, right down to her soul.

# CHAPTER THREE

Later, whilst the other guests enjoyed the scandal and refreshments in the Marble Hall, Rosa sought Beatrice out, where she was packing up the wedding and engagement presents.

'Good lord, what are you worrying about these trinkets for at such a time?' Rosa asked. 'Surely the servants will take care of it?'

Beatrice thought that the dazzling array of gifts laid out on the long table could hardly be called trinkets. Aside from the gold and silver plate, and the endless traditional tea sets, there was an extraordinary selection of jewellery: gold bracelets, and sapphire necklaces, and diamonds as large as a Fortnum & Mason sugared cherry. The servants had set out small cards beside each gift, stating who it was from, and the butler had compiled a neat list in a gleaming leather-bound book purchased just for that purpose.

'They h-have enough to d-do,' Beatrice replied. 'Besides, I want t-to get this f-finished.'

There were a lot of gifts to sort and Beatrice was grateful when Rosa sat down and silently helped her with the remaining pile. Finally there was only the clockwork peacock left, but Rosa wouldn't hear of taking it back.

'Don't be a goose!' she exclaimed. 'It's yours.'

'Thank you. I am t-truly d-delighted with him.'

Now that she examined the peacock again, Beatrice thought it was possibly even more beautiful than the one she'd seen in the Winter Garden. Rosa had not forgotten her earlier remarks, and took the opportunity to question her as to where exactly she had seen the other mechanical bird. Beatrice was forced to make up a story.

'I'm afraid you m-misunderstood me,' she said. 'It wasn't a r-real g-garden. It was in a ch-children's book. I thought you must have h-had the s-same one.'

'Oh.' Rosa looked disappointed. 'Well, I don't recall ever seeing a book like that.'

Beatrice was relieved to let the subject of the garden lapse, and to fall back into silence as they continued packing up the presents. By the time they'd finished, most of the guests were gone, including her Aunt Emily, who'd departed in tears. Beatrice could summon no sympathy for her, and was only relieved to think that the house would soon be hers once again. She ached for solitude in every limb.

Rosa reached for her hat. 'Thank you for the most thrilling day. Whatever will you do now?'

'T-Travel.' Beatrice looked out the window. 'I've n-never set foot outside E-England.'

*And I will find that Winter Garden.*

She didn't say the last part aloud, but the wish blazed like a star inside her chest. She'd spent years hoping the garden would return to Half Moon House, but there came a point when hoping and waiting weren't enough. The garden was out there somewhere – she knew it. And if it wouldn't come to her, then she would go to it. It wouldn't do to sit serenely in drawing rooms, fussing at embroidery when there were such wonders in the world. She had enjoyed studying the plants and insects in her own grounds, and had even attended some of the local horticultural shows and society meetings with her collections, but it was no longer enough. She felt a fierce rush of elation. Her father would have forbidden it, but with his death, her chains were cut, the cage door was opened. If she failed to fly out now, it would only be her own cowardice holding her back.

'It sure is the most marvellous fun to travel,' Rosa remarked, 'but, you know, it does seem a bit of a shame about Eustace. He's so thoroughly eligible. I'd marry him in a shot.' She snapped her fingers.

'I th-thought that you and James Sh-Sheppard seemed c-close?'

A brief shadow seemed to pass over her friend's face, so fleeting that Beatrice almost thought she must have imagined it. The next second, Rosa gave a merry-sounding laugh.

'An orchid hunter?' she exclaimed. 'Good heavens, Beatrice, I like James very much, but I have my sights set a little higher than that.'

'L-Lord Rupert then?' Beatrice said, naming another of Rosa's many suitors.

She pulled a face. 'If I married a second son I'd only get to share his courtesy title, and Lady Rupert Brannagh hardly has the same ring to it as Rosa, Duchess of Chalkley, does it?'

Beatrice knew that her friend had left a series of disappointed suitors behind her, both back in the States and when she'd recently travelled through Europe. She had famously turned down proposals from both Italian and French noblemen, and had confided in Beatrice that although she liked the men well enough, she couldn't get past the fact that many titles on the continent were newly created, with no real heritage to speak of. English family seats, on the other hand, could normally be traced back hundreds of years, and this was a prize that Rosa had set her mind upon. If the rumours were true, she'd even rejected a Polish prince, labelling him 'third-rate' when compared to a titled Englishman.

*The best, honey,* she had often said to Beatrice. *I want only the best.*

Beatrice shook her head. 'I d-don't think such things m-matter.'

Rosa laughed. 'Why, that's easy for you to say. You already have a title! I tell you, I'd give anything to be a duchess.'

'But wh-why?' Beatrice asked. 'Why is it s-so important?'

Rosa shook her head. 'You couldn't understand,' she said. 'Your family has always had money. Mine made their fortune within my lifetime. I know what it's like to be poor. And I know what it is to be cold and hungry. Two things you could barely imagine.'

Beatrice shook her head. 'A h-house this s-size is always c-cold,' she said. 'No m-matter how m-many f-fires you light.'

Rosa shrugged. 'Well, all right, but you're a person of quality. You've never been looked down upon, but I have. Money can't buy prestige and respect – not for a woman. Only a title can do that.'

Beatrice wanted to tell her friend that she had been looked down upon plenty of times, despite her title, but Rosa had warmed to her topic and was already moving on.

'Anyone with money can build themselves a fine house, but to live in an old, respected mansion like Raven Hall!' Rosa's eyes gleamed with ambition. 'To have one's own home featured within the pages of *Seats of the Nobility and Gentry*! I've always felt like I was born for that life. That it's meant to be.'

Beatrice frowned. She disliked the idea of lives being fated to play out in a certain way and she said so.

Rosa shrugged. 'Who can say? You know, when I was a little girl, my ma thought I might have a touch of second sight. It was small things, like I would know what my birthday present was going to be before I saw it. And I always told my folks I was going to be a duchess when I grew up. Isn't that the darnedest thing?' She laughed. 'This was back when we were poor as church mice and any kind of titled husband seemed an utter fantasy. Still, I suppose I shouldn't set my sights quite so high as a duke.'

She gave the clockwork peacock a wistful look, and Beatrice supposed Rosa was well aware that her proficiency in clockwork made her less desirable as a wife, her cleverness considered too intellectual and unfeminine.

Rosa shook herself and said, 'So do you really mean to set off by yourself, quite alone?'

Beatrice shrugged. 'I need n-no champion to p-protect me,' she said.

Rosa nodded slowly. 'I suppose you're right. A male companion would be sure to get in the way at any rate, flying into passions and making rows. Where do you intend to go on this trip of yours?'

'Ev-everywhere.'

She already hungered for it – basking in the rays of Eastern suns, seeing soft mists rise over cold mountains, getting lost in a sudden storm, smelling the sweet, strange perfume of unknown flowers. Beatrice planned to do it all.

'I wish I was going with you,' Rosa said wistfully. 'You'll write to me, of course?' She straightened the hat above her mass of blonde hair. Despite the wilting heat of the day, it had somehow remained perfectly fixed in the bouffants and rolls of its *coiffure caliste*, with a row of perfect rosebuds tucked into the *cache-peigne* at the back of her head. 'I want to hear all about your adventures, now that you've thoroughly scandalised everyone here,' she went on. 'You will write, won't you, Beatrice?'

'Y-Yes. I will.'

Later that afternoon Beatrice had changed back into her mourning dress and was about to go for a walk in the orchard when a maid knocked on her door saying that Mr James Sheppard requested a moment of her time. She was startled to hear that he was there. She had not imagined James would deliver the orchids for the wedding himself, but even if she had, she would have expected him to have left by now, with the others.

'He's waiting for you in the Blue Drawing Room,' the maid said. 'Shall I send him away?'

'N-no,' Beatrice replied. 'I will be th-there in a m-moment.'

She dismissed the servant and then made her way downstairs. She felt strangely nervous about seeing James again after all this time. She felt like he was an old friend, and she longed to greet him as such, but the reality was that he was the son of a gardener and had been her servant.

Whatever childhood fondness there might have been between them was better forgotten.

She opened the door and saw him standing by the open window, looking out at the grove of apple trees. He turned at her entrance and a smile spread over his face. It was the one thing that had remained from the child who had sat in the tree with her all those years ago. Certainly James was no longer thin. Even before he left Half Moon House, ten-hour days working outside had made him strong and lean. His brown hair was lightened by the sun and his skin was still tanned. But the change Beatrice noticed immediately was his nose. She remembered it being long and straight, but now it was crooked and bent at the bridge.

'What h-happened?' she blurted at the same time as James bowed and said, 'Good afternoon.'

He paused mid-bow. 'I beg your pardon?'

Beatrice flushed and touched her own nose.

'Ah.' James straightened and his smile became broader. 'A hazard of the job. Not all orchid hunters are honourable, I regret to say. This one objected to my reaching a mountain summit before him.'

Beatrice knew full well that some orchid hunters behaved very badly and had earned themselves a reputation for ruthlessness. They had no care for the land abroad, and once a discovery had been made, would strip it bare in order to thwart their rivals. Beatrice had read for herself the devastating effect on the native flower population, to say nothing of the trees upon which they grew and the wildlife that depended on them. And the tragedy of it all was that most of those orchids didn't survive the trip back to England anyway.

She hoped James was not one of those who behaved in such a way but, really, it was not as if she knew him at all any more. After her mother's death they had drifted further and further apart, until Beatrice only exchanged polite, formal greetings with him in the garden, if she acknowledged him at all. The distance between them had always made her feel a pang of sadness, and it was the same now. There were so many questions fizzing at the edge of her tongue.

*Did you ever manage to see all those different types of snail?*
*Which one was your favourite?*
*What made it special?*

With most people Beatrice found that she simply had no idea what to say to them, or how to create common ground, but with James – even after all this time – she had too many questions, too many areas of conversation she would love to enter into, especially since he was now a member of the Linnean Society, that most esteemed and venerable bastion of biology, botany, science and the natural world. Beatrice herself would have given anything to be admitted as a member but it was, of course, quite out of the question for a woman. Still, deep down, she could not help nurturing the hope that if she were to discover plants and flowers impressive enough, then the society might allow her to become a member one day.

She longed to ask him about the society, but was suddenly hesitant to mention her own continued interest in botany. The prizes she had won for her mushroom exhibits at the local horticultural shows seemed feeble when compared to the multiple gold Knightian Medals that James had received from the Royal Horticultural Society. His discoveries were frequently featured in *Curtis's Botanical Magazine* and the editor had credited James with collecting many of the finest specimens introduced into English gardens in recent decades, gushing that it had 'earned him the gratitude of the whole gardening world'.

'I d-did not expect you to d-deliver the or-orchids y-yourself,' she said, whilst inwardly cringing at her stutter. It seemed like a loss that she could no longer speak to him without her tongue tying itself into knots.

'Didn't you?' he returned. 'I would never have sent anyone else in my place to Half Moon House.'

Beatrice felt a faint glow of pleasure, thinking that he meant he had wished to see her again, but then he added, 'I could not pass up the chance to see the black apple trees. They're as spectacular as ever.'

The pleasure soured in Beatrice's stomach. Of course he had meant the trees, and not her.

'I thought you would not mind if I joined the other staff for the ceremony,' he went on. He paused, then added, 'Such as it was.'

Beatrice felt her flush deepen. She wondered what he must think of her after that scene, and then felt irritated that she should care about the opinions of a servant at all.

'Wh-what can I h-help you w-with, M-Mr Sh-Sheppard?' she asked, her voice coming out a little colder than she'd intended.

He smiled slightly at her tone – a tugging half-grin she recalled from when they were children.

'When I left Half Moon House I got the impression you were displeased with me,' he said.

This was true and Beatrice was annoyed that her feelings should have been so obvious. 'I c-cannot think what g-gave you that im-impression,' she said, stating the lie as boldly as she could.

He raised an eyebrow. 'You told me orchids are dull.'

'S-so they a-are.'

'Not this one.'

He bent down and picked up the Wardian case at his feet to set on the small table between them. The case was like a miniature glasshouse, large enough to hold only a single bloom – a pale orchid. Beatrice thought it had jagged petals at first, but when she stepped closer she saw that they were actually pointed teeth, each petal ringed with dozens and dozens of them. Silvery strings of saliva hung down from some of them, sparkling in the slant of afternoon sun coming through the window.

'It's a slug orchid,' James told her.

Beatrice recalled a time many years ago in the garden when James had held up a bright-yellow slug with blue tentacles for her to see. *The* Limax flavus, he'd said. *Each slug has twenty-seven thousand teeth! Can you believe it?*

She had been fascinated and delighted by such a fact.

'It is not worth much, I'm afraid,' James went on now. 'The fashion is for butterfly orchids.'

Beatrice had seen the pictures of the butterfly orchid that James had discovered. *Curtis's Magazine* had raved over the extraordinary flower, whose petals resembled butterfly wings. They were even said to be a favourite with the young Princess Victoria.

'But this one has a beauty of its own, and I thought you might be one of the rare people who could appreciate it,' James said. 'It's travelled all the way from Hawaii.'

In spite of herself, Beatrice felt warmed by the praise. Despite the fact that he was a servant, and someone she hadn't seen in years, James was one of the few people she had ever met whom she actually respected. As for the slug orchid, Beatrice thought it the finest flower she had ever seen.

'It is r-remarkable,' she acknowledged.

James smiled again. 'I am gratified to succeed in impressing you.'

'B-But since th-there was no w-wedding,' Beatrice said, 'I c-cannot accept any w-wedding g-gifts.'

'It is not a wedding gift, Lady Beatrice,' he replied. 'Simply a gift.'

Beatrice knew she ought to insist that he take the flower back. It would be quite improper to accept a gift of any kind, under the circumstances. But she liked it so very much. And given what she had already done today, this seemed a small impropriety in comparison. So she inclined her head in thanks.

Feeling a little awkward about the moment, she sought to change the subject. 'I r-read an article in *C-Curtis's* just this m-morning about Hawaii,' she said. 'And a m-man named B-Benjamin Smith. I b-believe you worked t-together in the p-past? He was an a-associate of yours?'

'Not an associate,' James said quietly. 'A friend.'

Beatrice inwardly shuddered as she recalled the article. How unspeakable to be gored to death in a bull trap. It made her wonder once again why James had picked such a dangerous profession when he might have been a gardener, safe and secure at home.

'I am v-very s-sorry.'

'Thank you,' he said.

'Did it h-happen r-recently?'

'Last year.'

'A t-terrible way to d-die.'

'It is something I hope never to witness again so long as I live.'

Beatrice stared. 'Y-You were *th-there*?'

'Yes,' he said briefly, before turning away and indicating the orchard through the window. 'The apple trees appear to be doing well.'

'It t-took some wh-while to f-find a g-gardener who w-would t-tend them,' she replied.

Most men wouldn't go near the black apple trees – they were too afraid of them. James was the only one who had seen them as Beatrice did. Once again she felt a flare of anger towards him for leaving. She knew the feeling was irrational, and that it stemmed partly from jealousy, yet it was too strong a feeling for her to master.

'I s-suppose you have s-seen f-f-far more impressive s-specimens on your t-travels.' She dearly longed to hear about them, and even as she spoke she wondered why she could not simply invite him to tell her all about it, rather than talking in such a remonstrative way. She despised herself for the sulkiness in her tone, and yet she could not seem to soften it.

James did not appear to notice, however, and his voice was pleasant when he replied. 'Certainly not. I doubt there can be anything more wondrous in all the world than them. Still . . .' He paused, then added, 'In certain circles abroad I have heard talk of a most unusual garden. One that's said to move around from place to place, filled with wonders such as your black apple trees. A magical garden where it is always winter . . .'

The moment slowed and stopped. Beatrice looked at James, to find him watching her closely. She had never known anyone allude to the Winter Garden in even the vaguest of terms before, and part of her wished to tell him everything at once. But it seemed too extraordinary a tale for anyone to believe. And he was an orchid hunter now – if he did believe her, could she be sure that he would not track down the Winter Garden in order to loot it? Magical flowers and extraordinary treasures would fetch a high price indeed at auction.

'Sounds like a f-fairy tale,' she said, making sure to keep any fond wistfulness from her voice. She would not allow herself to think of miniature snowmen, gnome-shaped cups or impossible tigers.

For a long moment it looked as if James might be about to say something more, but finally he nodded and said, 'Yes, I suppose it does.'

'Where did you h-hear such s-stories?'

'In auction houses, mostly. The Winter Garden is famous amongst orchid hunters. They say there's an orchid there that blooms nowhere else in the world.'

*The frost orchid.* Beatrice saw it once again in her mind, its iced petals crowned on top of a long, pale stalk, glittering behind the glass dome of its case.

'How c-curious,' she said.

'Indeed. Well, I will not detain you any longer.' He picked up his hat and jacket from the back of a nearby chair. 'I hope you will not mind if I say that it was good to see you again today, and that I admire very much what you did earlier. You showed great courage.'

Beatrice was both pleased and embarrassed by the praise, yet her own pleasure disturbed her. 'I do m-mind,' she said. 'You f-forget your p-place. As my. S-servant.'

She regretted the words as soon as they left her mouth. Why could she not allow herself to be easy with James, as she had been once before? Surely it did not matter what anyone else thought by now. Suddenly the lost ease of their childhood friendship made such a great ache press down on her chest. She almost hoped James would react with irritation – at least then she could see that her words had meant something to him. But he simply said quietly, 'I am no longer your servant, Lady Beatrice – or anyone's, thanks to the orchids. Financially speaking, I need never work another day in my life if I do not wish to, and I would live very comfortably. But I am truly sorry to have offended you. Please believe it was not my intent. Good day, Lady Beatrice.'

He offered her a bow and then took his leave. Beatrice looked at the slug orchid drooling its silvery slime and wished she could call James back and redo their conversation – do it right this time, rather than saying all the wrong things in all the wrong ways, as she seemed forever doomed to do. But it was too late for that, and once he'd gone it was a relief to finally have Half Moon House to herself.

She sighed, called Wilkie to her side and went out to walk with him through the orchard. A pink-and-purple sunset spread like a great bruise across the sky and Beatrice breathed deeply of the scent of apples and freedom, glad of the cooler breeze now that the stickiness was finally draining from the day. The apples shone as black as secrets, diamond drops of juice clinging to their skins. The sun dipped below the skyline and, right on cue, the dusk blossom rapidly bloomed along the branches of the trees, unfolding layer upon layer of petals in midnight-blue, steel-grey and shining indigo, ruffled at the edges, like petticoats. The air was immediately filled with a strange scent like evening rain, and cool soil, and bursting purple berries, and something else that Beatrice had never quite been able to identify – a sort of metallic tang that she could taste more than smell.

As soon as she stepped into the orchard, the nearest tree reached a spindly branch towards her, fingers of twig poking into her pockets in search of treats. She dug out a sugar cube, recalling how she'd painstakingly studied the trees as a child, learning all she could about how to care for them, mostly through trial and error, since they certainly featured in no book she had ever come across.

They didn't get their sustenance from the ground, so they didn't have normal roots, but something more like tentacles that allowed them to move around, if they had a mind to. Growing up alone at Half Moon House, the black apple trees had often seemed like the only friends Beatrice had; but, even more importantly, they were constant proof that she had not imagined the garden. If it weren't for the apple trees, then she might have thought she'd dreamed it all.

They could be hostile to people who irritated or threat-ened them, but they had always been affectionate towards

Beatrice, as if they recognised that she was the one who had planted and nurtured them. Once, when she'd been particularly low, they had even joined together to make her a magnificent treehouse that took up the entire orchard, forming a castle of rooms with their branches, and turreted roofs with their leaves, scenting every part with garlands of their strange blossom.

There was something in the scent that was quite irresistible to small animals and, sure enough, a tendril soon whipped out into the long grass faster than the eye could follow. There was a scuffle and it returned with a dead rabbit, which it drew to the base of its trunk. The craggy bark peeled back just far enough to push the rabbit inside. Beatrice caught the briefest glimpse of glistening teeth and a wet black tongue before the trunk closed over it again. The only sign of what had happened was the small trail of blood seeping slowly into the dirt.

The trees gathered close around her, and soon she had leaves and branches and tendrils curled around her shoulders and waist and arms. They squeezed her just a little tighter than she would have liked, and she knew they didn't want her to go. She saw their sorrow in the sticky sap that trailed like tears down to their crooked roots and in the way their thin leaves shivered in the still summer evening.

'Don't worry,' Beatrice said quietly, knowing that she would not stammer in front of her strange, spindly friends.

'And don't be sad. I might be gone for a while, but I won't be gone forever.'

How could she explain to the trees that, whilst she loved Half Moon House fiercely, sometimes she also wanted to be as far away from it as possible?

'I'll come back to you, I promise,' she said. 'And I'll bring the rest of the garden with me if I can.'

# CHAPTER FOUR

July 1836

Dear Rosa,

Hello from the Chrysalis Islands.

I admit I had a moment of self-doubt when I arrived in Liverpool to catch the steamer and the agent informed me they didn't issue return tickets for their West African line, as so few travellers manage to make it back. And in my cabin later that evening I wasn't much cheered to flick through my book of phrases in common use in Imago and found that the first one was 'Help, I am drowning,' closely followed by 'Why has not this man been buried?'

It was too late to turn back by that point, though, and I'm glad. I've been here three weeks now and wouldn't have missed it for anything, in spite of the mosquitoes.

Truly, it is another world. I'm staying in one of the large cocoa-growing districts and have seen butterfly species new to me every day. I've even been fortunate enough to see rare females laying ova. But I'm really here for one butterfly in particular. It's known amongst entomologists as the elusive ghost butterfly and several people have reported sightings of it in various locations throughout the islands. It's never been captured and some dismiss it as a myth entirely.

But local people say that it can pass through the barrier between our world and the next and can be persuaded to deliver a final message to someone who has died. One village I stopped at had a shrine to the creature, in the form of a tree hung with dozens of green butterfly shapes cut from banana leaves, each with a message handwritten on it. When I enquired as to their purpose, I was informed that the ghost butterfly delivers the missive by eating the leaf. One boy even showed me a message he'd found on his pillow some years ago, which he believes a butterfly brought back from his mother in the afterlife.

I sat and watched that tree for hours, but I never saw so much as a caterpillar. I think I might have glimpsed a butterfly down by the stream one evening in Luna, though. It was as big as my hand, a beautiful creamy-white colour with ivory spots and lacy wingtips. I happened to have my butterfly net with me and had just made up my mind to plunge across the stream to get it when it took flight and sailed away into the jungle beyond.

I suspected that collecting in the Cameroons was likely to yield great treasures, and now I'm certain of it. It's my keen ambition to be the first person ever to capture a specimen of this glorious creature.

For now, though, my candle is almost burned down and the relentlessness of the mosquitoes is wearisome. I hope you are well, Rosa, and I will write to you again soon.

Your friend,
Beatrice

*July 1836*

*Dearest Beatrice,*

*I have returned to my family's London town house for a brief time and have hardly had a moment to put pen to paper. Relying on the long-distance postal service can be such a bother in these circumstances, so I have put together the clockwork pigeon that you are hopefully gazing at now with much wonder! He will carry messages between us, and anyone else you care to write to. The pigeon will find you, no matter where you happen to be, and thus allow me to keep up with your wonderful adventures.*

*I have become rather specialised in clockwork birds of late. After we met at your wedding, the Duke of Chalkley commissioned our company to make a whole party of peacocks for his pleasure garden. I have to say, I find your old fiancé most charming.*

*The ghost butterfly sounds extraordinary! Happy hunting — I'm sure it will soon be yours!*

*Your most loving friend,*
*Rosa*

# CHAPTER FIVE

*July 1836*

Rosa had always had a plan, where marriage was concerned, and she wasn't going to be persuaded from it by anyone. It was therefore with an immense feeling of dismay that her own feelings had betrayed her at Beatrice's wedding. She'd just arrived at Half Moon House when she noticed her friend, James Sheppard, giving directions to the under-gardeners regarding the care of the orchids. The sun made his dark brown hair shine and his shirt was rolled up to the elbows, exposing forearms that were unfashionably tanned from his time abroad. And all of a sudden, out of nowhere, and to her dismay, it struck Rosa quite forcefully that he was the most handsome man at the gathering.

This was a notion she knew full well was not true. James was distinctly average-looking by any objective measure, and certainly he wasn't in any way fashionable. Normally he looked as if he'd just come straight from the stables, and Rosa had never seen him wear a shirt with so much as a single frill or flounce. He was frequently observed outside without a hat. And he never seemed to use a drop of Macassar oil to style his hair. The only explanation was that she was viewing him through a lens – one that was more than mere friendly regard. That she had, in fact, developed deeper feelings for him.

When Rosa had first employed James's services last year, she had thought nothing of inviting him to take tea with her whenever he delivered orchids to her family's town house. After all, being an American and an artificer, people didn't expect Rosa to abide by the usual social etiquettes. She enjoyed the freedom this allowed her, and thought of James as an equal. They both worked for a living, they had made their own fortunes and were both the very best at what they did. She loved hearing about his adventures abroad and discussing orchids with him. In turn, he appeared fascinated by her clockwork creatures and seemed to genuinely understand that Cookie was a real dog, even if he wasn't made from flesh and bone.

In a world full of small talk and flattery, it sometimes seemed to Rosa that her conversations with James were the only genuine ones she ever had in England. Yet at Beatrice's wedding she knew at once that the strange yearning she felt towards him was something she must steel herself against. Why, it was nothing more than a girlish crush, after all. James was interesting to her because his occupation meant that he was unlike any other man she had known. He lived a life of danger and adventure, spoke dozens of languages and was rumoured to be an expert shot with a pistol too. But that did not make him suitable husband material.

After recognising the situation last month, the sensible thing would have been to distance herself from James after Beatrice's wedding. Rosa promised herself she would do exactly that. She would find a new orchid hunter. Yet . . . she couldn't quite bear to do so. She told herself that James was the best in the business, but the truth was that she looked forward to his visits more than she cared to admit. And, after all, what harm was there in it? A couple of times a month they took tea together and discussed clockwork creatures and rare orchids. That was all.

And if Rosa felt a certain lightness and warmth infusing her body whenever he was near her, well, that was her secret and no one else need ever know about it. But deep down, she knew that it was more than mere warmth; it was a spark that had set her feelings on fire, and now a flame roared within her whenever James was nearby. She promised herself she was in control, that she absolutely would not get burned.

But then James arrived with her orchid delivery one bright morning in July and she invited him to tea as usual.

She was secretly glad she'd worn her day-dress with the Turkish sleeves and cream silk and cannelé stripes, as it was certainly one of her most fetching, to say nothing of the elegant ostrich plumes adorning her bonnet. But, irksomely, something seemed different about James from the moment he entered the house that day.

'You seem distracted this morning,' she finally remarked, a little peevishly.

'Do I?' He looked up at her.

'I should say so. You haven't even remarked upon my new clockwork canary.' She indicated the bird in the corner of the room.

His response was swift. 'How inexcusable. The bird is marvellous, of course, like everything you create. I would have remarked upon it at once, but there is another matter on my mind.'

It wasn't like James to be preoccupied in her presence, and Rosa was immediately curious as to what had stolen his attention away from her. 'Is it something I might be able to help with?' she ventured.

He smiled briefly. 'Oh, indeed. I dare say you can resolve the matter one way or another in an instant. But I wonder, do you think it's ever worth asking a question if you already know the answer?'

Rosa frowned, puzzled. 'If you already know the answer, then what would be the point of asking the question?' she asked.

'Quite.' James gave a half-smile that turned quickly into a grimace. 'And yet . . . I cannot seem to escape the conviction that sometimes it's important to ask the hopeless question regardless. Perhaps you owe it to the peace of mind of your future self. And certainly you must owe it to those who are no longer here and so do not have the privilege of being able to pursue their own happiness.'

'James, you know I adore talking to you usually, but I'm afraid I'm simply not following a word,' Rosa said. She was starting to feel rather annoyed. It wasn't like him to ramble, and she'd been looking forward to discussing the clockwork canary with him today.

'I beg your pardon,' he said. 'I'm making a terrible mess of this, but I doubt it will matter much in the end. Please allow me to make myself perfectly clear.'

He took something from the covered Wardian case at his feet and then, to Rosa's astonishment, went down on one knee in front of her, holding up a single flower. It was a galaxy orchid, speckling the room with the gentle silver-spangled shine of starlight. Rosa gasped. That type of orchid was extraordinarily rare and quite priceless, keenly coveted by orchid collectors all over the world.

'James, what on earth—' she began.

'I cannot provide you with titles and estates,' he said, 'which I fear is what you most desire. But I must tell you that I think you are the most wonderful and extraordinary person I have ever had the privilege to know.'

Rosa's breath caught in her throat. Was he really speaking to her in such a way? Was this actually happening? She knew she ought to stop him before he could go on, yet she sat as if transfixed, unable to interrupt him even if her life had depended on it.

'It would be my great honour to offer you love and devotion,' James went on. 'And a life full of adventure and flowers. If you would permit me, I would exert every effort in my power to make you happy. And so the question I must ask you, despite already knowing the answer, is whether you would ever consider accepting me as your husband?'

Rosa could hardly breathe. The flame inside her exploded in a firework of joy and, for a single blinding moment, she thought she might throw away all her ambitions, and hopes, and dreams for her glittering future and actually say yes.

But then the firework burned itself out, as fireworks must inevitably do, leaving behind only ash, and Rosa forced herself to straighten her shoulders and stiffen her spine. It was impossible, of course – a child's dream.

*Do not give in to any girlish sentiments,* her mother's voice echoed inside her head. *Or you will regret it for the rest of your life* . . .

And certainly she had not turned down the hand of princes and noblemen abroad in order to become the wife of a mere orchid hunter. Since her arrival in London she had often heard English ladies declaring that love was bourgeois – something for the lower classes and fools – and she couldn't help but agree. When she had a title, she would join the ranks of an established family. She would never again have to hear those hateful words: 'Oh, the Warrens? New money, you know.' And witness the nose-wrinkle that went with it, as if a bad smell had appeared in the room. She could not give up on her plans to rise to the very top of society for any man, not even for James.

'I can't.' The words slipped from her mouth and made her shiver with a sudden chill, yet it was a relief to say them all the same. 'Of course I hold you in very high regard—'

She began to recite the accepted speech, but James was on his feet in an instant. 'Please say no more,' he said, smiling easily. 'Your answer is as I expected. I had to ask the question, that is all. I hope you will keep the orchid regardless?'

He held out the flower, but she recoiled from it as if it were a snake.

'Oh, but I couldn't!' she said. It was so very valuable, and the thought of accepting it under such circumstances didn't feel right at all.

James paused. 'I hunted it for you,' he said. 'It had your name on it from the moment I first saw it. No one else would appreciate it as you will. Please. It is only a flower – nothing more.'

'You are very kind,' Rosa managed. 'But, really—'

'You have my word that I will not make a nuisance of myself, if that's what concerns you.' James's brown eyes watched her closely. 'In fact I will never raise this topic with you again. I hope you will accept the orchid as a token of friendship.' He raised an eyebrow. 'We *are* still friends, are we not?'

Rosa forced a smile to her face. 'Of course!'

Her voice seemed to ring in her ears like a hollow bell. She knew she absolutely could not accept the orchid, that it would be wrong and improper, and yet the flower was so beautiful, and she wanted it so very badly, and when her fingers closed around the stem, she wasn't sorry.

'Well, I believe I have taken up enough of your time, so I will take my leave,' James said, already reaching for his hat. He indicated the Wardian case at his feet and went on, 'I have left written instructions regarding the care of the galaxy orchid. They are quite particular flowers and prefer to be planted in books rather than soil.'

'Books? But how—'

'Simply fold it within the pages of a beautiful story for a few hours once a week or so,' James said, 'and the petals will shine all the brighter. I took the liberty of selecting an appropriate book. It's a children's tale I recently stumbled upon at an auction house. You'll find it in the Wardian case.' He offered a bow. 'Thank you once again for the tea and the conversation.'

And, with that, James took his leave. Rosa was certain she had done the right thing – that she had acted like an adult rather than a child – and so she couldn't explain why she felt a lingering sense of sadness that stayed with her throughout the afternoon. It might almost be enough to make a less determined person wonder whether they had made the right choice, after all. But Rosa had always known what she wanted from life, and she wasn't about to start doubting herself now.

Her resolve was rewarded when the Duke of Chalkley arrived at her home unexpectedly that afternoon. They took tea together in the drawing room, chaperoned by Rosa's lady's maid. Eustace wore a beautifully cut grey morning suit, the sleeves fashionably puffed at the top, along with a luxurious waterfall cravat fastened with a jewelled pin. His pale hair glinted in the afternoon sunlight slanting through the windows and when Rosa presented him with the sketches of peacocks, he gazed at them like he'd never seen a drawing of a bird before.

'But these are extraordinary,' he finally said, with unexpected warmth. He was usually so cool and possessed and proper – everything that an English duke should be. It was rare to hear emotion in his voice, and Rosa glowed with pleasure to hear his admiration for her skill.

'It is nothing, your grace,' she said modestly, waving the praise away as her mother had taught her to do. A gentleman must always be flattered and made to feel superior, wherever possible.

Eustace fixed his blue gaze on her. 'Can you really create something so beautiful?'

'You will have your party of peacocks before the end of the Season,' Rosa promised.

'I am astonished by your skill, Miss Warren,' he said frankly. 'Simply astonished.'

He handed the drawings back to her, and his mauve glove brushed against her hand, butter-soft. She wondered if the rumours were true that the duke changed his gloves at least five times a day, and that every pair was scented.

'I have not come here today to discuss the garden, however,' Eustace went on. 'In fact I came to see your father. And I'm pleased to tell you that only a short while ago he gave me his blessing to call upon you in an official capacity.'

Any lingering thoughts of James scattered like startled birds, as Rosa clasped her hands in her lap and tried to look demure as she thanked Eustace for the honour. She could hardly believe it, but there was a duke sitting in her drawing room wanting to court her, and Rosa knew exactly what she needed to say, how she needed to behave and who she needed to be in order to successfully reel him in. If she had her way, then she would have a proposal before the year was out.

*The Duchess of Chalkley* . . .

In the weeks that followed, she took to uttering the words to herself in private at odd moments of the day, and it seemed that no orchid had ever smelled as sweet as that title tasted upon her tongue.

*August 1836*

*Dearest Rosa,*

I am delighted with this clever clockwork pigeon. What a superb idea.

I'm afraid there is still no sign of the ghost butterfly, although you will doubtless be amused to hear that I fell into a gaming pit whilst chasing after another species last week. I'd travelled further than intended, when my guide indicated that the scratch marks on the trees surrounding us meant that there were leopards in the vicinity. I thought it judicious to turn back, and we were on the point of doing so when I fell straight through a clump of underbrush and found myself on a lot of beastly spikes some fifteen feet below ground in a big clay game-pit.

My guide soon hauled me out with a bush-rope, but those spikes must have been twelve inches long. It's at times like that you realise the blessing of a good thick skirt. Thankfully I was unharmed, save for the fact that I managed to lose my last hat-pin, which is quite a blow. Still, to you I will confess that falling into that pit was one of the most enjoyable experiences I've had in a long time. I doubt any other ladies of my acquaintance will understand, but I imagine you will. It was an adventure, infinitely preferable to morning calls. And we made it back to the hotel without being mauled by leopards, so it all ended well besides.

Your friend,
Beatrice

September 1836

Dear Beatrice,

How utterly thrilling your travels sound! If I ever found myself in a gaming pit, I think I would die of fright! I regret I have nothing so exciting to report here. Much of my time has been taken up with preparing the clockwork peacocks for the duke. I recently gave him a tour of one of our new London factories. Since then, we have spent a great deal of time together, tweaking the design to his preferences. I do so want him to be pleased with the birds and am determined that they shall be the crown jewel of his pleasure garden.

Speaking of gardens, how's this for a coincidence? I declare, you'll hardly credit it. You may be aware that James Sheppard sometimes favours me with small gifts — due to being his best client, you know — well, the other day he gave me an orchid planted in a book, and would you believe it was that children's book you mentioned on the day of your wedding? None other than The Winter Garden itself!

And gracious, Beatrice, I can certainly see why you were so taken with it. It's most beautiful, and an excellent example of a pop-up book. The pictures still spring up on their mechanisms just as well as they ever did. How you must have adored the story as a girl, to say nothing of the fact that the main character is called Beatrice! Why, she even looks rather like you. How very sad for the girl that she's a mute.

And the illustrations are simply exquisite. When I look at the pages they completely draw me in. I feel as if cold snowflakes really do brush against my cheeks, and I can smell the flowers, and hear the birds, and see the outline of the tiger's paw prints left deep in the sparkling snow. Sometimes I even fancy I can detect the scent of peppermint upon the crinkly old pages!

Anyway, I know that a child's pop-up book can't compare with tumbling into game-pits and fleeing from leopards and so on, but it was certainly the highlight of my week!

I hope to hear more of your adventures soon.

Your friend,
Rosa

September 1836

Dear Rosa,

I am extremely curious about the children's book you mention and would love to see it. If you could bear to part with it, might you be willing to send it with the clockwork pigeon so that I might take a look for myself?

Your friend,
Beatrice

September 1836

Dear Beatrice,

I would send the book, but I fear it is too heavy for the pigeon to carry such a vast distance, and I'd hate to trust it to the international post. It's so unreliable, and an old book like this would not like such rough treatment. It is quite delicate in places. Don't worry! It will be here waiting for you as soon as you return home to England. Certain developments mean that I may well be making England my permanent home in the future. I hope to say more of that in due course!

Your friend,
Rosa

September 1836

Dear Rosa,

I have decided to be frank with you. I was utterly astonished to receive your letter regarding the pop-up book. You see, I lied when I said that I had owned such a volume as a child. It was all I could think of when you questioned me about the peacock.

The truth is, the Winter Garden does not merely exist within the pages of a child's book — it is real. It came to the grounds of Half Moon House when I was only a girl, shortly after losing my mother. It was also around the time my father sent me for that dreadful surgical procedure, which was meant to correct my stutter but simply had the effect of almost robbing me of my capacity for speech for good. I could not speak a word at that time.

So, you see, the book you describe is my own story, and I do not understand how it can possibly exist in such a form. I never told another living soul about the garden, except for my nanny and father, neither of whom believed me.

Your perplexed friend,
Beatrice

September 1836

Dear Beatrice,

I was most charmed to receive your last letter. My dear, you can't honestly believe what you wrote to me about the garden? I'm sure you must be pulling my leg, you wicked creature!

Of course you must have owned the book as a child, and it so affected your imagination that I can well believe you would play at discovering the Winter Garden for real. But, honey, that's all it could ever have been — just child's play or a particularly vivid dream. How wondrous it would be if such a place could actually exist, though! I regret it cannot be so in this world of ours.

I hope you are keeping well and haven't fallen into any more pits full of spikes!

Your affectionate friend,
Rosa

September 1836

Dear Rosa,

You may believe me or not, but I tell you plainly that the garden was real and I visited it more than once. Nothing anybody says will ever convince me otherwise. In fact that is the true purpose of my travels abroad. I mean to find the garden.

My father refused to believe me and even threatened institution if I didn't abandon my claims, but I had hoped you might be more open to the idea, especially given the fact of the book. Surely the black apple trees within its pages are proof of what I am saying? I brought one of the apples back from the garden one night and planted the seeds in the grounds. How else can anyone explain their presence at Half Moon House?

Your friend,
Beatrice

September 1836

Dear Beatrice,

I confess I am more confused than ever and hardly know what to think. The book does contain some pictures of apple trees, and I suppose the fruit does look rather dark, but that could simply be because the garden is shown at night, with only lanterns and candles to illuminate it, and many of the pictures are in the form of cut-out silhouettes. Certainly there is nothing to indicate that the trees in the book are at all like the strange trees at your home. I cannot see that they have any teeth, for a start, and there's no suggestion that they move about at will, or gobble up rabbits, or unfurl peculiar blossom at dusk.

Really, my dear, extraordinary as those trees are, it seems far more likely that their appearance — together with this book and, of course, all the grief over your mother's death — caused you to dream up the magical garden when you were a child.

Having said that, no one would be more utterly delighted than I if such a garden actually existed and I'm sure the world is full of an abundance of things that we do not, and cannot, understand. So I am quite prepared to maintain an open mind on the matter.

How exactly are you planning to try to track down this elusive magical garden? Where on earth does one start on such a fantastic quest?

Your friend,
Rosa

*October 1836*

*Dear Rosa,*

I am beginning my search for the garden by seeking out the flora, fauna and animals I remember seeing there. I am also speaking to as many local people as I can along the way, in the hope that someone may have heard of the garden, or visited it themselves. I have already been rewarded by one child who claims to have been there, and whose account bears remarkable similarities to my own.

When Mr Sheppard attended Half Moon House for my wedding, he mentioned the Winter Garden to me, and said that he had heard rumours about it in auction houses. Of course I denied all knowledge of the garden, but I have since been making enquiries in auction houses myself and it turns out he is quite right. Many establishments have what they call 'shadow auctions' that are not open to the public, but to private collectors only. I have managed to gain entry to a few. They offer up only the rarest and most unusual of items, all of which are supposed to be vetted for authenticity, but I have my doubts as to whether all of these items are genuine. In India, for example, there was a mermaid's comb in the lot, as well as a haunted clock. Hardly likely to be real, I am sure you will agree.

But in Thailand I attended one such auction and found two items that I am sure did originate from the Winter Garden. There was a silver teaspoon stamped with the garden's crest, and a napkin from one of the midnight picnics. They both looked just as I remembered them. It seems there is quite a mania that surrounds these objects from the Winter Garden and much lore that has built up around it.

Please don't say anything to Mr Sheppard about the garden. Indeed, I would like to ask that you don't mention it to anyone at all. I have kept it a secret these past years and think it best that it remains that way for now. Unscrupulous people might try to raid it for profit, and I could not stand to have that upon my conscience. The garden appeared to me at the unhappiest time of my life and I owe it a great deal.

As you cannot send me the children's book, and I cannot spare the weeks it would require to return to England, perhaps you could do the next best thing and simply describe each page? I wonder if you would also be good enough to provide me with the details of the publishing house and the year it was printed, any distinguishing marks or inscriptions within the cover, etc.

Your grateful friend,
Beatrice

October 1836

Dear Beatrice,

I have some very exciting news that I am finally able to share with you! Eustace has asked me to marry him, and I have accepted! We are to be wed in the new year.

As you can imagine, I'm extremely busy making preparations, so I'm afraid the detailed description of the pop-up book will have to wait. I promise to get around to it as soon as I possibly can.

As for the author and publishing house, I have not been able to find mention of these anywhere in the book at all. It is as if it simply sprang into existence by itself. So perhaps you are right, honey, and there really is a magical Winter Garden travelling the world, filled with fairies and crowned frogs and other wondrous things. How marvellous if that were so! I feel I'm living in a fairy tale myself at the moment. If it's possible for someone like me to become an English duchess and have all their wildest dreams come true, then who's to say that your fantastical garden cannot exist also? I sincerely hope to see it one day for myself.

I do wish I could invite you to the wedding, Beatrice, but I'm sure you'll appreciate that would be quite impossible, given the circumstances. I hope you will think of me when the time comes, though, and give me your blessing.

All my love,
Rosa

December 1836

Dear Rosa,

Firstly, allow me to congratulate you. If marriage to
Eustace is what you truly desire, then I wish you every
happiness in the world. I am quite certain that you
will make a far better wife than I ever could. Certainly
you have my most heartfelt blessing, and I trust your
future will be filled with much joy and happiness.

   Thank you for your information about the book. If
you could get those page descriptions to me as soon as
you possibly can, I would very much appreciate it.

Your friend,
Beatrice

# CHAPTER SIX

*December 1836*

Rosa walked into the Winter Ball on the arm of the duke, Cookie trotting at her heels, and felt as if she might float away on wings of happiness. She wore a ruby gown specially sent from Paris for the occasion. The corsage was cut low enough to expose a hint of the cream chemisette beneath, the sleeves formed a triple bouffant and were adorned with elegant butterfly bows. A twisted bandeau of the palest ivory gauze ribbons adorned her hair, containing a single bird-of-paradise plume held in place with a sparkling ruby pin.

Rosa's friend, Lord Randolph, was known for his lavish parties, and the ballroom tonight was festooned with holly garlands and hundreds of white orchids. It was the event of the Season, and all the guests turned to look at Eustace and Rosa as they entered. This was their first appearance as an official couple since the engagement was announced and Rosa intended to enjoy every glorious moment.

The evening seemed to pass in a whirlwind of dancing and champagne. Rosa lost track of the number of congratulations she accepted from well-wishers. Whenever she stepped off the dance floor she faced an avalanche of girls, keen to prise details from her about the upcoming wedding. She would have danced all night if she could have done so, but Eustace was concerned for her feet and she finally allowed him to lead her to a chair for a rest. Cookie seemed glad of the break too – the clockwork pug wasn't as young as he'd once been – and flopped down beside Rosa's chair with a creaking of old hinges. She made a mental note to oil him as soon as they were home. He was by far the oldest clockwork creature she had, and mechanical animals required more care and attention as they got older, just as flesh-and-blood ones did.

'May I fetch you something?' Eustace asked. 'Some sweetmeats? Another glass of champagne?'

Rosa felt herself bask in the warm glow of his attention. He was always so very considerate towards her, forever mindful of her comfort, and attentive to the smallest hint of a desire. It seemed to Rosa that he was determined to provide her with anything and everything she could possibly want, the very moment she wanted it.

He went off to the buffet, leaving Rosa tapping her feet to the orchestra, impatient to join the dancing again as soon as possible.

'I hear congratulations are in order.'

She looked up to see James standing before her. She had known he was present – she'd recognised his flowers the moment she entered the house. Cookie immediately heaved to his creaking feet and greeted the orchid hunter with much excitement and tinny yapping.

'Hello, old fellow.' James crouched down to stroke the dog's metal ears before glancing back up at Rosa. 'And so you got everything you ever wanted in the end. I'm truly happy for you.'

There was a warm smile upon his face and Rosa returned it gladly. His proposal, and the uncertainty she'd felt over it, seemed a world away now. How fortunate that she had not allowed herself to lose her head, and how lucky that she had never betrayed her own brief infatuation, or else none of this would be happening now.

'Thank you,' she said, beaming. 'You'll provide the orchids for the wedding, of course? I want hundreds and hundreds of them. Thousands! And you know that Raven Hall has forty hothouses in the grounds?'

It was the part she'd loved best when Eustace had given her a tour. Some of the hothouses were home to the duke's vast collection of orchids, whilst the rest catered to the endless cycle of bedding plants that the estate required, as well as infant trees, beehives and out-of-season fruits.

'Just think how many extraordinary flowers you'll be able to bring me once I'm the duchess!' she said.

James smiled and stood back up. 'It would be my honour to provide flowers for your wedding, Miss Warren, of course – the most exotic and lovely blooms I can find. But after that, I'm afraid you must employ the services of some other orchid hunter.'

For a moment Rosa thought she must have misheard.

'Mr Sheppard! Don't tell me you're retiring from the business?'

She was shocked. James had often talked of how much he loved orchid hunting, in spite of the inherent dangers, even going so far as to say that it made him feel more alive than anything else in the world ever could.

He laughed. 'Indeed, no. I imagine I shall hunt orchids, in one fashion or another, until the day I die. My father considers the whole thing a mania, and perhaps he's right.'

There was suddenly a strange look in his eyes that Rosa didn't understand.

'A mania,' she repeated. 'Why, that's putting it rather strongly!'

James shrugged. 'I'm not so sure. If something brings you more grief and heartache than reward and pleasure, yet you persist in the endeavour anyway, then how else might one describe it?'

'You seem in a melancholy mood this evening,' Rosa replied with a frown. 'I thought you adored orchid hunting?'

'Oh, I do,' he said. 'Even when I don't.'

'I'm afraid I don't understand you.' Rosa was concerned. She might not fancy herself in love with James any more, but she still liked him a great deal. 'Are you quite all right?'

'Indeed, yes. Please forgive me. Some of the flowers I provided for the party tonight just reminded me of an old friend, that's all. He died in Hawaii last year.'

'I'm truly sorry to hear it. But if you have not given up the whole enterprise, then what is all this nonsense about not providing me with flowers after the wedding?'

'It is only that I must be quite particular about my clients, as you know, and I'm afraid the duke is not a gentleman with whom I can do business.'

'But why ever not?' Rosa stared at him. 'Gracious, he has the greatest orchid collection in the world! I should think most hunters would be pleased to work for him, especially as the king himself toured Raven Hall's hothouses last summer.'

She wondered whether the true reason could be that James was jealous of her upcoming marriage, but then surely he would not have agreed to provide flowers for her wedding if that were the case?

He seemed unconcerned by her surprise. 'I am not most orchid hunters; I am glad to say.'

'But this is the most foolish thing I ever heard, Mr Sheppard,' Rosa said. 'I can hardly credit it, because I know you are not a foolish man. You should be falling over yourself to provide the orchids for Raven Hall. I must demand an explanation.'

Cookie was nudging James's boots most insistently, so he leaned down to pet him once again.

'I would not wish to speak ill of your betrothed, Miss Warren,' James replied, 'but if you must demand an explanation, then it is perfectly simple. The duke mistreats his horses. I make it a rule not to work for any man or woman who does so.'

Rosa recalled that James had a great love of horses and had once told her that if he could not have become an orchid hunter, then he would happily have been a groom instead. She had been shocked by his remark, since a groom really was one of the lowliest jobs in service that one could do, but when she'd said as much, he'd merely laughed and made some ridiculous comment about generally preferring horses to people.

'I'm sure you are misinformed,' she said now. 'The duke is so kind and courteous – I cannot believe for a moment that he mistreats his horses. Besides, they're far too valuable.'

'Be that as it may,' James said, 'my orchids will not go to Raven Hall.'

Rosa opened her mouth to argue further, but just then another gentleman called to James from across the room and he took his leave with a bow. When Eustace returned with her refreshments a moment later, she recounted the conversation to him – omitting the part about the horses.

'I endeavoured to employ Mr Sheppard's services last year, but he declined,' he told her. 'No matter. There are other orchid hunters in the world.'

'But none so good,' Rosa protested. She felt suddenly crestfallen. After all, James really was the best in the business. No one else was ever likely to present her with a galaxy orchid.

Some of her dismay must have shown on her face, for Eustace said, 'Well, if it means that much to you, my dear, then I will speak to Mr Sheppard again.'

Rosa expected that he meant at some time in the future, so she was surprised when he immediately excused himself and crossed the ballroom right then and there. The two men spoke for only a matter of minutes before James gave a stiff bow, and Eustace returned to Rosa's side with a smile.

'It is done,' he said. 'Mr Sheppard will provide orchids for our hothouses.'

Rosa beamed. 'How clever you are!' she said. It was always wise to flatter a man's ego, of course, and she took every opportunity to do so where Eustace was concerned, but this time she was genuinely pleased.

'Not at all,' the duke replied. He looked suddenly serious. 'If there is ever anything you lack, no matter how small, then you must tell me at once. When you are mistress of Raven Hall, and my wife, you will want for nothing. That I promise you.'

Rosa smiled. Champagne and happiness filled her with tiny golden bubbles, and she felt as if she would burst.

And why not? In a matter of weeks she would have everything she had ever wanted.

And yet . . . when James left the ball a short while later, she noticed Cookie trail him across the dance floor and then sit motionless, staring expectantly at the doorway, as if hopeful that he would soon return. The sight of her little dog waiting patiently like that nagged at her in a way she could not fully explain. Eventually, she called the pug to her side. She would not allow herself to feel unsettled. Not on a night like this, when there were so many wonderful things to feel thrilled about.

# CHAPTER SEVEN

*Singapore – February 1837*

Beatrice sat in the auction hall and tried to cool her face with the large folding fan she'd obtained from the market. There were ceiling fans working above, but the heat was still intense – almost a physical burden that rested heavily upon her shoulders. The wooden chair was unforgiving against her legs and she could feel sweat soaking into her skirts. She had originally intended to be outside, exploring the flora and fauna along the rivers, but she'd heard of this shadow auction and managed to gain admittance at the last moment. So far it had been a disappointment, with nothing pertaining to the Winter Garden at all, but then the auctioneer announced the next item.

'Up next we have the Tiger of Stars, which is, of course, from the fabled Winter Garden with which many of our collectors will be familiar.'

Beatrice lowered her fan and sat up a little straighter in her seat. Two staff members wheeled out a trolley and removed a velvet cloth to reveal a glorious sparkling tiger. It was not made of stars, but from hundreds of tiny diamonds that sparkled and flashed in the sunlit space.

Just like that, Beatrice was a child again, back among the pines of the Winter Garden. The little domed ice house had peeked out shyly from amongst the trees at the very edge of the grounds. Covered in frosted moss, the building had seemed like something from fairyland, a home for trolls, perhaps, or ice witches. Even the trees surrounding it were lovely, with sugar mice and glass angels slowly twisting and turning from their branches.

The young Beatrice was well accustomed to ice houses – her own home's grounds had several of them hidden amongst the foliage – but this one belonged to the Winter Garden and so she had immediately hurried towards it, already marvelling at whatever delights she might find inside.

Before she could reach the open door, a tiger stepped out. Instead of black-and-orange stripes, it had shone with the light of a hundred tiny stars. Each whisker was a thread of moonlight, its fur was a haze of star-glow, its eyes were galaxies. Beatrice had thought the tiger the most majestic thing she had ever seen, or could comprehend. She was so shocked by the sheer size of him that she stopped and recoiled backwards, sitting down hard in the snow.

'Isn't he magnificent?' a voice had said behind her.

Beatrice had looked up and seen the Spider Queen. She wore a shawl of cobwebbed lace across her shoulders, and flakes of new snow settled in her greying hair. Her spiders were in the trees all around her, already spinning their extraordinary webs into the spaces between the branches, their silk as fine as fairy thread. Beatrice stood up and dusted the snow from her dress. She longed to ask questions about the tiger, but her tongue was still a useless lump of flesh in her mouth. Instead she pointed at the big cat, sparkling on the ice-house steps, and looked back up at the Spider Queen, who smiled. A spider – white as milk – crawled up her arm and settled itself on her shoulder.

'Some of the plants and animals in the garden come and go,' she said. 'But the tiger has been here since the beginning, and he'll be here until the end.' She looked down at Beatrice. 'Have you ever heard of navigating by the stars?'

Beatrice shook her head.

'People say there is one star in the whole of the night sky that doesn't move, called the North Star. If you find it in the sky, then you will always be able to locate true north.'

The spider ran down her arm onto the tree branch, where it began to spin an elaborate galaxy web in shining threads of silver – an entire daisy chain of stars.

'But what most people don't know,' the Spider Queen went on, 'is that there's a second star in the sky that is fixed, and that is the Tiger's Eye. It forms part of the White Tiger constellation and it marks the place where pure magic lives. Which is why you'll always find the tiger right here, in the garden. The most magical place in the world.'

Beatrice had never seen anything like the tiger before, yet as she stared at him she felt the most curious sense of déjà vu. Surely she had been here before, dazzled by the beauty of the tiger, and the magic of the garden, and the wonder of the universe?

Then there was the scraping of claw over stone, and the tiger began making its way down the ice-house steps towards them, his great body rippling with white light and silent strength. He seemed to become bigger and more beautiful with every step, until he stood only a couple of paces from Beatrice. His head was level with hers; he was close enough that she could see each individual whisker and the bright white fire burning in his eyes. They stood looking at one another for a long moment. Then the tiger padded slowly forward and rubbed his great head against Beatrice's shoulder in what was, quite unmistakeably, an affectionate gesture. She felt the burning coldness of his stars against her skin, the inky blackness of his stripes against her hand. And then he was gone, padding through the trees and into the garden.

Every night that Beatrice visited after that, the tiger sought her out and walked by her side for some of the evening. He would permit her to touch him and sometimes initiated the contact himself. When the Winter

Garden left, some small part of Beatrice had hoped that perhaps the tiger might have stayed behind to be with her. The loneliness of her new life without her mother might be a little easier to bear if she had the beautiful big cat for company. She had so dearly hoped to look out on the lawn and see the icy glitter of his stars. But he had left with the garden and she never laid eyes on him again.

Once she was older, she consulted the astronomy books in her father's library, hoping to find some information about the White Tiger constellation, but there was no mention of it anywhere. The sparkling diamond tiger before her now was the closest she'd got to finding him. The starting price was inordinately expensive, but Beatrice knew at once that she had to have it. It not only dazzled just as the real tiger had, but it also wore the same expression of quiet dignity and its huge paws seemed made for treading into deep drifts of snow.

Fortunately it was a long way out of the price range of most of the other collectors there, and Beatrice won it easily. When she went to provide her details to the auctioneer afterwards, she was disappointed to learn that the seller was not the creator of the item. She had been hoping to speak to someone else who had been to the garden.

But as she made arrangements for the tiger to be shipped back to Half Moon House, she felt sure that she was making progress, and getting closer to the garden, bit by bit. Surely she would see it again for herself before the year was out.

# Part Two

# CHAPTER EIGHT

*March 1837*

Rosa, Duchess of Chalkley, gazed out the window and onto the grounds of Raven Hall.

'I am happy,' she told herself. '*I am.*'

Her wedding to Eustace had been one of the most glittering events anyone on either side of the Atlantic had ever seen. The New York newspapers had gone into raptures over it, sending reporters to cover every last detail. There had been fifteen hundred guests, two hundred clockwork turtle doves and a fifty-piece orchestra. The church aisle was an avenue of Rosa's favourite white orchids, and the stone columns, arches and wooden pews were adorned with a record-breaking abundance of lilies, roses and chrysanthemums.

At the wedding breakfast at Raven Hall later on there were more than twenty thousand sprays of lily-of-the-valley and enough orchids that if they were laid end to end they would cover a distance of some eight miles. James Sheppard had been true to his word and had provided Rosa with countless exotic blooms, and everyone who attended the wedding agreed that it was one of the most spectacular ever celebrated in England.

Her clockwork pigeon fluttered up to her, ever hopeful that she was ready to send a letter. Rosa had created the bird to deliver messages to Beatrice, and yet she hadn't sent any in months. She didn't know what she could say to her old friend, but she knew that she must write to her soon. Just last week Beatrice had sent a letter by regular post saying that she might return to England to see the pop-up book for herself, and that was something Rosa could not face – to have to see her old friend again and pretend that all was well. She must send Beatrice a note with a white lie about the book. Perhaps she could say it had been lost.

In the two months since her marriage, Rosa had tried to will herself into happiness, but it was no use. Misery had sunk deep into her bones. She felt no love or tenderness whatsoever towards the baby growing inside her. This felt like the greatest failure of all, for Rosa had always wanted children, and had promised herself that she would be nothing like her own mother: so cold, and distant, and resentful.

Rosa and her brothers had received more love from Maggie, the slave who had cared for them in the nursery. Even now, Rosa still felt a twinge of grief when she recalled the day Maggie had been sold to another family.

How strange it was now to think of the excitement with which she had walked down the aisle on that January afternoon. Eustace had been so attentive and charming to her throughout the day. Everyone was so admiring, and her family was so delighted, and her entire world became a glow of delight. When she walked through the front doors of Raven Hall as its mistress for the first time, she could barely breathe. There were only thirty dukedoms in the whole country, and she had managed to capture one! Of course she did not love Eustace, but then she had never expected to. She liked him, and he seemed to like her, and that was enough. Plenty of marriages had been built on far less.

'You mustn't expect too much from a new husband,' Rosa's mother had counselled on the day of her wedding. 'Especially when it comes to considering your various wants and whims. In all likelihood, this will not even occur to him. You should try to think of him as an egg – so full of himself that he is incapable of holding anything else.'

Rosa seemed unable to find common ground with her mother on most things, but she thought this sound advice. And she did not mind in the least. After all, their marriage was a business arrangement. She had signed over her wealth and fortune, and in return she had received the title that she coveted so fiercely, as well as a place in the history books and the right to call a grand ancestral hall her own.

Rosa had been slightly nervous about the wedding night, but she knew the facts of 'the unfortunate side of marriage', thanks to a rather scandalous book she had found during a trip to New York, and her hands only trembled a little as she changed into her new silk nightdress and slipped between the sheets.

But when Eustace came to her bedroom, the golden bubble burst as soon as he touched her. Rosa didn't think that he particularly intended to hurt her, it was more that he simply didn't think of her as a person at all during those moments. When it was over, he rolled away from her without a word, and suddenly Rosa no longer wanted to stay in the same bed with him, so she got up and slipped into her dressing room.

She was afraid he might follow or object, but there was only silence and stillness from the bed and she realised he didn't care where she went, or what she did, or how she was feeling. She wrapped herself up in a rug and fell into a fretful sleep upon the chaise longue.

When Eustace found her there the next day, he exclaimed in surprise, as if he had not the least comprehension as to why she was not in bed. He wasn't angry. Far from it. In fact he enquired after her health most attentively, questioning her to check whether the bed, or the mattress, was not to her liking, and asking what he could do to make her more comfortable.

Rosa had begun to wonder whether the night had really been as bad as she imagined. Perhaps Eustace had not been particularly kind, but he hadn't been overly cruel, either. Had he? Her mind was a blur of confusion, and queasiness roiled in her stomach. She wasn't sure what was usual in such circumstances. All she knew was that she had hated every sweating, grunting moment, and had no wish to repeat it ever again. She tried to tell herself that she would become accustomed to it in time. She had to.

But the next night was just as horrible. And so was every night that followed. Rosa came to shudder at the very idea of Eustace's touch. His scented gloves made her feel ill, and the overpowering reek of the Macassar oil that he put in his hair was even worse. In the dim light of the bedroom lamps he did not even look like himself, or like any man at all. He seemed to her more like a pig, a boar – ugly, and red, and straining.

Now Rosa stood up from her writing desk and paced the drawing room. In spite of her unhappiness she still wanted to be a duchess, and she wanted Raven Hall and all it stood for. She wanted the collection of Canalettos and Rembrandts, the ormolu horses and Flemish tapestries, the Sèvres vases and Waterford chandeliers. And, of course, she wanted the hothouses full of her favourite flowers, the exotic and expensive orchids, the most coveted flower in the world. The bloom that men died for abroad every year. This was the position and status Rosa had been aiming for her entire life. Yet suddenly her corset felt too tight and there was no air in the room. Something had to change. Perhaps it was merely a question of *talking* to Eustace?

She froze as the idea occurred to her. Of course it was utterly unthinkable to broach such a subject. Her mother would probably faint away at the idea. And yet . . . what was it Eustace had said to her that night at the Winter Ball last year?

*If there is ever anything you lack, no matter how small, then you must tell me at once . . .*

Perhaps she only needed to explain to him how wretched she felt and he would be utterly appalled and would probably apologise profusely. She could see it in her mind's eye already. He would be quite bereft at the idea that he had hurt her, however unintentionally. Rosa would be gracious in her forgiveness, and things between them would change for the better. Yes, surely this was the solution.

Before she had time to second-guess herself, she went down the corridor to Eustace's study and knocked on the door. He called for her to enter, and she stepped inside to see him answering correspondence at his desk.

'Rosa,' Eustace said, looking up. 'Is everything all right?'

'No.' She forced herself to say the word. 'It isn't. I need to speak with you.'

Eustace laid down his pen at once. 'But what is amiss?'

She cleared her throat, summoning her courage. 'I am unhappy.'

There. She had said it. The words could not be undone. And just as she had imagined, Eustace was staring at her with an appalled expression. 'I am dismayed to hear this,' he said quietly. 'Why on earth did you not speak to me sooner? Whatever it is that you lack, you have only to tell me and I will see to it at once.'

Rosa felt a sudden giddy relief at his words, but was suddenly unsure how to express the problem delicately.

'Is the house not to your liking?' Eustace went on, speaking too quickly for her to have the chance to respond. 'Has one of the servants been impudent? Is your pin-money not sufficient? I'm sure we could increase it slightly.'

Rosa felt a deep flush spread across her cheeks. 'It is nothing of that sort,' she said.

'Then what?'

He spoke with such utter incomprehension that Rosa felt the old fear flare up inside her again.

*One of us is surely mad.*

*Could it be me?*

But surely he *must* know? He simply had to be aware of how wretched he made her feel in the chilly silence of the night. If nothing else, he must feel how tense she was, he must notice when she flinched. There had even been the occasional sob that she had been unable to stifle.

She took a deep breath. 'I am referring to the way you treat me in the bedroom.'

Eustace's eyes widened slightly. Her words seemed to suck all the oxygen from the room, leaving her light-headed. Eustace had gone completely still, staring at her with an unreadable expression. The silence stretched on and on, until Rosa thought she would not be able to bear it a moment longer.

'How dare you, madam,' Eustace finally said, his voice dreadfully quiet. 'Have you no delicacy of mind? No well-bred woman would dream of speaking of such matters. I will overlook this just once, in recognition of the fact that your condition may have caused you to become hysterical.'

Rosa's fists were clenched at her sides. She didn't notice that her pug, Cookie, had nudged the door open and had sat himself down companionably by her side, laying his favourite ball at her heels, already wagging his clockwork tail in anticipation of a game.

'Whilst I have you here,' Eustace said, 'I have been meaning to speak with you about the new clockwork creatures for the garden, when we open to the public in July. I've decided that this year we should have a pair of swans to go with the peacocks. You may make a start this afternoon.'

Rosa glared at him. She knew the sensible thing would be to agree and quietly leave the room but suddenly it seemed important, in this moment, to make herself heard, or else a pattern for their lives would be set that she knew she'd never be able to escape. She no longer felt nervous, or afraid of what Eustace might say or think. Now she simply felt angry.

'No,' she said.

'I beg your pardon?'

'As well you should,' Rosa replied. 'But I said no, and I will say it again. If you will not give me what I want, then I will do the same to you. You have made me feel like a . . . a thing. I am not a whore, sir – I am your wife, and I'm trying to tell you that you're making me miserable. I will not produce another piece of clockwork for you until that changes.'

Rosa turned, intending to leave the room with an air of dignity, but Eustace was out of his chair in the blink of an eye. Moving faster than she had ever seen him do before, he reached her side in seconds, and she flinched in readiness for a blow that never came. Instead he snatched Cookie up from the floor.

'No!' Rosa cried, already starting forward. 'Oh, please, don't!'

It was too late. Eustace dashed the clockwork pug so hard against the wall that springs, wires and clockwork flew out in all directions. The dog's yaps abruptly stopped.

*It's all right,* Rosa thought. *He can still be repaired; I can bring him back . . .*

But then Eustace struck him against the wall a second time, and a third, and after that third blow there was no longer a clockwork pug in his hands at all, only a collection of cogs falling through his fingers.

And then there was the ghastly ring of silence, broken only when Rosa let out a choking sob.

'Do not carry on,' Eustace snapped. 'We both know you can rebuild him in a day.'

He smoothed back his hair. A fat vein bulged in his forehead and, for the first time, Rosa saw the boar beneath the mask surface outside the bedroom. It made her sick. She knew there was no point trying to explain. She could make another clockwork pug certainly, but even if she built him to be identical, he would be a different dog with different experiences and a personality all his own. It would not be the same loyal companion who had accompanied her to barbecues and fish-fries in Georgia and had stayed by her side all the way from America – the one precious piece of her old life she'd still had left. Most people would have called it heresy, but Rosa truly believed that clockwork creatures had souls too. And now Cookie was gone, and gone for good. All that was left of him was the ball, still lying on the floor where he had dropped it.

'If you ever speak to me that way again,' Eustace said quietly, 'then we will have serious difficulties.' He straightened his cuffs. 'Really, madam, I have no wish for us to be out of sorts with one another. Let us try again. Do you understand my instructions, and will you follow them to the letter?'

'Yes, Eustace,' Rosa said, staring at the floor. 'I understand and I'll do as you say.'

'Good.' He returned to his desk. 'Might I suggest that you make time this week to read the book my mother so kindly presented to you as a wedding gift.' His mouth pinched into an expression of distaste. 'She tried to warn me that admitting Americans into the English aristocracy could only damage it, but I would not listen. I assured her that you would not do, or say, anything vulgar or coarse. Now I see quite plainly that you have much to learn about being an English duchess, to say nothing of a mother and wife. Like most of your kinsfolk, you speak so fast that no one can understand a word. You do not curtsy correctly. And that ridiculous business with the children's party last month. Extremely embarrassing.'

Despite the winter weather, Rosa had been keen to make a good impression on the tenants and had thought it would be a nice gesture to throw a fete for the local children, introducing them to American treats such as ice cream. She'd imagined they would be delighted, but the English palate was not so used to rich, sweet food, and soon the children were complaining of stomach aches and asking if there was any hot tea instead. Rosa had noted the snide looks and sniggering from the tenants, and knew that the dowager duchess was not the only person who disapproved of an American marrying into the aristocracy.

Eustace flicked a glance at her now, before frowning down at his desk. 'I cannot look at you. Please remove yourself from my sight.'

Rosa turned and walked from the room without a word, pausing only to pick up Cookie's ball, then closing the door quietly behind her. She went straight outside to the aviary where the ravens were kept. Since moving to Raven Hall, Rosa had come to appreciate that a garden could be a solace to the soul, and she spent much of her time outside. The aviary was one of the most beautiful buildings she'd ever seen. The sprawling cast-iron struc-ture took its inspiration from the trelliswork pavilions of palatial French gardens, like those at Versailles. The ravens fluttered and swooped between their perches in the lofty space overhead as soon as Rosa entered the building.

An *unkindness* . . .

That was the collective noun for them. It seemed strangely fitting for the birds that lived at Raven Hall. Still, Rosa liked them and had taken to spending a great deal of time in the aviary recently, even using it as a sort of workshop to sketch out her clockwork designs. Most days it was bitterly cold, but today she preferred to be bundled up in her winter furs with the birds than inside the same mansion as Eustace.

She went over to the feeding station and dipped the ravens' biscuits in bowls of blood, just as they liked them. They descended in a flurry of black wings, silken as petticoats. Yes, Rosa thought. The ravens would work perfectly well for what she had in mind.

Using the feeding station as a makeshift desk, she pulled out the workbook and pencils she'd stored there. Recently she had been working on plans for a winter carousel. She had adored them ever since riding one as a child at the Mechanical Museum on Coney Island, and had entire sketchbooks filled with hundreds of designs. For years she had dreamed of creating a spectacular carousel of her own – something that was more than mere cogs and clockwork, something that was truly magical. It was the dream that had first ignited her interest in becoming an artificer, even though everyone said it was a domain that women should not enter.

In her latest clockwork sketch the horses all had silver ribbons in their manes – all except one, which had a golden ribbon instead. The gold-ribboned horse was special somehow, in a way Rosa had not yet worked out. There were sleighs and polar bears on the carousel too, and twists of ice that hung down from the circular roof and dripped from the horses' flailing hooves.

But it was no longer the time for beauty and magic, so she put the carousel to one side, turned to a blank page and began work on a new mechanical sketch. Several hours passed, her back aching and her stomach grumbling with hunger, but still she worked and worked, adding details here, refining the design there. The sun was low in the sky by the time she'd finished and it had turned even colder in the aviary, but she was pleased with her efforts.

She glanced at Cookie's ball and her hands tightened on the paper. She would pay Eustace back. It would take a little time, and she would have to work in secret, but she would hit him harder than he'd hit her. As the ravens cawed overhead, Rosa smiled grimly down at the clockwork plan before her. Whatever it took, she would have it ready for the day Eustace's pleasure garden opened.

# CHAPTER NINE

*March 1837*

That night Eustace came to Rosa's room as usual. She thought he must be quite mad if he thought to share her bed after what had happened earlier, but it turned out that saying no wasn't an option. The struggle between them was brief, strangely silent, and over in a matter of minutes. Shortly afterwards Rosa closed the door of her bedroom and turned her back on it, trembling in every limb. Too late, she realised she had made a dreadful mistake. Far from clearing the air between them, trying to discuss the matter with Eustace had made the situation a hundred times worse.

Her wrists ached where Eustace had gripped them, and her hands shook as she took a candle and matches from her dressing-gown pocket. She lit the wick, but one small flame did not do much to dispel the house's shadows.

She set off down the corridor, walking and walking, with no idea where she was going. The mansion was muffled in freshly fallen snow, like an ancient dowager in her prized furs. Fires were kept burning in the main rooms throughout the day, but the house remained colder than a crypt. Beatrice had been right – it was simply impossible to heat a building of this immense size.

As she walked, it seemed to Rosa that the corridors stretched on endlessly, like a maze from which there could be no escape, always leading to another crooked staircase or another shut-up chamber. Antlered skulls loomed out of the shadows, and the vast oil paintings seemed filled with the sightless eyes of slaughtered deer and the limp wings of blood-stained pheasants. Many of the rooms had not been occupied in years and mouldered away beneath their Holland covers.

On nights like this, the windows rattled in their frames as the darkness pressed up close against them. The flag-stones beneath Rosa's feet were slabs of ice that drove blunt blades through her legs, slicing at the skin of her aching thighs. Her damp nightdress seemed to freeze into a single sheet, stiff as a paper doll's dress. The beating heat of her family's plantation in Georgia seemed a million miles away. She hadn't known such cold could exist in the world. Even the inside of her mouth was cold – her tongue, and her cheeks, and the roof itself. There was blood on her nightdress and she felt unlike herself – an actor in a play who has forgotten their lines, a tapestry that has been unpicked thread by thread. For the first time in her life, she simply had no idea what on earth she ought to do next.

To make matters worse, she soon became hopelessly lost. It was almost as if the rooms moved when she wasn't looking. As if the mansion was against her, taking spiteful pleasure in her confusion. Too late, she recalled how the housekeeper had revealed that she still went about her day with a map of the mansion tucked into her apron pocket, despite the fact that she had worked there for years. And there were several maids who, in their first days, had been driven to despair and had to ring servants' bells in order to be found and rescued from whatever part of the house they had wandered into. Rosa thought of this and her smoulder of panic quickly turned into a blaze of horror inside her chest. Time was moving on and she simply could not be found like this in the morning, sweating into her bloodied nightgown, freezing and fright-ened as a lost child.

It did not help that the house was full of clocks – hundreds and hundreds of them – their round faces peering out at her from every shadow, shining like minia-ture moons. When the servants had been presented to her upon her arrival, she recalled how there had been one footman whose sole duty was to wind and maintain Raven Hall's many timepieces. The task of getting their mechanisms all to strike at precisely the same moment proved to be impossible, however, and Rosa found that the bells and chimes clashed on, at war with each other, for a good five minutes after the hour had passed.

She could almost feel the walls breathing. The air felt moist. The windows were watchful. She thought she heard someone crying, and wondered whether it was her or the house. Shadows flickered up in the rafters and made it seem as if feathers rained down upon the staircase. There were fifteen staircases in the house, and Rosa paused part of the way up one, wondering whether this was the one that Lucy Hamilton, the Tenth Duchess of Chalkley, had broken her neck tumbling down some fifty years ago.

She'd quickly discovered that the duchesses of Raven Hall were a fated group, apparently doomed to ill fortune. She knew the servants whispered about curses and engagement rings. It was bad luck for a woman to wear any opal, they said, but especially a blood opal, and especially a duchess within Raven Hall. She had not believed them, until now.

Rosa quickened her pace and, to her great relief, eventually found herself outside the Long Gallery. From here she could get her bearings and make it back to her bedroom. But before she could walk on, she heard a noise ring out suddenly in the darkness. There was no mistaking it – surely it was the sound of a child crying.

She frowned. How strange to think that a child was wandering the house at this hour. She supposed it must belong to one of the servants. She paused outside the door of the Long Gallery, listening. It sounded as if the child were just on the other side of the door.

'Hello?' Rosa reached for the handle.

Immediately the crying stopped and she thought she heard small feet running along the floorboards.

'It's all right,' she said, opening the door.

Her feeble candle flame did very little to illuminate the great long space, and her eyes struggled to adapt to the leaping shadows.

'Hello?' she called again.

There was no sign of anyone else in the room and Rosa's mind went foolishly to ghosts. She walked slowly down the gallery, peering anxiously into shadows. The painted duchesses watched her from their frames – the only other women who could truly understand what it was like to live at Raven Hall. The blood opal glittered on Rosa's finger and she suddenly felt like she wasn't her own person at all, but merely a copy of these other women – the same soul living the same cursed existence over and over again.

The boy was so still that she almost missed him. He was hunched on the floor right at the end of the row, beneath Rosa's own portrait. His back was pressed up against the wall and his arms were wrapped around his skinny legs. He looked straight down, his head pressed firmly against his knees, so utterly motionless that he could almost have been a statue.

'Hello,' Rosa said softly. 'What are you doing here?'

The boy looked up with eyes that seemed huge in the dimness. She could clearly see her candle's flickering flame reflected back in each dark pupil. There was a sunken, sallow look about his face and one of his arms was withered.

'I live here,' he said. 'What are *you* doing?'

'Why, I live here too,' she said, surprised that the boy didn't recognise her accent, if nothing else. 'I'm the new duchess.'

The boy narrowed his eyes at her. 'No, you're not.'

'But I am. Look, you're sitting underneath my portrait.'

The boy shook his head vehemently.

'Why are you crying?' Rosa asked, trying a different approach.

'I'm trying to find the carousel,' he said. 'Do you know where it is?'

His eyes were suddenly bright with an odd hunger Rosa didn't understand.

'I'm not sure what you're talking about,' she said. 'What carousel?'

But the boy only scrambled to his feet. 'I have to go. I'm not supposed to be here.'

Rosa called for him to wait, but he ran off into the shadows of the gallery and his footsteps faded away. She assumed he must have gone back below stairs.

The next morning she questioned her lady's maid, Jill, about him, but the girl only looked baffled.

'None of the servants have children, miss.'

'But then where did that boy come from?'

Jill only stared at her. 'Raven Hall is no place for children.'

When Rosa questioned the housekeeper, Mrs Wright, she received the same answer.

'Well, *someone* must know who he is, if he's living here in Raven Hall,' Rosa said, frustrated. 'He was quite small, with a greyish tinge to his skin, as if he'd been ill. He had a withered arm.'

'I'm very sorry, your grace,' Mrs Wright replied. 'I don't know what you want me to say.'

Rosa knew that the boy *had* been there. One did not have conversations with wraiths. The most likely explanation seemed to be that whichever servant he belonged to did not have permission to have him in the house, and so Rosa didn't mention the boy to Eustace, in case she got anyone into trouble. Besides which, the thought of seeing her husband that morning made her feel literally sick.

She didn't see the boy again, but as the days went by, she often heard him, crying quietly during the night. And it seemed to her that he was perhaps the only other person at Raven Hall who was as unhappy as she was.

*April 1837*

*My dear Beatrice,*

*I am sorry for my long silence. I have been having such a glorious time since our wedding that I cannot seem to find a spare moment for correspondence these days. In addition we have been most blessed and are expecting our first child in December, so I expect I shall soon be busier than ever.*

*I am sorry that I have not replied to your many queries over the past months about the pop-up book. Sadly, I am afraid there is little point in your returning to England to see it. The truth is that it was somehow lost in the move to Raven Hall I am not sure how it happened — only that I have not seen the book since our arrival here. I am sorry.*

*All my love,*
*Rosa*

# CHAPTER TEN

*Sarawak, Malaysia – May 1837*

Beatrice leaned back in the canoe, taking in the sights and smells of the river. The water was simply alive with boats. Little wooden houses clustered at the bank, raised up on tall stilts and almost lost within the lush foliage of areca and cocoa-nut palms. The scene was everything she had hoped it would be, everything she was travelling for in the first place. And yet she could not summon up any wonder or joy at the sight.

She'd felt a dark mood hovering over her all day, that familiar feeling of a broken angel's wing draped across her shoulders that she'd felt as a child when her mother had died. The feeling had been building and building over the last few months. She'd felt that angel's melancholy embrace as she toured the Great Gardens of Japan, and when she'd gone on to see the snow monkeys of Yudanaka. The feeling had been there when she'd watched the dance of the red-crowned cranes and experienced the snow festival of Hokkaido. And now it had followed her to Malaysia as well.

How much more straightforward it was to bear a physical illness or malady. You need not do anything but rest, and the body simply healed itself. Miseries of the mind, however, were quite another matter; they were a sticky spider's web, and Beatrice had learned that the more you struggled against them, the tighter the strands seemed to bind you.

She ought to have known by now that travelling to a different part of the world would not help. The relentless sun warmed the air, making it smell swampy. Sweat ran down her back and dampened her underarms, but she didn't mind the discomfort. It was all as far away as she could imagine from any English drawing room, which was a blessing at least. There wasn't a dainty teacup in sight.

Her guide handed her a pineapple with its top cut off and a wooden spoon with which to eat it. Soon enough her fingers were sticky with juice, but she didn't dare dip them in the river to wash them because she'd been warned there were alligators in the water.

They were approaching the town of Kuching, and she strained her gaze down the river for her first glimpse of the town's tiled houses. But a different sight met her eyes.

Instead of the village, Half Moon House sprawled there on the riverbank, its windows gazing sadly down at her through the thickets of the mangrove swamp. It was unmistakeably her home, but not as she remembered it. The windows were choked with leaves and the roof was crawling with vines. Dark feathers and strange flowers clogged the chimney pots. The doors were covered with mushrooms and moss. It was being swallowed up by nature.

Beatrice jerked upright. 'That house!' she gasped, pointing it out to her guide. 'Where did it come from?'

She frowned. How strange that she hadn't stuttered once. There was a flurry of wings overhead and she looked up, expecting to see a Pacific golden plover or a Bornean wren kingfisher, but the blue dome of sky was empty of colourful plumage. Instead a lone raven circled like a vulture, croaking out its ugly cry. It was quickly joined by a second raven, then another and another, until the sky darkened with black feathers.

'What house?' a voice enquired.

But it wasn't her guide who'd spoken; it was her father. Beatrice looked back to see him sprawled in the boat where the guide had been moments before. His long legs were stretched in front of him and he held a newspaper in his hands.

'I am ashamed to call you my daughter today,' he said, not taking his eyes off the paper. 'Because of you, your mother left this earth broken-hearted. You are a wicked child . . .'

Beatrice closed her eyes. Her mother's wasted face rose up in her mind. There had been a flickering light of pleasure in her expression when the bed curtain first parted to reveal her daughter, but Beatrice had extinguished it the moment she stepped back. Once again she saw her mother's tired face crumple with raw hurt.

'Oh, please . . .'

The hand reached towards her, seeking comfort that Beatrice had been too cowardly to give. She heard that cry once again as she turned her back on the person who had loved her most in the world, and ran from the room. If only she could do it once more, she would behave so differently. She would take her mother's dear hand and hold it tight, and keep on holding it, right up until the very end. The weight of the regret felt like a great boulder that she must carry upon her shoulders for the rest of her life.

'Please don't cry.'

Beatrice looked up and saw that her father had been replaced by the Spider Queen. Clad in a cobwebbed gown, she sat in the guide's seat, trailing her fingers lazily in the water, apparently unconcerned by the presence of alligators. Around her, several white spiders spun beautiful pictures in the spokes of the boat's steering wheel, and in the gap under the bench, and between the sticks of the Spider Queen's hair comb.

*There is no need to fear the spiders, Beatrice*, the queen's kind voice whispered inside her head from all those years ago. *Their only wish is to consume your nightmares and protect your dreams . . .*

'I didn't say goodbye,' Beatrice said now. 'When I had the chance.'

The Spider Queen looked up, delicate white spiders dripping like diamonds from her slender fingers. 'We each have our own peculiar heartbreaks,' she said. 'And we all ask why it must be so. But remember the garden? Life needs dark leaves in the wreath. It is the way of things.'

'Why can't I find you?' Beatrice asked. 'Over a year of searching, and I have come nowhere close to the Winter Garden.'

The Spider Queen sighed. 'It only appears when people most need it,' she said. 'You know that.'

'But I *do* need you,' Beatrice said. 'Badly.'

The Spider Queen made no response, and Beatrice's gaze fell upon the three webs. One spider had spun an image of a key. The second, a horse. And the third, a plum. She was about to press the Spider Queen further when a hand on her shoulder gently shook her awake and she found herself back in the canoe with her guide. The queen and her spiders were gone. Beatrice realised she must have dozed off as they made their way back down the Sarawak River.

The dream left her feeling unsettled and cloaked in a darker mood than ever. She could feel herself perilously close to that deep pit she had been in before and had no wish to return to. It was a pit she thought had been a consequence of her stifling life at home, and not one she had expected to encounter whilst travelling. She tried to tell herself there was no need to feel low. Even if she never found the Winter Garden, she was living the sort of life she had always wanted, and she was free. Was that not enough? Still, every nerve felt strained to its limit by the time she got back to the hotel.

A letter from the Linnean Society awaited her there. She had written to them weeks ago with news of several marvels she had discovered during her travels, each more wondrous and spectacular than the last – far more impressive than anything Sir James Edward Smith could possibly have conceived when he first founded the society. She had also sent a package containing dried specimens and sketches, two envelopes of seeds and an entire Wardian case of live plants as examples.

How excited she had been to show her discoveries to others who shared her interests – botanists, mycologists, ornithologists and lepidopterists. She'd asked permission to present a paper of her findings and also offered to bring back specimens for the society to put on display, alongside her highly detailed botanical illustrations. It had been months since she sent the package, but Beatrice knew the international post was notoriously slow and felt a small glow of excitement now as she tore open the envelope.

It was a flat rejection. Not only that, but it took pains to make clear that Beatrice would never be considered a peer, and that membership was quite out of the question.

They would not put her findings on display, they would not allow her to present her paper and, furthermore, she was denied access to the research library and would not even be permitted to attend the presentations of scientific papers given by the society's learned male members. She was absolutely barred, the door slammed and locked in her face, affixed all over with padlocks and chains. They seemed quite outraged that she had ever sought admittance in the first place.

She put the letter down. The hotel would be serving dinner in the dining room downstairs by now, and Beatrice hadn't eaten anything except the pineapple since breakfast, but she had no appetite. She could not even bring herself to move from the chair. Suddenly she found herself wondering what on earth all this was for? The scandal, the reprobation, the uprooting of her life, the social disgrace. Perhaps the adventure simply was not worth the candle.

She was no closer to finding the Winter Garden. And no matter how many wondrous discoveries she made, she would not be able to share them with the people back home. She was barred from making any meaningful contribution to her country's knowledge and learning, as she so earnestly desired to do. How stupid and naïve she must be, to have travelled to the other side of the world when she did not, and could not, have a free hand to work at the things she cared about most. She was suddenly struck with the fear that when she reached the end of her life, she would look back on it all and think only, *It was a waste of time.* For she had made all the wrong choices and taken all the wrong paths.

As the room darkened, the angel's wing about her shoulders got heavier and heavier until it pinned her to the chair as effectively as any manacle. Beatrice sat there all night, dozing fitfully, dreaming about her mother and longing for the Winter Garden. She could sense pieces of herself floating away until she seemed to become someone else altogether: a stranger she barely knew. It frightened her to feel her own sense of who she was unravelling like a ball of string, until she teetered right on the edge of that familiar black pit – forever eager to swallow her whole once again.

# CHAPTER ELEVEN

*June 1837*

At last, the opening night of Eustace's pleasure garden had arrived and the preparations had all been made. There were three hundred bottles of champagne, fifty barrels of porter, fifty baskets of strawberries, a thousand Eccles cakes and endless roast chickens. Fifteen different foreign wines were available from the cellar, from Burgundy to Spanish Fontcarrel. Coloured oil lamps lined the pebbled paths and tree-lined avenues, the supper booths were set up in a circle around the bandstand, and the orchestra was due to arrive later that day with their instruments.

During the Season Eustace liked to refer to his weekly party as a *fête champêtre* but, in truth, the only thing separating it from a common pleasure garden was the entrance price. The aristocratic guests enjoyed the exclusivity of such a venue – not having to rub shoulders with mantua-makers' girls and grubby little lawyers' clerks, to say nothing of fashionably dressed women of loose character and quick-fingered pickpockets. Opening night was the perfect opportunity for dealing Eustace the blow that Rosa had been itching to deliver for weeks.

That evening she was laced into her gown as tightly as her swelling stomach would permit. The champagne-coloured satin was decorated in beautiful floral sprays and gold-edged leaves, trimmed with lashings of blond lace, and fashionably left much of her arms and shoulders bare. It was exactly the kind of dress Rosa had imagined wearing as a duchess, but she found it hard to take any pleasure in it now.

Whilst her maid arranged her hair, Rosa watched the supper booths being set up on the lawn. The previous Season there had been magicians and mesmerists, as well as carefully staged *poses plastiques*, who resembled statues both in their dress and in their uncanny ability to remain utterly still for hours. Indeed, the guests had had quite a hard time distinguishing those performers from the garden's actual statues.

Rosa had no idea what the new entertainment would entail, but she was looking forward to unveiling her own clockwork creation later. Fortunately the duke's business in Parliament had kept him regularly occupied in London, so he had not had the time or interest to inspect her work. In all likelihood, it did not even cross his mind for a moment that Rosa would do anything other than obey his wishes exactly. Rosa smiled grimly to herself at the thought of the surprise that lay in store for him.

Finally there was no powder left to apply, no hair left to curl, no skirts to brush. The sun was setting and Rosa went downstairs to join the duke. He wore a heavy silk-lined opera cape, his hair slicked back, his moustache waxed, his silver walking cane clasped in one gloved hand. Rosa tried to find the handsome nobleman she'd first met, but all she could see now was the boar beneath, and the cape reminded her of a painting she'd once seen of the devil. There were some things you could not unsee once they had been revealed.

She could tell that Eustace was in high spirits, looking forward to the garden's opening night and the chance to show off both his wife and her clockwork. Rosa made sure to keep her own excitement buried deep within, where it belonged. It was, after all, a twisted, miserable sort of feeling and not one she should take any pleasure in.

'Your father has sent one of his artificers to us for the weekend,' Eustace told her. 'Should you receive any questions about the design or inner workings of the clockwork, you will direct these enquiries to him.'

Rosa frowned. 'But they are not his designs. They are mine—'

'Rosa, please.' Eustace pinched the bridge of his nose and closed his eyes for a moment, as if she were tiring him beyond reason. 'Now that you are a married duchess, you must see that it would be quite unacceptable for you to be lecturing our guests on the subject of mechanics, of all things. You will deport yourself with femininity and confine yourself to commenting upon suitable subjects.'

'Such as?' Rosa asked coldly.

She saw a flicker of anger cross his face before he mastered it. 'Good God, surely you do not require me to tell you? Philanthropy, social engagements, the weather, fashionable hats. You know.'

She would have argued the point, but tonight she had bigger fish to fry, so she merely spoke through gritted teeth. 'Very well, Eustace.'

'Come. Let us greet our guests.'

He offered her his arm, Rosa reluctantly placed her gloved hand in the crook of his elbow and they went outside. There was applause when they emerged, eager eyes turning towards them in the dark, necks craning for a glimpse of the esteemed couple. Rosa smiled and inclined her head in acknowledgement, amazed at how easily the old gestures came back, startled by the familiar buzz of conversation and the cold press of a champagne glass through her silk glove.

And what a transformation in the gardens – like a dark butterfly unfurling its wings as it emerged from a night-time chrysalis. The first and most overwhelming impression was created by the sparkling lights: hundreds and hundreds of them. Coloured oil lamps hung among the trees, candles flickered on tables, but best and brightest of all were the clockwork peacocks.

The blue-and-green eyes of their spectacular feathers blazed with an astonishing brilliance that surpassed all else. Sparks of sapphire and emerald flashed inside the female guests' diamond necklaces, and a blue haze bathed the plumes of ostrich feathers in a ghostly glow. The peacocks' elegant blue heads and necks shone with an iridescent sheen, as if they'd been dipped in oil, and their golden eyes glowed just as brightly as the ones on their feathers.

Rosa and Eustace took their dinner in one of the supper booths. They were situated in a grove of flowering *Aesculus* χ *carnea*, or pink horse-chestnut trees – the only ones in the whole country. Plenty of homes and gardens had horse chestnuts, but none that flowered pink. They were one of the many exotic specimens that Eustace's plant hunters had brought back from the continent last year.

The orchestra's music seemed to float through the air on wings. Patriotic paintings lined the wooden walls of the booths, showing heroes bloodied in victorious battle. Beyond the lights, the silhouettes of the monkey-puzzle trees were dark sentries gazing down at them. The food was as excellent as ever, yet the chicken skin seemed to sit greasily in Rosa's stomach, the champagne created too many bubbles, the syllabub – normally her favourite – was a slimy sludge in the crystal-cut bowl. Her pregnancy had ruined so many of her favourite foods for her, but she forced down as much as she could, before the ordeal of mingling with their guests began.

There were perhaps two hundred people there, and Rosa and Eustace spoke to each and every one – including, unfortunately, the dowager duchess Margaret, who had made a special trip down from London for the event. Rosa found herself mentally switching off as Margaret expounded on what she must, and must not, do during her confinement. Truly she had never known a woman to be an expert in so very many areas; and, in her sweetest voice, she said so. Eustace missed the edge in her tone and looked pleased, but Margaret was a little sharper than her son and knew it was no compliment.

Despite Eustace's concerns about them being last year's spectacle, it was immediately clear that the peacocks were still the highlight of the event. Guests crowded around the clockwork birds, exclaiming in delight every time one of them fanned out their tail, showering the onlookers with sparks of sapphire and lighting up the surrounding sky with a pale blue haze. People congratulated Eustace on the clockwork peacocks again and again, exclaiming at their colours, their beauty, the intricacy of their clockwork mechanics.

The remaining guests buzzed like bees around the pagodas and follies where the new entertainment was to be found. Eustace had employed an ever-popular freak show, composed of people who were too tall or too short, too thin or too fat, too hairy or completely bald. This seemed to go down extremely well with their guests, but Rosa didn't care for it. The eyes of the Giraffe Girl were sad behind her smile, and it seemed cruel the way the guests tugged and tore at the hair of the dark-skinned Woolly Woman, although the sign invited them to do just that: *She is genuine; you are at liberty to take hold of this lock of hair and pull it* . . .

Rosa felt herself growing tenser with each performer they viewed, until she was as brittle as a twist of ice. The laughter from the guests seemed too shrill, the smell of perfume and Macassar oil was overpowering, the red lips of all those smiling mouths were sickening. Beneath her corset, her skin was slick with sweat and her stomach felt tangled up in knots.

'Please,' Rosa said, digging her fingers into Eustace's arm. 'Might we take a stroll through the dark walk? The noise and the lights . . . they're making my head ache.'

She looked longingly at the other end of the garden where an unlit path wound through an arboretum of Scots pines, with only the moonlight filtering through the branches to show the way. How blissful it would be to lose herself in the canopy of that cool, quiet foliage, just for a few moments. But Eustace turned her away, saying, 'We haven't seen all the entertainment yet. I've saved the best until last.'

He steered her through the trees to a hermitage. This building had the largest crowd of all, but it parted to let the duke and duchess through. The small stone building was lit with a single oil lamp, and Rosa saw it was occupied. At first she thought two elderly women sat side by side at a table, but then she gasped at the realisation that the women were joined at the shoulder.

'Conjoined twins,' Eustace said, delighted. 'Are they not grotesque?'

The twins had a beaded shawl wrapped around their bony shoulders, carefully arranged to show off the part where they joined. Their dark eyes seemed to glitter out of the shadows at them.

'Good evening, Duchess,' one of them said in a low, throaty voice, whilst the other grinned a toothy smile. 'Would you care to have your fortune read?'

Rosa instinctively recoiled.

'Oh no, thank you, I—'

'Good heavens, Rosa, don't be so uptight,' Eustace said. 'Ladies love having their fortunes read and these twins are renowned all over Europe. In fact they're the very reason I employed this troupe. I thought they would please you.' He gave her a little push forward and Rosa clenched her jaw. She did not believe that for a moment.

'Do not worry about your swans,' Eustace said. 'There's plenty of time before we unveil them.'

His voice brimmed with excitement, eager for the outpouring of praise he fully expected to come his way when the clockwork birds made their debut. He went out, closing the door behind him, leaving Rosa alone with the twins.

'Sit down, child,' the first woman spoke again, indicating a chair on the other side of the table. 'I'm Gwendolyn and my sister is Alice. We are both gifted with second sight.'

Reluctantly, Rosa took her seat, her heavy, satin skirts rustling against her legs. She saw that Gwendolyn wore her hair in a bun, whilst Alice's was long and loose down her shoulders, making her look curiously child-like, in spite of her wrinkles and liver spots.

'How fortunate that the party was tonight, your grace,' Gwendolyn said. 'One day later and it would not have happened at all. We would all have been searching for our mourning attire.'

Rosa had no idea what she was talking about and simply stared.

Alice shook her head. 'They say women spend most of their lives in mourning, one way or another.'

Her voice was startlingly different from her sister's, high and fluting as a girl's.

'How true that is.' Gwendolyn fixed her eyes on Rosa. 'Most people believe the future stretches ahead of them, shrouded in fog, but we see time as a loop. Everything that has ever happened to us has already happened some-where in that circle.'

'We see the barbecues and fish-fries of your past,' Alice said, although she made no move to touch the cards at her elbow.

*Georgia.*

155

'The wild animal stalking your present,' Gwendolyn put in.

*The Boar.*

'And as for your future . . .' Alice trailed off and looked at her sister.

'You carry new life inside you,' Gwendolyn said.

Rosa automatically looked down at her dress. She was larger around the middle, it was true, but her pregnancy was not yet public knowledge and she'd thought it would be a while before it became obvious. She wondered whether Eustace had told them. In fact this entire performance had probably been carefully staged by him in order to bring her pain. These women were in his employ, after all, and she knew she could not trust a word they said.

'The twins of joy and sorrow,' Alice went on. 'You cannot have one without the other.'

'I see a small gravestone before a year has passed,' Gwendolyn said.

Rosa had yet to feel any tenderness at all towards the baby in her belly, but those words sent a cold shudder through her, as if she'd just slipped between the icy sheets of a frozen bed.

*It's not real,* she told herself. *It is only Eustace finding new ways to punish me.* Very soon, though, it would be his turn to be punished . . .

'I see a winter garden,' Alice said.

'Two gardens, in fact,' Gwendolyn chimed in.

'One of snow and magic,' Alice said.

'Another of fire and clockwork.'

'I see a tiger made of stars.'

'Showers of opals and orchids.'

'Purple rain.'

'And a carousel upon a frozen lake.'

Rosa realised her hands were bunched together in her lap. It felt hot and airless inside the folly, which suddenly seemed to spin gently around her. 'What are you talking about? Did my husband tell you to say these things?'

'The Carousel of Icicles,' Alice said again. 'The world has never seen its like before.'

Rosa thought of the aborted plans for a winter carousel buried in her workbook – the hundreds of icicles. She was about to question the twins further, but nausea gave a sudden lurch in her stomach and she stood and turned around, stumbling over her skirts in her haste to get out. The blood opal blazed upon her finger as she gripped the handle and opened the door. She hurried away to the outskirts of the garden, where she could shelter beneath one of the trees and take deep gulps of the cool night air.

She had lost her taste for the garden and had just decided to return to the house when she saw James Sheppard standing a short distance away, beside a display of orchids. True to his word, he had continued to provide Rosa with orchids after she married, but he never came to Raven Hall himself, and Rosa had not expected to see him tonight. The last time she'd laid eyes on him had been at the Winter Ball, when he'd congratulated her on her engagement. It felt like a lifetime ago, like something from a dream, and now Rosa felt a strange mixture of sorrow and gladness at the sight of him. Before she could hurry away, he noticed her across the lawn and smiled. Rosa was dismayed by the sudden ache that she felt at the sight, a hopeless longing. When he bowed to her, she might simply have inclined her head in return and moved on, but instead she found herself crossing the lawn towards him, as if in a trance.

'Good evening, your grace,' he said. 'Being a duchess suits you. Of course I knew it would. You look as beautiful as ever.'

Rosa wished he would say instead: *You look wretched. What is wrong? How can I help?*

*Run away with me . . .*

'Thank you, Mr Sheppard,' she replied, marvelling that her voice could come out sounding so ordinary. 'I am gloriously happy.'

'Naturally.' He glanced at her feet. 'But where is your charming dog?'

Grief immediately filled Rosa's throat and she had to swallow it down with an effort. She was suddenly very afraid that she would not be able to speak of Cookie without crying. 'He . . . he was very old,' she managed. 'And even clockwork creatures wind down eventually.'

James winced and put a hand on her arm. 'I am so very sorry.'

Rosa couldn't bear his kindness and pulled away from his touch, afraid that it would unravel her completely.

'Isn't this divine?' she asked in an overly bright voice, desperate to change the subject. 'The garden, I mean.'

James looked out across the lawn. 'It is certainly a spectacle.'

She raised an eyebrow. 'It is not to your taste?'

'Pleasure gardens are my bread and butter,' he replied. 'But it seems to me that they are very often ugly affairs.' He glanced at her. 'Your clockwork peacocks, though – they are quite lovely. You must be very proud.'

Rosa said nothing. She could not stand the sight of them. James would see soon enough that the ugliest thing in the garden had come from her. She had created her own monstrosity. She had allowed herself to get drawn into the depravity. She felt a flash of regret, but it was too late to go back now. She was determined to see it through.

'Thank you,' she said. 'But I believe your orchids are the loveliest thing here by a long way.'

No longer content with hunting orchids abroad, James had also set up a garden laboratory in England and had begun experimenting with creating hybrid flowers. The tray at his feet held rainbow orchids, and their multicoloured petals were not found anywhere in nature.

'Thank you. I sense the duke's design on these gardens more than your own,' he said. 'If you were to have a free hand, what would your ideal garden be?'

No one had ever asked her that, but Rosa wasn't surprised that James should do so. Back when they used to take tea in her town house together, he was forever asking her questions and, furthermore, listened carefully to the answers. He had always seemed genuinely interested in her thoughts, and opinions, and preferences.

He was watching her and waiting quietly for an answer now, so Rosa said, 'Perhaps something like the Winter Garden. The magical one from the book you gave me. Except it would have more clockwork.' She glanced at him. 'Do you think it could be real? The Winter Garden, I mean?'

'Well. It hardly seems plausible, does it?'

'Beatrice says she has been there.'

That got his attention. James's eyes fixed on her in the dark.

'She asked me not to tell you,' Rosa went on, thrusting down the guilt she felt at doing so. 'But I know she's looking for it. Perhaps you are too?'

He nodded slowly. 'I would dearly love to see it,' he said. 'But I do not think I have ever come anywhere close. If the stories are to be believed, the garden only appears to people in their darkest hours.'

Rosa tried to prevent her mouth twisting into a grimace. Surely she had already had her darkest hour? Far darker than anything Beatrice had experienced in her sheltered life. She knew her friend's mother had died, but everyone lost their mothers eventually. It was the natural order of things.

'Why do you think that some people get to see the garden, whilst others don't?' she asked. 'It doesn't seem fair.'

'Perhaps not,' James replied. 'But I do not think there are many who would claim that life is in any way fair. For now, I think I am better off searching for orchids rather than looking for the Winter Garden. I have the feeling that if it does not wish to be found, then you won't see so much as a leaf, and I'm determined to have something spectacular to present to the Linnean Society when I return from my next expedition.'

'You're going abroad again?'

'I leave next week.'

'For how long?'

'I hope to be back by Christmas.'

'Well, I wish you luck. And I hope you will consider selling some of your new flowers to me upon your return.'

'You shall have the first pick, your grace. It is a great pleasure to provide orchids to someone who appreciates them as much as you do.'

'I think they are truly the most beautiful, extraordinary flower in the world.'

'As do I.'

She glanced at the rainbow orchids surrounding them, their colours bold and wonderful in the dark.

'Please take these back to the hothouse, Mr Sheppard,' she said suddenly.

He paused. 'But no one will see them there.'

Rosa wanted the flowers out of the way so that they would not be damaged later. Ruining the flowers was not part of her plan. But she could hardly say that to James.

'They are too special,' she said. 'Too beautiful. You will think me a selfish creature, but I wish to keep them all for myself.' She glanced out at the garden and her lip curled slightly. 'These people will not appreciate them properly, at any rate.'

James gave her a curious look, but did not probe.

'Very well,' he replied.

He called over two gardeners to help him. They had just removed the last orchid by the time Eustace had gathered everyone at the edge of the lake for the grand unveiling. Servants had wheeled out the crate, and it stood beside the duke, covered in a red velvet drape.

It was a picturesque spot, and during the day Rosa enjoyed watching the kingfishers and moorhens, goldcrests and treecreepers that flourished there. The birds were all back in their nests now, chased away by the noise and lights. Rosa knew that Eustace would be searching for her, expecting her to be at his side for this moment, so she skirted around the edge of the garden, keeping close to the trees where she wouldn't be seen. She was almost back to the house by the time someone gave the signal for the orchestra to cease, and Eustace addressed his guests, his voice carrying across the still airlessness of the garden.

'I'm afraid my wife has become so mesmerised by our display of freaks that she has lost track of time,' he said, to polite laughter. 'But it is my great pleasure to unveil the latest masterpiece from Warren's Clockwork Creatures on her behalf. Ladies and gentlemen, if you thought the peacocks were impressive, then prepare to marvel at these glorious clockwork swans.'

Guests shuffled forward for a closer look, craning their necks and jabbing their elbows into each other's sides, all wishing to be the first to see them. The air smelled of spilled champagne and crushed strawberries, and Rosa was glad she'd done what she had. Now was her last chance to call out a warning, but instead she merely took the last few steps to the terrace and said nothing.

The next moment Eustace removed the velvet cloth and unfastened the hook to release one side of the crate. This was clearly the signal for the fireworks to begin too. They'd been set up at the edge of the lake, and Rosa supposed Eustace thought they would be a fitting backdrop to the beauty and grace of the swans.

But the thing that lumbered out of the crate on four stubby legs had no beauty and no grace. Its back was broad; its neck was thick. It was a huge, muscled beast of a pig, with bristled wire fur all over its body, and mean-looking eyes that glowed red in the darkness.

For a strange, still moment, everyone simply stared at it. They all thought there must be some mistake, some explanation for this monstrosity. They had been promised a spectacle of beauty, after all, of wonder and loveliness. Instead, noses were starting to wrinkle in distaste and lips curled in disgust.

*What is amiss?* Rosa wanted to ask. *Is this not the kind of freak you came here to see?*

She looked at Eustace, their eyes suddenly meeting across the lantern-lit lawn. Even from this distance she could see how incensed he was, but in that moment she didn't care. Whatever came later would be worth it, to have triumphed over him, just once. To see his carefully laid plan break into pieces at his feet.

The boar stood sniffing the air for less than a minute before the first peacock strolled by. Immediately its deep-set eyes burned a brighter red, its ears flattened against its head and its lips parted, to reveal the cruelly sharp teeth that Rosa had spent many hours labouring over, carefully filing them to razor-points.

The pig gave a bellowing cry so fearsome that Eustace stumbled back and tipped right over the edge of the pond, landing in the murky water with a splash. The boar lowered its head and charged forward, scattering the crowd. Panicked shrieks filled the air as people ran from its path, but the boar was only interested in the peacocks. One by one, it rooted them out and tore their delicate clockwork bodies to shreds of scrap metal. Its thick body barrelled through everything and anything that got in its way, whether that was a table, an entire supper booth, a chair or a person. And, all the while, the firework display continued in the background, lighting up the sky in great fire-flowers of crimson, and jade, and blossoming violet.

There were very few injuries to speak of afterwards, although you would have thought half the guest list had been mauled, with all the fuss they made. Still, the boar surpassed Rosa's expectations. She had fully intended for it to destroy the peacocks, and had assumed that a few flowers might also be trampled, but she had not realised that the clockwork pig would demolish most of the garden as it chased after the birds, uprooting plants and turf with its hooves, splintering the infrastructure and even toppling several lanterns, which quickly set the trees alight. Rosa watched, fascinated, as pieces of ash drifted through the night sky to grace the ladies' hair arrangements, like silver hair combs.

By the time the boar finally lay down in the middle of the lawn, with sapphire feathers sticking out between its teeth and oil running down its bristled chin, most of the garden had been wrecked, and a team of servants was fighting to put out the fires. She saw James among them, his sleeves rolled up past his elbows and soot in his hair. She wondered whether he would ever agree to work for her again after this.

The carriages had all departed, taking the last of the angry guests with them, and the grounds of Raven Hall smoked and smouldered quietly. Rosa had not moved from the terrace, enthralled by the display. She looked around as Eustace stamped towards her, still dripping wet, his fine suit ruined, his hair stinking of pondweed.

'Well,' she said, 'that was certainly an even larger spectacle than last year, would you not agree?'

For once, Eustace seemed quite speechless.

'Dear husband, whatever can be the matter?' Rosa asked, in her most innocent voice. 'I thought you'd be pleased.'

Eustace moved to stand very close to her.

'I will demonstrate my feelings to you, madam,' he said quietly, 'quite clearly – the moment I am assured that the fires are out, and we are alone again inside. I don't know what possessed you to act in such a way but, upon my word, you will pay dearly for this, I promise you.'

The little laugh seemed to burst from Rosa quite without her meaning it to and caused Eustace to look at her askance.

'Have you lost your reason?' he demanded.

'I apologise,' Rosa said. For a moment her voice trembled with the effort of not giving in to more mirth, but she gathered herself and went on. 'Why, it is just too absurd, you know, to imagine that you might have the power to hurt me any more than you already have. So pray do not talk to me any further in that imbecilic manner. If you had the sense God gave a goat, you'd realise I am not the least afraid of you – or of anything you can do.'

Eustace went red. She could see the veins beneath his skin, bulging like engorged worms, fat from the graveyard. 'We will see about that,' he snapped.

She turned her back on him and went into the house. From her bedroom window she watched as they burned the boar on the final remaining fire – the remnants of a supper booth that had been set alight. The boar did not resist when the nervous servants approached it. Rosa hadn't designed it to attack humans, only peacocks. Much as she had desired to punish Eustace, she did not want or intend anyone to be hurt. So the pig squealed into the dark as its metal body melted, and the fire crackled and spat out molten lumps of iron.

By the time the duke stormed his way up the stairs, he was in the most murderous temper. When he discovered that she had locked him out, his shouts echoed around the house, but Rosa cared not. The blood opal on her finger blazed hotter than ever. One way or another, she knew, he'd eventually find another key from somewhere, or break down the door. And if he wanted to fight, well, so did she. And she was ready for him.

# CHAPTER TWELVE

Eustace raged out in the corridor for an hour before finally calming himself enough to go and find a spare key. The door unlocked with a soft *click* and swung slowly forward. Rosa stood by the window, where she'd been watching the ruins of her clockwork boar smoke in the grey morning air. She turned away from the window now to face Eustace across the room. His eyes were bloodshot and all reason had gone from his face.

'You should know that we have some new ravens,' Rosa said. 'The chimneys are packed full of them.'

Eustace breathed hard through his nose. He looked as if he'd never even heard of a raven. 'What in God's name are you talking about?'

Rosa called them. She called the ravens waiting up on the chimney pots, and the ones clustered around the crib in the night-nursery, and in the aviary. She called the birds in the Long Gallery and the White Drawing Room, and perched on the gables of the follies out in the grounds. From all over the house they appeared, pouring in through the door and the windows, coming down the chimney in a cloud of dark wings and greedy eyes. Only these birds weren't made from feather and bone, but from clockwork and cogs.

So many weeks of work, but it had been worth it to create not only the boar, but fifty ravens as well. There was barely space for them all in the room. Their eyes glowed a deep, gleaming red, their beaks were razor-sharp, their claws were talons. They looked as if they could tear a man's throat out with one swipe.

'What is the meaning of this?' Eustace asked in a voice of ice.

'It is quite simple,' Rosa said. 'You are a worthless sort of a man and I knew you would not listen to anything I had to say unless I forced you to—'

She did not manage to finish before he lunged at her, but he had no chance to lay a finger on her before several of the ravens descended on him in a flurry of metal wings and iron claws. His face was hidden from her view in the dark storm, but she could hear his shrieks, and saw blood splatter on the floor and clumps of hair fly out in all directions.

'Enough!' She snapped her fingers and the birds immediately swooped back to their perches.

Eustace was on his knees on the rug, breathing hard. The birds had ripped into the flesh of his hands and face with their beaks and pulled out entire chunks of hair. For the first time since she'd known him, he looked not just angry, but afraid as well. When she stepped closer, *he* shrank back from *her*, and she felt a sick pleasure at the sight.

'I will carry this wretched child of yours,' she said. 'But when it is born I will have nothing to do with it. It must be part monster, if it came from you. We will employ nannies and wet nurses, but the raising of this creature will not involve me. And there will be no further children.'

Eustace made to protest, but Rosa cut him off immediately.

'Will you be silent; I am not finished!' she thundered. 'From this night on, you will never enter my bedroom again. You will not touch me. You will speak to me only when necessary.'

'You are insane,' he whispered, glaring up at her with bloodshot eyes. 'My conjugal rights are—'

'They are finished, sir!' Rosa was trembling from head to foot, only it wasn't from fear this time, but from some other strange tangle of emotions. Exultation perhaps, and triumph, and a bitter sort of heartache. 'If you ever lay a finger on me, you will have the ravens to answer to.'

The bird shuffled on their various perches, eyes red as devils as they cocked their dark heads this way and that, listening to every word. The soft click and whir of clockwork filled the room.

'I have designed them to rip out a man's throat in one go,' Rosa said. 'And to attack the eyes. This is the last time you will see them assembled together, but you will always know that they are here, inside the house, or out in the grounds, watching you. Do not think of trying to hunt them, because even if you manage to catch one or two, you'll never get them all. If you have me locked away, they will come for you. They are programmed to have but one purpose, and can travel over many miles. They do not need to sleep or eat. They would find you, no matter where in the world you might go.'

She snapped her fingers again, and the ravens disappeared up through the chimney – all except one, which remained perched on Rosa's shoulder.

'Now,' she said quietly, 'get out of my bedroom. And leave that key where it is.'

Even now she had not been quite sure that it would work, but to her delight Eustace stood up, making no move to touch her. He no longer looked quite so handsome, with a torn face and bald patches where the ravens had attacked his scalp. He turned and walked towards the door without a word.

'Oh, and those conjoined twins,' Rosa said. 'Did you instruct them to say those things to me? About tigers and twins and winter gardens?'

Eustace didn't turn round. 'I have not the faintest idea,' he said, 'what you are raving about. They were performers, hired to entertain. I thought they would please you. That is all.'

He walked out, closing the door quietly behind him. Rosa tried to feel a sense of triumph. She had played his dreadful game, and she had won. An ugly dawn light was creeping into the room and she was exhausted in every limb, so she locked the door, drew across the drapes and fell into bed, safe in the knowledge that her raven kept watch from the top of her four-poster.

It was late in the day by the time she rose and rang for tea and fresh washing water. When Jill arrived, she said nothing of the previous night's events, although Rosa knew the servants must all be ablaze with gossip about it downstairs. In fact Jill wouldn't meet her gaze at all, and Rosa realised the girl was frightened of her. Or, at least, afraid of the clockwork sentry still perched upon the post of her bed.

'Do not worry about the ravens,' Rosa said gently. 'They will not harm any of you below stairs.'

Jill shot her a brief look, before staring back down at her hands. 'Is it true that the clockwork birds are all in the chimneys, your grace?'

'Yes, but you need not be afraid of them. They are here only to protect me.'

Jill bobbed a curtsy and turned back towards the door, only to pause and return.

'One other thing, your grace. I don't know whether anyone has informed you.'

'Of what?'

'It's the king. He died this morning. In the early hours.'

She curtsied again and took her leave. Rosa frowned, recalling what the twins had said about how the pleasure garden's opening night would have been cancelled, if it had been held just a day later. And it seemed they were right. A period of general mourning would now be announced for the king, and opening a pleasure garden during such a time would have been quite unthinkable.

Rosa told herself it was only a coincidence. The rest of the words the twins had spoken to her had been a total muddle and she felt sure Eustace must have been behind it anyway. Last night had been a triumph. She had managed to put Eustace in his place, and she was not about to let any fortune-telling babble detract from that. And yet . . . she did not feel as triumphant as she had expected. In fact she didn't feel triumphant at all.

Suddenly, something broke apart in her chest and Rosa began to cry. Her soul ached and ached. She wept for Cookie. She wept for herself and the miserable cage that her life had become. She wept for the life of happiness she might have had as James's wife. And she wept for the unborn baby inside her, whom she had always wanted, but now feared she would never be able to truly love. She felt ashamed of the words she had spoken to Eustace about the child, but she had meant every one. She felt ashamed that, for the first time, her clockwork creatures had invoked fear rather than delight. But there had been no other choice and she would do it all again if she had to. That did not make it easier to bear.

Finally she dried her eyes, bathed her face and went into her dressing room to apply new powder. As she did so, she noticed the *Winter Garden* pop-up book inside one of the drawers. She felt a sudden thirst for an escape into magical gardens, and pretty snow, and flickering lanterns, so she took it out and set it on the table before her, carefully moving the galaxy orchid to one side.

Rosa had always loved books – and old books most of all, delighting in the feel of the thick-cut paper beneath her fingers, the smell of binding glue, and ink, and memories. The pages were slightly worn and yellowed at the edges, as if many children's hands had turned them over the years, marvelling at the wonders within.

It was not a long book and Rosa had been through it several times, after what Beatrice had said about it. She knew the story by heart now, and so she could not explain why, this time, a new part of the book sprang into life before her eyes: an entirely new page that had never been there before. A pale carousel rose up on its paper mechanisms, and for a long moment Rosa simply stared. This carousel was *hers*. It had the icicles, and the sleighs, and even the horse with the golden ribbon. She heard the twins' voices once again.

*A carousel upon a frozen lake . . .*

*The world has never seen its like before . . .*

In every way the carousel looked identical to the one in Rosa's workbook. Her eyes went to the text printed on the page:

*But perhaps the most wondrous thing in the Winter Garden was the Carousel of Icicles. For the horse with the golden ribbon had a special gift – she could take a person back, to change just one decision they regretted . . .*

Rosa's hands clenched, her nails dug into her palms. She knew at once what decision she would change. She would go back to the day Eustace proposed. And instead of saying yes, she would turn her back on him, as Beatrice had done. She would run away as fast as she could. Some ember of hope sparked into life inside her.

She recalled a clockwork fortune-teller she had seen once at the Mechanical Museum. Locals knew her to be more than just cogs. Somehow she really could see into the future. Rosa thought of Cookie and her other clockwork animals. They had souls, just as flesh-and-blood animals did. Could such a carousel as the book described truly be created? She turned the page to the next one in the story, which was just as she remembered it. But when she turned back to the previous page, the Carousel of Icicles was gone – vanished, as if it had never existed at all. But the idea had been planted in Rosa's mind.

Over the next days and weeks she started work on her own carousel once again. If there was a way to create such a thing, she was determined that she would achieve it. Here, at last, was a way out. She would put right the ghastly mistake she had been fool enough to make. Meanwhile her clockwork ravens did an excellent job of shielding her from Eustace. As she had promised, the birds themselves were rarely seen, but their shadows were an ever-present sight in Raven Hall, and you could often hear them scrabbling in the chimneys or scratching around in the gables.

Eustace couldn't bear them and fled to his London town house, but Rosa sent a few of the birds there after him, determined that he would not get off that easily. And if the servants whispered of reports that the duke frequently woke from nightmares that left him screaming and sweating with terror, well, so much the better. It was no less than he deserved.

She wrote several letters to Beatrice, admitting that she had found the pop-up book and explaining that it appeared to be enchanted. Sometimes the Carousel of Icicles page was there and sometimes it wasn't. She enquired about Beatrice's own search for the Winter Garden but, strangely, she never heard anything back from her friend – the clockwork pigeon always returned empty-handed.

There was little time to dwell on this, however, because Rosa was so busy working on her carousel. It was by far the largest undertaking she had ever attempted. There was no chance of it being completed before the baby arrived. So far she had constructed only four basic horses and one polar bear, but there did not seem to be anything special or magical about them at all, and she despaired at ever re-creating the carousel from the pop-up book. And she still couldn't understand how her design could have appeared within its pages in the first place. Yet it seemed she had no choice but to keep on with her work, in the blind faith that, eventually, she would create something magical.

# CHAPTER THIRTEEN

*August 1837*

Beatrice sat in the doctor's surgery and waited for her name to be called. It had felt like giving up, to return to England, but her bleak mood wasn't lifting and she had finally admitted defeat. She had never been brave enough to seek help before. Perhaps it was simply a matter of asking. She had to try at least, although she shuddered at the thought of attempting to describe the dark, hopeless moods that sometimes descended upon her. The broken angel's wing. The chains that bound her to the bed. The despair that she would never feel any better.

Her palms were clammy by the time her name was finally called. The doctor was a serious-looking man with a neatly trimmed white beard. He invited her to sit on a hard wooden chair in the middle of the cold room. Beatrice felt somehow smaller and more stupid, and diminished, as soon as she did so. Her hands were too large for her lap, but she did not know what to do with them. For the first time in her life she wished she could be dainty. The clock on the wall ticked too loudly and the air felt thin.

'Thank you for coming in to see me, Lady Sitwell,' the doctor said. His voice was as dry as sawdust. 'What is it that troubles you?'

Beatrice swallowed hard. She knew her stutter would be bad, even before she opened her mouth. 'I h-h-have b-been s-s-suffering with a l-l-low m-m-mood,' she managed, spitting the words out like stones.

'Indeed? Well, that is not so very unusual. We all experience sadness from time to time.'

Beatrice shook her head, already despairing at how to make herself understood. 'It is m-m-more than being s-s-sad,' she struggled through the stammer. 'It is a f-feeling of c-c-c-complete d-d-d-despair. S-Some d-d-days I c-cannot get out of b-bed.'

*Or eat. Or sleep. Some days I don't feel like a human being at all. Some days I feel like a shell that has had everything sucked out of it.*

'I see,' the doctor said, although Beatrice could tell that he didn't see at all. 'And have you recently suffered a bereavement or something of that nature?'

Beatrice shook her head.

The doctor frowned. 'So, what is the cause of this despair you describe?'

*Everything.*

*And nothing.*

She felt a headache begin to stir behind her eyes.

'There is n-no p-p-particular c-c-cause,' she managed.

That was part of the problem. She tried to go on, but her tongue froze and the words jammed in her throat, even though she knew what she actually wanted to say.

*Winter makes me sad sometimes. So does summer. The despair might be set off by recalling a moment from the past, or by feeling out of place in a crowded room, or by the nightingales returning in May. It makes no sense. It's a sadness that can creep up on me, even in my happiest hours. Because this sadness has legs and it follows me wherever I go, and whatever I happen to be doing, and whomever I'm with. It might be triggered by a genu-inely upsetting event but, most of the time, there is no reason to it, no logic – no discernible cause at all.*

'There is always a cause, Lady Sitwell,' the doctor said. 'It is only that sometimes we are not able to recognise what it might be.' He glanced at a page of notes on his desk, then looked back at her and said, 'You are unmar-ried, I believe?'

'Y-Y-Y-Y—'

'You know, of course, that spinsterhood is an unnatural state,' the doctor said, rather sternly. 'It is well known to us in the medical profession for causing all kinds of health problems in women, from uterine disorders and selfish tendencies, to brain fever and hysterical outbursts. It sounds to me as if you are simply suffering from a feminine case of the vapours.'

Beatrice's face burned. Could he possibly be right? Might this be something she had brought upon herself with her unnatural behaviour? Yet he had not asked her how long she had had these wretched spells, and she wanted to explain that she'd suffered from them since her early teenage years, in case that made any difference to his prognosis. But her tongue was a lump of welded lead in her mouth and she doubted she'd be able to get any further words out in front of this man now.

'I shall prescribe you a dosage of opium,' he said, turning back to his desk. 'I'm confident that will help to some extent, even if we cannot treat the underlying cause.'

The spinsterhood, in other words – one of the greatest shames a woman could own. Beatrice left the building with her head down, her cheeks flushed and her glass bottle of little pills clutched tightly in her sweating hand.

# CHAPTER
# FOURTEEN

*August 1837*

Rosa looked up from her sketch as the clockwork pigeon landed on her work desk. She'd tried sending another letter to Beatrice but, as expected, the pigeon had come back empty-handed. At first Rosa had felt irritated by her friend's long silence, but now she had started to feel concerned instead. What if something had happened to Beatrice? She seemed to travel about as she pleased, like a seed caught in the wind, with no set schedule that Rosa was aware of. If some accident were to befall her, then who would be any the wiser? She felt as if she ought to notify someone, but who? She didn't even know which country Beatrice was currently in . . .

But then something pieced together in her head and she stared at the pigeon in surprise. It was normally gone for days, if not weeks, whenever she sent a message to Beatrice, but this time it had been gone for barely an hour. Furthermore, there were traces of dark blossom on its wing tips. A blossom that smelled of rain and purple berries. Could Beatrice possibly have returned to Half Moon House without telling anyone?

Rosa wasn't going to waste any time before finding out. She had reluctantly given in to custom and gone into confinement, now that her pregnancy was apparent. To her dismay, the doctor had told her he thought she was carrying twins, and she was already large enough that she could never get comfortable for very long.

Modest women did not go visiting at such times, or appear in public at all, but she wasn't about to let a thing like that get in her way now. She packed away her workbook and went straight to the carriage house. Ignoring the shocked expression of the groom, Rosa gave the order for the carriage to be made ready and a driver to be summoned. A short while later she was seated in the velvet interior as the carriage jolted its way to her friend's home. She instantly knew Beatrice was indeed there, because of the black apple trees. They were not in the orchard as usual, but clustered beneath the window that Rosa knew to be Beatrice's bedroom. She frowned as she recalled something her friend had once told her about how the trees only did that when they were worried about her. So perhaps something was amiss after all?

When the carriage stopped in front of the main entrance, Rosa didn't send her driver in with her card but climbed awkwardly down from the carriage instead, wincing at a twinge in her lower back. The slightest exertion seemed to make her out of breath these days, and she was puffing slightly by the time she'd climbed the steps to the door. A butler answered it promptly at her ring and could not have looked more aghast to see Rosa there than if she had been stark naked.

'Good afternoon,' she said, forcing a smile. 'Is Lady Beatrice home?'

The butler began to shake his head and make excuses, but Rosa cut him off. 'I don't mean is she "at home" to visitors, I mean is she physically present in the house? Because if so, then I will not leave without seeing her, even if it means I have to sit on these steps all night.'

She very much hoped she would not have to follow through on her threat, because she had no idea if she'd be able to heave herself upright again, once she was down. To her relief, the butler invited her to take a seat in the lobby whilst he conveyed her message. And a short while later she found herself announced into Beatrice's study.

Beatrice was seated behind Lord Sitwell's desk, slowly turning the pages of a book about mushrooms. She looked up at Rosa's arrival and an expression of genuine pleasure brightened her face. Rosa noticed immediately that Beatrice was thinner than when she'd last seen her and had a sallow look to her skin.

'G-Good afternoon,' Beatrice said, rising to her feet. 'I am s-sorry for n-not replying to your l-letters. I h-have not b-been w-well.'

'You look rather peaky now, if you don't mind my saying so,' Rosa said, peering at her.

'I am m-much recovered,' Beatrice replied.

Rosa doubted that was entirely true, but she crossed the room to take both Beatrice's hands in hers anyway. 'Honey, it is so good to see you. I can't tell you how much I have missed having an intelligent and interesting friend to call upon.'

She hadn't quite realised the truth of her words until that moment, but it struck her quite forcibly now. The women in the circles in which she moved were all so dull to her, not to mention gossipy, judgemental and snobbish.

Beatrice flushed slightly and looked embarrassed, but she squeezed Rosa's hands in return. 'I f-feel the s-same.'

'You are not too dreadfully shocked at my visiting you in this state, I hope?' Rosa gestured to her belly, feeling the need to acknowledge it in some way.

Beatrice frowned. 'Wh-Why should I b-be? P-Pregnancy is p-p-perfectly natural. And c-congratulations. Of c-course.'

Rosa gave a tight smile.

'P-Please t-take a s-seat,' Beatrice said. 'I w-will r-ring for t-tea.'

Rosa waited until it had been served before launching straight into the matter of the Winter Garden. She told Beatrice about how the Carousel of Icicles had appeared, first in the pages of her own workbook and then in the pop-up book.

'So, you see, I believe you about the garden,' Rosa said. 'I believe that you visited it as a child and, honey, I'm just desperate to hear all that you know about the carousel.'

Beatrice looked up from her teacup. 'B-but there w-was no c-carousel. N-Not that I s-saw.'

'Oh.' Rosa had not expected this and found herself flailing for an explanation. 'But how can that be? Was the garden very large? Might it have been tucked away in a corner you didn't see?'

'It is p-possible.' Beatrice looked up at her. 'The g-garden was . . . n-not b-big, but n-not s-small, either.' She shook her head. 'It is d-difficult to explain. In the g-garden th-there was f-forever the s-sense of unseen w-wonders. Hiding. In the. Trees.'

'So you can tell me nothing about the carousel at all?'

Beatrice shook her head. Rosa set down her teacup with a clatter, trying to master her disappointment.

'Wh-why does it m-matter to y-you?' Beatrice asked. 'S-Surely you h-have n-nothing you w-wish to ch-change?'

'Darling, everyone has something they wish to change,' Rosa said, purposely keeping her voice light.

'But you are h-happy?' Beatrice pressed. 'At R-Raven Hall?'

'Oh, divinely,' Rosa said briskly. 'It is only that I should like to make my own carousel, you see. Just like the one in the book. It would be quite the marvel, would it not? I'm an artificer, after all, and the Carousel of Icicles sounds like quite the challenge. But if you haven't seen it, then you cannot help me, so I guess I'll have to figure it out by myself.'

Beatrice looked as if she might be about to ask further questions, so Rosa hurriedly changed the subject.

'Now what was this illness you suffered from? Some tropical fever or something, I suppose?'

Beatrice nodded, but her eyes slid away from Rosa and she offered no further detail.

'Did you ever find the ghost butterfly?' Rosa asked.

'N-No. I c-came to the c-conclusion that it d-does not exist.'

'That is a pity. I should love to have seen it. Still, I suppose you brought home lots of other marvellous specimens that I might admire?'

'I b-brought n-nothing,' Beatrice admitted. 'There s-seemed no p-point. The L-Linnean S-Society r-refused to exhibit my w-work.'

'That stuffy old bunch of coots! What do you want to be bothering about them for?'

'The p-point was to sh-share my d-discoveries,' Beatrice said. 'With the w-world.'

'But you enjoy travelling and discovering for its own sake too, don't you?'

'Well, y-yes—'

'Then that's all that matters. No one can take that away from you. When are you returning abroad?'

Beatrice paused. 'I m-may not go b-back at all. P-Perhaps it is b-better if I s-stay h-here.'

Rosa stared at her. 'Better for who? Are you saying you may give up travelling altogether? It isn't like you to be such a ninny! Whatever happened to the woman who walked out of her own wedding and damn the conse-quences? And what of the woman who travelled the world by herself, scorning any chaperone?'

'P-Perhaps that w-was the a-aberration,' Beatrice said. 'And the r-real me. Is the. Ninny.'

'That is not true!' Rosa exclaimed. 'The thought is beyond absurd. For heaven's sake, you managed to break free, and now will you really lock yourself back up in a cage, just because some stuck-up society won't display your flowers?'

To her surprise, Beatrice suddenly hunched forward, burying her face in her hands. 'I do n-not know. What to d-do.'

Rosa reached out for her hand and held it tightly. 'It is hard to go on sometimes,' she said. 'I understand. Do you imagine I never faced opposition in my ambition to become an artificer? You have to be so good that they can't say no to you. You have to fight for it with every breath.'

'One c-can b-become t-tired. Of f-fighting,' Beatrice said, yet she spoke with less conviction than she had previously.

'Yes, I know that too,' Rosa said. She felt suddenly very tired herself. It was a blow to find that her friend could offer her no help or information when it came to the carousel, and Rosa suddenly longed to be back in the peace and quiet of the aviary, surrounded by her ravens.

'Rest here a while, if you must,' she said, 'but, Beatrice, it would be a travesty if you did not return to doing what you love. I admire you so much for what you did.'

Beatrice looked startled. '*Y-You?*' she said. 'Admire m-me?' She gave a small laugh.

'Well, why is that funny?'

'It is j-just that I h-have always l-longed. To be. Like you.'

Rosa released her hand and leaned back against the settee.

*Careful what you wish for,* she thought.

'How kind,' she said aloud. 'But, you know, that is only because you see my triumphs rather than my mistakes.'

Beatrice frowned. 'S-So much t-talk of m-mistakes,' she said. 'Are you qu-quite c-certain that all is w-well?'

'Quite,' Rosa said brightly. 'You must forgive me, Beatrice. If I seem restless, it is only because I am tired of pregnancy, and more than ready for the babies to be born. It is so very uncomfortable, you see. On that note, I think I'd best return to Raven Hall.' She looked up at her friend. 'Think about what I said, please? Promise me that you'll at least do that?'

Beatrice nodded. 'Y-yes,' she said. 'I w-will.'

Rosa stood up and Beatrice did the same. 'Take care of yourself, honey. If you stay in England, then perhaps I will see you again, but I very much hope that will not prove to be the case and that we won't see each other for months and months.'

Rosa was almost at the door when the other woman spoke her name and she turned back.

'Th-Thank you,' Beatrice said. 'For s-seeing me. As I. Am.'

Rosa smiled. 'No,' she said. 'Thank *you*. For sharing the secret of the Winter Garden with me. And for showing me there's another way to live. I always fancied myself a bit of a rebel, but, Lady Sitwell, I'm nothing on you.'

She took her leave. The short walk to the carriage seemed to go on forever. She was uncomfortable sitting down, but she was uncomfortable standing up too, and lying flat, and everything in between. It was a blow to have gleaned no new information about the carousel, but she had enjoyed seeing her friend, regardless. The days passed uneventfully after that. Once a fortnight had gone by, Rosa was pleased to receive a letter from Beatrice saying that she had decided to return to travelling after all. The clockwork pigeon resumed carrying messages between them; or, rather, from Beatrice. Rosa increasingly found that she lacked the energy for letter writing, and what was there to say anyway? Her life was not like Beatrice's. She rarely had anything of interest to share.

Soon enough, though, November arrived. Snow came to Raven Hall and Rosa suffered from a severe bout of homesickness as she recalled the sleigh rides she used to take in Central Park when her family went to New York for Christmas. The Warren sleigh was always one of the grandest, with its polished runners and dark-blue paintwork. The liveried footmen sported matching shades in the piping of their furred collars and the tops of their shining boots. The horses were resplendent with their elegant feathered aigrettes unfolding from their glossy heads. Those had been happy days, full of sleigh bells and laughter, and Rosa longed for them hopelessly, wishing that she had never left America.

But then she gave birth to twin girls, and everything changed.

# CHAPTER FIFTEEN

*November 1837*

Esme was small and pretty, whilst Ada was ugly and angry, yet Rosa loved both of them fiercely. She didn't know how she could ever have thought that she didn't want them. Her plans for the carousel were put to one side, and the clockwork horses and polar bear were dismantled. Her previous hopes of changing the past filled her with guilt. For although she still loathed her husband, she no longer wanted to erase him from her life, even if such a thing were possible. Without him there could be no babies. And they were her entire world.

And yet . . .

Loving them was not the problem – she loved them both with her very soul. The problem was that they did not appear to love *her*. From the beginning Rosa had insisted on feeding and looking after the babies herself, earning all kinds of baffled looks from the servants.

'This is quite ludicrous, Rosa,' Eustace had said. 'What do you know about caring for infants? It simply is not done, for a duchess. We shall be a laughing stock if word gets out. Servants gossip, you know.'

But Rosa did not care. She dismissed the wet nurse that Eustace had employed. She was almost euphoric to find that she was able to love her daughters after all. And love, surely, would be enough. She expected she would know instinctively what to do, how to meet their needs and make them happy. Yet it was all so much harder than she had ever imagined.

The babies seemed to cry incessantly. They never laughed or smiled, as Rosa had imagined they would. Instead their little faces seemed to be forever screwed up in an incandescent rage that nothing would soothe. All they ever wanted from Rosa was her breasts, but feeding was so intensely painful that she would often weep as she was doing it. She began to feel hollowed out, exhausted with the effort of trying to please two tiny monsters who could never be satisfied. Even holding them did not come naturally. Their heads fell back too easily, their limbs were too uncoordinated, they were forever scratching at their own faces, leaving deep, vicious welts there, as if devils had been at them in the night.

In the dark hopelessness of the endless days, Rosa even wondered whether perhaps they sensed, somehow, that she had not wanted them to begin with. Might they have been able to feel her emotions whilst still in the womb? Might that explain how keenly they seemed to dislike her? Even worse, perhaps they somehow knew that she had been working on a carousel to erase them from existence. Maybe this was what they could not forgive her for.

'I'm sorry,' she whispered, over and over again. 'I do want you. I *do*.'

She even made them another carousel – not a cold-hearted one built from icicles, but a brightly coloured music box, with a cheerful circus tune and friendly, prancing ponies in vibrant ribbons.

Eustace was, naturally, disappointed the twins weren't boys and took little interest in them. This would not have bothered Rosa in the slightest if it hadn't meant that he broached the subject of a male heir once again. One night he even had the nerve to knock on the nursery door. It was late and Rosa was already in her narrow fold-out bed. The twins had finally stopped crying and she was just drifting off to sleep. For a moment, in the confusion of coming properly awake, she thought Eustace was in the room with her, imagined she felt the touch of his fingers, hot and slick and greedy on her skin.

She jerked upright, gasping for breath, but he was nowhere near her bed and her ravens knew well enough what they must do. The duke yelled as they descended upon him in the corridor, and she heard his footsteps retreat as he fled to the safety of his own bedroom, like a rat disappearing back down its hole. The noise had awoken the twins, who began to bawl once again. Exhausted, Rosa dragged herself from her bed to take them from their cribs. She could no longer remember what it felt like not to be tired.

The next morning Eustace had a deep cut beside his eye, but he said nothing of what had happened. In fact he did not speak to Rosa at all, and left for London immediately after breakfast. She was glad to be left alone once more. At least now Eustace would not be there to witness her absolute failure as a mother, her total inability to do it properly.

A few mornings after he'd left, Rosa was slumped in the rocking chair in the nursery, two crying babies cradled in her arms. It had been another endless night, and a grey dawn light was finally pushing its way through the windows, but Rosa knew the nightmare would continue. It seemed as if this endless cycle would just go on and on. There was blood on her nightdress where her nipples had been bitten raw. Tears ran from her bloodshot eyes, but she was hardly aware of them. Truly this seemed the cruellest punishment imaginable – to want the babies, only for them to not want her.

She barely even noticed when Jill entered the room with her morning cup of chocolate, until the girl set down the tray and then came to crouch beside the chair, into Rosa's line of sight. Dimly she realised that the maid had been talking to her and she had not been taking it in. Rosa realised, too, that her aching breasts were exposed, yet even if her arms had not been full with the twins, she doubted she could have mustered the energy to cover herself. What did any of it matter?

'I'm sorry, Jill.' Her own voice seemed suddenly strange to her. 'What did you say?'

'I offered to help, madam,' the maid repeated, although she looked terribly uncertain. 'With the babies. I have three of my own and it doesn't have to be . . . like this.' She gestured vaguely. 'I can show you, if you like, how to make it easier? I mean . . . if it's not impertinent?'

Rosa looked at her maid properly for the first time then. There was kindness in the girl's face, but she looked worried too, as if afraid she might be dismissed on the spot for even making such a suggestion.

'Oh.' Rosa felt her heart clench painfully with a small spark of hope. 'Oh, would you?'

'Of course, your grace.'

Suddenly Rosa's tears turned to sobs. 'What's wrong with me? Why am I so bad at . . . at everything?'

Jill tentatively laid a hand on her back and rubbed it gently. Rosa did not think she had ever been so glad in her life to be touched by another person, yet it only made her cry harder.

'Feeding isn't easy, madam, not for anyone,' Jill said. 'Not at first. And especially not if you have two little ones. You just need someone to show you how to do it properly. That's all it is.'

Jill did as she had promised and, from there, things started to get a little easier, bit by bit. It was still difficult, and exhausting, and frustrating at times, but Jill told her that was just as it should be, and it didn't mean she was doing anything wrong. She showed Rosa how to breast-feed so that it wasn't agony and explained that the babies were too young to smile yet, let alone laugh. She simply had to persevere. And so Rosa did. And there were moments when it became less difficult. And there were moments of peace when they could simply enjoy being together. And, eventually, there were even moments of happiness.

'I can never thank you enough,' Rosa said later to Jill. 'Whatever your salary is, I will see that it is increased.'

The maid blushed and fidgeted uncertainly with her hands.

'You don't have to do that, your grace. But thank you.'

Rosa duly consulted the housekeeper and had Jill's salary doubled, but even that hardly seemed adequate. Perhaps nothing ever would. After questioning Jill about her favourite animal, Rosa made her a clockwork hedgehog. No upper-class lady had ever seemed as delighted with their jewelled songbird as Jill seemed with her little hog.

Rosa's health continued to improve as she recovered from the birth. Even when the twins grizzled, it seemed to her that they were worth every wretched moment with Eustace. They were what her whole life had been building up to. And if her happiness was marred every now and again by thoughts of the cryptic words whispered by those wretched sisters in the smoky darkness of that hermitage, well, she did not let it bother her for long. All of that sorrow was in the past and Rosa had drawn a line under it. Life would be better, now that she had the twins. There was love in the house for the first time. Certainly there would be no small gravestone. Rosa would not allow it.

Every evening, when they retreated to the night-nursery, Rosa closed the door and wound the carousel music box. The ponies spun round and round, shedding sparkling diamonds of light around the room. And then, one day, the *Winter Garden* pop-up book turned up in the nursery too. Rosa later learned that Jill had taken it from her dressing table and put it there, thinking it might be easier for Rosa to read to the babies, since she had confessed that she never knew what to say to their serious little faces.

When Rosa first saw the book, she wasn't sure she wanted it in the nursery. After all, it reminded her of the Carousel of Icicles, and her own guilty ambition that would have erased the twins entirely if she had succeeded. But Jill had explained it was good for the babies to hear her voice, so she opened up the book and started to read.

'*Once upon a time, there was a sad, lonely little girl called Beatrice.*'

The twins were far too young to understand the story, of course, but they stared solemnly at the pictures as they rose up out of the pages. Rosa had learned that, of the two of them, Esme had the gentler nature, and cuddling often seemed to quieten her. Ada was usually much more difficult to please, but even she appeared to be interested in the book, so Rosa kept on reading.

'*One night she was feeling especially alone because an angel had taken her mother. But then the ice clock chimed, the white frog appeared on her pillow and ice roses filled her bedroom . . .*'

Rosa often returned to the book when the twins were hard to settle. Ada, in particular, would sometimes cry disconsolately for hours in the evening, and there seemed to be nothing that Rosa could do or say that would soothe her – except to read from the *Winter Garden* book. Ada's red, outraged face would soften and her tears would dry up, as the pages seemed to emit faint scents of candied fruit and frosted pine.

Then one night something extraordinary happened. Rosa had finished the story, the twins were both asleep at the same time for once, and Rosa was keen to crawl into her own bed for an hour or two before one of them inevitably woke. But when she tried to turn off the carousel's music, the mechanism got stuck. The key refused to move and the lullaby continued to play.

And then, one by one, the tiny ponies left the carousel. Rosa stared. She had not designed them to do that, but she knew from experience that sometimes her clockwork creatures could take on a life of their own. It usually happened when they had existed out in the world for a little while and had begun to develop their own souls.

They stepped off the carousel's platform straight onto the window ledge. One of the ponies kicked the frame beyond the bars and the window swung open – only a few inches, but it was enough for the ponies to tumble out onto the ledge.

Rosa lurched after them with a little cry of dismay, but before she could stop them, they'd leapt from the edge, to be swallowed up by the deep snow in the grounds below. She quickly closed the window. Esme had been looking a little sickly the past few days, and the last thing she needed was icy air blowing into the room.

Rosa checked to make sure the twins were still asleep before tiptoeing out into the corridor and down the stairs. It had taken her many hours of patient work to craft the carousel, and she didn't want to have to make replacement ponies. She paused long enough to pull on her furs and winter boots, then went out through the front door and round to the back of the house where the horses had fallen. The night was ferociously cold, but clear and still – heavy with the promise of yet more snow. She reached the spot beneath the nursery window, half-fearing that she would find only a collection of broken cogs and clockwork.

Instead there were tiny hoof prints, leading straight into the arboretum of Scots pines. Rosa sighed, but pressed forward. The ponies' mechanisms would freeze if she left them overnight and could damage them. She frowned as she trudged through the snow, wondering what could have possessed them to behave like that. She'd never had clockwork creatures run away from her before. Truly, it was most puzzling. And if she'd known they were going to trot off so fast, she would have been sure to bring a lamp . . .

Just as the thought occurred to her, there was the soft flicker of lamplight up ahead and she stopped in surprise. It was past midnight. Surely there could not be anyone else out at this hour? Even the groundskeeper and gardeners would be tucked away inside their cottages. And yet there were certainly lanterns hanging from the branches, clearly marking out a path through the pine trees.

The snow crunched, deep and soft beneath Rosa's boots, as she made her way further into the arboretum. Between the stark outline of the spindly branches, she thought she glimpsed the white blur of some large shape up ahead. A familiar tune suddenly drifted through the darkness, icy notes hanging in the air like stars to guide her way. It was the lullaby melody from the carousel. Only Rosa hadn't brought it with her – it was waiting inside the house. But the tune sounded different somehow: no longer tiny and tinny enough for music boxes and nurseries, but fuller and clearer and somehow coloured in, as if it formed part of the real world now, instead of a child's frosted fairy tale . . .

Rosa turned a corner of the path and stopped abruptly. She had found her little ponies. And she had found the Carousel of Icicles.

# CHAPTER SIXTEEN

Rosa stared up at the carousel glittering before her in the lamplight. It was just as she had imagined it. The white horses were life-sized. Hundreds of icicles hung down from the cream-and-gold striped roof. As it rotated, Rosa saw that these horses all wore silver ribbons in their manes and tails. And there were two stationary sleighs, adorned with silver bells and pulled by white polar bears. It all sparkled in a coat of tiny diamonds. The music spilling from it was sad and sweet and exactly the tune her music box played. Yet how could that be, when it was an entirely original song that Rosa had composed herself especially for her young daughters?

*The Carousel of Icicles. The world has never seen its like before . . .*

'No.' Rosa shook her head. 'No, I didn't make you.'

She felt a horrible rush of guilt, as if the twins might be able to sense that the carousel was, impossibly, suddenly here. She walked slowly forward, past her small clockwork ponies, who were frolicking in the big carousel's shadow. She touched the side of the carousel, half-expecting it to turn to smoke and disappear, but it was cold and real enough beneath her hand. How could this be? She had dismantled her horses and put away her plans. Yet here the carousel was, completed and beautiful and terrible.

'You mustn't be here,' Rosa whispered. 'You're not needed. I don't want to go back and change what happened with Eustace. I don't regret that decision any more.'

There was nobody in sight – either on the carousel or operating it. It stood quite alone amongst the snow-dusted trees; impossibly lovely, impossibly strange, like something from a cherished childhood dream.

Rosa gripped one of the icicle poles, wincing at its coldness, and pulled herself up onto the revolving platform. Mirrors surrounding the fairground organ reflected her image back at her, a lone winter princess amongst her herd of white snow horses. She walked among them, examining their faces, and saw that they were all unique. Each had a slightly different stance, or expression, or style of livery. And Rosa knew them all well, for each and every horse was perfectly replicated within the pages of her workbook. Now here they all were, brought to life before her.

She reached up a hand to place on the nearest horse's muzzle and, although it did not move, Rosa felt as if it recognised her. The animals were all made of white clockwork. The detail was exquisite, but they were completely artificial, and so she was at a loss to explain why she suddenly thought she heard a sudden snort behind her, as if from a real horse. She turned round, but only clockwork steeds pranced in her wake.

She continued moving through the carousel, looking for one creature in particular. In no time at all she had found it – the one horse on the entire carousel that had a golden ribbon tied into its mane:

*The horse with the golden ribbon had a special gift – she could take a person back, to change just one decision they regretted . . .*

Rosa looked into the horse's eyes and they seemed almost accusing.

'What are you doing here?' Her words were a whisper. 'I don't want you. I changed my mind. You must leave. Go back to wherever it is you came from.'

The horse's eyes hadn't changed, but all at once they seemed sad rather than accusing. Sweat tingled on Rosa's skin, despite the iciness of the night. The carousel seemed suddenly dreadful to her, as if its mere presence might somehow snatch the twins from her grasp.

'Did you hear me?' she hissed. 'You're not wanted here! Go! Get away!'

The next second, inexplicably, the carousel was gone. Rosa tripped over herself in the air and fell, crumpling into the snow. A church-like hush whispered over the scene, and flakes of fresh snow thickened the sky. One by one, the lanterns winked out and then vanished, leaving the scent of candle smoke twisting in ribbons through the naked branches. Fingers of moonlight filtered through the trees, making everything seem silver and surreal.

And Rosa was left alone in the clearing, with only her tiny clockwork ponies for company. She scooped them up and thrust them into her pocket, before running out of the trees and across the lawn to the house. It seemed to take an age to climb the stairs to the nursery. At last she threw open the door, terrified that she might find empty cribs. But everything was just as she'd left it and her baby daughters slept quietly.

Rosa breathed in to steady herself, waiting for a sense of relief that never came. Instead there was only a dark dread that one day, somehow, her daughters would be snatched away from her.

The next day Rosa was in the morning room, just finishing a letter to Beatrice about the carousel, when a footman announced that James Sheppard was outside and had enquired whether she was at home to visitors. She hadn't seen him since the night of the pleasure garden, but she recalled now that he had promised to give her first choice of his plants when he returned from abroad.

'Oh yes!' Rosa exclaimed. 'Yes, show him in. Has he brought orchids?'

'I believe so, your grace.'

The footman showed James in and Rosa moved forward immediately, delighted to see him, as well as the large Wardian case placed by his feet.

'It's so good to see you, Mr Sheppard, I can't wait to see your new orchids. Tell me, have any of—'

But that was as far as she got before Ada let out a piercing shriek. Rosa flinched. She had forgotten they were there for a moment. The noise woke Esme, who had been sleeping peacefully, and soon both babies were crying. Ada had only just settled moments ago and already she was upset about something.

'I'm sorry,' Rosa said, raising her voice above the din. 'One of the servants will remove them.'

'Please don't on my account.'

Rosa tried to stifle her rising panic. It was bad enough when the servants saw her with the twins, but with James the shame would be even worse. She knew she would not be able to quieten them, and then all her ineptitude as a mother would be laid bare.

*You do not know the first thing about infants,* Eustace sneered inside her head.

But before she could say anything, James had walked over to the cribs and was leaning over them, talking to the twins. Rosa went to pick up Esme, who immediately stopped crying in her arms. The babies were now too big for one person to pick them both up at the same time whilst also supporting their heads, but Rosa knew there would have been no point in picking Ada up anyway. Once she started crying like that, nothing would make her stop.

She was therefore astonished when James reached a hand into the crib and Ada wrapped her own hand tightly around his finger and fell silent.

'Beautiful,' James said softly, looking down at her.

*I wish she was yours . . .*

The thought seemed to ring loudly in Rosa's head. She had always thought of Ada as being ugly, but perhaps that was because she only ever saw her with her face screwed up in anger. Now, as the baby blinked her large eyes up at James, she seemed suddenly lovely.

'I wanted to get them each a present, but I could only find one, so perhaps they might share it?' James reached into his pocket and drew out something in a miniature glass dome. It was a star that fitted snugly in the palm of his hand.

Rosa gasped. She recognised it from the pop-up book. The pages were littered with these beautiful, sparkling, impossible stars. They shone in the snow, and glittered amongst tree branches, and dusted the ice-house steps. It seemed that they fell from the Tiger of Stars, just as a real beast would shed its fur.

'Have you been there?' Rosa asked quickly. 'The Winter Garden?'

James glanced at her, looking surprised by the eagerness in her voice.

'I have not,' he said. 'This was just another auction find, I'm afraid.'

Rosa thought of the carousel, shining there in the dark amongst the pines. 'Have you ever heard of just one small piece of the garden appearing by itself?' she asked.

'I cannot say that I have,' James replied. He straightened from the crib to turn round to her. 'Why?'

Rosa heard herself give a strained laugh. 'There was . . . I thought I saw a carousel last night.'

'A carousel?'

'The Carousel of Icicles.'

James looked blank.

'You never saw it?' Rosa asked. 'In the pop-up book you gave me?'

James frowned. 'I don't recall any carousel. Perhaps you are thinking of another children's tale?'

She shook her head. 'The page is not always there,' she said. 'Oh, I know it sounds strange but . . . it seems to appear at random. The book says that if you ride the horse with the golden ribbon, then you can go back and change a decision you made in the past.'

'What a wonder that would be,' James said slowly, his eyes gleaming. 'But I regret to say I have never heard of such a carousel – either in the Winter Garden or anywhere else.'

He was echoing what Beatrice had already told her. Their conversation was cut short then, when the door opened. Rosa looked round, expecting to see one of the servants, but it was Eustace instead. She had known he would not stay at his town house forever, but it was a blow to have him back again so soon, especially as his face was pale. She knew this meant that he had a headache and he was always more bad-tempered when he suffered from one of those. He stood frozen in the doorway, staring at them aghast, as if witnessing something grotesque.

'What are you thinking of, receiving this man without a chaperone? It will not do, Rosa.'

Rosa felt a rush of heat spread over her face. 'Mr Sheppard is an old friend who has merely come to—'

'He is your former beau,' Eustace cut her off. 'Did you stop to think for even a moment about what people would say?' His eyes narrowed. 'How long has this been going on?'

Right on cue, Ada began to cry, but Rosa could not pick her up without putting Esme down, and there hardly seemed much point in doing so when she knew that nothing she did would calm her. The baby wailed unattended in her crib.

'I am here to sell my orchids, sir,' James said mildly. 'And to congratulate an old friend on the safe arrival of her daughters. If you think anything improper has occurred, then that is more of a reflection on you than it is upon your wife.'

Eustace turned to him, his lip curling in dislike. 'Surely you would not deny that you proposed marriage to Rosa?'

'Why should I deny it?' he asked. 'I would think any man with an ounce of sense would wish to marry such an accomplished lady. But as she turned me down, I was certainly gentleman enough to accept her refusal.'

Eustace took a deep breath and took a few steps into the room. 'I want you out of my house,' he said. 'If you do not leave at once I shall have you thrown out.'

Rosa didn't think she had ever felt such fury; it was a fist clenched in a strangling hold around her throat. Ada's crying went on and on in the background, and she longed to scream with her. 'How *dare* you—' she began, half-choking on the effort to get the words out.

'It's all right,' James said quietly. He set the star carefully down on the mantelpiece. 'I will go.'

Eustace's eye fell on the Wardian case. 'Kindly take your weeds with you.'

'The orchids are a gift,' James said, looking at Rosa rather than Eustace. He bowed. 'Good day to you, Duchess.'

She flinched. In that moment she would have given anything to not be a duchess. And then James was gone, closing the door quietly behind him. Before she had time to think, Rosa had put Esme beside her sister and was going after him. She ignored Eustace's barked command for her to remain where she was and caught James up outside on the drive beside his carriage.

'I am so sorry,' she said. 'I hope you can forgive that shocking display.'

He turned towards her. 'There is nothing to forgive, your grace—'

'Please!' Rosa's voice came out harsher than she'd intended. 'Would you do me a favour? Would you call me "Miss Warren", as you used to?'

She had a sudden longing for someone to call her by her old name, even though such a request would doubtless seem strange.

'Certainly, if that is what you would like.' James paused. 'I hope this doesn't seem impertinent, but I must ask: are you all right? Here, I mean. At Raven Hall. Because if there is something amiss – anything at all – then you have only to say. I won't ask questions. I won't pass judgements. I won't breathe a word of what you tell me to another living soul. I want only to help in any way that I can.'

For a wild moment Rosa thought about telling him everything, the whole sorry lot of it. She wanted to apologise for placing importance on all the wrong things. She wanted him to know how highly she thought of him. She wanted him to know the truth of what her life had become. Most of all, she wanted to ask James to take her with him, no matter where it was he might be going. He was looking at her in that quiet, steady way, and she sensed that he would do it, if she asked. She could climb right up into the carriage with him now and never look back . . .

But she could not leave her daughters behind. She would not.

'Why, I am perfectly content,' she heard herself say, whilst her heart seemed to shudder inside her chest at the lie. 'Eustace is a boor sometimes, but that's the aristocracy for you.' She laughed. 'So accustomed to having their own way.'

James breathed a sigh. 'I'm relieved to hear it,' he said. 'Well, I believe I've taken up enough of your time, Miss Warren, so I'll bid you good day. I hope you are pleased with the orchids.'

And with that, he climbed up into his carriage and put his hand out the window in a wave as it set off down the drive. Rosa kept the awful smile pasted to her face until the horses disappeared through the gates, then she whirled on her heel and stormed into the house back to Eustace.

'You wretched creature,' she hissed. 'How dare you behave in such a manner to my guest?'

'It is you who are at fault, madam,' he said, bitterness dripping from every syllable. 'Perhaps that is how things are done in America, but we have higher standards here. For heaven's sake, will you not quieten the child? Or better yet, call for the nanny to take them to the nursery where they belong.' He glared towards the crib where Ada continued to howl. 'I have the most sickening headache.'

He crossed to the servants' bell and tugged it so hard he was in danger of snapping the cord.

'If our presence offends you so much, then perhaps I shall return to America and take the girls with me!'

Rosa was not sure if she really meant the threat. Being a duchess and living in such a house had been her dream once, and she still wanted that life desperately, in spite of everything.

'Do not speak nonsense,' Eustace snapped. 'They are my children. They will remain at Raven Hall, and so will you. Confound it, I cannot hear myself think with that din!'

He strode over to the crib and, before Rosa realised what he was going to do, he reached in and pinched Ada hard on the arm. Her plaintive wail for attention immediately transformed into a frightened scream of pain.

It was a ghastly sound – one that Rosa had never heard her make before. It felt like a knife passing through her gut and she gasped, but the air was suddenly too thin and her heart seemed to clench and cramp, making her entire chest ache. She snapped her fingers and the raven on her shoulder flew at Eustace, its metal talons going straight for his eyes so that he staggered back with a yell and had to put up his hands to protect them.

Rosa hurried straight to the crib and snatched up Ada. She rocked her daughter in a futile effort to soothe her, but her small body was rigid, her arms flailed, her face was scarlet. Tears streamed down her round cheeks and she continued to scream so loudly that Rosa had to raise her own voice to be heard above it.

'I will not remain in this house with you another day!'

She ought to have confided in James, after all. She suddenly felt it had been a mistake to let him leave like that. He might have helped them to depart . . . But, no, she had no right to ask such a thing of him. She had to get out of this mess herself. She clicked her fingers again and the raven returned to her shoulder. Eustace had shielded his face, but Rosa felt a fierce rush of pleasure at the sight of the bleeding welts on the backs of his hands. 'We are leaving. All three of us. This moment.'

She refused to think about the fact that, by law, she simply wasn't allowed to walk out on Eustace, never mind take his children from him. She had become his property when she married him, and he would be within his rights to break down the door of any house that harboured her. Well, let him try and he'd see what happened! She had an unkindness of ravens to protect her and she wasn't afraid to use them. She had to get her daughters out of this house – she had to. She would not be shackled to unhappiness like some meek little mouse. Beatrice had had the guts to set herself free, and Rosa could certainly do the same.

A servant arrived in response to Eustace's bell then, so Rosa ordered them to help her take the twins up to the nursery, along with the book, the star and the orchids. Eustace did not protest – or if he did, then she didn't hear him over her daughter's cries. Once in the nursery, she dismissed the servant and examined Ada's arm. A small bruise had formed already, but it did not appear to be a serious injury. Relieved, Rosa attempted to quieten her, but nothing worked. The baby sobbed for hours.

By the time Ada finally fell into an exhausted sleep, it was too late to leave Raven Hall. The thought of going anywhere other than a comfortable chair was beyond shattering to Rosa anyway, so she had to accept that they would be spending another night in the house after all. But she promised herself it would only be the one. There was nothing worth saving here. As soon as morning came, they would go. And they would never return.

Later that evening both twins were sleeping, and Rosa had snatched the opportunity to nap on the narrow bed alongside them when there was a knock at the door. She jerked awake with a start and could have wept when Ada awoke too and started to cry again. Was it too much to ask to be left alone just for a few hours? To sleep for more than five minutes at a time? Her mind felt fogged with the need to rest, and her stinging eyes were like peeled grapes in her head.

When she opened the door she found Eustace on the other side. The colour had returned to his face, which meant that his headache had gone. Rosa's, on the other hand, throbbed and throbbed within her skull.

'I am sorry I frightened the child,' he said quietly.

Rosa was startled to hear him apologise. He had never done so before, in all the time she had known him. But it was too late for such words.

'I don't care about your apologies.'

His remorseful expression soured instantly, as she had known it would. 'Mother thinks that the children need a firmer hand.'

'They are not children. They are babies.'

'You coddle them, Rosa. They should not even be in the downstairs rooms at all; it is not natural for them to spend so much time with you. We have an excellent nanny with the most perfect references, who sits upstairs doing nothing. Mother says you will spoil the twins if you continue that way.'

'She ought to know, I suppose!' Rosa shot back. 'Since she did such an excellent job of mothering you!'

Eustace looked baffled. 'Of course she did.'

Rosa felt that chill once again as she was reminded that Eustace didn't realise he was a boar at all, but truly thought he was a gentleman. Suddenly she felt tired down to her bones, hollowed out by all the hours of crying she had endured with Ada. Sometimes it felt like she wasn't even a person at all, only a husk filled with dust.

'We are leaving this house tomorrow,' she said. 'And nothing you say will change that. If you attempt to stop us, the ravens will tear you to pieces.'

She braced herself for the raging and remonstrance that were bound to follow, wondered whether he might even threaten to set the law on her and have her dragged back to the house like a dog. But instead his face seemed to crumple.

'Please,' he said, so quietly she could barely hear him. 'Don't go. I will be a laughing stock.'

'I cannot even tell you how much I do not care about that.'

She stepped back into the nursery and closed the door in Eustace's face. He was unlikely to return that night, but she locked it anyway, just in case. As usual, Ada's cries had woken Esme, and now she had two alert babies on her hands. Wearily she sat in the rocking chair with a daughter in each arm and settled herself to the long task of feeding, cuddling, singing and soothing. That endless cycle, which seemed to have become her entire life. If she was lucky, then one of them might fall asleep, although she had practically given up hope of them both sleeping at the same time. Perhaps she ought not to have dismissed that wet nurse Eustace had employed. Perhaps she ought to accept the help of the nanny. It was just that Rosa no longer trusted anyone but herself to take care of her daughters.

In the end, though, the twins miraculously quietened. Rosa didn't dare stand up to put them back in their cribs, and fatigue seemed to weigh down her limbs like blocks of lead, so she remained in the rocking chair with them, promising herself she would only stay for a moment. The star from James shone softly inside its glass dome, twinkling over the orchids. For a blessed moment, all was quiet and peaceful and beautiful, and Rosa could breathe, and she could breathe, and she could breathe.

The star filled the room with a silvery glow that dappled, like light shining through water, and Rosa thought she was looking at a flickering shadow at first. Then her focus suddenly sharpened and she realised with a jolt that she and the twins were not alone in the night-nursery. Sitting upon the floor on the other side of the room, playing with one of the tin soldiers, was the boy with the withered arm. The one she had seen in the Long Gallery so many months ago. The one who had first spoken of the Carousel of Icicles.

# CHAPTER
# SEVENTEEN

Rosa felt the shock of adrenaline like an icy slap. How long had the boy been there, quietly playing at her feet? He was partially obscured in shadows and sat sideways-on to her. The tin soldier clicked softly across the wooden boards as the boy marched him across the floor. And the child was humming. It was a tune Rosa recognised – the one from the carousel itself. She glanced at the door but it was still shut, with the key in the lock.

'How did you get in here?' she whispered.

'I live here,' the boy said, without looking up from his soldier.

'No, I mean how did you get into the nursery? I locked the door.'

The boy offered no reply and Rosa's head buzzed. The melody he was humming seemed to burrow deeper and deeper into her mind. She knew she had locked the door. Surely he could not have been in here all along? She would have noticed him before now. Perhaps she had drifted off and he had entered with a spare key.

She longed to get up and take him by the arm, to turn him to face her and somehow *make* him talk, but she shuddered at the thought of waking the twins again. She didn't think she could take any more crying tonight. She would go mad.

'When we met before, why were you looking for the Carousel of Icicles?' she asked, trying to keep her voice low.

The boy stopped humming but continued to stare at the soldier in his hands. He was silent for so long that Rosa was about to repeat the question when, finally, he said, 'I don't think I'm supposed to be here.'

Rosa shook her head impatiently. 'Never mind that. Where did you learn about the carousel?'

He dropped the soldier, which fell with a thud to the boards. Rosa winced, but the twins didn't stir.

'From the book.'

'You've seen the page too?' Rosa was suddenly eager. She spoke a little too loudly and Ada shifted in her arms.

The boy did not reply, so Rosa nodded at the pop-up book and spoke in her most authoritative voice. 'Bring it here. Show me.'

To her relief, the boy got to his feet, picked up the *Winter Garden* book and brought it to her. He opened it and the Carousel of Icicles sprung up on its folded mechanisms, just as it had before. In the silver light from the tiny star, it looked even more lovely than it had previously.

'Please,' the boy whispered. 'Tell me where it is?'

Rosa looked at him, startled. He was close enough that she could see each individual freckle across the bridge of his nose.

'But I have no idea,' she said. 'It appeared in the grounds the other night and then vanished again.'

He looked confused. 'But *you* must know where it's gone?'

'Why should I?'

'It's your carousel.'

'No, it isn't.'

'Why did you draw it in your workbook then?'

Rosa flushed. 'How have you managed to go through my workbook?' she demanded. 'It's in a locked drawer in my dressing room.'

The boy bent down and put the book on the floor as carefully as if it were made of glass.

'I shouldn't be here,' he said. 'My father will be angry.'

'Don't worry about that. I will speak to your father, if you tell me who he is.'

Rosa expected him to give the name of one of the footmen, or perhaps the man who wound the clocks, or one of the many gardeners.

'His name is Eustace Hamilton,' the boy said, turning away from her. 'The Duke of Chalkley.'

Rosa thought she should perhaps not be as surprised as she was. It was not unknown for the gentleman of the house to visit a servant's room at night. Still, it came as a shock.

'Whatever happens,' the boy said, 'don't let her ride the carousel.'

'Who?'

But he was already turning to leave.

'Oh, please don't go!' Rosa cried. 'Tell me who your mother is.'

It was no use. The boy was already at the door. He unlocked it, slipped out and closed it quietly behind him. Rosa finally risked putting the twins back in their cribs and then hurried after him, but by the time she opened the door, the corridor was empty. She sighed. The child probably knew the endless rooms and corridors of Raven Hall far better than she did. It was pointless trying to search for him. Instead she returned to the *Winter Garden* book and sat down in the rocking chair with it on her lap.

Her fingers fumbled over the pages, worried that the carousel might vanish again, but it sprang up as it had before. And this time she noticed something else about the page. There was a pull-down tab in the sky above the carousel. Rosa had seen this on other pages scattered throughout the book. One pulled the tab down to reveal a previously hidden detail, like a fairy, or an orchid, or a frog. She was almost certain that there had not been a tab on this page before.

Slowly she reached out to pull the tab. Since it was in the sky, she expected to reveal a picture of a star or perhaps one of the many birds or butterflies that filled the garden. Instead the tab revealed two words written in the sky: *Dear Rosa*.

She stared at them and, before her eyes, more words appeared written in stars in the night sky, until an entire message sparkled before her on the page:

### *Dear Rosa,*

*You are invited to enter an unusual competition.*

*I am looking for the most magical, spectacular, remarkable pleasure garden this world has to offer. A garden that brings wonder and amazement to people's lives.*

*The winner will be picked at the end of next year, upon New Year's Eve.*

*They will be required to give up the most wondrous part of their garden. In return, the prize will be one wish — from the last of the Winter Garden's magic.*

*Yours sincerely,*
*The Spider Queen*

Rosa's hands trembled upon the page. If she'd still had any doubts about whether the Winter Garden actually existed, they now melted away. Her mind blazed with how such a thing was possible, how the book could speak out to her personally like this. More than anything else, one question scorched itself into the darkness inside her head: how much would she be able to transform her life with one wish? She glanced over at the twins sleeping in their cribs. If she won that competition, then surely she could use the prize to fix everything?

She even wondered fleetingly whether she would have the nerve to wish for Eustace to die, but it was no use. She shuddered at the wickedness of it. And Rosa had wanted a husband all along, as she had wanted to be a wife and a mother and a duchess. Perhaps she could wish that bad, rotten part of him away? Like removing a core from an apple. She could make him decent and gentle, and then they would be happy at Raven Hall and her life would be what she had always longed for.

Some small part of her wondered what might be left of Eustace if she took away all that was wrong with him, but she thrust the thought aside. When it came to magic and wishes, surely anything was possible. Anything at all.

Of course it would mean staying at Raven Hall. If Rosa was to leave, she would not be able to return to her family in Georgia ever again. Her mother would see to that. She would have nowhere to host a garden, and no money to create one. But at Raven Hall she had a seemingly endless supply of funds via Eustace, as well as extensive grounds.

The only question was: was it worth staying for? She might not win the competition. Indeed, for all she knew, there was no contest at all, simply words written in stars in a book. Within the hour they had melted away as if they'd never existed. Rosa thought about it, round and round, all night.

Finally her mind settled on the notion that perhaps the carousel sometimes appeared in the book because she was destined to win the competition with it? After all, if she could create such a thing, then surely it would be a wonder worthy of winning the competition? And how else might one explain how her own design kept appearing in the book, yet no one familiar with the garden had ever heard of a Carousel of Icicles? She must create it for real – and put it on display for the whole world to see at Raven Hall.

The next morning she called her clockwork raven to her shoulder and went straight to Eustace's study. She entered without knocking and found him seated behind his desk. He looked gaunt, as if he had hardly slept, and she was glad that he had suffered as she had. The moment she walked through the door, he rose from his seat and began earnestly entreating her to reconsider her decision to leave.

She held up her hand to silence him and said, 'Why did you not tell me you had another child here at Raven Hall?'

He frowned. 'Another child? But what do you—'

'There is no use lying to me about it. I have seen the boy around the house after dark. He was in the nursery with us last night. So which unfortunate maid was he fathered upon?'

If she could get the mother's name, then she could find the boy and perhaps finally get to the bottom of what he knew about the carousel. She expected Eustace to be sullen and resentful as he admitted the truth to her, but she felt sure his fear of the ravens would compel him to do so.

Instead he looked utterly appalled. 'I don't— I have not the least notion what you are referring to. How dare you suggest such a thing to me?'

Colour tinged his cheeks and Rosa realised he was telling the truth. Or, at least, the truth as he saw it. Perhaps he genuinely did not know about the child? Perhaps the maid had kept it from him, worried about losing her position? But then . . . surely it would have become obvious at some point? Rosa frowned. She supposed that if the housekeeper was particularly understanding, then the girl might have been allowed to return to her family on the pretence of recovering from an illness of some kind, and then had come back with the child later?

'Tell me which maid has been spreading these grotesque falsehoods!' Eustace said, a nerve twitching at his temple. 'She will leave Raven Hall today. She will never work for a titled family again.'

'I already told you I do not know who his mother is,' Rosa replied. 'And when I asked Mrs Wright, she told me there are no children here.'

'There aren't, so far as I am aware.' He met her eyes and said, 'Perhaps your wedding vows meant nothing to you, but they meant a great deal to me. I would never . . . commit myself in that fashion. Never.'

Rosa could hardly believe he imagined she was concerned about such a thing. 'It matters not one jot to me whether or not you are faithful,' she said. 'You may woo anyone who will have you – in fact I encourage you to do so. Besides, this child must have been seven or eight years old, so would have been born long before we met.'

'I will speak with Mrs Wright,' Eustace said. 'And get to the bottom of whatever this is.'

'Good. Oh and, by the way, I have decided to stay.'

He stared at her. 'You . . . you have?' She saw astonishment and then a brief flash of delight pass over his face.

'On one condition.'

He looked wary. 'Yes?'

'I want a garden.'

Perhaps there was no competition or, even if there was, maybe another garden would win. But Rosa had always believed you needed to fight for the things you wanted. The trick was to fight longer and harder than anyone else. You had to still be there, over and over again, slogging away long after everyone else had given up and gone home. You had to drag yourself up after every single fall, even when you were exhausted and bleeding. That was how you ended up with everything you had ever wanted. That was the only way to win, in the end.

'Very well,' Eustace replied. 'Although I'm not sure why you go through the pretence of asking me, when it appears I have little choice in the matter.'

He looked at the clockwork raven on her shoulder and his eyes were full of a seething resentment that startled Rosa. She had seen it before, but there seemed something wilder about it this time, as if whatever control he had of himself was wearing thin. She told herself it did not matter. She would enter the competition, she would win that wish and she would use it to fix whatever was wrong with her husband.

# CHAPTER
# EIGHTEEN

*December 1837*

**B**eatrice stood in the hallway of the Linnean Society and shook with outrage. Her hands were gripped so tightly around the document in her hand that she was in danger of ripping the paper. Her anger was a fist clenched around her throat that made it even harder than usual to get any words out.

'H-How c-c-can you kn-know my p-paper has no w-worth?' she struggled. 'You h-haven't e-even g-g-glanced at it.'

The secretary sighed. 'Madam, this is a men's establishment for real scientists. I'm sure your mushrooms seem most interesting to you, but—'

'Lady Beatrice,' a voice called.

Beatrice turned to see James Sheppard walking over to her across the shining tiles. She felt no anger towards him this time for leaving her employ. Instead she felt a pang of shame as she recalled the nature of their parting at Half Moon House the year before. She had been terse with him, perhaps even rude. She had said all the wrong things and regretted them later. But if he nurtured any grudge, it did not show on his face, which was as amenable as ever.

'This is a surprise,' he said, smiling. 'I did not know you were back in England.'

'Only b-briefly,' Beatrice said. 'I h-hoped to p-persuade the s-s-society to ch-change their m-minds about my w-work. But I c-c-cannot even g-gain an audience.'

She waved her hand vaguely at the frowning man behind the desk.

James glanced at the paper in her hand and said, 'May I?'

Beatrice hesitated, then handed it over to him.

He flicked quickly through the pages and she saw his eyes widen – as well they should. The paper was filled with such wonders: a flower that could bring rain, another whose scent could remove physical pain, a bird whose song bestowed visions of other lives, and a frog who could catch nightmares right out of the sky.

James looked up at the secretary and said, 'Please be so good as to fetch the president.'

The man gave a startled laugh. 'Oh, but he will not—'

'I am not joking, sir; fetch him at once,' James said, his voice sharp.

Beatrice felt a flare of resentment as the secretary gave a bow and hurried away. For almost half an hour she had stood here arguing with him, to no effect whatsoever. It was galling to have James sweep in now and take charge of things, even if he was trying to help her.

'These discoveries are extraordinary,' James said, passing the paper back to her. 'You must be immensely proud.'

She inclined her head, but said nothing. A few minutes later the secretary reappeared with the society's president, a thin man with a neatly trimmed white moustache, named Sir Harold Monker.

'What is all this, Mr Sheppard?' he asked, ignoring Beatrice entirely. 'I hear it is most urgent?'

'Sir, I have the honour of introducing Lady Beatrice Sitwell,' James said, before turning to her. 'May I present Lord Monker, the president of the Linnean Society?'

In spite of the difficulty in getting him here, Beatrice felt a hum of excitement to be standing before him at last.

'H-H-How d-do you d-do, s-s-sir?'

Lord Monker gave her a bow. 'It is a pleasure to meet you, Lady Beatrice. Forgive me, but I'm not sure quite how I—'

'Lady Beatrice has travelled widely over the last eighteen months,' James said. 'She is a fine botanist and mycologist and has come to present a paper to the society. I highly recommend that you read it.'

Lord Monker looked astonished. 'But my heavens, we cannot possibly—'

'Please be so good as to at least glance at the pages, sir,' James said.

The president sighed and flicked through the paper in his hand. His movements were impatient at first, but he quickly slowed down and his expression changed to one of interest. Finally he looked back up at James.

'Well,' he said. 'This is most interesting, I must admit. In light of the . . . ah, the significance of some of these finds, we might, perhaps, permit you to present the paper on her ladyship's behalf?'

Beatrice felt her blood boil in her veins. That Lord Monker should speak to James Sheppard – the son of a gardener – as if he were a social equal, whilst she was passed over as if she were invisible. It was intolerable!

'No,' she said, before James could speak for her. 'I p-p-present it m-myself. Or n-not at a-all.'

Lord Monker shook his head. 'It is quite out of the question, I'm afraid.'

He handed the paper back to her. Beatrice had no energy left for speech, so she offered only a curt nod before turning and leaving the room.

'What a rude woman,' she heard the secretary exclaim behind her.

'No manners at all,' the president agreed.

'Certainly there was shocking rudeness, sir, but I do not think it was on the part of Lady Beatrice,' James said, his usual mild tone replaced with one of irritation.

Beatrice ignored them all and didn't stop until she was out of Burlington House on the streets of Mayfair. There were far too many people about and she longed desperately for solitude. Her carriage was parked a little way down the road and she began to walk towards it, trying to ignore the stares of passers-by. She had become so accustomed to travelling on her own abroad that she had almost forgotten how unacceptable it was for a lady – especially one who was unmarried – to walk unaccompanied in the street in England.

In addition she couldn't fail to notice that her French walking dress was hopelessly out of fashion. The huge puffed gigot sleeves of only a couple of years ago seemed to have vanished entirely and Beatrice felt suddenly ridiculous, as well as irritated that she should have to bother about such things in the first place. She vaguely recalled Rosa mentioning in one of her letters that the tastes of the new Queen Victoria had drastically changed women's fashion since she ascended to the throne, but being completely disinterested in the subject, Beatrice hadn't paid it much attention.

Was it really so much to ask to be able to leave the country for a year or two and return to find the same wardrobe still serviceable? She was rich enough not to be particularly bothered by the expense of ordering a new one, although it still seemed a terrible waste, but the time required for measurings and fittings and the endless choosing of different ribbons and ruffles was the most irksome thing of all.

She had also forgotten how dirty London was. Smuts stained her clothes and cold mud soaked through the toes of her boots as soon as she stepped outside. When James called out to her a few moments later, Beatrice's instinct was to ignore him and continue walking, but it felt too childish, so she reluctantly stopped and waited, committing yet another dreadful faux pas, if anyone happened to be watching. One must never stop to speak to a gentleman in the street. If he had something of pressing importance to say, then he might be permitted to say it as he walked, but stopping to gossip was not done. Beatrice was wearied by all the many rules, however, and they suddenly seemed to matter to her even less than they'd ever done before.

'I only wanted to apologise,' James said, stopping before her. 'I took over and spoke for you in there, which I realise I had no right to do. It was quite wrong and I hope you can forgive me.'

Beatrice shook her head. What did it matter anyway? Even without her stutter, she could not speak for herself in such a place and would have had no contact with the president at all without James's intervention.

'You w-w-were t-trying to h-help,' she said.

'It is a disgrace,' he said quietly. 'That's all there really is to say about it. I am sorry.'

'I expected as m-much from their l-letters,' Beatrice replied. 'I h-hoped if I c-came in p-person it m-might h-help, but . . .' She trailed off. 'At least. I tried.'

She had owed it to herself to do so, but still the disappointment was bitter.

'W-Will you c-come?' she asked suddenly. 'To see my f-finds? I should l-like to sh-show them. To s-someone. Who w-will appreciate them.'

Suddenly she dearly longed for *somebody* to marvel at them. She'd invited Rosa to her home several times after receiving that startling letter about the carousel, but her friend seemed to be permanently occupied with the twins these days. And if it was improper to extend such an invitation to an orchid hunter, Beatrice simply no longer cared.

'Yes,' James said at once. 'I will come. I should be honoured.'

'Next T-Tuesday,' Beatrice said. 'At eleven o'c-clock.'

He nodded. 'Until next week then.'

He offered her a bow and Beatrice inclined her head before continuing on to her carriage. What a relief it was to climb up into the soft hush of the velvet interior and close the door upon the world.

Later, when she was back at Half Moon House, the opium bottle lay beside her, Wilkie snored softly at her feet and the golden haze of almost-happiness filled her body, making her feel that she could float right out of the window and rise far above the house's chimneys, like one of those spectacular hot-air balloons they sometimes sent up from Vauxhall.

Beatrice recalled the first time she'd ever seen one, just a couple of years before her almost-wedding, when she'd been in London for the Season. How astonished she had been by the balloon's beautiful blue-and-gold colours, and the majesty of its slow rise into the star-filled sky. How she longed to go up in a balloon herself, rather than merely watching from the ground. But then the balloonist had performed his next trick to the adoring crowd by releasing two miniature 'balloons' from over the side. They looked like tiny versions of the real thing, except they weren't really balloons at all, only parachutes that came down too quickly and tilted at too much of an angle, giving the crowd a good look at the terrified eyes of their two occupants.

There was a monkey in one and a puppy in another. The little monkey died when his balloon crashed to the ground, but the puppy survived, although his wicker basket was destroyed. Ignoring her aunt's cries, Beatrice had pushed through the crowd and gathered the puppy up in her arms. The small creature trembled from head to foot and its urine spread in a warm patch down the front of her dress.

There was a great fuss when the balloonist came back down and tried to take the puppy from her, but nothing would persuade Beatrice to part from him, and eventually the man left with a payment that was double the dog's worth. The dog had returned to Half Moon House with Beatrice after the Season, and she'd loved Wilkie ever since.

As she lay on the bed hours later, it occurred to Beatrice that opium was rather like a balloon. It took you up very high – for a while – but eventually you had to come back down, usually with a crash, and the breaking of bones, and the splintering of debris that would fly out and impale you to the mattress, so that you couldn't move when the dead monkeys came, half-mad on their opium nightmares.

And when the monkeys touched her with their rotten fingers, the nightmares became her own and she couldn't move to escape them. She could only lie there and relive, over and over again, the despicable thing she had done in this house when she'd turned her back on her own mother.

Many hours later she lay in the cool darkness of the bedroom, which twinkled in the silver light of the stars shining through the window. The monkeys had gone and there was only the white frog, sitting on her pillow and staring at her with its over-large eyes. It was the same creature she had seen almost twenty years ago. A golden crown shone upon its head, and in its mouth it held an envelope with her name penned in an elegant script across the front.

Beatrice stared back at it for some time, believing it to be a last remaining fragment of her opium dream. But the minutes and the hours stretched slowly by and the frog didn't move, or fade from existence. It only sat there, looking at her and waiting. Finally she sat up and reached a hand out towards it. The frog immediately dropped the invitation into her palm and then jumped from the bed, hopping across the room and squeezing through the gap beneath the door.

Beatrice scrambled after it, her heart bursting with hope, already imagining a trail of dancing golden mushrooms, but when she threw open the door the corridor remained still and dark. There was no sign of the frog, either. Beatrice closed the door and went to the window, to be faced with another disappointment.

No lanterns flickered upon the lawn, no fairies fluttered through the dark silk of the night sky, and the winter picnics didn't offer up delicious scents of savoury pies and sweet jam puffs. Beatrice looked back down at the card in her hands. Suddenly she worried that perhaps it would be a reprimand. Perhaps the Spider Queen was angry with her for searching for the garden. She broke the seal and drew out the letter. She saw that it was, in fact, an invitation, only of a very different type from that which she had been sent before:

*Dear Beatrice,*

*You are invited to enter an unusual competition.*

*I am looking for the most magical, spectacular, remarkable pleasure garden this world has to offer. A garden that brings wonder and amazement to people's lives.*

*The winner will be picked at the end of next year, upon New Year's Eve.*

*They will be required to give up the most wondrous part of their garden. In return, the prize will be one wish — from the last of the Winter Garden's magic.*

*Yours sincerely,*
*The Spider Queen*

Beatrice gazed at the letter. The last of the garden's magic? What could that mean? It had never occurred to her for a moment that the garden would ever be any less wondrous than when she had seen it. The thought made her feel profoundly sad. And yet . . . what a prize on offer! She knew at once what she would wish for. She would go back to that dreadful day at Half Moon House and do it all differently. She would wish that she had had the courage to say goodbye to her mother when she had the chance.

A golden glow of hope warmed her body and made the ends of her fingers tingle. Surely she already had a head start, with all the discoveries she had made? How could anyone else's garden possibly compete? And, best of all, she had an entire year to get everything ready.

# CHAPTER NINETEEN

In the days after learning about the competition, a plan
formed in Beatrice's mind. She had already found many
remarkable and spectacular things on her travels, but
displaying those wasn't enough. She knew what she had
to do. The only snag was that she would require James's
help to do it.

She took special care to make sure everything was ready
for his arrival. She recalled that James had a particular
fondness for walnut cake and gave orders for the cook to
prepare one, alongside a full tea tray. She waited impatiently all morning and, to her relief, he arrived promptly
at the hour they'd agreed. A footman showed him into
the study and, to Beatrice's surprise, he was accompanied
by his driver, who carried a large wrapped parcel, the size

and shape of a painting. After setting it down against the wall, the servant took his leave.

'Good afternoon, Lady Beatrice,' James said, offering her a bow.

'G-Good afternoon.' She indicated the parcel. 'What is th-that?'

'We spoke of the Winter Garden once before,' he said. 'Do you recall? It has been quite fascinating to me ever since I first heard of it. And, in my own small way, I'm a collector of those items that occasionally appear in auction houses. Much like that dazzling tiger over there.'

Beatrice glanced over at the diamond tiger she had purchased in Singapore.

'You th-think the t-tiger has something t-to do with the g-garden?' she asked.

'Perhaps we might be frank with one another,' James said. 'I know about the Tiger of Stars. I know the Winter Garden exists and that you have been there.'

Beatrice did not deny it this time; in fact she was pleased to hear him bring it up in this way. It would make it easier to raise the subject of the competition with him.

'Last week I stumbled across something at Mr Stevens's Auction Rooms,' James went on. 'I'd like to share it with you, if I may?'

He went to the parcel his driver had brought in, tore off the brown paper and turned it round to face her. Beatrice stared at it for long silent moments. It was an extraordinarily beautiful painting, depicting a girl and a tiger facing each other, their gazes locked across the snow. The tiger's body was made up entirely of stars. The silver-and-white paint used to create his galactic stripes seemed to shine right out of the canvas. The tiger was more than mere paint somehow – he was a reminder of the spectacular wonder of the universe, and all the mysteries of life, and the deep magic to be found in love and sorrow.

The girl was about eight years old, with a solemn face and very dark hair. She wore a mourning dress and her black parasol was trimmed with dark lace and hung loosely from her hand, the tip dragging in the deep drifts of sparkling snow that surrounded them. It so glittered with minute crystals of ice and frost that Beatrice felt sure the canvas would feel cold if she touched it.

And, indeed, she couldn't help herself. She crossed the room to do just that. There was only oil and canvas beneath her fingertips, yet the painting's spell seemed to blaze right out of the frame at her. The skeletal forest surrounding the girl and the tiger was just as she remembered it, hung with glass angels and sparkling sugar mice. Pale spiders spun their dreams between the long white branches and she could even see the corner of the ice house at the edge of the frame.

'Images of this child appear time and again in connection with the Winter Garden,' James said. 'Sometimes in paintings. At other times it's in picture books. There was a bronze statuette once. And the painted lid of a music box. The girl is you, of course. I recognised her immediately.'

He looked at her closely. 'We were friends back then. Why did you not tell me you were the first visitor to the garden?'

Beatrice looked at him with a frown. '*F-First* v-visitor?'

He indicated the brass plaque at the bottom of the painting. It read: *The Tiger of Stars and the First Visitor.*

Beatrice stared. The girl was certainly her, but she'd had no idea that she was the garden's first visitor.

'You didn't know?' James asked.

Beatrice shook her head.

He frowned. 'Then you are not aware of the myths that surround the first visitor, either?' At her blank look, he went on. 'She is supposed to be important to the garden somehow, and to the tiger.'

Beatrice's mind went to the invitation in her bedroom upstairs and the opportunity it offered. Before she could mention it, the servants brought in the tea tray that she had organised.

'Are we having tea?' James looked surprised. His eye fell upon the walnut cake and he suddenly looked strangely pleased. 'You remembered,' he said, glancing at Beatrice.

For some reason she felt suddenly flustered. Was it an odd thing to have remembered? Did it make her look a little pathetic? She frowned and, rather brusquely, invited him to be seated. Then she dismissed the servants. Of course there ought to have been a chaperone present, but this was not a conversation Beatrice wanted overheard.

'Well, this is cosy.' James raised an eyebrow. 'What's the occasion?'

Beatrice plunged straight in. 'I p-plan to open a p-pleasure g-garden,' she said. 'Here. At Half M-Moon House. And I w-will n-need flowers. The m-most spectacular and b-beautiful in the w-world. Wonderful enough. To impress. The S-Spider Queen herself.'

She took a deep breath and told him about the competition and the invitation she had received.

'I w-will p-pay you, of c-course,' she said. 'If we c-can come to s-some agreement on the terms.'

'Certainly!' He took the slice of cake she offered. 'I should like to help you win that competition very much.'

The feeling in his voice took Beatrice by surprise and made her suddenly suspicious. 'If we are t-to w-work t-together in this endeavour, I m-must h-have your w-word that y-you will n-not attempt to p-p-pillage the g-garden for your own p-profit.'

For a moment James said nothing at all. Then a flush crept over his face and he carefully put down the cake. For the first time since she had known him, he looked angry.

'Pillage?' he finally said. 'I am sorry you think so little of me.'

'Orchid h-hunters s-strip the l-land b-bare,' she said. 'You c-cannot d-d-deny that.'

'There are many unscrupulous orchid hunters,' James agreed. 'Men chasing riches, who care nothing for the flowers themselves and have no respect for the foreign lands they travel through. I'm not one of them.'

Beatrice suddenly recalled the care and respect James had always shown towards the grounds of Half Moon House, and the genuine, steadfast friendship he had given her during the years of their childhood. She was painfully aware that he was the only friend she had ever really had, other than Rosa. Guilt slithered in the pit of her stomach and she knew she ought to apologise, but couldn't quite work out how to phrase it without making herself look foolish.

'If I seem eager to help you,' James went on, 'it is only because, of all the people I've ever known, I can think of few more deserving of a wish than you.'

Beatrice flushed uncomfortably. What was that supposed to mean? Was he *pitying* her? Her desire to apologise suddenly evaporated and she felt irritated and ashamed instead.

'If I am ever fortunate enough to visit the Winter Garden,' James said, 'I would not remove so much as a leaf.' He looked at her closely. 'You have my word on that. It is as good as any gentleman's, I believe.' He picked the cake back up and took a bite. 'Well, this is excellent,' he said with a smile. 'Even if I only got it because you want something from me.'

Beatrice wasn't sure what to say to that, since he was perfectly correct. She would not have dreamed of taking tea with him like this if it wasn't for the competition, and the help she required.

But for some reason her mind went to the way she and James had often pinched cake from the kitchen as children and run off giggling into the grounds to eat it in their favourite tree. That girl seemed a million miles away from who she was now. Beatrice couldn't remember the last time she had giggled. Or enjoyed the company of any person apart from Rosa. The memory made her feel suddenly very lonely.

'I u-understand you have a g-garden l-laboratory at your h-home,' she hurried on. 'To c-create h-hybrid or-orchids.'

'Yes.' James set down his empty plate.

'W-Will you t-teach me? It w-will not b-be enough to c-collect s-specimens. I m-must p-produce s-something entirely n-new.'

'I will gladly share with you everything I know if you think it will help.'

'I am d-delighted to h-hear you say s-so, b-because there is s-something. In p-particular. I n-need.' She took a deep breath. 'I w-want a f-f-fate orchid.'

'Ah.' James gazed at her steadily for a moment. 'But, Lady Beatrice, you know I don't deal in fate orchids. Not for anyone.'

This was common knowledge. It was the only rare orchid that James refused to hunt, no matter the price. Beatrice had never seen the flower in real life, but she was familiar with the almost legendary plant, found only in India. Its petals were made of paper but it smelled of rain and, most of the time, the flower remained tightly closed, as if it were not yet ready to bloom. But if a person held it by the stem, then its petals would unfurl to reveal the story of their lives, from beginning to end.

'It may seem wondrous,' James said. 'But I have known that flower to ruin lives. It does no one any good to know the future. Besides which, the whole concept of fate is distasteful to me. We must be agents of our own lives, or else what is the point?'

'I m-must have one,' Beatrice said. 'I must.'

'But why?' James looked genuinely puzzled. 'I saw your paper at the Linnean Society. I know the extent of the incredible discoveries you've already made. Why is the fate orchid so important?'

'It is one of the t-two m-most m-magical s-specimens kn-known in the w-world. I w-want it for my h-hybrid. I already t-told you, I m-must c-create something entirely n-new to w-win.'

'You mean you would not display the fate orchid itself?'

Beatrice shook her head.

James still looked unconvinced. 'Well, what is the other plant? The one you hope to combine it with?'

'A p-plum t-tree.'

'What kind of tree is this exactly?'

'I d-discovered it in Ch-China.'

Beatrice had learned that plum blossoms were one of the most beloved flowers in that part of the world, featuring time and again in art and poetry going back centuries. They were admired because they bloomed most brightly against the winter snow, making them a symbol of strength in adversity, perseverance and hope. There was an old tradition of viewing them by moonlight, and Beatrice would never forget the first time she had seen them, so ghostly and beautiful and perfect against the sparkling ice.

'The beautiful women of the forest and moon,' James said, startling her. 'Is that not how Ji Cheng referred to them in his journal? From the Ming Dynasty? You needn't look so surprised. I have travelled widely in China, remember.'

'I thought y-you only h-hunted orchids.' Her tone was almost accusatory.

'I am interested in many things.'

'So, you h-have s-seen them t-too?'

'I'm familiar with the trees of which you speak, yes. The plum juice bestows knowledge on whoever drinks it. They might become fluent in a whole new language, or an expert mathematician, or an advanced scientist.'

'Then you m-must agree they are a w-wonder?'

He gave a slight shrug. 'I suppose I'm very boring, but I would rather earn my knowledge the old-fashioned way. To be given it in the space of a moment, with no effort or discipline exerted at all, has always seemed to me to be rather . . . hollow.'

Beatrice frowned, displeased. But what did James know about it anyway? It was her garden. It was *her* thoughts and tastes that counted – no one else's.

'I think y-you are w-wrong,' she said. 'Kn-knowledge is the g-greatest g-gift. Will you h-hunt me the orchid?'

'On the understanding that you will not display it in your garden,' he said. 'Or ever touch it yourself.'

Beatrice resented being given instructions in this way, but since it was something she had already pledged to herself to do, she gave a curt nod.

'I hope you know what you're doing,' James said. 'And, at any rate, it will take some time to find such an orchid. Hardly any exist.'

'I h-have every f-faith in you,' Beatrice said. 'Y-You are the b-best in your f-field.'

She had meant it as a statement of fact rather than a compliment, but James smiled and said, 'Thank you.'

'There is s-something else,' Beatrice said. 'I n-need advice.'

'Go on.'

'Many h-hunters have g-great d-difficulty t-t-transporting their f-flowers back alive. You h-have a m-much h-higher-than-usual s-success r-rate.'

'I do.'

'If it's p-possible to s-safely t-transport a f-flower, m-might it b-be p-possible to transport a t-tree?'

James raised an eyebrow. 'An entire tree would present its own unique challenges,' he said.

'Not j-just one t-tree,' Beatrice said quietly. 'I n-need a f-forest.'

'You wish to bring these plum trees back from China?' He looked dubious.

'The c-contest is only a y-year away. Even in h-hothouses, I d-do not have t-time to g-grow the t-trees from the s-seeds I c-collected.'

James leaned back slightly in his chair. 'You wish to take a forest,' he said. 'And yet only a short while ago it was you who accused me of pillaging.'

Beatrice flushed, appalled. Suddenly the accusation of pillaging seemed like the worst crime a person might be accused of, and she regretted suggesting to James that he was guilty of such a thing.

'I a-a-apologise for th-that,' she said stiffly.

'I appreciate it.'

'I w-w-would n-n-n-never p-p-p—'

All of a sudden she could not even say the word. Her distress was making her stutter worse, so she took a deep breath, relieved that James stayed silent and gave her the chance to compose herself.

'I w-would not d-do that,' she finally said. 'I h-have b-been in c-correspondence with a p-private c-collector in Ch-China. They are p-prepared to s-sell me their t-trees. The p-problem is b-b-bringing them s-safely h-home.'

'I see. In that case, please allow me to apologise also. I ought to have known better, but we are all of us fools sometimes. What you wish to do will be difficult, but I believe it can be done. It will be devilishly expensive, of course.'

Beatrice waved a hand. Price was no object. She had plenty of money – it was expertise she lacked.

'In order to help I would need to be present for the journey,' James said.

Beatrice shook her head. 'But I w-wish to f-fetch the t-trees myself. C-Can you n-not just p-provide me w-with instructions?'

'It is not as simple as that, I'm afraid.'

Beatrice felt an old resentment beginning to stir. 'They are *m-my* trees,' she insisted. 'And I m-must be th-there to t-take c-care of th-them. I want them to t-trust me. Anything y-you have d-done with y-your orchids, I c-can do t-too, if y-you will only t-tell me how.'

'Regrettably,' James replied, 'I cannot simply tell you how to speak Chinese. Forgive the presumption, but I expect you are not fluent in Mandarin?'

Beatrice shook her head. She had picked up a smattering of several languages during her travels abroad, but she did not have an ear for languages and had found Chinese quite impossible to get her tongue around, even for the most basic of phrases.

'There are no shortcuts for some things,' James said. 'Of course you could drink the plum juice in the hope that it bestows you with the skill, but my understanding is that the knowledge the plums give you is quite random. You may learn how to speak Chinese, but you might just as well learn how to dance the can-can.'

Beatrice had no idea what he was talking about. 'C-Can-can?'

He waved his hand. 'Never mind. Just something I saw in a French music hall once. Quite scandalous, and equally enjoyable.' His expression turned serious. 'There is no complicated magic to the way I transport more living flowers than most orchid hunters. It is just that I spend a great deal of time with the flowers and talk to them every day. They enjoy being spoken to in any language, of course, but the native tongue of their country is more familiar and therefore more comforting to them. And you'll need all the help you can get when attempting an ocean voyage of that length. Flowers dislike being at sea. I cannot think that trees will be any different. Especially given that it won't be possible to take them from the ship's hold to soak up the sunshine on the deck.' He shook his head. 'No, if you have any hope of this working at all, then you will need me to come with you.'

'V-Very w-well,' Beatrice said. 'I s-suppose it c-cannot be h-helped.'

James gave her a sudden grin. 'That's the spirit,' he said. 'It'll be like old times.'

To Beatrice's surprise, he held his hand out to her as if she were an equal. There was an amused gleam in his brown eyes, and she wondered if he was testing her in some way. Of course he must know they were not equals. Despite their ill-advised childhood friendship,

Beatrice was still a titled lady, whilst James was the son of a gardener. Yet if he would persist in viewing them as the old play-fellows they once had been, there wasn't much Beatrice could do about it. It didn't change the fact that she needed his help, so she took his hand and they shook.

'Thank you for the tea and cake,' James said. 'We have much to plan and discuss, but I have some business of my own to tie up before embarking on any new expedition, so I hope you will excuse me.'

'Of c-course. Perhaps y-you m-might c-call again n-next week?'

'Yes, I'll do that. Thursday? Three o'clock?'

Beatrice nodded and James stood up, already reaching for his hat and coat.

'Orchid h-hunting is h-highly d-dangerous,' Beatrice suddenly said. 'You s-said you had l-lost a f-friend yourself. Any s-sane m-man needs a r-reason. You s-said other h-hunters ch-chase riches . . .'

James looked at her. 'Are you trying to ask me a question?'

She could hardly believe she was about to ask something so personal, yet she was intensely curious about the answer. What had drawn James away from Half Moon House, when by rights he ought to have stayed, done the job his father had trained him to do and looked after her black apple trees?

'What d-do you ch-chase?'

James paused. 'Various things,' he finally said. 'Adventure. Seeing the world. But, mostly, I wish to participate in the race.'

She frowned. 'What r-race?'

'The race against what's coming for all of us. You and I have cause to know how fleeting life is. I still feel my mother's absence every day, as I'm sure you feel yours. Losing someone important when you're still very young . . . well, I think it puts a restlessness in you. Sometimes it feels like England suffocates me, but when I'm travelling abroad I have the small consolation of knowing that I'm wringing every last drop from my life, whilst I still can. Before the inevitable day when everything I hold dear is ripped away.' He glanced at her. 'Isn't that partly why you wish to find the garden? It's not only the wish – you were searching long before news of the competition. I imagine that experiencing something so wondrous makes you feel truly alive in a way that few other things can.'

Beatrice nodded slowly. Perhaps he did understand a little better than she'd thought, after all.

'What was it like?' James asked then. 'In the garden? Did you really see the Spider Queen? The Frost Orchid? The Book of Lost Souls?'

'I s-saw it all,' Beatrice replied. For a moment she was back there, in the icy swirl of stars and snow. 'And it was p-pure magic.'

# CHAPTER
# TWENTY

For the first week after the carousel appeared, Rosa had looked out the frosted windows of Raven Hall, half-hoping to see the Carousel of Icicles on the lawn, or the glow of lantern light from between the branches of the Scots pines, but the carousel did not return, and her small clockwork horses made no further attempt to leave their music box. She knew that Beatrice was back in the country to spend Christmas at Half Moon House and very much wanted to see her to discuss the carousel, but then Esme became unwell. What Rosa had originally thought was a mere chill worsened into something more serious. Her breathing became rattling and laboured and, finally, Rosa sent for Dr Livingstone.

She had crossed paths with him several times, and did not care for the man at all. Whenever he had attended her in the past, it had been quite clear that he was not on her side and Rosa hated being examined by him, despising the press of his cold fingers on her skin. The last time she'd seen him had been shortly after the twins' birth, when he'd come to discuss the delicate subject of marital relations with her and the fact that enough time had passed for it to be perfectly safe to resume her duties as a wife. Rosa knew full well that the visit had been instigated by Eustace, and the doctor made it clear that he believed she would be putting her own health at risk if she did not allow their relationship to return to 'normal'.

'Spinsterhood is not good for a woman's insides,' he had said. 'Creates all sorts of problems and afflictions. Don't think I exaggerate when I say that it may even cause you to lose your health altogether.'

'Thank you for the advice, Doctor,' Rosa had replied. 'I will consider all you have said.'

Of course she did no such thing. The ravens afforded her the privilege of saying no. But when Dr Livingstone came to examine Esme, his prognosis was grim indeed. He said she had a complaint of the lungs, that there was little he could do and that she would, in all likelihood, not survive. Life seemed to grind to a halt.

Rosa's mind returned to the words spoken by the fortune-telling sisters, and one phrase burned itself into her mind: *I see a small gravestone before a year has passed . . .*

But she couldn't accept it. She would not. Whilst Eustace said there was clearly nothing to be done except pray, Rosa made tireless enquiries and obtained multiple second opinions. Mostly the other doctors agreed with Dr Livingstone, but one of them finally told Rosa of a physician who was a specialist in cases such as Esme's. It seemed that if anyone could give her a chance, it was him. He was based in Switzerland.

Rosa made all the arrangements for their trip herself. She entered into correspondence with the doctor, who agreed to treat Esme. She organised their travel and booked their hotel. She made the decision to take Ada too, because she couldn't bear the thought of leaving her at Raven Hall to be cared for by the servants. And so she and Eustace found themselves travelling by brougham with their daughters, across the Alps to Switzerland. Rosa began the journey feeling hopeful and glad of the action they were taking – glad to be doing *something*.

But it was all for nothing. When they arrived, the Swiss doctor told her gently that it was too late and, indeed, Esme died later that same day. Rosa felt something unravel inside her as she held her for the last time. She wished she could be anywhere else in the world but here, experiencing this unspeakable loss. She'd fought so hard, but it had all been for nothing. There was nothing to do but make arrangements for the body and then return home the way they had come.

The snow had forced them to stop on the mountain path for what seemed like the hundredth time. Ada grizzled in the crook of her arm, but Rosa couldn't comfort her. Her bones had turned to lead. Her heart was a stone. It could not be possible that she was returning home with only one baby rather than two. It simply could not be possible. And yet the fact was that she would never hold her daughter again, never see or smell her. Esme was truly gone. Rubbed out like she'd never existed. A small footnote in the book of their lives.

The door opened and a blast of cold air blew into the stuffy interior, along with a flurry of snow, as Eustace climbed up. The small carriage rocked beneath his weight and Rosa caught a glimpse of the swirling ice crystals and glittering frost in the frozen world beyond, before the door slammed shut.

'We've dug out the carriages,' he said, each word smoking before him in the dimness. 'Are you sure you don't wish to get out and move around a little before we start off? It might help to warm you.'

Rosa shook her head. She'd removed her travel gloves in order to hold Ada closer, and the blood opal gleamed like an eye in the darkness. The brushed-velvet curtains stiffened in their coats of ice at the windows. The cold bit deep into her bones like teeth of broken glass, but she was barely aware of the discomfort. Esme was cold, so she would be too. Coldness was nothing.

Eustace sighed and rapped on the roof of the carriage. Rosa heard the driver speak to the horse and then there was a jerk as the brougham started forward, rattling them around inside like popcorn in a popper.

If only Esme had been one of her clockwork creatures, then Rosa could have opened her up and fixed her. How many times had she brought some clockwork rabbit back to life after all the other artificers had given up? But there were no cogs and wheels inside Esme, and a stopped heart wasn't a stopped clock. No one and nothing in the world could fix this. No key could wind back what had happened.

'How long until we reach Turin?' Rosa asked in a small, hoarse voice that didn't sound like her own.

'The driver thinks another five hours,' Eustace said.

That would make eleven hours altogether. Eleven hours of jolting around in this carriage with the man she despised most in the world.

*I cannot bear it*, Rosa thought. *I will go mad before we get there.*

She was struck with a sudden wild fear that the journey would never end. The carriage smelled of the stale stickiness of leaking breast milk, along with frozen metal, damp velvet and the polished leather of Eustace's boots. She found it difficult to recall what her life had felt like before. It was as if there had only ever been this moment, trapped in the upholstered confines of the brougham. Rosa simply couldn't recall what it felt like to be warm and happy. She couldn't remember the taste of fried fish at a barbecue, or imagine it being so warm that she would shelter in the shade of a papershell pecan tree on her family's Georgian plantation and call for palmetto fans and mint juleps. In fact she could no longer recall at all what it was like to be Rosa Warren rather than the Duchess of Chalkley.

Ada grizzled in her arms and, with a sense of dread, Rosa knew that she would begin wailing soon, and that the cries would be even shriller and more unbearable than usual in the small space. She would be quite unable to stop them. In contrast, Esme had become more and more settled in the weeks before their trip, perhaps even content. She rarely cried and, when she did, Rosa could immediately quieten her simply by picking her up. But that did not work with Ada. If anything, her incessant crying had worsened, and if Rosa tried to cuddle and comfort her, this only seemed to enrage her further. Her arms would flail, her back would arch and the tears just would not stop.

*It would have been better if Ada had died instead of Esme.*

The thought rose only once in Rosa's mind before she quickly smothered it, appalled at herself for thinking such a thing. Yet the notion seemed to echo round and round her head. It was a truth that made her feel cold to her bones. She shivered where she sat. What a wretched, wicked creature she must be. Eustace was right – she was a despicable excuse for a mother.

As if on cue, Ada drew in the trembling gasp of air that Rosa had grown to dread, before letting out a thin, heartbroken cry. Normally Eustace flinched away if one of the babies so much as whimpered, but this time he indicated Ada and said, 'Shall I take—'

'No!' Rosa snapped. 'Do not touch her!'

Eustace closed his eyes for a moment. 'Please, Rosa,' he said quietly. 'I am aggrieved by what has happened too.'

'*Don't!*' she hissed. 'Don't pretend that you loved Esme. Or that you care for anyone but yourself.'

The words burst from her, each one dropping like a stone between them, into that open, empty space – a well with no bottom. Her chest ached with the effort of keeping her screams locked inside, her fingers itched to tear at Eustace's face. In the moist sickliness of the carriage he drew a deep breath. There were circles beneath his eyes and his face was grey. For a moment Rosa wondered whether she had done him a disservice. Perhaps he *was* distraught by Esme's death. Perhaps he did care. Perhaps he was about to reach out to Rosa, try to comfort her in some way, even apologise, ask if they might start again. For a moment she longed for him to do so – to make some attempt to put right all that was so wrong between them.

But instead his mouth pinched into a thin line. 'Mother is right,' he said. 'You're as uncontrollable as a horse without a bit in its mouth.'

'Your mother doesn't know the half of it,' Rosa spat. 'Do not forget about the ravens, for they have not forgotten you!'

She was pleased to see Eustace shudder at the mention of the birds. Several of them had come on the trip and, much to the driver's consternation, were riding with him on the roof of the carriage.

She turned away, angling her head so that her travelling bonnet partially shielded her face from Eustace's view. She yanked back the curtain to stare blindly out of the window. It was so cold inside the carriage that she thought her tears would freeze to her cheeks, but they ran towards her chin and she had to lean down to wipe them on the sable-fur trim of her cloak. Ada howled and howled as Rosa futilely tried to soothe her. Her arms burned from holding her. She wished with all her soul that Ada could be quietly content, just once, just for a few moments of blissful peace.

The snow was storming so thickly outside that she couldn't see the mountains at all, but she could feel their presence, the silent sentries who cared nothing for the small human miseries passing through them. The invisible valley felt suddenly sinister, shrouded in a sort of doom that made the air heavy and hard to breathe.

The snow smothered everything with a graveyard hush, the only sound the rattle and creak of the carriage, the snorts of the exhausted horse. There was a feeling of pressure in the air, a sense that they had passed out of the real world entirely and into some strange, impossible place, the cruel realm of a heartless ice queen where everything was shards and splinters and spite.

The carriage bumped and lurched its way along, and Rosa's eyes settled for a moment on a large white butterfly hovering right in front of the window. The ghost butterfly emerged from the snow just as Beatrice had described it, with lacy wings and ivory spots.

She gasped and suddenly the air was full of them, falling and fluttering and dancing in the icy mountain air. Rosa pulled down the window with her free hand, ignoring Eustace's cry of alarm. She was desperate to catch one of the butterflies, but her fingers were so cold that she could barely move them.

It didn't matter, because an entire kaleidoscope poured straight in through the open window, with every available surface of the brougham covered in delicate, white, frost-tipped wings. They were on the curtains and the uphol-stered seats, perched upon the luggage rack and fluttering against the glass of the other window.

'What in heaven's name are you doing?' Eustace demanded, raising his voice above Ada's cries. 'Do you want us all to die on this road?'

He reached past her to draw the window closed. For a moment Rosa saw a ghost butterfly perched on the brim of his hat, but then it seemed to crumple and melt away until it was merely a clump of snow. When she looked around the rest of the carriage she saw only crusts of ice and lumps of slush. On the other side of the window there was a brief flutter of pale wings, but then a gust of wind blew sprays of ice across her vision and the butterfly was lost back into the blizzard. The shock of the icy draught momentarily hushed Ada, and the sudden quiet was almost more shocking than the crying.

'For God's sake, Rosa,' Eustace muttered. 'What were you thinking of?'

Rosa tightened her hold on her daughter and wondered what she would have said to Esme, if she could have sent her a message:

*You were loved.*
   *You mattered.*
*You were my world.*
   *I am so desperately sorry.*

But even Beatrice had not been able to track down a ghost butterfly and there was no evidence that they'd ever existed at all. She told herself it did not matter. There was still the Winter Garden competition and the prize of one precious wish. All thoughts of using it on Eustace had vanished. There was something more important now.

*I wish that my daughter had not died . . .*

# CHAPTER
# TWENTY-ONE

When they arrived back at Raven Hall, Rosa watched the house being dressed for mourning with a strange sense of detachment. The servants glided about, covering the mirrors and stopping the hundreds of clocks guarding the corridors, but it didn't feel real. The house was dreadfully silent without the discordant echoes of ticks and tocks, and the covered mirrors meant the rooms were even gloomier than usual.

The funeral went ahead on a grey, dull day. Esme's coffin was placed on a miniature white hearse, surrounded by sprays of ostrich feathers and the most exotic orchids James Sheppard could lay his hands on. There was an abundance of mourners, a mixture of family, friends and the mutes Eustace had paid for, to make the mourning even more of a spectacle. Rosa found their presence particularly objectionable, since they'd never set eyes on Esme, let alone cared about her. Their tragic expressions were put on in exchange for coin, which they would surely spend in the nearest tavern as soon as the service was finished. But she lacked the energy to argue with Eustace about them. In fact she seemed to lack the energy to do anything at all.

Getting out of bed was so sickeningly difficult that the effort made Rosa sweat. She couldn't sleep. She couldn't sit still. She couldn't think. She could only hurt and hurt. With every mile that they had travelled closer to home from Switzerland, her determination about the competition seemed to have slipped through her fingers, despite how hard she tried to hold on to it. By the time they arrived at Raven Hall, there was nothing left of it at all. Her workbooks and carousel plans lay untouched. The pop-up book remained unopened in the drawer of her dressing table.

She felt so exhausted that it sometimes seemed perfectly plausible that she might simply die quietly in her sleep. Magic gardens and wishes seemed an absolute fantasy. Real life surely did not contain such things. It was preposterous. The slimmest of slim chances. Even if there was such a place, and even if the competition was real, and even if she entered it, who was to say she would win? Who was to say the wish would work? The dead did not come back to life. That was the one constant truth, the resounding peal from a bell that would not stop ringing inside her head. Esme was gone, and she was gone forever.

It took all Rosa's remaining strength to persuade Eustace that she would be attending the funeral. Under usual circumstances, women were not permitted to do so. Funerals were thought too much of a strain for them and it was unseemly for an upper-class woman to show her grief openly, but Rosa didn't care what anyone else thought, or if her tears offended them – she was going to say goodbye to her daughter.

The coffin was impossibly small and the loss was impossibly hard. Rosa wept and didn't care who saw her tears. She had refused to wear a mourning veil, and as soon as her tears began to fall inside the church, Eustace touched her elbow and attempted to quieten her. She tried to believe he was concerned for her, but she knew he was only embarrassed by what people would say, so she put both hands on his chest and pushed him away so forcefully that he staggered into a nearby pew. It screeched loudly as it shifted along the stone floor, and everyone turned to look. This was, Rosa reflected, the first time she had willingly touched her husband since their wedding night. How strange to think that they'd been married in this very place almost a year ago. Surely a hundred years had passed since then. There were shocked murmurs and gasps from the other mourners as Eustace straightened his jacket, and Rosa loathed them all.

After the service she watched as the coffin was lowered into the frozen ground, trying to withstand the finality of the goodbye, and to accept that Esme would never have the chance to become an adult with a life of her own. She was a candle that had been snuffed out the moment she tried to burn.

There seemed to be an endless stream of people wanting to express their condolences, but Rosa found she could not face speaking to anyone, and slipped away to return to Esme's small grave. Her heart felt as if it had been split open. For the first time in her life, she wished she had never been born.

'Miss Warren.'

She turned. James stood before her in the snow. He was dressed all in black and there was such a look of utter sorrow in his eyes that she wanted to weep. Esme's own father cared less about her death than this man who had only met Esme once, and just for a matter of minutes. This man who could have been her husband and made her happy, if only she had let him.

'There are no words that will help,' he said quietly. 'I know that. But I wanted to tell you that I am so very sorry.'

Rosa couldn't speak. Her whole body trembled and she wanted so desperately to be alone that it was difficult to breathe. Suddenly she wished she had worn a mourning veil after all, so that the agony of it all would not show so plainly on her face.

'I have not come to disturb you,' James said quickly. 'I only wanted to bring you this.'

He opened his hand and Rosa saw a single seed resting in his gloved palm. She stared at it. How could he possibly imagine that she cared about plants at such a time? Beatrice had sent a wreath too, along with a heartfelt letter of condolence, but Rosa hadn't replied to it. She had no wish to see anyone, not even her friends.

'It comes from no ordinary flower,' he said quietly. 'But from a mourning orchid. One of my hybrids. The seeds can only be planted by someone who is grieving. Their love for the lost person nourishes the flower. I thought, perhaps . . . it might be a fitting way to honour Esme.'

Rosa found herself strangely pleased to hear him speak her name and realised that hardly anyone had done so today. She was always 'the baby' or 'the child' or 'the poor dear soul'. It was good to hear her name – to hear someone else acknowledge that she had been a real person, even if she'd only been able to stay with them a very short while.

She recognised the kindness in his gesture, but the truth was that she didn't care about the orchid. It would not bring Esme back or change what had happened. She took the seed from him only because it seemed to be the fastest way of ending their conversation. She dimly registered that it felt warm through her black glove, before slipping it into her pocket. She realised she ought to thank James, but if she tried, she knew she would begin crying again, and a hundred years would pass before she was able to stop. Fortunately he did not seem to expect a reply.

'Life can be so very hard,' he said softly. 'I wish it were otherwise. Is there anything at all that I can do?'

He was so close to her. Close enough for her to see each of the smile lines around his eyes, to notice the way his brown hair curled over the edge of his collar. Close enough to glimpse that other life she might have had – the one he had offered full of adventure and flowers and love. But in her wisdom, she had chosen ravens and sadness instead, and now there was no turning back. His proximity and the concern in his eyes were suddenly unbearable to her. In that moment she honestly hoped she would never see him again.

'Please,' Rosa said hoarsely. 'Just leave me be.'

To her relief, he left at once. Soon after that, she and Eustace returned to Raven Hall, and Rosa went to the nursery to see Ada, in the hope that her surviving daughter might be some comfort. But the infant started to cry as soon as Rosa took her from the nanny. The sound was like nails across her skin, blades in her gut. Esme's empty crib was a horror that seemed to scream at her with its resounding, accusing silence. This was not right. There should be two babies here, not one. Not one.

Ada howled out her rage, and Rosa wondered whether her surviving daughter knew somehow that her sister was gone, whether she missed her too. The little girl seemed to be forever looking over at the other crib and screwing up her face in a frown, as if offended not to see her sister gazing back at her. Either way, it seemed that Ada and Rosa had no love or comfort to offer each other. Rosa's eyes slid to the empty crib once again, and the longing to hold little Esme in her arms was so overpowering that she really thought she might vomit. Wordlessly she handed Ada back to the nanny and returned to her own room, where she gathered her clockwork ravens about her and locked herself in.

She must find some way to rewrite the story she had had so clearly in her mind, of herself with her twin girls. Esme's absence left a slashed, dark space in that story, and it was impossible to stitch up the gap without distorting the entire page around it. The pieces no longer fitted together. The story did not make any sense. Now it was a book that had been half-ravaged by fire, all charred around the edges, with great chunks missing, and scorch marks blurring the meaning of the carefully chosen words.

It was not fair.

Worst of all, with Esme's absence, all her love for Ada seemed to shrivel away into nothing. As the days crawled by, she could not look at the child without being reminded of Esme's loss. She no longer found any delight in Ada's tiny hands, even when they gripped tightly around her own fingers. She didn't marvel at her deep-blue eyes when they fixed searchingly on her own. She no longer even seemed to feel the warmth of Ada's small body when she held her in her arms. The baby almost ceased to feel like a living, breathing thing at all. She might as well have been a doll made from wax. The orchids in the hothouses and the clockwork ravens in the rafters seemed to have more soul than Ada.

Rosa knew something was wrong with her but, deep down, she was glad. If Esme's death had proved anything, it was that this kind of love was too huge and terrifying. It was too powerful and dreadful. Better to feel nothing. Perhaps better simply not to exist at all. She began to spend less and less time with Ada, surrendering her care to the nanny who was so eager to take her anyway.

But then, a week after Esme's death, Eustace remarked that he was pleased she had finally seen sense where Ada was concerned, and some small spark of defiance shot to life inside Rosa, like a green shoot from a plant believed dead. That afternoon she ordered the nanny to put Ada in her pram so they could take a turn around the grounds.

'Oh, but it's freezing outside, your grace,' Hannah replied.

'I am aware of that, thank you.'

In fact, she had been quite *unaware* and it came as a complete surprise to her to look out of the window and see there was still snow on the ground, that it was still winter.

'Wrap her up warm,' Rosa instructed. 'We will not be outside for long.'

Hannah was reluctant, and as soon as Rosa stepped into the grounds she could see why. Not only was it far too cold to be outside, but it was impossible to push the pram through the snow. Not prepared to admit defeat so soon, Rosa scooped Ada up in her arms and took her to one of the hothouses.

Warmth enveloped them as soon as they stepped inside the glass structure. It was a muggy heat, unlike anything naturally found in Britain, or even Georgia, and Rosa imagined that the air of tropical islands must smell and taste this way – lush and alive. She had not been inside the hothouse for weeks, although she knew that James had potted more of his orchids there. She paused at the entrance for a moment, with the snow still melting from her boots and her fingers tingling from the cold.

Surprisingly, Ada had not made a fuss about being taken from the house, and Rosa noticed that the orchids appeared to have caught the child's interest. From the cradle of her mother's arm, she regarded them with her solemn blue gaze.

'Shall we see what new flowers James has brought us?' Rosa asked.

They walked down the centre of the glasshouse, admiring the various orchids in their beds and baskets. The sight of them pleased Rosa more than she had antici-pated. *Truly*, she thought, *orchids must be the loveliest blooms in the world*. She particularly admired a new one James had brought, with its vivid orange-and-black tiger stripes, as well as an orchid that hummed softly when you stroked its petals.

Her thoughts returned to the dreadful morning of Esme's funeral and the seed James had given her. She was wearing the same coat she had worn that day and she put her hand in the pocket. She had not thought of the seed since that moment and worried that it might have fallen out, but her fingers quickly found it. She'd assumed beforehand that it must have been warm from James's touch, but she realised now that the seed was emitting a heat of its own.

'What do you think?' Rosa said quietly to Ada. 'Shall we plant this together for your sister?'

They were alone in the hothouse and Rosa liked the idea of it being just them – the only two people in the world who had truly loved Esme. She found an empty plant pot, put in a handful of soil from a nearby bed and then pushed the seed beneath the surface. She was just looking for a watering can when, to her surprise, a green shoot suddenly poked up from the soil. The next second the shoot lengthened, turning gracefully into a long stem. A bud formed and ripened at the end, the leaves peeled back and petals fanned out from the stalk like a peacock spreading its tail. In less than a minute there was an entire orchid before them.

Rosa stared at it, spellbound. Her spare hand was still frozen in the act of reaching for a watering can. Her other arm burned with the effort of carrying Ada. The mourning orchid was, in some ways, one of the more modest in the hothouse. There were no vivid patterns, no particularly exotic perfume, and it did not sing or sparkle. It was, in most respects, rather plain and ordinary – except for the fact that its petals were an entirely new colour.

Rosa searched her mind for the right words to describe it, or other colours to compare it to, but it was hopeless. She had to accept that this was a colour she simply didn't have a name for. All she could think was that it was darker than black and more beautiful than purple. The edges of the petals were laced in a creamy ivory shade. Somehow it seemed to gentle her soul in a way that nothing else had since Esme's death – not the mourning clothes, or the ostrich plumes, or the hideous wax mourning doll that Eustace had ordered for the grave. All those things had made her feel worse, like a cloak that kept getting wetter and heavier about her shoulders. But this flower was perfect and beautiful. Rosa looked down at Ada to see what she made of it – only her daughter wasn't looking at the flower. She was looking straight up at her. And she was smiling.

For long moments Rosa could hardly breathe, afraid of doing the wrong thing, of breaking the spell. At first she thought Ada must be looking past her, at some flower or the sparkle of sunlight on glass, but no, she was definitely looking at her, and this was a real smile, the first proper one Rosa had ever seen. She could hardly believe it. Not only was angry, spiky, discontented Ada actually smiling, but she was smiling at *her*!

Rosa had thought that Esme might have smiled a couple of times, but those expressions had been nothing like this. The smile reached Ada's eyes. And as she looked at Rosa, it seemed as if she really *saw* her, that she was looking *for* her rather than staring at some random spot.

'Oh.' Rosa let out her held breath. 'Oh. Hello.'

It seemed a feeble response, but Ada's smile immediately deepened. A dimple flashed in one rounded cheek and her mouth opened wide enough to glimpse pink gums. The tiny girl looked delighted, right down to her soul. Rosa did not think anyone, in all her life, had ever smiled at her like that – as if she were the most wonderful, miraculous thing they had ever seen.

Something clicked and fell into place as Rosa glimpsed the soul inside Ada, the small human, the person she would one day become. She had once heard James talk about the hybrid orchids he grew, and how you never knew how a seed was going to turn out, or whether it would even grow at all. You planted it and then you watered and nurtured the soil, patiently and diligently, hoping that, in the end, something would flourish.

Sometimes, James had said, the seed failed to sprout at all. But at other times you were eventually rewarded with the sight of a bright, green shoot poking up through the dirt. And then you knew you had *something*, even if you didn't yet know exactly what that something might be. It was the best moment, he'd said, because it meant that all the love, all the care and attention that you'd poured in had not been wasted. And then you were glad that you had kept faith with it, after all, even when it appeared as if nothing whatever was happening.

Now, at last, Rosa could see that there was some part of Ada that *did* respond to her, that needed and appreciated her, that was even delighted and comforted by her, that perhaps even loved her. And suddenly she didn't care that the baby would probably be crying inconsolably again in a few minutes, and that she would not know what exactly had changed, or what she had done wrong, or how to fix it. Here, in this moment, right now, Ada was smiling at her, and nothing else mattered in the entire world.

'Oh my goodness,' Rosa breathed. 'I would walk through such fires for you.'

She'd thought the love she felt had been big, and powerful, and terrifying before, but that was nothing compared to these waves that felt like they could sweep her away entirely. She would give up her whole soul to make Ada happy. She would do anything to keep her safe. And she would do the same for her lost sister too.

The orchid showed off its impossible colours there at the edge of her vision, and it no longer mattered that the Winter Garden competition was the slimmest of slim chances. She would grab it with both hands.

'We'll enter that competition, won't we?' she said to Ada. 'And we'll win it. For Esme.'

# CHAPTER TWENTY-TWO

*January 1838*

'The Duchess of Chalkley is at the front door, my lady,' the footman said, presenting a card on a silver dish. He was impeccably trained and looked quite unbothered by the fact that there was a frog perched on the toe of his polished boot, and another steadily making its way up his trouser leg.

Recently Beatrice had taken to wandering the gardens of Half Moon House, despite the thick snow that lay upon the ground and the icy frost that glittered on the bare branches of the trees. The specimens she'd brought back from abroad had required a lot of work to settle them into their new home in England, and Beatrice was anxious to ensure that all was well before she returned abroad.

Today she had put on her pale-blue winter cloak, lined in warm mink fur, and had come out to the newly created frog pond.

She looked up from this now, surprised. She had written several letters to Rosa since learning about her daughter's death, but her friend had not replied to any of them. Recalling how she had felt in the time after the loss of her own mother, Beatrice had guessed that Rosa might wish to be left alone, so in her final letter she had simply said that she would give her space, but would be very happy to hear from her any time she felt ready.

'Sh-show her into the h-house,' Beatrice said quickly. 'Actually, n-no, b-bring her h-here. And ask M-Mrs Hamble to s-send a t-tea t-tray to the s-study.'

'Very good, madam.'

The footman delicately removed the frogs with pristine gloves before going to fetch Rosa. He returned with her a few minutes later, a clockwork raven perched on her shoulder. Her Paris carriage dress had been dyed black for mourning, but she still looked very modern compared to Beatrice in her old-fashioned gown. Rosa's golden hair shone brightly against her black cloak, but she had deep, dark circles under her eyes and was much thinner than the last time Beatrice had seen her – almost gaunt. A shadow of her former self.

Beatrice was dismayed and hurried forward to put her arms around her friend – the first time she had ever hugged anyone, apart from her mother. After a moment of surprise, Rosa returned the embrace, and they stayed that way for several minutes, surrounded only by the frogs, and the skeletal trees, and the sparkling snow, and the quiet, before finally pulling apart.

'It is g-good to s-see you,' Beatrice said, hoping Rosa could hear in her voice how sincerely she meant every word.

'And you.' Rosa smiled, and looked at the pond. 'But what darling frogs!'

They were unlike any found naturally in England. Instead of a drab green or brown, they were a brilliant white, shining brightly against the dark pebbles of the pond. Beatrice bent down and scooped one up in her gloved palms so that Rosa could inspect it more closely.

'Why, they have a minty scent!' she exclaimed, peering down at it. The large eyes bulging from its face were a pale blue and stared boldly back at her.

'I w-was l-looking for the ghost b-butterfly in J-Japan, but f-found these instead,' Beatrice explained. 'They are m-mirror f-frogs.'

'Mirror frogs?' Rosa said. 'How curious.'

'They c-can allow you to s-see what a p-person r-really thinks of you.'

'But what can you mean?' Rosa asked, gazing back down at the frog in Beatrice's palm. 'How does it work?'

'When t-two p-people hold the f-frog together,' Beatrice said, 'it l-lets you s-see their hon-honest opinion of y-you.'

Beatrice watched her friend carefully. She expected many people would shy away from these pretty little frogs and what they could do. In a world of insincere courtesy and forced politeness, of façades and fakery, she did not expect that many people would allow another person to know how they truly felt about them.

But a delighted smile crept over Rosa's face and she met Beatrice's gaze at once. 'Shall we?' she asked.

'J-Just p-put your h-hands under m-mine.'

Beatrice held out her cupped palms and Rosa lifted her hands so that her black mourning gloves rested against Beatrice's powder-blue ones. At once there was a sudden shift behind Beatrice's eyes, and she knew her friend would be experiencing the same thing – the slightly disorienting sense of a looking glass being flipped.

And then she saw herself through Rosa's eyes – not awkward, and ugly, and hopeless at all. Indeed, Rosa didn't even view the stammer as evidence of any mental weakness. Beatrice felt an intense rush of glorious warmth flow through her as she realised that Rosa viewed her as rebellious, and intelligent, and kind, and courageous, and strong, and that she truly liked her more than any other woman she'd met in England. She thought of her as a friend and cared deeply about her.

Beatrice knew that Rosa would also be experiencing all the admiration and respect and regard that Beatrice had for her; that she would feel how Rosa had inspired her to be a better, stronger, more confident person than she'd ever dreamed of being before.

Finally the looking glass righted itself again and the two women had no one's thoughts or views inside their heads but their own. For a moment there was only a deep, frozen silence before Beatrice bent to replace the frog carefully at the edge of the pond.

'Incredible,' Rosa breathed. She looked pleased, and a little embarrassed. 'I hope I can be half the person you believe me to be. What an extraordinary frog.'

'There is m-much m-more to sh-show you,' Beatrice promised. 'But l-let's take t-tea first.'

They returned to the house, where the housekeeper had left a tray in the study. After pouring the tea, Beatrice felt she had to acknowledge Rosa's loss in some way, so she took a deep breath and said, 'I am s-so s-s-sorry.' It was impossible not to wince at how inadequate the words were. 'About your d-daughter.'

Rosa managed a weak smile. 'Yes, I know,' she said. 'Everyone is dreadfully sorry. But that doesn't help me in any way. It does not bring Esme back. It does not seal up the place where my soul has been ripped in half.' She met Beatrice's gaze and said softly, 'It has undone me, Beatrice. That is the truth. In fact the old me has died. I'm someone else now altogether. That is why I have been feeling so strange, I think – I am no longer me at all.'

Beatrice nodded. She knew how it felt to be ravaged by grief but she could not think what to say, so she echoed the Spider Queen's words from all those years ago. 'L-life needs d-dark l-leaves in the w-wreath.'

The thought took her back and suddenly Beatrice was a small girl again, there in the frosted haven of the magical Winter Garden. It was her fourth night of visiting, but she was still discovering new things and tonight she had come across a red-brick wall hung with wreaths.

For long moments, Beatrice stood and admired the summer colour bursts of scented stocks and radiant sunflowers, the tiny white flowers of gypsophila, the delicate sweet peas and violet-blue cornflowers. And there were winter flowers too: an abundance of sunshine-yellow winter aconites, pale-purple cyclamens, star-shaped jasmine and the pink cup-shaped blooms of Japanese quince.

'Lovely, aren't they?' the Spider Queen said beside her. 'Each one represents a person's life. The good times and the bad.' She glanced at Beatrice and went on, 'If you're like most people, then I expect you were drawn to the flowers, but I have always thought the foliage more striking.'

She stepped closer and ran her fingers gently over the greenery.

'See how the glossy leaves of scented myrtle and cascading ivy provide a backdrop to these purple primulas? And this Christmas rose would be quite overlooked, were it not surrounded by delicate wisps of tree fern, and the grey-and-blue leaves of eucalyptus. The different types of foliage all have their parts to play: honey bracelet, Italian *Ruscus*, lemon leaf and moss. Only look what happens when a wreath is made from flowers alone.'

She pointed at a couple near the bottom of the wall. They had hardly any greenery, but they didn't have many flowers either, and what blooms there were appeared drained of colour, feeble and limp, like they'd wilted in the sun.

'Alas,' the Spider Queen said softly, 'life needs dark leaves in the wreath. There cannot be true joy without sorrow, or real happiness without loss. They come as a pair. It is simply how it must be, if one is to live a full life. Take my own wreath, for example.' She pointed at a particularly striking one made up of foliage so dark it was almost purple and black in places, but brightened with spectacular bursts of scarlet poinsettia.

'I first saw the poinsettia in Mexico,' she said. 'The *Euphorbia pulcherrima*, to give it its botanical name, but it's also known as a "Christmas star" because of its red pigment, so vibrant and bold. I would not give up my dark leaves if it meant losing the poinsettia,' she said.

The garden faded away now, taking the memories of the flowers with it.

'I w-wish there was s-something I could d-do,' Beatrice said helplessly.

'Well, actually,' Rosa said, 'there's nothing you can do, but there may be something *I* can do. In fact that's why I've come here – to discuss it with you.'

She proceeded to tell Beatrice about the night the Carousel of Icicles had appeared in the frosted grounds of Raven Hall. She told her, too, of the strange boy who roamed the house at night and what he had said about the carousel. And, finally, she told her about the invitation itself.

'And of course I intend to enter that competition,' Rosa said fiercely. 'I intend to build the carousel, and win, and get my daughter back. I'd like you to tell me everything you know about the Spider Queen. About her likes and tastes and preferences. Anything at all that might help me to win.'

Beatrice stared at her friend in silence. She longed to help her in any way she could, and yet she felt nothing but despair at the news that Rosa was entering the competition too. There was only one prize. They couldn't both win it, and a wish was not something that could be shared. She would have given Rosa almost anything that she asked, but not this.

'I c-can't.' She forced the words out like stones.

Rosa looked confused. 'Can't what?'

'I c-cannot t-tell you anything about the S-Spider Queen.'

'Why in the world not?'

'We are t-to b-be c-c-competitors.'

Beatrice told her about the invitation she had received herself and the plans that were already under way to open a garden of her own.

'Oh.' Rosa looked suddenly stiff and brittle, like one of the sugar figurines Beatrice had received at Christmas – a sparkling shepherdess who might snap in half, if not handled carefully. 'And I cannot persuade you to withdraw?'

Beatrice couldn't believe she'd heard correctly at first. 'W-Withdraw?' she repeated, feeling suddenly slow and stupid.

'From the competition.'

'But . . . the p-prize is a w-wish. It is t-too m-much to ask anyone t-to g-g-give that up.'

'And yet, here I am asking you anyway,' Rosa said. 'Beatrice, please. I've explained how important it is. You know how much it means to me.'

Beatrice thought of her mother's haunted eyes, the misery and loneliness of her death. She couldn't give up the chance of making things right, she just couldn't.

'I am s-sorry,' she said. 'But I c-cannot withdraw. I h-have my own r-reasons for wanting that w-wish.'

'But this isn't fair!' Rosa cried, her voice suddenly breaking. 'You have the advantage. You've been to the Winter Garden before. You know the Spider Queen. You've already experienced the magic of the place. Why not let someone else have a chance?'

Beatrice looked at her sadly. Just a few minutes ago she had basked in the warmth of the regard Rosa felt for her but, beneath that, she'd felt something else too – something altogether less pleasing. She realised that Rosa felt she had had a safe, sheltered, pampered sort of life, one that did not involve any serious suffering or sorrow to speak of at all.

And Beatrice knew that was true, up to a point, but she also knew that she'd felt about as lonely, and misunderstood, and isolated as it was possible for any one person to feel. She did not have things as easy as Rosa believed, not by a long way.

'There are th-things you d-don't know,' she said. 'About m-me. H-hardships I have f-faced and—'

'Oh, Beatrice, please!' Rosa suddenly looked disgusted. 'Are you really going to sit there and say such things to me now? When I'm in mourning for my child? To say nothing of—' She broke off abruptly, as if she'd been about to say too much. 'Well, never mind all that. Look, I'm not trying to say you haven't suffered. Only that there are different types of suffering. Mine exceeds yours, that's all, and it would be selfish of you to enter the competition under these circumstances, especially with all the advantages you hold.'

Unable to sit still any longer, Beatrice rose to her feet. She already felt a hopeless futility in making herself understood, but for the sake of their friendship she knew she must try.

'You r-recall l-last y-year,' she said desperately. 'When I w-was ill? It was n-no t-tropical f-fever. It was a d-d-disease of the m-mind. A terrible m-m-melancholy. I c-could not s-sleep, or eat, or—'

'Don't you *dare* talk to me about melancholy!' Rosa hissed, rising to her feet too. 'If anyone knows about that, it's me, not you! For heaven's sake, Beatrice, everyone faces hardship in their life. You have to fight your way through it, not wallow in it!'

Beatrice felt a raw stab of hurt. She ought not to have confided this secret to Rosa. Like everyone else, she saw it only as weakness. 'This s-sadness,' she managed. 'Was not. Like that.'

'No,' Rosa said. She suddenly sounded more tired than angry. 'I suppose it was special because *you* were the one feeling it.'

Beatrice clenched her teeth. That wasn't what she had meant, either, but it seemed that any attempt at an explanation was doomed. It felt to her as if their friendship was unravelling at her feet, but she couldn't think of a way to repair it. Not without giving up her chance of winning that wish. But before she could think of what to say, her attention was suddenly caught by the painting on the wall behind Rosa – the one James had given her of the tiger.

She had spent many hours staring at it, drinking in every detail, relishing the memories it brought back. She knew every brushstroke, so she saw at once that the painting was not as it was supposed to be. Instead of looking at the girl in the mourning dress, the tiger had turned its head and was gazing right out of the painting – looking straight at Rosa.

Rosa pressed her lips together. Her hands were clenched into fists at her sides. 'I can see there's no reasoning with you,' she said, reaching for her gloves. 'So I'll return to Raven Hall.'

'P-Please,' Beatrice stood up too, 'do not g-go like th-this. At least st-stay for another c-cup of— Oh!'

She'd reached her hand out towards her friend, but the clockwork raven on Rosa's shoulder snapped at her fingers so menacingly that it seemed it would have bitten them clean off, if it could.

'Thank you, but I have much to attend to,' Rosa said coldly. 'As, I am sure, do you.'

She walked out of the room without looking back. A few moments later Beatrice heard the crunch of her carriage wheels upon the gravel. She realised her hands were clenched so tightly that her nails dug into her palms. Why did Rosa, of all people, have to receive an invitation? Beatrice was dismayed at the blow to their friendship, but she was suddenly also afraid of how many other gardens she might be competing against. She had assumed her win was assured, but now she felt the first stirrings of doubt. Her eyes went back to the painting, but the tiger was looking at the girl once again, as though it had never changed the direction of its gaze at all.

# CHAPTER
# TWENTY-THREE

*At sea – April 1838*

The trees had disliked being loaded onto the ship, and as Beatrice had stood on the dockside in Shanghai and watched it happen, she had wondered whether she was making a mistake after all. Trees were not meant to be cooped up inside a box. These ones thirsted for snow, and ice, and cool, silver moonlight.

But it had been too late to turn back. The arrangements had all been made, the trees had been carefully dug up and potted in large containers. It had taken a large team of strong men to move Beatrice's forest all the way to the docks and into the ship's hold. She couldn't very well call it off after that – she'd have looked like a fool. The idea of people laughing behind her back haunted her. Besides which, she needed that wish.

They'd been at sea for two weeks, but there were still months to go, and they would be required to change ship several times along the way. It was hard not to feel despair. The journey would use up precious time and there was no guarantee the beautiful trees would survive the trip. They would die, it would be Beatrice's fault and all of this would be for nothing.

Despite her original objections, she was glad that James was with her. It was reassuring to have someone to share the burden with. They both spent a great deal of time in the hold with the trees, as there was no way of getting them up on deck for fresh air and moonlight. Fortunately James had brought a galaxy orchid with him, and the flower nourished the trees with its speckled starlight.

But Beatrice felt uneasy throughout the voyage, especially as they were sharing the ship with several orchid hunters. It was impossible to hide the existence of the trees from them. They had all seen them being loaded, and gossip spread quickly around the ship. The hunters didn't know what exactly the forest could do, but they knew it could do *something*. Magic poured off the trees like a scent. And although that part of the cargo hold was out of bounds to all but James and Beatrice, the bright glow of the plum blossom shone out beneath the cracks in the door, day and night.

'We must be watchful,' James remarked early on. 'I know the other orchid hunters, by reputation, if nothing else. Most of them are all right, but Horace Johnston is a bad sort.'

Beatrice had tried not to flinch at the name. She'd not mentioned anything to James, but she'd overheard Johnston mocking her to the other orchid hunters in the canteen one evening.

'B-B-Bovine B-Beatrice!'

He was neat and tidy, always much smarter-dressed than the other hunters, but there was a meanness in his eyes and a permanent smirk seemed to linger around his mouth. More than that, there was a sulkiness about him that Beatrice recognised. He was the type who believed the world owed him something, and that type of man could be dangerous. When he'd realised that she had overheard his remark in the canteen, he hadn't even had the grace to look embarrassed. Perhaps he was one of those men who believed it bad luck to have a woman on board a ship.

'Y-You d-don't th-think he would h-harm the t-trees?' she'd asked, alarmed.

James had lifted his shoulders in a shrug. 'I don't think he would miss an opportunity to make money, that's all.'

So Beatrice had taken to sleeping in the cargo hold, beneath the canopy of the plums. It was no less uncomfortable than her cramped cabin, and she liked being near the trees. She tried to object when James first joined her, but he wouldn't be moved on the matter.

'It isn't safe for you to be here alone,' he insisted. 'No one would hear you if you called out. I promise I will behave like a perfect gentleman at all times, if that's your concern. Besides, it will be good for the trees to have the company at night. I'll even sing them a Chinese lullaby.'

Beatrice smiled, in spite of herself. 'You kn-know one?'

'Madam, I know several, and I've been reliably informed that I sing them very well too. And trust me, it's quite difficult to sing in Chinese.'

Beatrice didn't object again. It wasn't as if her reputation wasn't already in tatters, thanks to travelling alone with him in such a way. She simply didn't care. She knew James wasn't a threat to her and she trusted him.

She had cause to be thankful of her choice when, a few days later, she woke in the middle of the night to the rough press of a hand over her mouth, and Horace Johnston's greedy eyes gleaming at her in the soft glow of the plums.

'Don't shout,' he whispered. 'I just want to talk.' He removed his hand and jerked his head towards the trees. 'Tell me what they can do.'

Beatrice knew at once that she would not be able to utter a word. To her horror, she recalled that tonight, of all nights, James wasn't there. He was playing poker with some crew members and she had no idea when he'd be back. Perhaps Johnston already knew this, maybe it was exactly why he'd picked tonight to sneak down here.

He gripped her arm, squeezing it tightly. 'Speak, woman!' he growled.

She could smell the reek of alcohol on his breath and, for the first time in her life, felt truly afraid. She knew they docked at Hong Kong the next day, and suspected that Johnston meant to take some of the plums and try to sell them. He gave her a little shake, causing a shock of adrenaline to race through her like electricity and silence her speech even further.

'Don't stare at me like a halfwit,' he snarled. 'Tell me about the plums or I'll—'

'Take your hands off her,' said a cool voice from the doorway. 'Now!'

Beatrice felt a sob rising in her chest at the sight of James standing in the doorway, a pistol in his hand.

'Don't be a goddamned fool!' Johnston sneered. 'You're just as likely to hit her as me.'

James tilted his head slightly, but kept the pistol aimed steadily at him. 'Is it possible you don't know who I am? Allow me to introduce myself. The name is Sheppard.'

Johnston gave a small gasp and released Beatrice as quickly as if she'd just turned poisonous.

'I . . . I meant no harm,' he stammered. 'I'm just interested in the trees, that's all.'

James ignored him and looked at Beatrice instead. 'Did he hurt you?'

She shook her head, although her arm still throbbed where he'd grabbed it.

James turned his attention back to the orchid hunter. 'Who gave you a key to the hold?'

Johnston took a step away from Beatrice, both hands raised before him. 'I b-bribed a crew member.'

'I'll have his name. Then you will apologise to Lady Beatrice and get the hell out,' James said, in a voice so icily calm that even Beatrice shivered. There was a hard look in his eyes that she had never seen before. 'And if I ever see you within fifty feet of this hold again . . .'

He didn't even have time to finish his threat before Johnston offered a fumbling apology to Beatrice and then fled from the hold. To her great embarrassment, Beatrice realised she was trembling, and gratefully accepted the whisky flask James handed her. Fortunately he didn't try to speak to her right away, but gave her a moment to gather herself. A sudden lurch of the ship made it seem as if the trees rustled softly around them, and Beatrice found herself comforted by the soft, deep haze of their purple glow.

After a few minutes she handed back the flask and tried to thank James for his help, but he blanched and said, 'Don't thank me for that. It should never have happened in the first place – I'm sorry.'

'N-not. Y-your. Fault.' She gestured at the pistol. 'I d-didn't know y-you c-carried one.'

'It never leaves my side when I'm travelling,' he said. 'And it's got me out of some tough scrapes in the past. I hope it doesn't bother you?'

She shook her head.

'May I?' James indicated the space beside her and, when she nodded, he sat down.

'Wh-Why,' Beatrice said. 'Did h-he react to y-you. L-like that?'

James was silent for so long that she began to think he wouldn't answer her at all. Finally he said, 'There was an incident in Hawaii. You recall the article you read in *Curtis's* about the man who was gored to death in a bull trap?'

Beatrice nodded, remembering how she had read about Benjamin Smith the morning of her wedding. 'You s-said he was a f-friend.'

James nodded. 'He was a decent and honourable man. As always, there is a story behind the story, but I doubt if *Curtis's* mentioned that Ben fell into that pit because of another orchid hunter. We were given misleading information, you see, which sent us the wrong way into the mountains. The other hunter knew that the area was dangerous. He knew there were hidden bull traps everywhere.'

Beatrice frowned. 'You h-held him r-responsible,' she said. 'So wh-what did y-you—'

'Careful,' James said quietly.

It was the first time Beatrice could ever remember him interrupting her. His eyes flicked towards her in the soft purple light. 'Be careful what you ask me next. Yes, I held him responsible. It all happened so quickly. One moment Ben was there beside me, the next . . .' He looked away from Beatrice then. 'No one should have to die like that. No one. It could just as easily have been me who fell in and Ben who survived, but that day still changed my life forever, changed *me* forever. No person could witness such violence and remain unaltered. I will be marked by it until the day I die. If you feel you must know the details of what happened next – what actions I felt justified in taking – and why a man like Johnston has had cause to hear my name and be unwilling to cross me, then certainly I will tell you. I only urge you to consider whether these are things you truly want to know.'

Beatrice was silent for several minutes after he spoke. Her heart ached for him. To lose a person you cared about in such a senseless, ghastly way was beyond her comprehension. It suddenly seemed to her that she had no right to judge James for anything he did, or did not, do in such a situation. How could she possibly know how she might have reacted herself?

'I will not p-pry,' she finally said. 'It is y-your own b-business. But wh-whatever h-happened, I am s-sorry.'

James nodded, and that was an end to it. They never discussed the subject again. He looked up at the forest shining above them now and said, 'It's likely to be a difficult voyage, I'm afraid. I hope it will be worth it in the end and that you'll create something beautiful back at Half Moon House. I want to believe that life is more than something nasty, brutish and short. That it can be something magical, wonderful and precious instead.'

'It c-can,' Beatrice replied. 'I've s-seen it. And I w-will c-create it again.'

The truth was that she felt more determined than ever before.

# Part Three

# CHAPTER
# TWENTY-FOUR

*November 1838*

That year boasted a summer of gardens. It seemed you could not move for learning of another grand opening. Rosa attended several of them. She had no idea whether they were anything to do with the Spider Queen, but either way she meant to keep an eye on any potential competitors. Of course it was not possible to visit every garden – some were too far away or, indeed, not even in the same country.

One particular garden in Paris caused quite a stir during the Season. Rosa heard enraptured stories of how it put on spectacular hot-air balloon shows every night, the balloonists returning to the ground with jars full of moon-light. A second garden in Spain boasted a flock of golden songbirds whose beautiful voices freed listeners from the bitter pain of any old grudges they had allowed to fester. Yet another garden had opened around the canals of Venice, and was said to be filled with the mysterious beauty of actual mermaids, whose grey pearls could do such extraordinary things that the people who had experienced them would only speak of the garden in hushed voices.

But Rosa was not intimidated by such talk. Plans for her own garden had progressed well. She had worked diligently on the carousel and – whilst it was not quite the same as the one she had read about in the pop-up book – it was, she felt, still singularly remarkable. It was difficult to imagine that anyone else could have a wonder capable of topping it.

Everything had been ready for some time, but she had deliberately chosen to wait until winter before opening. Her garden needed the cold and darkness to show off the spectacle of its fire and clockwork. After their quarrel, Beatrice had sent Rosa a couple of letters attempting to repair the rift, but since she'd made no mention of withdrawing from the competition, Rosa had refused to respond. For the last eight months Rosa had had no contact with Beatrice at all. She knew she'd been abroad for much of the year and that, scandalously, James Sheppard had accompanied her for some of it.

She felt a sharp sense of hurt about that, which she knew was unfair. Beatrice did not know how she felt about James, nor was the orchid hunter aware that he was helping an adversary of Rosa's. But still. The one consolation was that so far there had been no garden at Half Moon House, and Rosa nurtured a faint hope that perhaps her old friend had thought better of entering the competition after all. Either that, or perhaps she had failed in whatever it was she'd been trying to bring back.

But then, one morning, a large purple butterfly startled Rosa at the dining-room window whilst she was taking breakfast. For a long moment she stared, dumbstruck. She'd never seen anything like it, and would not have thought such a specimen could exist in England at all. It was easily as big as her palm and looked as if it belonged in a tropical jungle on the other side of the world.

But even more striking than its size was the fact that it carried a creamy envelope attached by a golden string. Rosa leapt up from her seat at once and opened the window. Could it be a message from the Spider Queen?

The butterfly dropped the envelope into her hands and then fluttered over to land on the back of a dining-room chair, where it spread its magnificent wings. As Rosa watched, they proceeded to change colour, cycling through dusky lilac to snowy white to ice-blue – an entire rainbow of winter colours. And the creature seemed to affect the objects around it too, because the chair on which it perched changed shades along with the butterfly. Finally its wings turned ivory with lace-tipped edges, and it flew back out of the window to be swallowed up by the sky, which was almost bursting with the promise of further snow.

Rosa turned her attention to the letter in her hands. As soon as she drew out the card, she saw that it was not from the Spider Queen after all. In her haste to open it, she hadn't noticed that the seal on the back was different. Instead it was another invitation, bordered in tiny pressed flowers:

*Lady Beatrice Sitwell is pleased to invite you to the grand opening of her winter pleasure garden tonight.*

*Prepare to be amazed.*

*Prepare to be enchanted.*

*The gardens of Half Moon House are for those who desire more magic in their lives, and will open at 11 p.m. for one hour only.*

Rosa frowned. One hour? Most pleasure gardens opened in the afternoon and continued until early morning. Eustace's pleasure garden had closed at 4 a.m., and the popular gardens like Vauxhall and Cremorne had similar hours.

She flipped over to the back of the card to see if there were any further details, but found only a handwritten note from Beatrice: *I am sorry we quarrelled. Please come.*

And then the flowers on the border of the invitation started to move. Before her eyes, their pressed petals slowly unfurled and the dainty flower heads grew up towards the sky on a long green stem, until the card contained an entire miniature garden, filling the air with a delicate perfume. Rosa wondered whether Beatrice had selected the flowers especially for her, because they were a mixture of purple hyacinths, the flower of forgiveness, and chrysanthemums, the flower of friendship.

Rosa set the invitation down on the table and smiled grimly. She had no doubt that Beatrice had many spectacular things in her garden, but so did she. And she was fairly confident that a few magic flowers couldn't possibly compete with the wonders of her clockwork.

After breakfast she went straight to her workshop. The morning stretched on into the afternoon and she was just putting some final touches to one of her new clockwork creations when a footman came to inform her that the family doctor was waiting for her in the drawing room. Rosa had not seen Dr Livingstone since the dreadful time when Esme had fallen ill, and she shuddered at the thought of speaking to him again now.

'But I didn't send for him,' she said. 'Why is he here?'

The servant had no answer to that. 'The duke is with him, your grace,' he offered.

She and Eustace now had an unspoken agreement to cross paths as little as possible and, in a house the size of Raven Hall, it was not difficult to avoid one another. Eustace knew nothing of the pop-up book, or the Spider

Queen, or the Carousel of Icicles. Rosa had not spoken of the competition to him, either. So far as he was concerned, she was reopening the garden simply because she felt like doing so. They had barely exchanged more than a few words in weeks, and sometimes Rosa almost forgot she had a husband in the house at all.

She sighed and set down her instruments, calling her favourite clockwork raven to her shoulder before she departed. The ravens accompanied her everywhere around the house and she was comforted by the sound of them, even when she couldn't see them.

When she arrived in the drawing room, she was surprised to see that someone had brought Ada down from the nursery. She was balanced upon Dr Livingstone's bony knees, her small face scrunched up with worry. Rosa disliked seeing the doctor's long fingers curled around her daughter, and the way he held her at arm's length, as if she was something distasteful.

Eustace stood on the other side of the room by the window, an unreadable expression on his face. She could not quite recall when she had last spoken to him, but she was surprised by his appearance. He looked gaunt but, more than that, there was something about the hollowness of his face that was almost haunted. He and the doctor had been talking when she walked in, but fell abruptly silent at her appearance. Rosa felt certain they had been discussing her, and her skin prickled with warning. She felt suddenly ambushed.

'To what do we owe this pleasure, Doctor?' she asked, trying to keep her voice level. 'And why is Ada here? She has not been unwell.'

'Ma!' Ada exclaimed, forever eager to use one of the few words she knew.

'I thought the doctor might as well take a look at her whilst he was here, my dear,' Eustace said. 'One cannot be too careful, especially after what happened to poor Esme.'

'She appears to be in good health,' Dr Livingstone admitted, sounding almost disappointed by the news.

'Of course she is.'

Rosa couldn't help herself – she walked over to scoop Ada up in her arms. The little girl snuggled into her, and Rosa tried to feel reassured by her solid warmth. Her daughter had turned one the week before. Rosa had hoped that after a year of being a mother, she would know exactly what she was doing, but there were still difficult days, times when she felt she was failing at everything, that she was not being the mother she so desperately wanted to be. After one whole year, the only thing she knew for sure was that motherhood was exhausting, terrifying and nerve-racking, and every day seemed to force her to learn anew what she must do. Yet it was also the most rewarding adventure of her life, and she thrilled at the thought of all that lay ahead – which made up for all the moments when she was laid low with uncertainty and doubt.

And so even when Ada was in the darkest of tempers, throwing tantrums, crying without reason or whining incessantly, Rosa was there, still loving her, refusing to be pushed away. And when Ada smiled, or let out a shriek of joyful laughter, or wrapped her arms around Rosa's neck, squeezing tight, Rosa knew she was on the right track, even though it often didn't feel like it. Whatever she might get wrong, she loved her daughter more and more each day.

'It strikes me, however, that you are looking rather tired, your grace,' the doctor said, although Rosa noticed that he barely looked at her, but glanced at Eustace instead. 'Are you feeling quite well?'

'Perfectly, thank you,' Rosa replied. 'I have simply been keeping long hours. We are about to reopen our pleasure gardens, you see.'

The doctor paused. He glanced at Eustace again, but the duke seemed suddenly keenly interested in the view from the window.

'I will speak plainly, if I may,' the doctor said.

'Since I very much doubt I can stop you, please do,' Rosa replied, her voice hard. She already knew that nothing good could come of this.

'I have called upon you today at the request of your mother-in-law, the dowager duchess. She has expressed concerns about your health.'

Rosa looked sharply at Eustace. 'Did you know about this?'

The duke turned from the window and shook his head. 'Mother did not discuss it with me.'

'The duchess has become concerned,' the doctor said. 'She noticed certain . . . irregularities when she stayed with you last week.'

*That shrew!* Rosa thought bitterly. She and Eustace normally kept up the façade of a married couple during their public appearances, but it was certainly true that she had made little effort to conceal the disdain she felt for Eustace during his mother's stay. Not having to pretend had felt delightful, in a twisted sort of way. She'd even gone so far as to offer the dowager duchess a few home truths too.

'The vast majority of the time,' the doctor went on, 'motherhood is beneficial to women. But in some rare cases it can have the effect of unbalancing their natural inclinations and creating disturbances of the mind. Sadly, it is not unusual for the mother to unjustly place the blame for these changes upon the husband, turning cold and unfeeling towards him, which only serves to exacerbate the problem further. It is not a natural state for either party and can cause great unhappiness and stress on both sides. Fortunately there are treatments available.'

'And what might they be?' Rosa asked, forcing the words out through her gritted teeth.

'I have discussed your case with your husband,' Dr Livingstone said. 'We have agreed it would be beneficial for you to take a restorative trip abroad together. There are several sanatoriums in Switzerland that I could recommend. A month or two out there and you will be back to yourself in no time.'

Rosa's arms tightened around Ada. 'And what about my daughter?'

'Come, Rosa,' Eustace muttered, with a gesture of impatience. 'You know perfectly well that she would be adequately cared for here. She has an army of nannies and nurses who are willing and eager to do their jobs, if only you would step aside and allow them to do so.'

'Excessive attachment to one's child is another symptom, I am afraid,' Dr Livingstone said. Rosa noticed how his whiskers were yellowed with tobacco stains, and her insides seemed to shrivel up in disgust.

'I have already lost one daughter,' she said. 'I do not intend to lose another.'

'Your grace—'

'I fear you have wasted your time, sir,' Rosa said. 'I am not leaving Raven Hall. Certainly not now when I have a garden to attend to.'

'The garden can wait,' Eustace said. 'It is not the done thing to open in winter anyway. Why not delay until next summer?'

Rosa shook her head. She had no intention of explaining about the competition deadline to Eustace.

'It would only be a temporary absence, your grace,' Dr Livingstone said. 'Until you feel more yourself. I should think you would be glad to hear that there is a medical reason behind your restlessness and that it can be cured.'

'Indeed,' Eustace said. 'It was very kind of Mother to look into this on our behalf.'

'Your mother knows nothing of our marriage and ought not to be sticking her uncommonly large nose into our affairs,' Rosa said sharply.

Eustace gave her a sullen look but, when he spoke, he addressed Dr Livingstone. 'You see how it is? She becomes overwrought and quite vicious, without the least reason. One never knows when she is going to throw out some new threat or insult.'

'Yes, I see the situation plainly enough, your grace.' Dr Livingstone stood up too and moved a little closer to Rosa. There was a hard lack of pity in his eyes that chilled her blood. 'I realise this might be distressing to hear,' he said. 'But it is my medical opinion that treatment at this time would be highly beneficial, not just for you, but for your entire family. Should your condition go unattended, it could develop into hysteria. Of course the duke is ultimately responsible for your health and well-being and must be called upon to make decisions on your behalf, if your condition means you lack the capability to do so yourself. We thought to seek your involvement as a courtesy, but I must tell you that I have only to sign the necessary certificate and all the arrangements will be put in place.'

Rosa stared at him. 'Do you *dare* try to tell me that I would be sent off somewhere against my will?'

'A break from the child would be for your own good, and the good of those around you,' the doctor said sternly.

Rosa looked at Eustace. 'Do I need to remind you what would happen, should such an event occur?' she said.

Eustace rubbed the back of his neck. 'My dear,' he said. 'I understand your reluctance, but we both know you are not happy. Dr Livingstone and I are only trying to help you. What harm could it do to give the treatment a chance?'

'If you wish to be a responsible mother, it is the only course of action available,' the doctor put in.

Something snapped inside Rosa then. She could see it happening so easily – the crunch of carriage wheels arriving under the hushed cover of night, strong hands taking her from her bed and forcing her into some strange, cold, pitiless place. Ada would be handed over to servants who did not love her. And Rosa would be absent from Raven Hall right at the time she most needed to be there – her chance to win the wish ripped from her hands.

'Thank you for your concern, Dr Livingstone,' she said. 'Now please leave this house. The ravens will show you the way.'

The doctor frowned. 'What ravens?'

'The ones who will make your life a misery if you ever lift a finger to have me removed from my daughter.'

She snapped her fingers and a fury of ravens descended down the chimney like locusts, surrounding Dr Livingstone in a dark, angry cloud. Rosa felt a swell of triumph as she heard his yells from within the mass of birds. In that moment she didn't care if he lost his eyes. She simply wanted him out of the house, and it thrilled her that she had the power to make it happen.

Eustace rushed to the doctor's aid. In one movement he threw his own jacket over the man and tried to usher him from the room, whilst the ravens clawed at his head in a furious frenzy of metal wings and slashing beaks.

The commotion had upset Ada, who started to cry, so Rosa took her back to the day-nursery to soothe her. She spent the remaining afternoon up there, delighting Ada with the collection of clockwork fairies she had made especially for her. Eustace did not bother her and she did not seek him out to see what damage the ravens had done. She dined alone that evening, as usual, before retiring to her bedroom to get ready for Beatrice's pleasure garden.

Her winter cloak had been brushed and laid out in readiness, the violet-coloured velvet trimmed with ermine fur and finished with silk tassels. She was just fastening the cloak's jewelled brooch beneath her chin when there was a knock at her door and Eustace spoke her name from the other side. She frowned. Despite what had happened earlier, she hadn't expected him to come to her room. Indeed she had assumed they would slip straight back into avoiding one another, as before.

'If you don't wish to have your eyes pecked from your head, I suggest you remove yourself from my door,' she called through the wood.

'Rosa, I must speak with you,' Eustace said. 'It is urgent.'

She scowled and threw open the door. She rarely felt any fear of Eustace any more, only a stale sort of loathing, like a wound that refused to heal and had turned fetid. Yet there was something about being this close to him late at night that touched some old, cold sense of dread deep within her.

'What is it?' she snapped.

'I have something to ask you,' he replied.

His voice sounded oddly hoarse, and Rosa noticed again the alteration in his appearance. When had this happened exactly? How had she failed to notice? The new cuts on his face from the ravens did not improve matters, either.

'Please,' he said quietly. 'Call off the birds. I cannot bear to go on hearing the scrape of their wings inside the chimney, or the rap of their beaks on glass, or their claws scrabbling upon the slates of the roof. For the love of God, enough! I have done all that you asked, complied with every request, no matter how unreasonable. It is enough to quite undo a man.'

After all Rosa's grief over Esme, her heart was a stone and whatever pity there might have been to spare for Eustace evaporated at his choice of the word 'unreasonable'.

'The birds will not disturb you so long as you leave me alone,' she said. 'If you behave honourably, then you have nothing to fear.'

His shoulders slumped and Rosa felt an ugly surge of satisfying power as she pushed past him. In that moment she felt the echo of every unkind word he'd ever spoken to her, each bruise from those crushing fingers, all those occasions when he'd made her feel that she was unravelling into pieces at his feet.

'We cannot go on in this manner,' he said behind her. 'How do you imagine it will end?'

Rosa had no answer to that, for she did not know herself. He was right, of course. It was quite clear to her that her marriage was dead and could not be revived, especially since she intended to use the wish to get Esme back, if she should win, and so could no longer attempt to change Eustace in any way. Whether she won or not, the competition would soon be over, and what then? She could continue to remain living at Raven Hall within this resentful and uneasy truce or she could pack up her bags and leave. A great scandal would surely follow, but Beatrice had borne it, and so could Rosa. With her ravens for protection, she could start a new life somewhere with Ada. And Esme, she added. That was the point of the competition after all – to get her other daughter back.

Yet, as the opening night for her own garden approached, Rosa found herself feeling increasingly uncertain. Esme was dead and had been given a good Christian burial. Perhaps interfering with that was the last thing she ought to be doing? She had no answers, so she offered none to Eustace, but continued past him into the corridor.

'Where are you going?' he called after her.

'To Beatrice's pleasure garden.'

He made no move to follow her as she went down through the darkened house. At this time of night the great mansion had the feel of a ship floating through a mysterious sea filled with secrets, and Rosa was glad to leave Eustace behind and go out to where her carriage was waiting. Ribbons of frozen fog wound about the horses' legs and made the carriage seem ethereal and strange in the lamplight, as if it were heading to a destination that was altogether not of this world.

# CHAPTER
# TWENTY-FIVE

Rosa arrived at Half Moon House shortly after eleven
o'clock. There were several carriages there, and
guests wrapped in their sumptuous winter furs, paying
for entrance tickets at the gate. When Rosa handed over
the invitation to the footman, he immediately gave her a
ticket and waved her through without payment.

It was bitterly cold, but the fog had vanished and the
air was sharp and clear as a cut diamond. Rosa shivered
as she pulled her cloak tighter around her and tucked her
hands a little deeper into her swan-down muff. The sky
was a glittering net filled with stars, and wishes, and bright
hopes for impossible tomorrows, yet she could feel a soft
sadness creeping over her.

She trailed the other guests as they followed the signs erected on the lawn, guiding them round to the back of the house in a swirl of lamplight, like a golden paint-stroke from a magician's paintbrush. As she walked, Rosa was puzzled by the quiet. She had expected music – perhaps a band or orchestra in full swing, the stamp of feet upon a dance floor, the laughter of couples twirling beneath the stars. Instead there was only a frosty hush, as if the snow had soaked up all sound.

There was not even a golden glow in the sky from lanterns, and lights, and leagues of endless candles. It was as if there weren't really a pleasure garden here at all. Had it not been for the other guests, Rosa might have wondered whether she'd got the days muddled up and come at the wrong time.

But when they went round the corner, the people in front of her gasped. The East Garden had been transformed into a sparkling fairyland of flowers, and ice, and candles hung in glass jars from the crooked branches of the black apple trees. Their baby lights flickered sweetly in the darkness, casting a ghostly sheen across the blue snow, adding glitter to the frost and smudging smoky shadows into the edges of the garden.

A decorative arch marked the entrance and was covered in dozens of ice roses that threw back the candlelight in speckles and glints of golden confetti. Rosa thought at first that the flowers must be a carved sculpture, but as she approached she saw that they were living blooms. It was possible to make out the fine hairs upon the thorny stems, the lines of the leaves and the delicate stamens within the folds of ruffled petals. There was a scent too, faint but fragrant, of sugared petals, and frosted pollen, and the minty snap of something icy cold. As she watched, a blue-and-silver striped bee suddenly wriggled free from one of the roses and took off, making a lazy trail through the air.

'Welcome to the winter garden of Half Moon House.'

Rosa turned in the direction of the speaker, a liveried footman carrying a stack of gold-edged pamphlets. He continued to address the group in front of her.

'Lady Sitwell hopes you will find the visit delightful and informative,' he said. 'But before entering, please be aware of the three garden rules: first, touching the botanical specimens is strictly prohibited unless you are invited to. Second, guests must not leave the designated path. And finally, do not approach or pester any of the animals. If they come up to you, then you may interact with them, but you must allow them to retreat as soon as they wish. Anyone found breaking the rules will be asked to leave immediately, with no exceptions. Now, would you care for a pamphlet to guide you through the wonders you will find within?'

When it was Rosa's turn, she took a guide from him, but found it difficult to pay much attention to it when her eyes were so drawn to the displays around her. The path the footman had indicated was made of dark-blue marble and branched off in multiple places, so that guests had to choose which to follow. It was rather like a maze, twisting and turning through the trees, making it impossible to see what was coming up ahead until you were face-to-face with it.

There were several guests already in the garden but they were moving quietly and almost reverently, with none of the usual raucousness found in pleasure gardens. Rosa quickly understood why. The extraordinary plant and animal life seemed to invite a hushed cathedral-like atmosphere somehow, as if to speak too loudly would be to break whatever spell hung over the place. Certainly the apple trees disliked too much noise, shying away and taking their light with them if people got too loud.

Rosa was glad of the quiet. It made it easier to drink it all in. At every turn there was something to marvel at – pale butterflies, mirror frogs, glowing blossom, humming tulips and even a few miniature rabbits made from delicate china. No larger than a kitten, their bodies sported an elegant blue-and-cream willow pattern, yet they hopped and frolicked in the snow as nimbly as their flesh-and-blood brothers.

Rosa longed to touch one, but recalling what the footman had said, she forced herself to keep to the path. The apple trees, though, did not stay still. They wandered about the place and sometimes temporarily blocked the way. A couple of them did so now, one up ahead of Rosa and one a little way behind, sealing off this part of the garden so that she was the only person in it.

She froze as one of the rabbits hopped closer, raising itself on its haunches to peer up at her inquisitively, its nose twitching as it sniffed the frosted air. Its eyes shone brightly in the candlelight and its pale ears were very long, decorated in intricate twists of flowers. Slowly Rosa withdrew one of her hands from the muff and reached carefully down towards the nearest rabbit, thinking it would probably flee. Instead it hopped right up onto her palm.

Its body was icy against her bare skin and, for a handful of seconds, Rosa and the rabbit simply stared at one another. There was something in the rabbit's gaze that was unmistakeably friendly and intelligent, as if it had deliberately sought Rosa out and picked her from among all the guests in the garden.

Yet Rosa barely had time to take the animal in before it changed, its body moving and shifting so suddenly that it was hard to follow what was happening. All Rosa knew was that, in the space of a few heartbeats, she no longer held a rabbit in her hand at all, but a perfectly beautiful teacup. It sported the same willow pattern, with an intricate design of flowers and vines, minuscule petals painted along the arched handle. The only sign of the rabbit was in the form of a painted one, right at the bottom of the cup. Rosa stared at it, momentarily unsure whether she had done something she shouldn't have. But then a voice behind her said, 'Congratulations, your grace. You've been invited to the supper booths.'

She straightened up and turned round, the teacup still carefully clasped in her hand. The apple tree had moved out of the way and another liveried footman stood on the path behind her, with several curious guests peering over his shoulder.

'I beg your pardon?' she asked.

'There is not enough space for all the guests to attend the midnight tea,' the footman explained. 'The teacup rabbits therefore choose who is invited to stay on in the gardens after closing time. There is more information on page three of your guide. You will need to keep hold of the teacup and present it at the supper booths.'

'Thank you,' Rosa said.

The footman moved on and Rosa immediately found herself surrounded by the guests who had been behind him, all exclaiming enviously over the teacup, with one gentleman even offering to pay Rosa a handsome sum for it.

'It would do you no good,' a lady in a crimson cloak said, peering down at the guidebook. 'It says here that the teacup can only be used by its chosen recipient, whose name will be painted on the base.'

Everyone peered over Rosa's shoulder as she turned the cup over. Her name was indeed stencilled there in curling teal letters: *Her Grace, Rosa Hamilton, Duchess of Chalkley*.

'I could hardly have parted with it at any rate, sir,' Rosa said, trying to make her smile seem genuine. 'Who would give up the chance to experience the supper booths in a garden such as this?'

It was wondrous and extraordinary, yet her heart was a stone as she watched a few of the other guests try to coax over one of the remaining rabbits. She had barely set foot in the garden, and already she feared that it would provide stiff competition for her own.

The cold air rippled around her like a length of chilled silk as she ventured further into the maze. She could see why the lighting was kept so soft, since practically everything in the garden was best viewed in the dark.

She marvelled at a fairy ring of violet mushrooms glowing brightly, immediately recalling childhood stories of how such a ring was supposed to mark the place where fairies had danced, or grew over the spot where one of their underground towns was to be found. When she located the mushrooms in her guidebook, it confirmed that they did indeed grow above fairy villages, and that these mushrooms were particularly attracted to music:

*The fairy ring marks the spot where the fairies have their music hall. Step into the ring, and the mushrooms will allow you to hear the strains of fairy harps far below your feet.*

Rosa saw that the path went straight through the middle of the mushroom ring rather than around it. With mounting curiosity, she stepped inside and almost dropped the rabbit teacup. Part of her had not truly believed it was possible, yet the moment she was within the ring, the fairy harp music surged up through the ground and washed over her in waves and waves.

This was harp music as Rosa had never heard it before, filled with wild abandon and carefree joy. Not only could she hear it clearly, but the music seemed to assail all her other senses too. She could taste luscious fairy fruits upon her tongue, feel cool dew between her toes, glimpse the glittering lights of a fairy hall and smell the smoky scent of their peat fires.

It was so enchanting that she could barely breathe and her entire body trembled. For long minutes she stood transfixed, not wanting ever to leave the circle. It was only the other guests crowding impatiently behind her that finally made her move away. As soon as she stepped outside the ring, the harp music was abruptly lost, and the snow-covered quiet seemed to echo strangely inside her head.

She thought of the clockwork fairy orchestra she had laboured over back at Raven Hall, and all her pride turned to dust. So many hundreds of hours wasted. It could not begin to compare with what she had just experienced. But it did not matter. Extraordinary as all these flowers and animals were, surely none of them could compare with her carousel and what it could do.

She continued along the path towards a fountain – a beautiful structure made from multiple tiers of shining white marble. She quickly spotted bright flashes of gold within the frothing water. There were orange-and-white fish in the bottom, darting to and fro among the bubbles. And a little basket hung from the edge of the ledge. It contained pennies, along with a written invitation to make a wish and throw one in.

Rosa thumbed through the printed guide until she found the relevant page, which explained that these were wish-fish, discovered high in the Himalayas. As the fish were only tiny, their magic was also small, and the wishes they were able to grant could only be of the most trivial kind. The guide suggested wishing for a hair comb, as this was something the fish were apparently particularly good at.

Rosa took a coin and tossed it into the fountain. Despite what it had said in the book, she couldn't resist wishing for the thing she *really* wanted – for Esme to be returned to her – but when the nearest fish swallowed up her coin, it promptly spat it back with such force that it came right out of the water and landed on the edge of the fountain. Sighing, Rosa picked it up and wished for a hair comb before tossing it back. This time a fish gobbled the coin down eagerly and, for a moment, it glowed bolder and brighter than all the rest, so that its light seemed to reach right up out of the fountain and created a golden pool on the marble ledge.

The next moment an exquisite hair comb appeared beside Rosa's hand. Made from mother-of-pearl, it featured gold-and-white wish-fish swimming amongst a bed of pearls and silver coins. She slipped the comb into her purse, and as she moved through the garden, she noticed that many of the women wandering through had the same comb clutched in their gloved hands or tucked into the ribbons of their velvet bonnets.

The time passed quickly and, in what remained, Rosa took in a pond, populated with fat golden toads that created a peculiar, croaking music as they slid about on the frozen surface. Then onto a little grotto, the ceiling alight with dozens of glimmering glow-worms. She knew there were birds in the garden too, because she sensed the fluttering of their wings overhead, but they always moved too quickly for her to see them properly.

'What is magical about this bush?' she overheard another guest ask a passing footman, pointing at a plant with vivid red leaves.

'It is a poinsettia, madam,' the footman replied. 'Lady Beatrice's favourite plant.'

'Yes, but what does it do?'

'It does not do anything, madam. Lady Beatrice simply has a great liking for its leaves. They require periods of darkness in order to take on their red colour.'

The guest seemed disappointed, but Rosa thought there was something very lovely about the plant. Every time she took one path, she knew she was missing out on several others that would take her to equally marvellous things. There was forever the sense in the garden that there were wonders hiding just out of sight, and invisible eyes watching her from the foliage. Beatrice was nowhere to be seen, but it wasn't long before she spotted another familiar face – James Sheppard was on the path up ahead.

Rosa had not spoken to him since Esme's funeral and felt a sudden burst of regret at the way they had parted. He was the first and only person who had shown her any kindness that day, and she ought to have been more gracious. It had been too painful to be near him then, and Rosa sensed that same ache stirring inside her now. She yearned to be near James, even though his presence was a bitter reminder of everything she might have had if she had chosen more wisely. She had gone too far down another path to wish to turn back time now – she wouldn't give Ada up for anything. James and that other life were lost to her forever, but she wished to thank him for the flower, so she called his name and he turned round.

His eyes met hers across the garden and he smiled, causing the lines around his eyes and mouth to deepen. As he walked over, it struck Rosa that he was a man who smiled often. She did not think Eustace had a single one of those lines.

'Rosa,' he said. 'How good to see you. You look well.'

'Thank you, I am,' she replied. 'How are you?'

'Better than ever.' His smile broadened. 'In fact there's someone I'd like you to meet.' He beckoned over a nearby lady, who left the glowing blossom trees she'd been admiring and came to stand by his side. She wore an emerald cloak with a matching bonnet and was startlingly pretty. She was also, to Rosa's surprise, brown-skinned.

'Jani, this is Rosa Warren,' James said. 'Well, the Duchess of Chalkley now in fact.'

'Of Warren's Clockwork?' Jani asked, in lightly accented English.

'The very same,' Rosa replied. 'How do you do?'

The other woman smiled. 'I am delighted to meet you. I am Jani Sheppard.'

'Sheppard?' Rosa repeated, confused.

'We married in India in the autumn,' James said.

'Oh.' Rosa felt as if someone had struck her. Her insides clenched with such sudden force that she felt queasy. It took all her will power not to let the pain show on her face.

*He could have been mine . . .*

She felt the absurd urge to say the words aloud right here and now, to make Jani understand that James had proposed to *her* first, and that the only reason Jani had him at all was because Rosa had said no. The thought made her feel hollow and she hated herself.

'I have seen your clockwork creatures,' Jani said. There was something lovely about her quiet, measured voice. 'They are exquisite. You must be very proud.'

'Thank you, yes, I am,' Rosa managed. 'I'll make something for you, if you like.'

'That is most kind.'

'What is your favourite animal?'

'A snail.'

'Jani and I met through Beatrice,' James told her. 'I provided the orchids for the garden and Jani provided the snails. Have you seen them?'

Rosa shook her head.

'There is too much to see in one night of course,' James said. 'Perhaps you will come back? It would be a shame to miss the snails. They're incredibly special.'

James glanced at his wife and they exchanged a quick smile. The moment passed between them in seconds, but it was enough for Rosa to see that their marriage was completely different from her own and Eustace's. They loved each other. She was happy for James, she told herself. But heartbroken for herself. She could feel envy and bitterness stirring to life inside her, but was determined that none of that would show in her face or voice.

'You shall have your snail, Mrs Sheppard,' she said in a cheerful tone. 'And I promise it will be the most beautiful clockwork snail ever created. It may not be until next year, though. I am quite busy at the moment with preparations for my own garden.'

'Ah, yes, Beatrice mentioned that you were opening one,' James said.

Rosa wondered how much he knew and whether Beatrice had told him about the competition. She longed to ask, but felt reluctant to mention the Winter Garden in front of Jani.

'I plan to open next week,' she said. 'You must both come.'

'Thank you for the invitation – we would have loved to see it,' James said, 'but we are returning to India in a few days. We intend to make our home there.'

'Oh.'

It was yet another blow. She wanted to tell him that he couldn't go. She wished she could ask him to stay. But she knew she'd lost the right to do so, and bit her tongue instead.

'I was going to send you a note tomorrow,' James said, a little apologetically.

He had not been back to Raven Hall since the day Eustace had ordered him out, although he had continued to send orchids from time to time. Rosa understood that his work for Beatrice had kept him very busy during the past year.

'I can continue to have orchids shipped to you, if you like,' James offered.

Rosa nodded dumbly.

'And I wish you luck for the competition, of course.'

Rosa was startled. 'You know about it?'

'Beatrice told me.'

Rosa's eyes slid to Jani, wondering how much she might be aware of.

'Jani knows all about it too,' James said quietly. 'She has been to the Winter Garden.'

'You have?'

'Many years ago,' Jani replied. 'As a child.'

Rosa felt another surge of jealousy. What made Jani so special that the garden had appeared to her when it had never shown itself to Rosa?

'Did you . . .' She licked her lips, which were suddenly dry. 'Did you ever see a carousel there?'

'James told me about your Carousel of Icicles,' Jani replied. Rosa flushed, wondering what else he had told her. 'I never saw anything like that in the garden.'

Rosa thought briefly of asking Jani the same favour she had asked of Beatrice – to tell her all that she knew about the garden and the Spider Queen – but what good would it do? James had already told her that they had met through Beatrice, and so Jani's loyalty would surely lie there.

Before they could continue their conversation, a bell chimed somewhere to signal that the allotted hour had come to an end.

'It was good to see you,' James said.

'And you. Oh, and I wanted to say thank you. For the mourning orchid. It . . . it was a great comfort to me.'

He looked at her, and for a moment she felt as if she was back there in the graveyard, taking the seed from him in the snow, feeling the warmth of it through her glove.

'I am glad,' he said. 'Truly. I hope Ada is well?'

Rosa smiled at him, pleased that he had remembered her name. 'She is no longer a baby. She has grown into a darling little girl.'

She gestured with her hands as she spoke, and James's eye fell on the teacup. A faint frown line appeared between his eyes.

'You have been invited to the supper booths,' he said.

'Yes.'

He hesitated. 'A word of caution,' he said. 'Do not go into the plum rain. Whatever you see there . . . cannot be unseen.'

Rosa had no idea what he was talking about, but was unable to question him further. The apple trees were moving around, shepherding people out of the garden and there was one on their path that was most insistent. So Rosa said goodbye with a heavy heart. As she walked back towards the entrance gates, she tried not to dwell on the fact that this was probably the last time she would ever see James.

'Thank you for visiting the pleasure garden,' the footman said as they filed out. 'If you were fortunate enough to be invited to the supper booths, then please make yourself known to my colleague by the Rose Gate. Otherwise, your carriages await to take you home, and Lady Beatrice sincerely hopes you had an enchanting evening and that you will visit the garden again soon.'

Rosa looked round to where another footman waited beside the gate with the ice roses. A few people holding blue-and-cream teacups already clustered around him. Rosa walked over to join them and, soon enough, there were perhaps forty guests assembled there.

'I believe that's everyone,' the footman said. 'If you are all ready, then please follow me.'

Rosa expected them to pass under the Rose Gate and walk back through the garden, but instead the footman took them round the corner of the house to where a second gate waited. Like the first one, this formed an archway, but rather than being decorated with ice roses, it was adorned all over with fat, ripe plums. Their purple skins showed through coats of frost that were like sparkling crystals of sugar.

The footman stepped back, waving a gloved hand at the arch. 'Please do go through,' he said. 'On the other side of the Plum Gate you will find servers waiting to escort you to your tables.'

A hedged walkway stretched beyond the gate, making it impossible to see what was coming up ahead, but Rosa thought she heard the soft splash of fountains and the trilling call of a songbird. Just off the path, a single golden feather lay on the snow, impossibly bright and beautiful – the most golden thing that could exist in the world. As she followed the other guests through in a whisper of cloaks and anticipation, Rosa clasped her teacup a little more tightly in her hands, partly thrilled and partly dreading what new enchantments she might find beyond.

# CHAPTER
# TWENTY-SIX

Having already spent an hour exploring the gardens, the other guests were in such a state of excitement that the icy air seemed to crackle with it. They hurried down the path, greedy for more wintry delights, not even pausing to notice the magic along the way, but Rosa's gaze took in everything.

The path was lined with ornamental bramble, only these weren't fat, white berries gleaming within the bright winter bark, but elegant spiders with legs pale as milk. When Rosa peered more closely, she saw that they were spinning webs of frosted gold between the branches, and a quick glance at her guidebook told her that these spiders didn't catch flies in their webs, but bad dreams instead.

Rosa saw that she had fallen behind the group and hastened to catch them up. She emerged from the hedgerow and found herself in the middle of the supper booths. They were located in a grove of plum trees, their slim trunks topped with bursting crowns of flowering blossoms that shone with a vibrant light of their own against the deep winter sky. There was every possible shade of purple there – swirls of amethyst, speckles of periwinkle and bold strokes of violet. There were several signs warning guests not to eat the plums themselves.

*Please beware: one does not consume the plums – the plums consume you.*

There was a cluster of tables covered in pristine white cloths and laid out for tea, set in the snow within the orchard. Strangely, a whole canopy of parasols hung from the branches of the trees, attached by their opened-out tops, creating a ceiling of silk and lace, walnut handles and velvet tassels. There were folding-handled carriage parasols and gentlemen's walking umbrellas, children's black mourning umbrellas and cream lace bridal brollies.

It was an odd sight, and Rosa wondered what the point of them could be. It was far too cold to rain, after all, and they would prevent the person seated at the table from looking up at the purple blossoms. Perhaps, at last, she'd found a design flaw in Beatrice's garden, but it hardly detracted much.

Great blooms of strange blue flowers surrounded the supper booths, rising up on stalks almost as tall as a person, their heads leaning down towards the tables slightly, as if they meant to eavesdrop on the conversations. Shafts of purple light pushed through between the gaps in the parasols, shining like spotlights upon a stage, and several more of the white spiders she'd seen previously spun their golden webs between the umbrellas.

Now that she could see them more clearly, Rosa realised that the webs were far more intricate than ordinary ones, with the most exquisite designs woven into them, as if the spiders were artists and the spider thread was their paint, creating artwork just as remarkable as those adorning the booths at Vauxhall. Many of the webs had intricate flower designs, but there were a few that had tried something different: a lady's winter gown, a castle, a reindeer, a star, a sleigh decked out in ribbons and bells.

Most of the guests were already seated, but a waiter was just showing one couple to their table when the lady noticed the webs and gave a whinny of distaste. Her companion promptly used his cane to destroy the web – which had contained a detailed image of a tiger – and the spider fell to the floor, narrowly missing getting stamped on as it hurried away in search of cover.

The effect was immediate. The couple's teacups were confiscated and a second footman appeared, to ask them to leave the gardens for breaking one of Lady Sitwell's rules. The couple were outraged and tried to argue, but

the footman was having none of it, and they found themselves bundled away very quickly. In the meantime, one
of the waiters greeted Rosa and indicated the table the
other couple had just left.

'I'm afraid your companions have had to depart,' he
said. 'Would you like me to see whether we can add you
to a different table?'

'No, that's all right,' Rosa said quickly. 'I'm perfectly
happy to dine alone.'

She took her seat beneath an emerald shot-silk walking
parasol with ruffled-trim edging. Her place was already
laid with silver cutlery and china that matched the rabbit
teacup, which she set down upon the cloth. Slim silver
tree trunks surrounded her on all sides, some of which
had lime-spotted mushrooms growing up them. If she
leaned right back in her chair and craned her neck, she
could just peer past the cover of the umbrella to the
spectacular show of blossom above and the frozen stars
beyond, twinkling like iced gems against black silk. Within
minutes, a host of gloved waiters brought out tea services
upon oval silver trays to each table. Rosa could tell from
the scent that there was no ordinary tea inside.

'Tonight the winter garden is serving smoky bonfire tea,
your grace,' her waiter told her. 'With honeyed milk, and
toffee-apple-flavoured sugar cubes.'

It was unlike anything Rosa had tasted before, but she
found it quite delicious, relishing the hints of bonfire
smoke and the crispness of the apple skins. Aside from

the tea service, a small silver carriage clock stood upon each table, and Rosa scowled down at hers, hoping it wasn't about to do anything extraordinary. She'd already had her fairy orchestra ruined; she couldn't afford for her collection of clocks to be spoiled too – but as the minutes ticked by, it remained a perfectly ordinary timepiece.

She sipped her tea and slowly flicked through the pages of the guide, realising that it was, in itself, the most beautiful thing. The pages were decorated with Beatrice's own artwork: exquisite drawings of the animals, and painstakingly accurate botanical illustrations of mushrooms and other plant life. It was quite clear from its pages that Rosa had seen only a fraction of what the garden had to offer. As for the plum trees themselves, it appeared they were a hybrid of two other plants, although it didn't say which ones.

Rosa closed the guidebook and more waiters arrived with tiered silver plates filled with cakes. Like everything else in the garden, they were delicate, frosted and impossibly pretty – tiny treasure boxes studded in jewels for some fairy queen.

'For your pleasure this evening, your grace, we have songbird tiffin.' The waiter indicated slices of canary-yellow finger cakes. 'As well as butterfly biscotti.'

These were beautiful lavender biscuits decorated with piped white icing, and Rosa took one of them first. It crumbled into sweet, buttery pieces on her tongue, and she was sure she could feel the flutter of tiny wings inside when she swallowed them. But the real star was the songbird tiffin. Before she could even touch the cake, it broke apart to reveal a pair of tiny white birds with bright-yellow chests. They fluttered together to the handle of the teapot and sang duets there for the remainder of the evening.

When the carriage clock on the table struck midnight, a footman called out, 'Ladies and gentlemen, the plum rain is about to begin. Anyone who wishes to participate should read the instructions.'

Rosa was about to turn to her guidebook, thinking the instructions would be found within its pages, but then she noticed that her teacup had transformed once again into a china rabbit, and the animal was pushing a little scroll of paper towards her with its nose.

She unrolled the scroll and read the words painted there, as the carriage clock sounded out the hours with a clear chiming of icy bells:

*At the hour of midnight, for one minute only, the plum rain falls.*

*You are welcome to relax in your chairs beneath the parasols and enjoy the show. Or, if you would like to experience their magic for yourselves, simply reach a hand out into the rain.*

*The first drop that lands on your skin will show you another life. A life that might have been yours, if you had taken a different path.*

*Beware! This can be a fascinating glimpse, but it can also be the most shocking thing you will ever experience.*

*The choice is yours.*

The moment Rosa finished reading the note, the plum rain began in soft, whispered sheets. The violet drops sparkled all the way to the snow and, to Rosa, they looked as dangerous as glittering daggers. She knew she had not made good choices in her life. She didn't need any magical plum rain to tell her that. And yet . . . the chance to see how life might have been different was just too tempting to pass up. With a sort of wondrous horror, she watched herself reach a hand out into the rain and felt the curiously warm splash of a purple drop upon her fingertip.

At once, church music flowed through the air, wrapping itself around her like lengths of scarlet ribbon. The purple plum trees and the rain melted away, revealing the new picture that had been hidden beneath: bright sunlight streaming through a kaleidoscope of jewelled windows.

Rosa sat on a pew, flanked by her children and grand-children, with an ancient and creaking Cookie at her heels. Times had moved on regarding women at funerals but, even had they not, Rosa would have insisted on attending this one. Nothing in the world would have kept her away. It was, after all, the last chance to say goodbye to her soulmate – the person she'd loved most in all the world, the other half of her soul.

Oh, certainly they had argued sometimes, and they had disagreed sometimes, and they had hurt each other sometimes. But all that was immaterial. As the years passed, Rosa had known that she was happy, of course, but perhaps it was only possible to well and truly appreciate just *how* good it had all been now, when it was finally over forever.

It was impossible for her to imagine James inside the coffin. Impossible to imagine that her husband would never take her by the hand again, or kiss that particular spot on her neck, or laugh at some shared joke, or wrap his arms around her to hold her close and tell her how precious she was to him.

She could not stop the flood of memories. The first time he made her shiver with pleasure. The arrival of their first baby, and the pride and wonder with which James had gazed into the crib. The time she accompanied him to India and they had eaten papayas on the veranda of a white marble hotel until the juice ran down their chins. All those countless other adventures they had taken all over the world in pursuit of orchids. How their home had been filled with the scent of them, and how people had travelled from miles around to marvel at the unusual, fantastic specimens in their garden and hothouses. A life filled with flowers and love.

Naturally there had been dark times too – the dreadful weeks she wept for their six-year-old son, Henry, snatched away by influenza. But at every step James was by her side to share her grief. He was an old man by the time he died, his skin lined, his body thin. But, to her, he would always be that dark-haired adventurer, laughing at some joke she had just cracked as they made their way to their next exotic destination. Throughout their lives there seemed always to have been some whistle blasting impatiently in the background, and when Rosa closed her eyes, even now, she could still feel James's warm hand on her arm, his head bent close to her ear as he said, 'Come on, Cogs, we don't want to miss the train.'

Rosa couldn't remember when he'd first started calling her Cogs, although she knew it was to do with her affinity for clockwork, and was always spoken in warm tones of affection and admiration. She'd always loved the name, always felt a pleasant sensation of warmth whenever he'd affectionately called her by it, even in front of guests and distinguished visitors.

Shoulder-to-shoulder – that was how they had faced the world, a team. And now he was gone, and she was alone, and it was anguish, the worst thing imaginable; and yet it was still better than the alternative, better than never having known or loved him at all. She would do it all again, exactly the same way: every minute, every word, every choice. Even during those times when he infuriated her, when he saddened her, she had still loved him to distraction, and James, in turn, had kept his promise by making her happier than she had ever thought possible. And if this agony was the price to pay at the end of a life well lived, then it was worth every tear, it was worth every single tear. Better to lose such a love than never to have had it at all.

It was a good, clean sorrow that Rosa felt – pure as snow – as she prepared to say goodbye to her husband for the last time. But then, to her surprise, a fat, ripe plum fell into her lap, impossibly purple against the black of her mourning dress. She looked up and saw several branches growing along the church's roof, all coming from a tree in the centre of the aisle – a plum tree heavy with fat, frosted fruits, its roots growing straight through the floor tiles, splitting them into broken pieces.

Rosa nudged her eldest son, Albert. 'What is that tree doing in here?' she asked.

He glanced round. His eyes were the same shade of brown as his father's. 'What tree?'

Rosa gestured impatiently back at the aisle, but then another plum fell into her lap, followed by another and another. She looked up in time to see the church roof peel back, exposing a dark winter night sky filled with lacy parasols and thousands of stars. Snow blew in across the floor, and the straightforward sorrow she'd felt warped into a complicated tangle of regrets and bitterness, thorny as briars.

The next moment the real world won the battle altogether and the what-might-have-been vanished in a last groan of organ music and the funeral incense of extinguished candles. Rosa was back in Beatrice's garden, gasping at the shock of the icy air and the wrenching loss as that other life was torn away from her. Surely it would have hurt no more to have her very spine ripped out?

She could not prevent the strangled cry that escaped her lips, but fortunately no one else noticed, as the air was filled with the exclamations of others who had experienced the plum rain. Some were laughing, others were weeping, whilst some people simply looked dazzled, as if their eyes could not adjust to the lantern glow of the pleasure garden after whatever it was they'd just been looking at.

A footman was thanking them for coming, and guests were rising to their feet to leave. Rosa hung back and let them go first, desperately trying to catch her breath and to thrust all the pieces of herself back together again. Her hands shook with anger. How could she have been stupid enough to touch the plum rain, knowing full well that nothing good could come of it? Now she had simply given herself another burden to carry – one more rock to make her already-unbearable load even heavier.

Even worse was what this meant for the competition. She'd been so certain that she would win, but now, for the first time, she felt a thorn of doubt slide beneath her skin. She was struck again by the sparkling beauty of Beatrice's garden – the snow was a perfect carpet, the candlelight lapped at the night, like a cat licking cream, and the darkness meant that the sky was a net full of trapped stars. She worried that her own garden seemed brash and fake, and too bright, in comparison.

Finally she stood up from her table, snatched up her muff and the guidebook and quickly followed the other guests towards the exit. The carriages were already starting to rumble down the drive, and Rosa was just about to climb up into her own when a voice spoke behind her.

'Hello, R-Rosa.'

She turned to see Beatrice lingering on the dark steps of Half Moon House, wrapped up in winter furs. It was strange to see her again after all this time.

'Why are you lingering out here like this?' she asked. 'You're the hostess. You ought to be in the garden.'

If their roles had been reversed, Rosa would certainly have been out in the middle of it all, basking in the triumph of her success, soaking up every adoring, rapturous moment. It was such a waste that Beatrice had merely skulked at the outskirts, like an intruder at her own party, and Rosa felt an unreasonable flare of irritation towards her.

Beatrice shrugged, then seemed to hunch deeper into her furs. It seemed to Rosa that there was something different about her. 'Too m-many people,' she said. 'They make me f-feel t-trapped.'

345

Rosa frowned. 'Why are you looking at me like that?'

'Like wh-what?'

'I don't know, like . . . like you're seeing me for the first time or something.' She put a hand to her face. 'Do I have something on my cheek?'

Beatrice's eyes slid away from her. 'I d-don't know wh-what you m-mean. D-did you like the g-garden?'

Rosa shook her head and, even in the dim light, she saw Beatrice flinch slightly.

'I didn't like it,' she said softly. 'I loved it. It is exquisite. Simply the most magical, wondrous thing I've ever seen.'

Beatrice smiled suddenly, and Rosa wondered whether it might have been the first time she'd ever seen her do so.

'I did think the plum trees cruel, though,' she added. She could feel her irritation turning into something stronger, angrier, as she went on. 'What is the point? We can't undo our choices, so why torture ourselves with visions of what might have been?'

'And y-yet you ignored the w-warning and ch-chose to. Experience it. Anyway,' Beatrice said.

Rosa had no answer to that and the fact that she only had herself to blame just made her anger even hotter.

'It is h-human n-nature,' Beatrice said. 'To l-look in all the wrong p-places, focus on all the w-wrong th-things and s-seek out that which is b-bad for us. It's why so m-many of us. Are so. Unhappy.'

'Including you?' Rosa hazarded. 'I suppose you know there was much gossip about you and Mr Sheppard whilst you were away. Going off together like that, quite alone . . . Why, there were even people who thought the two of you might have eloped.'

Beatrice flushed. 'J-James is m-married.'

Rosa raised an eyebrow. 'James, is it? So you did nurture feelings for him. Bad luck that he chose someone else in the end.'

Rosa had no idea why she was speaking in such a way. She felt suddenly sick.

Beatrice gave her an odd look and said, 'I am h-happy for h-him. He d-deserves every h-happiness and h-has b-been a g-g-great f-friend to m-me. But a-as you k-know, I d-do not w-want to m-m-marry anyone. Ever.'

Rosa shrugged impatiently, suddenly desperate to change the subject. 'Well, I don't know what instructions the Spider Queen gave you, but I understood our gardens were supposed to amaze and delight people.' The thought gave her a sudden surge of hope. 'You've no more sense than a June bug, if you think your plum trees do that. I don't imagine you will win the competition this way.'

She was pleased to see a flicker of uncertainty cross Beatrice's face and hoped that she had touched a nerve.

'Your garden is extraordinary,' she said. 'But mine is better. You must come when it opens next week. Until then, I'll wish you goodnight.'

She climbed up into her carriage and was about to rap on the roof to signal the driver to go, when Beatrice suddenly reached in through the window and gripped her wrist.

'Gracious, what are you doing?' Rosa stared down at her. There was such a strange look in her friend's eyes – a sort of desperate sorrow that Rosa did not understand.

'I j-just . . .' Beatrice began. 'I w-wanted to t-t-tell you . . .'

'What?'

Beatrice looked up at Rosa and frowned. Some inner process seemed to take place inside her head and the next moment she released Rosa's wrist and stepped back.

'N-Never mind,' she said. 'It d-doesn't m-matter.'

'Really, Beatrice,' Rosa said. 'You act most strangely sometimes.'

She rapped on the roof and the driver clicked his tongue to urge the horses forward, leaving Beatrice alone upon the frozen steps.

# CHAPTER
# TWENTY-SEVEN

Beatrice watched Rosa drive away with a nagging feeling in her stomach, sharp as teeth tugging at her guts. Should she have told her what she had seen in the plum rain? But it was such a shocking thing to speak of, and Beatrice was not sure she had the words.

She sighed and walked out into her garden, wanting to be sure that everything was being attended to correctly. She had a horrifying fear of fire breaking out and so always checked and double-checked that all the candles and lanterns had been extinguished. She'd spent most of her time that evening up on the roof of Half Moon House. From there, she had a good viewpoint down into the gardens, and it certainly seemed as if it had gone well and that most people had behaved themselves properly.

The black apple trees had been excited to be involved, but seemed to have worn themselves out, because they'd finally gone still enough for icicles to form along their crooked, dark branches. The footmen had done an excellent job of clearing the supper booths – not so much as a crumb remained, and all the lights had been extinguished, leaving only the pleasant smell of candle smoke and canary-coloured marzipan upon the air.

It was pleasant to have the garden to herself once again and Beatrice enjoyed walking through in the snow-muffled silence. Just her, and the flowers, and the stars. The plant life would, of course, stay where it was, but the animals had all been relocated back to the temporary habitats built for them on the other side of the house.

She paused in the forest of plum trees, recalling the night she had first experienced them. After James had shown her how to create hybrid plants, she had laboured tirelessly to make something new and unique – something that the world, and the Spider Queen herself, had never seen. Finally her hard work paid off and, when she stepped into the purple rain for the first time, she glimpsed another world. In fact it was Rosa's world, for she had seen what her life would have been like had she gone ahead with her marriage to Eustace. She had swapped lives with her friend.

She still shuddered as she recalled the way Raven Hall had sprung up around her like a prison and she had felt at once that she was another person – that this was her home, and had been for years. Too many years. At the back of her mind was the vaguest recollection of how, in the early days, she had tried desperately to keep hold of who she was, clinging to the frayed edges of her identity with bloodied fingertips. But time and suffering had chipped her inner self away bit by bit until nothing remained, and now she was only a husk, with no opinions of her own, no thoughts in her head, save for a cringing horror of the man who slept beside her each night.

Within the purple rain she found herself outside Eustace's study door, her hand raised to knock on it. She was there on some trivial matter, some humdrum house-keeping issue that she needed to get his approval on. And yet, the thought of entering that room filled her with such dread. The door seemed to get darker and more defined, the longer she stared at it, scorching itself into her eyes until it was the only thing that existed in the world. She saw the whorls and knots in the solid oak and they appalled her. In every way it was an unremarkable door, and yet the sight of it made her want to turn and run, and keep on running. But no matter how far she ran, she would only ever find herself back here, in Raven Hall, before this very same door.

A bitter taste flooded her mouth, even worse than the time she'd been so unwise, as a girl, to lick one of the black apple skins. She gagged. She could feel her thinness in the way her bones pressed through her skin. She was completely hollow. If only she had never met Eustace. If only she had never walked down that aisle, knowing full well that she shouldn't. But now all her choices boxed her in and bound her to this cursed house in the heaviest of chains . . .

She took a stumbling step back from the door, but instead of stepping into an empty corridor, her back pressed against something. She turned and saw that there was a tree inside the house. Not one of her beloved apple trees – Eustace had had those chopped down and burned years ago. No, this was a plum tree, impossibly beautiful, filling the corridor with the scent of its amethyst blossoms as its elegant branches grew along the corniced ceiling and its roots pulled up the polished floorboards.

A fat, ripe plum fell to the floor, followed by another, and another. The ceiling peeled away to reveal the outline of a hothouse against a starry night sky. Purple rain fell into the room and snow blew across the floor.

There was a sudden icy gust of air, and the last of the corridor was driven away. Raven Hall dissolved back into the nightmare it had come from, and Beatrice was in the garden laboratory once more.

*I'm so sorry,* she had wanted to say to Rosa when she got into her carriage earlier. *I know what your life is like, and I'm so, so sorry.*

Beatrice was culpable. She felt that in her bones. If she had married Eustace like she was supposed to, then Rosa would be in some other life right now. Beatrice thought it strange, and sad, and a little scary, how every tiny thing one person did – every single choice and act – could ripple out to have an impact on the people around them. And you could never quite know how many people you affected, or in what ways, or how your life might have touched theirs for the worse.

Her heart ached for her friend. Becoming trapped in an unhappy marriage was one of the most desperate and dreadful lots that could befall a woman, precisely because there was no escape, no magical key that would lead to a way out. She wished with all her heart that she had not seen that other life in the plum rain; that she had not seen what kind of a man Eustace was, or the rottenness within Raven Hall. She had always disliked the house. Now she was more convinced than ever that there was something wrong with those old stones. Perhaps it was simply that it had seen so much misery over the years. Either way, Beatrice did not think it possible for anyone to be truly happy there any more.

She turned away from the forest of plum trees now and returned to Half Moon House. As always, she went straight to the painting of the tiger that James had given her. Only it was not a painting of a tiger any more, but a girl alone, gazing across the snow at nothing. The tiger had left the frame months ago.

After Rosa's visit, Beatrice had kept a close eye on the painting. And on several different occasions she had seen the tiger move. It was never by much. His head would be at a slightly different angle, or one great paw would be an inch to the left, or a whisker would catch the moonlight in a slightly different way.

'It looks the same to me,' James had said, when she mentioned it to him.

'He has moved,' Beatrice insisted.

The orchid hunter looked doubtful, but she knew it was true and did not require anyone else to confirm it to her.

And then, one day, the tiger vanished from the frame altogether. Everything else remained the same: the solemn-faced girl in mourning, the black parasol, the snow, the stars, the sparkle of magic between the bare branches of the winter trees. But the tiger was gone, leaving not even a paw print behind. When James next visited Half Moon House with more orchids for the garden, he could hardly believe it, but Beatrice took it in her stride. Such a thing was nothing compared to the wonders she'd seen in the Winter Garden itself.

'But where did the tiger go?' James had asked.

They were in the garden laboratory that he had helped her set up in the grounds. Beatrice finally felt like she was getting somewhere with the plums and did not appreciate the need to make conversation with James just then.

'He's in the house,' she said, not taking her eyes off her work.

Whilst they'd been travelling together she had, somewhere along the way, returned to her old ease in front of James and no longer stammered in front of him at all. It was rather nice, to have one person in the world to whom she could express herself properly.

'But that's extraordinary!' James said. 'You've seen him?'

She glanced up. 'I hear him mostly. He wanders around. At night.'

'But . . . why is he not in the Winter Garden? By all accounts, he's the most important part of it.'

By now James had met another couple of people who claimed to have been to the garden, including Jani, and they had both said the same thing. The tiger was the heart of the garden, but he did not approach anyone. Nobody touched him. Not ever. No one except Beatrice.

'What is it about you that's so different?' James had asked.

But Beatrice had no answer. Now she gazed at the painting and felt frustration tangle up her insides. Even the tiger seemed to have changed towards her. She'd told James the truth about hearing him move around the house. Every night there was the creak of his great paws upon the floorboards, and sometimes she would find a star that had fallen loose, sparkling softly in the dark. But she had not seen him properly since she left the garden, let alone touched him. She seemed to be always just behind him, always just missing him, barely catching the flicker of his shadow as he left the room before her.

She turned away from the painting now and made her way up to the roof to retrieve the flask she'd accidentally left there. It had started to snow again when she stepped outside, and the pale flakes fell all around her as the frosted turrets rose up like the spires of a fairy-tale castle. The coldness of the flask seemed to burn Beatrice's skin more than any flame, and she quickly slipped it into the pocket of her cloak, but not before James walked out behind her, carrying a tray of violet orchids. These flowers required feeding with moonlight rather than water, and so they had created a nursery for them on the rooftop.

Beatrice did not regret asking James and his wife to stay at Half Moon House tonight – it was not as if there weren't plenty of guest rooms – but she wished he would not stick his nose into her affairs. From the look on his face, she had a horrible feeling he was about to do so now.

'Do you think it wise to be indulging in opium so high on an icy rooftop?' he asked.

'Must we do this now?' she asked, suddenly weary. She glanced at him. 'You are here to scold me.'

'I thought I would urge you to reconsider one last time, before I leave.'

Beatrice had told Rosa the truth when she'd said she had no romantic feeling towards James, or anyone else, but they had become close during their travels and she would miss him when he left. He had gone away once before and it was hard not to feel a little hurt that he was doing so again, and more permanently, even though Beatrice knew she had no claim on him in that way.

'Please,' James said quietly. 'Remove the plum trees from the garden.'

She made an impatient noise of dismissal. They had had the conversation – the argument – before and she was tired of it.

'I must show the Spider Queen a wonder she has not seen before.'

'But that's just the problem,' James said. 'Whatever those trees are, they're not a wonder. Beatrice, they were a mistake. We should never have created them—'

'*We* did not create them! I did!'

'All right,' James replied. 'But I showed you how to produce hybrids, so I feel responsible.'

'You regret helping me.'

'I do,' he said quietly. 'Very much.'

Beatrice felt a cold flash of resentment. James had only gone into the plum rain once, and she suspected he had only done so because he did not truly believe what they could do. She had no idea what he had seen, but after that, he had sworn never to go near the trees again.

'I will show the Spider Queen something new,' Beatrice repeated. 'That is how I will win.'

'Look, after tomorrow I don't know when I will see you again,' James began. 'Perhaps never. And I wanted to say something to you privately before I go. Whatever wonders the Winter Garden might have, I'm not sure that any wish could really fix what happened all those years ago with your mother. Some things – some mistakes . . . Well, we just have to live with them, that's all. And there's no shortcut or magical solution that will undo them.'

Beatrice flushed. There were things she had told James during their travels together that she had never told anyone else. Something about being abroad seemed to break down the barriers between them, especially after he came to her aid the night Johnston broke into the hold.

'Thank you for the unsolicited advice.' She turned away from him to look out at the garden. 'I hope you find every happiness in India. Now please. Leave me alone.'

'Very well,' he said quietly. 'I'll speak to you in the morning. But, please – at least think about what I've said.'

Beatrice didn't bother to respond and, at last, she heard the door close as James left the roof. Snowflakes settled on her eyelashes and the cold wind tugged gently at her cloak. James was wrong. He had to be. The Winter Garden could deliver the wish it had promised. And Beatrice was going to win it. She lingered on the roof for a few moments more before returning to her bedroom, where she put the laudanum flask carefully in one of the drawers before undressing for bed.

When she slipped beneath the sheets she tried to summon up some pleasure at the success of her garden's opening night, but her mind was a carousel of worries and regrets; and, finally, she was forced to retrieve the laudanum flask. She knew by now that it was no medicine – that it was, in fact, a vice that did her no good whatsoever. But by the time she had truly appreciated this, it was too late. Her body craved it as it craved air. In winter especially she often could not get through the long nights without it.

The familiar euphoria rushed in soon after taking it, warming her so thoroughly that even the open window was not enough to cool her down. So she took her furs and went back up to the roof where the world was not on fire.

It was cold and still there, and she could finally be comfortable and at ease with herself as she watched the snowflakes turn into winter fairies that danced and spun around her. For a long time it was the most beautiful show, played out across the vast stage of the night sky, with icy stars for spotlights and the flowers below for an audience. At one point she was sure she even saw the rippling icy glitter of the tiger walking between the turrets.

But then the fairies vanished, frightened away by the white ravens that appeared in their place, vicious creatures with gleaming red eyes full of hatred, and Beatrice knew that Rosa had sent them. She tried to shoo the birds away as they swooped at her, but her arms were like lead, her entire body refusing to obey her commands. When the birds realised she couldn't move, they flocked about her on the freezing roof. Beatrice tried to shout for help, but her voice was a wisp with no power in it at all, and who would come to her aid anyway? She had made all the wrong choices in her life, each stemming from that one dreadful act of cowardice when she'd been summoned to her mother's deathbed. And if there was no one to help her now, then it was no more than she deserved.

Still, she wept as the white ravens tore pieces of flesh from her legs, gobbling them down like starving creatures until the bones had been picked entirely clean and she was a skeleton from the waist down, never to walk or run or dance again. And perhaps never to see again, either, as the birds started on her eyes next, digging their sharp beaks into the jellied softness, knowing she could not lift a finger to stop them.

Then the door to the roof opened and James was there, and Beatrice realised that one of her eyes at least must be mostly intact because she could see the angry expression on his face: the way his mouth was a hard, thin line and his eyes were shards of flint. She supposed he had returned to berate her – about the plum trees, or Rosa, or the wish – and she tried to speak, to beg him not to do so when she was feeling so sad about the loss of her legs, but her lips were sealed together. Perhaps blood from her eyes had trickled down there and frozen. All of a sudden she realised how very cold it was.

The white ravens scattered as James walked through them. He dropped down by her side to gather her up in his arms.

'Curse that imbecile doctor,' he muttered. 'I wish I could take a strap to him.'

She wanted to tell him about the ravens, but the words simply wouldn't come. Her entire body trembled with the shock of seeing her legs eaten away and she could only whimper for the hideousness of the loss.

James straightened up and walked towards the door.

'It's all right, Beatrice.' His voice was gentle. 'We will soon have you warm. All will be well.'

# CHAPTER TWENTY-EIGHT

Rosa's mind was still full of Beatrice's winter garden as her maid dressed her the next morning. Much to her irritation, her dreams had been full of enchanting images all night long, almost as wondrous as those long-ago childhood visions of snowflakes and sugarplums on Christmas Eve. She'd slept in later than she'd meant to, after getting home in the early hours, and so she took her breakfast quickly, eager to get to her workshop as soon as possible. But first she went upstairs to see Ada, as she did every morning.

She walked into the day-nursery, only to find the room empty. Not only was Ada not there, but both this room and the night-nursery had been stripped bare. The toys and books were gone, the wardrobe stood empty, the crib's sheets had been removed. The empty cot reminded Rosa of that dreadful day eleven months ago when they'd returned from abroad without Esme. She felt the shock like a punch and reeled back straight into Hannah, the nanny.

'What is the meaning of this?' Rosa demanded. 'Where is Ada?'

Her heart clenched in the sickening fear that Hannah would say her daughter had died in the night but, instead, the woman looked confused and said, 'Why, she's gone to stay with her grandmother, your grace. As you instructed.'

'As *I* instructed? I did no such thing! When did this happen? How?'

'One of her grace's servants collected her first thing this morning,' Hannah said. 'I packed up her things to be sent on, like you asked.'

'I did *not* ask you to do that!' Rosa exclaimed.

Hannah frowned. 'But . . . the duke passed on your instructions himself—' she began.

Rosa didn't wait to hear any more, but stormed down the stairs to Eustace's study, which she entered without knocking. He sat in an armchair, perusing the morning paper.

'How dare you send our daughter away without consulting me?' she demanded.

Eustace put down the paper with dreadful calm. 'You left me no choice,' he said. 'You heard what the doctor said yesterday. It is for your own good.'

Rosa silently cursed herself for not programming the ravens to act to prevent such an occurrence.

'I will not stand for it,' she said. 'I will fetch her home at once. Today.'

'You will not,' Eustace said quietly. 'Mother has kindly agreed to take Ada on holiday for a spell – to a location that we have agreed shall not be made known to you. There are going to be some changes around here, Rosa.' He leaned down to open one of his desk drawers, drew out a piece of paper and held it out to her.

'What is that?' she asked.

'Read it,' he said. 'It is a copy of the letter I sent last night to be held by my solicitor, with instructions that it should only be opened if something were to happen to me.'

Rosa took the letter from him and scanned down it, trying to make sense of the words, which seemed to shift like serpents across the page:

*To whom it may concern,*

*In the event of my death, or any debilitating injury, I would like to plead mercy for my wife. In every way, Rosa is sweet, loving, attentive and an utterly devoted mother.*

*I remain hopeful that, with patience and time, she can be returned to full health, and I take full responsibility for disregarding Dr Livingstone's recommendation and allowing Rosa to remain at Raven Hall. The fault is mine alone.*

*The doctor will attest to the fact that her mind became fragile after the birth of our twins and was put under further strain when one of our daughters passed away unexpectedly. If it makes her life easier to bear to blame me for this tragedy, then I am happy to accept her condemnation. Should her grief at what happened take a more violent turn, then I would like the authorities to know that I categorically do not want any action to be brought against her.*

*Furthermore, I am confident that our daughter, Ada, is not at risk in any way. It is true that some of Rosa's clockwork creatures have exhibited worrying tendencies in the past, but so long as my wife is not permitted any access to the workshops, I have every confidence that she will be a safe and suitable mother and that Ada should not be removed from her care.*

*Eustace Hamilton*
*Twelfth Duke of Chalkley*

Rosa's hand trembled upon the page. 'This . . .' She was so furious that the words stuck in her throat like burs. 'How dare you! This is a monstrous falsehood!'

'It is hardly that, madam,' Eustace said. 'Have you not tormented me with those wretched birds for months now? Have you not threatened to have them peck out my eyes? Truly it is you who has the dark soul, not I. Exactly which part of my letter is false?'

'You have left out the most pertinent details!' Rosa cried. 'You have not mentioned the fact that I would never have raised a hand to you, had you not struck me a hundred times first.'

'I have asked the authorities to treat you mercifully.'

'Knowing full well that they could not possibly accommodate your request! The very point of asking was merely to point an accusing finger at me.'

'Well, I am sorry you see it that way. I am only trying to help you. That is all I have ever attempted to do. If you believe otherwise, it is only because your own mind is so corrupted and warped.'

'You are despicable!'

What a fool she had been to think she had the situation under control. Instead she had played right into Eustace's hands. Hundreds of people had witnessed her clockwork boar destroy the pleasure garden last year, and a few guests had incurred injuries. Very minor ones, but injuries nonetheless. And she expected that she had made an enemy for life of Dr Livingstone, whose testimony would be the most damning of all against her.

She felt the doors slamming closed, the dirty chains winding tighter, the great padlocks clicking quietly shut as the key was tossed into the ocean, to be swallowed by the waves and snatched away by the skeletal hands of all those who had drowned before her. She could almost feel all the painted duchesses in their gallery upstairs, shaking their heads sorrowfully for her. It seemed she had misplayed her hand.

Her life seemed to stretch endlessly ahead, and it wasn't the one she had planned or chosen. It was a grim existence behind bars, whilst Ada grew up without her, twisted and moulded by the likes of Eustace and Margaret, taught to believe that her mother was unhinged, that she didn't love her, that she'd abandoned her.

Rosa looked at the ravens. A few had followed her into the room and more came down the chimney in a shower of soot. In that moment she longed to set the birds upon her husband, to have them tear chunks from his flesh until he begged her for mercy and vowed on his knees that he would never challenge her authority again.

'I know what you're thinking,' he said quietly. 'And I would think again, if I were you. If those birds attack me now, then that letter will be opened, and I imagine you are correct when you suggest that my pleas for mercy on your behalf would be ignored. It would be a shame if you were forced to spend your days within the walls of some filthy asylum, although I admit it has crossed my mind that perhaps a brief stay in such a place might make you a little more appreciative of all the many riches you are fortunate enough to enjoy here with me.'

He stood up and Rosa forced herself not to step back as he approached her. His eyes were hard, his mouth a flat line of dislike.

'I regret to say that you are dreadfully spoiled, my dear,' he said. 'Your parents were far too lenient with you, and God knows Americans have some strange ways, but that will be tolerated here no longer. I have provided you with money, a title, an extraordinary mansion and an enviable position in society, yet still you refuse to behave properly, and only complain incessantly about what you do not have. What a wretched creature you are.'

Rosa took a deep breath. There were dark birds of rage trapped within her, desperate to get out and rip Eustace apart, but she knew she must control them. She could not allow things to spin out of control. Eustace blew as red hot as she did herself, and if either of them lost control in this moment, then they'd be racing together down a dark tunnel from which there could be no turning back.

'What do you want, Eustace?' she asked.

'You know full well what I want,' he replied. 'An heir.'

'That is never going to happen.'

'Then Ada stays where she is,' he snapped. 'And we'll see which of us breaks first.'

'If you try to do battle with me on this,' Rosa said, 'One way or another, you will lose.'

Eustace slowly smiled. 'I do not see how,' he replied, 'when I hold all the cards.'

*Not all of them,* she thought silently. *Not quite.*

She still had the Winter Garden. The competition. And the chance of winning a wish. At one time she had hoped to use it to fix whatever was wrong with Eustace. Then she had hoped to bring Esme back. But now her thoughts went to Ada. She found herself blinking rapidly. Surely the world would not be so cruel as to force her to choose between her daughters? She would not think about it. Not now. All that mattered was that a wish was up for grabs and, however she used it in the end, it must surely go some way to putting right the many things that had gone so wrong in her life. And if a wish could not do so, then surely nothing in the world could.

'I do not have time to talk nonsense with you,' Rosa said. 'I have work to do on the garden.'

She turned and left, but not to her workshop. Instead she called for her carriage and went directly to Margaret's home in London. She had at least to try and see her daughter, but in the end the two-hour journey was fruitless. The duchess was not there, nor was Ada. The footman said he could not possibly pass on the precise details of her whereabouts without the duchess's permission.

Despite Rosa's best efforts, he would say nothing further, so she returned to her carriage, sick with frustration. Even if she'd found Ada there and taken her home, what then? She could not keep the child with her all the time, could not watch her every hour of the day and night. Eustace would eventually find an opportunity to snatch Ada away again, and could pay a servant to hide her somewhere

– anywhere. Indeed, even now she might not be in the country at all.

Still, Rosa did not trust Margaret with her daughter. She did not trust her to take care of her properly, or to treat her kindly, or to cherish her. Ada would not understand where Rosa had gone or why she did not come when she cried for her. Duchess Margaret had made her thoughts on crying babies known several times during previous visits.

'It does them no good at all to rush to their side every time they whimper,' she'd said. 'Children ought not to be mollycoddled. They must learn to be self-sufficient. And if they cry and carry on, then they must be punished. Spare the rod, I always say.'

The thought of anyone striking Ada and then leaving her to sob alone in a chilly, darkened room rose up like a spectre in Rosa's mind. The image was a hundred pairs of icy hands clutching and squeezing at her insides, poking frozen fingertips down deep into her soul. She gritted her teeth, gave the order to return home and climbed up into the carriage.

It was dark by the time she returned to Raven Hall. She refused offers of food and refreshments from the servants and went straight to her dressing room, where her thoughts turned to the clockwork pigeon. As she had told Beatrice, if the bird was given a letter, it could deliver it to a recipient wherever in the world they happened to be.

Yet it would not help now. Ada wasn't old enough to read a letter, far less write one back to Rosa to tell her where she was. It was hopeless.

Instead Rosa took out the pop-up book. When her garden opened, it would have a magnificent carousel but, in spite of all her efforts, it was not quite the carousel from the book. She went through the pages again now, turning them slowly in the hope that some previously overlooked detail might jump out at her, or an entirely new page rise up to shed light on her dilemma. But the book had shared no new secrets since the invitation.

She had even given up looking for the strange, sad little boy with the withered arm. She had not seen him since that night in the nursery, and Eustace's conversation with Mrs Wright had proved futile. She was adamant there were no children at Raven Hall.

Finally Rosa put the book away. It was late, but she could not sit in her room doing nothing, so she took the ravens with her and went down to her workshop in the aviary. A team of artificers from her father's company had worked tirelessly alongside her for the last three months and it had been pleasant having them there, almost like old times. But now they'd all returned to the States, leaving Rosa alone once again.

She sat down at her workbench and tried to push the events of the day, and her worries about Ada, out of her mind. They would not serve her now, and so she must tidy them away into a grim little box, lock it up tight and bury it down deep. There were plenty of other matters to concern herself with, not least how she might lure guests back to the gardens of Raven Hall. People knew that one of her clockwork animals had gone berserk last time, that people had been hurt and property destroyed. And then, to crown it all, the house had become overrun with clockwork ravens, and a baby had died, and people feared the mechanical bird that guarded her grave.

*The unlucky duchess.* Rosa knew that was what people called her, and she'd never cared before, but now she needed them to come to her pleasure garden. It didn't matter how extraordinary and wonderful it was, the Spider Queen was hardly going to award the prize to gardens that no one attended. Rosa knew she had to find a way to entice people back.

She simply needed to focus, even if dragging her thoughts from Ada tore bleeding strips from the inside of her mind. There was clockwork to be prepared, inventions to be inspected and improved, and invitations to be designed and sent.

She picked up her tools and began.

# CHAPTER
# TWENTY-NINE

What a relief it had been upon that first morning for Beatrice to wake up and realise she still had her legs and her eyes after all. Swiftly followed by the agonising shame of realising that James had witnessed her at her lowest ebb, and not for the first time. It had been impossible to hide her opium use from him whilst they were abroad, and in the end Beatrice had given up trying.

'You cannot go on like this. You're aware of that, I suppose?' he asked at breakfast after Jani had left the table.

Beatrice knew well enough that he was correct, but she had not the least comprehension as to how she might go about setting her life on a different course. That dark angel still dogged her steps, trying to curve its great wet wing about her shoulders, and the opium was the only thing that kept it at bay, if only for a short while. She so dreaded the angel that she would rather have the opium nightmares, even if it meant white ravens feasting upon her legs while she watched, powerless to stop them, or dead monkeys reaching for her with their rotting fingertips.

'What would have happened if I hadn't been there?' James went on.

'Why *were* you?'

'I couldn't sleep, so I thought to check on the orchids. How will you manage in this house by yourself?'

'The laudanum helps me to unwind,' she said.

'It will help you straight into an early grave,' James replied.

'Whatever lines may have blurred between us abroad,' she said in an icy tone, 'I'm still your employer. I'll thank you to remember that and keep your impertinent remarks to yourself.'

James stared at her for such a long moment that Beatrice felt a prickle of shame creep over her skin. She was well aware that this was a poor way of repaying the service he had done her last night, one for which she had not uttered so much as a word of thanks. To say nothing of how he had helped her with the garden. And even been a friend in her lonely childhood and awkward adulthood. So many debts that she could not repay.

'As always, Lady Beatrice, you make your feelings perfectly clear. I am sorry to be such a bother to you.' James rose to his feet, tucked his paper under his arm and walked towards the door, where he paused. 'You ought to know, however, that it is no use being so prickly with me, since nothing you say will convince me that we are not extremely good friends.'

Beatrice was glad to hear him say so. He was departing for India later that day and she knew she could not leave things this way.

'Wait,' she said quietly when he was almost at the door. He paused and turned back.

'I want to thank you. For looking after the trees. And me. Whilst we were away.'

'I enjoyed every moment.'

'So did I,' she admitted. 'You are one of the finest men I have known. And I will always be grateful. For your many kindnesses.'

James looked at her, surprised. She had never spoken to him in such a way before, afraid that acknowledging she had needed his help might make her seem weak in some way. Yet in this moment she knew it was the right thing to do – the words made her feel strong rather than weak, and she was glad she had not left such important things unsaid.

James offered her a bow. 'The honour has been all mine,' he said. 'I hope you win that wish.'

'You said once you thought I deserved a wish more than anyone you knew,' Beatrice said.

'I remember.'

'What did you mean by that?'

It was a question that had niggled away at her ever since, like a worm in a piece of rotting wood. She worried that James pitied her, and the idea was curiously unbearable.

'I suppose what I meant is that some people are born out of place in the world. I ought to know, as I'm one of them myself. If you and I had lived in a different place – or perhaps a different time – then perhaps the world would have suited us a little better. It's a hard thing, and unfair.' He shrugged slightly. 'It only seemed to me that a wish might go some way towards rectifying that.'

Beatrice nodded. He was right, of course, and she was glad that he had not spoken out of pity – that he thought it was the world that was at fault, rather than her.

Later that day he and Jani left for India and then she was truly alone at Half Moon House.

As the week progressed, it seemed that every night was a triumph for the garden. The staff reported that one or two more guests had had to be removed for breaking the rules, but word seemed to have got round about that; and, once people realised she was completely in earnest, no further rules were broken. Due to the garden's limited capacity and opening hours, there were not enough tickets for everyone who wanted one as it was, and nobody was prepared to risk squandering their chance to see the winter wonderland about which they'd heard such extraordinary tales.

A week after opening night Beatrice was relaxing in the Winter Smoking Room. It was one of her favourite rooms, with its white marble and the handsome drinking cabinet. Most of all, she adored the stained-glass windows. They depicted a host of seasonal birds, from red-breasted robins and clever nuthatches, to tiny goldcrests and pretty bramblings, gorgeous in their winter plumage.

Beatrice had settled herself in a window seat, with Wilkie at her heels, and passed the hours by turning the creamy pages of one of her sketchbooks, admiring all the many non-magical mushrooms she'd seen over the years. To her, they were just as wonderful as their more spectacular brethren on show in the garden, but she knew people weren't interested in paying to see these types. So she admired them alone, drinking in the jelly ears and the scarlet elf caps, the blushing wood mushrooms, amethyst deceivers and shaggy parasols. She was just about to ring for tea when a footman entered bearing a silver tray. On it was a small golden box, beautifully wrapped in scarlet ribbons.

'A messenger brought this, your ladyship,' the footman said. 'From Raven Hall.'

Once the servant withdrew, she turned her attention to the parcel in her hands. It was, indeed, from Raven Hall, as evidenced by the tiny black raven painted on the corner of the lid. Beatrice tugged the ribbons free and removed the lid from the box. Inside was a nest of tissue paper, from which glowed a pair of tiny eyes, red as rubies. The next moment a clockwork bird erupted from the box in an explosion of crimson-and-gold sparkles, like a miniature firework. It held a tiny scroll in its beak, which it dropped in Beatrice's lap before spreading its magnificent wings and flying several times around the room.

Eventually it landed back on the wooden armrest of Beatrice's couch and looked up at her, cocking its head expectantly. She couldn't tear her eyes from it. It was quite the most beautiful creature, with a golden framework, a fiery crest upon its head and brilliant feathers adorned with an array of sparkling rubies and garnets.

'But what can you be?' Beatrice wondered, peering down at the bird.

Certainly it was like no creature found in England – the robins and nuthatches in the stained-glass window looked dull in comparison. Yet there was something about it that was familiar, although Beatrice couldn't think where she might have seen such a creature. She was still racking her brain when suddenly the golden bird spread its wings once again, only this time it didn't take flight, but froze motionless, as if it were an ordinary ornament.

Beatrice marvelled at the sleek tips of its golden wings, each feather edged in dazzling scarlet. She assumed the clockwork mechanism had wound down, and was about to turn her attention to the scroll when, without warning, the little bird burst into flames. Beatrice cried out and leapt to her feet, stumbling back a few steps.

The flames looked white-hot, with a blazing blue heart, but they lasted only a moment or two before dying out completely. The bird had vanished, leaving a small, smoking egg in its place. Beatrice reached out to grab it, then paused, fearing it might burn her. Very carefully she touched it with the tip of her finger. It was not at all hot; in fact it was cool to the touch. She picked it up and saw that there were no scorch marks left behind on the wooden arm of the sofa. The fire had been a clever illusion.

As she held the egg carefully in her fingers, it cracked, and she could make out the small shape of a clockwork baby bird inside. The next moment it began to wriggle, poking its little beak through the top of the shell and squirming its scruffy body free. Beatrice stared down at the golden chick. It strutted up and down on her palm for a moment, before leaning down towards the shell pieces and gobbling them up as if they were seed.

'A phoenix,' Beatrice breathed.

She'd seen the birds depicted in artworks during her time in China and Japan. The mythical creature was said to rise from the ashes of its own destruction in a never-ending loop. So far as she knew, they did not exist anywhere in the world for real.

'Extraordinary,' she said, carefully setting the baby bird down on a side table where it continued to wander up and down, taking a few experimental jumps to flutter its tiny wings.

Beatrice felt a glow of admiration for her friend as she finally opened the scroll and an invitation unfolded before her eyes:

*The Duchess of Chalkley is delighted to invite you to the newly reopened Fire Gardens at Raven Hall.*
*Expect the unexpected, where nothing is quite what it seems.*

*And be prepared for:*
*Fantastic clockwork creations*
*Explosive fireworks*
*Cunning illusions*
*A pinch of danger*
*And only the very best champagne.*

*(Note: Not for the faint of heart or timid of disposition.)*

At the bottom of the page the house's address was printed, along with the date and time of the garden's opening night. It appeared it would open its doors in one week's time, from 7 p.m. to 4 a.m.

Beatrice smiled slightly. How clever her friend was. She must have realised that people would still be nervous about Raven Hall's gardens after what had happened last time, and rather than uselessly seeking to assuage such fears, she had turned them to her advantage. There was, after all, nothing that people – and especially those from the upper classes – secretly loved more than to be shocked and scandalised by a spectacle. It was the only thing better than being delighted and enchanted. Certainly freak shows and séance parties never seemed to lose their appeal. The fascination of terror was a strong pull indeed.

Still, Beatrice did not think it possible that Rosa would pose a challenge to her own garden. Her friend might be a master artificer, but the things she made were not alive or magical or real – they were artificial inventions made from cogs and clockwork. She had not spent more than two years travelling in search of all the most wondrous plants and animals the world had to offer.

Feeling a sudden thirst for the company of her magical plants and animals, Beatrice fetched her cloak, called Wilkie to her heels and walked out into the crisp, cold air. She could see the occasional tiny footprint left in the snow by fairies, the golden toads shone even brighter in the winter sunshine, and gigantic butterflies perched on the crooked branches of the apple trees, their extraordinary wings spread to soak up the warmth. Without ever setting eyes on Rosa's garden, Beatrice felt absolutely certain that hers must be superior in every way.

# CHAPTER THIRTY

*December 1838*

Beatrice fastened the velvet ribbons of her bonnet beneath her chin. The clockwork phoenix and the peacock that Rosa had made for her wedding gift had formed a friendship, and she had to shift them to one side to get to her velvet gloves on the dressing table. Over the last week the baby phoenix had grown bigger and bigger until it was the same size as the peacock. Beatrice expected it would probably burst into flames and start the process anew again, any day now.

She'd decided to go to Rosa's garden as soon as it opened. That should give her time to see everything and still be back at Half Moon House before her own garden was occupied. Although she never ventured amongst the guests, she kept careful watch over things from the roof, and wouldn't dream of not being physically present on the property whenever her specimens were being viewed.

It was another cold, clear evening, and Beatrice was glad of her winter furs as her driver handed her up into the waiting carriage. They reached Raven Hall shortly after seven o'clock, and there must have been more than a hundred carriages lined up on the drive already. Beatrice recognised many of the families from the crests painted on the doors, and realised some of them had come from miles away.

She was pleased for Rosa but, at the same time, shrank from being forced to mingle with such a large number of people. Nevertheless she climbed down from her carriage and walked with them towards the garden's wrought-iron entrance gates. They were guarded on each side by a six-foot-tall suit of armour. Each gripped a flaming torch in one gauntleted hand, as if they were guarding the entrance to a dungeon rather than a pleasure garden. The suit on the left held a tangle of pocket watches dangling from their chains, all showing different times, their ticks and tocks out of sync with one another. The suit on the right held, strangely, a silver platter piled high with fans. A card invited people to help themselves.

The female guests were doing so as they walked through the gate, chattering and laughing with their companions. Already the gardens were far noisier than Beatrice's. She could hear the strains of an orchestra mingled with the excited exclamations of guests. The air smelled of engine oil and bonfire smoke.

During the next lull in the crowd, Beatrice made to walk through the gates, but as she approached a suit of armour, she noticed it wasn't empty, as she'd assumed. Eyes glittered out at her through the visor, making Beatrice jump.

'A fan, my lady?' a muffled voice came through the helmet.

'In this w-weather?' Beatrice asked, recovering herself.

The suit of armour held out the platter of fans a little closer to her.

'Beyond these gates,' he said, 'nothing is what it seems.'

'How m-mysterious.'

Beatrice selected a fan and opened it up to reveal a beautiful red silk design held on ivory sticks and trimmed in cream lace.

'Thank y-you,' Beatrice said, before walking through into the garden.

She showed her ticket and then followed the marked path curving round to the back of the house. The noise and music got louder with each step, and when at last the guests turned the corner and found themselves on the veranda of Raven Hall, the grounds spread beneath them like a picture book. Unlike the maze of her own gardens, which only revealed themselves one small piece at a time, Rosa's garden was all on display at once, and the effect was dizzying, making it every bit as impossible to take in.

Rosa hadn't called them Fire Gardens for nothing. Vibrant flames seemed to dazzle out of every corner, so bright that they left white imprints on her eyes whenever she turned her head, and somehow they only served to deepen the dancing shadows at the outskirts. But the sight that immediately arrested Beatrice's attention was the dozens of miniature hot-air balloons suspended in the night sky above them.

One floated close by where she stood on the veranda, and Beatrice saw that the balloon was powered by a mechanical jet that blasted a tiny flame into it at intervals. It was intricately painted with English flowers, and the basket was only large enough to hold a single clockwork fairy. She was dressed in a velvet ballgown and held a tiny violin in her hands. Music poured from the balloon, getting louder as it approached them and softening as it floated away.

Beatrice looked up at the other balloons and realised they held an entire orchestra of clockwork fairies, each playing a different instrument. The fact that they kept moving about created an undulating tone to the music, which spilled out over the garden in waves.

There was no snow left on the lawn, having all melted away beneath the force of the flames. Perhaps Beatrice would need that fan after all. It was already clear that Rosa's garden was to be no fairyland. Everything was fire and clockwork, with not a single pretty butterfly or frosted flower in sight. Even the music from the floating orchestra was more surreal than beautiful. Beatrice didn't recognise any of the compositions she heard. Either these scores were by some obscure composer that she was unfamiliar with or they were entirely new.

She walked down the steps, her cloak dragging along the frozen stones. She took the first path she came across and quickly learned that Rosa's garden was full of mechanical marvels, from clockwork mermaids in the fountains to a miniature steam train that slowly wound its way along the grass on a special track. It proved to be one of the most popular attractions in the garden, thanks to the fact that each carriage carried a selection of champagne saucers, all filled to the brim with sparkling golden bubbles. Guests laughed in delight as they reached down to help themselves.

Occasionally some careless person would stand in the train's way, causing it to hoot out an indignant blast on its whistle. Even when it was blocked by skirts and trousers, it was possible to mark the train's progress by the small puffs of smoke drifting up from its funnel.

And there were dozens of clocks. Within a glittering maze of mirrors Beatrice found a wall of skeleton clocks with their innards exposed, pale and smooth as bone. Guests were invited to wind them and, when they did so, their double in the mirror aged before their eyes. It was both horrible and fascinating, and it did not stop until only the bones of a grinning skeleton stared back from behind the glass.

Beatrice hurried out of the hall of mirrors as quickly as she could. Next were the impossible clocks, which drifted through the air like snowflakes and had a most startling effect every time they chimed out the quarter-hour. Anyone who happened to be touching the clock when it chimed would be able, for a brief time, to see the garden as it had once been. Some saw it looking as it had only a year or so ago, others saw the fateful night when the clockwork boar had run amok, whilst a few even saw garden parties from a hundred years past.

And, of course, there were animals, all made from clockwork. Rosa had rebuilt her peacocks, which strutted through the grounds shedding their sparkling sapphire light over everything. Beatrice spent some time watching a fire magician perform various tricks, to the delight of the watching crowd, along with a couple of fire acrobats performing stunts on stilts whilst balancing precariously atop a tightrope strung between two trees.

Beatrice felt a little anxious watching them. She'd seen more than one performer suffer an accident at Vauxhall. It was easy to get distracted by the flashing lights of fireworks or the noise of the crowd. It was one of the reasons she'd never even considered hiring human performers for her own garden. In her opinion, the plants and flowers ought to be more than enough, but she suddenly worried that people might find her quiet candlelit grounds a little dull compared to all this fire and dazzling showmanship.

The heat from the magician and acrobats was overpowering and she took out her fan. But it seemed that this was all part of the act too. As soon as she opened it, the ivory sticks folded back to reveal clockwork innards. There were exclamations of delight all around as the fans folded over and over again, rearranging themselves until they were no longer fans at all, but birds with bright-red plumage. They flew from the ladies' hands to join the magician, forming part of his next act as they cartwheeled through the sky, releasing miniature fireworks that filled the air above their heads with glowing red stars.

By far the most impressive fire act, though, was the clockwork dragon. About the size of a large dog, it was covered in metallic red scales that glinted and gleamed in the torchlight as the dragon blew out plumes of fire so fiercely hot that it could even set fire to ice. It was a spectacular display, and yet when Beatrice looked into the dragon's glowing emerald eyes, she felt only a strange chill of dread, slithering beneath her skin.

She turned away from the fire shows and continued on into the garden. Just when she thought it was impossible to cram any more delights into the space, she found the crowning glory at the heart of the garden. Rosa had created an entire frost fair on the frozen surface of her lake.

# CHAPTER THIRTY-ONE

Beatrice was not old enough to remember the great frost fairs of years gone by in London, but as a child her mother had told her wonderful tales of them. How the Thames used to freeze solid and they would have a carnival on the ice, with all kinds of shops and stalls and entertainments. There would be drinking, and dancing, and dining, and playing nine-pins, and roasting oxen over a great open fire, the flames of which would leap even more joyously than the visitors.

The Thames had not frozen like that for some years, and frost fairs were a thing of the past now. Some said they would never come again. But Rosa had re-created a little slice of that forgotten world upon her lake. Beatrice tied on a pair of skates before venturing onto the ice.

There were stalls selling goblets of mulled wine, roasted chestnuts piping hot in their crinkled paper bags, juicy oranges begging to be unpeeled and eaten without delay, trays of Turkish delight cut into soft, sugared squares and the most extraordinary range of gingerbread houses, from tiny woodcutter cottages to entire fairy-tale castles. The air was filled with the scent of orange peel and Christmas spices.

Rosa had also put on a clockwork-pets stall that included every type of animal imaginable, from dainty poodles to miniature lions. Beatrice saw more than one fur-wrapped lady skating around the fair with a clockwork monkey perched upon her shoulder or a metallic mink poking its snout from the fur cuff of her sleeve.

But the clockwork did not stop at miniature pets for fashionable ladies. Also to be found on the ice were life-sized clockwork reindeer pulling sleighs festooned with silver bells and piled high with furs and blankets. Delighted passengers took the sleighs in tours that swept all the way around the perimeter of the lake.

And Rosa presided over it all from a magnificent sleigh at the edge of the ice. It glittered golden in the light from the flaming torches and, unlike the other sleighs on the lake, it was not pulled by reindeer, but by a great clock-work bear. It was a huge beast – the largest of its kind that Beatrice had yet seen. A small crowd of guests had formed around the sleigh, and Rosa looked animated as she chatted with them effortlessly. Beneath her velvet winter cloak sparkled a gown trimmed in gold lace. Seated beside her, Eustace looked washed out and pale, as if he'd been unwell.

The air was filled with chatter, and laughter, and the swoosh of skates on ice, and the clinking of silver cups and the otherworldly music from the fairy balloons. But there was something else weaving underneath it all, too – something delicate, and sad, and wondrously, hopelessly special.

Finally Beatrice found herself in the very centre of the lake where, for a long while, she only stopped and stared. The supper booths had been built right upon the ice in a circle and several guests sat at them now, partaking of roast dinners brought out by sure-footed skating waiters. The seating was plush with reindeer furs and velvet cushions, and saucers of champagne that seemed to sparkle more than the stars themselves.

And at the centre of the lake was an extraordinary carousel, dripping in icicles. Beatrice immediately recalled the day Rosa had asked her whether she'd ever seen a carousel in the Winter Garden. Although Beatrice never had, she thought this looked exactly like the kind of wondrous thing one might find there. It was impossibly beautiful, with its twists of ice glittering in the torchlight. And the horses! They were more than clockwork, somehow. It seemed to Beatrice that they surely had souls. There was too much life in their eyes, too much joyfulness in their prances, too much alertness in their twitching ears. Surely they would step right off the carousel at any moment and trot into the frosted dark walk through the Scots pines.

It was beautiful indeed, but Beatrice was surprised by the size of the queue. Guests formed a line so long that it wound halfway around the lake. But then she overheard some of the chatter from the people waiting. She frowned, thinking she must have misunderstood – or that the guests had – but then she skated over to one of the signs that people had gathered excitedly around:

*The Carousel of Icicles*
*Can take you back*
*To any memory*
*You would care to relive*
*Every detail*
*Every moment*
*Just as it was.*

Beatrice felt her breath catch in her throat. Could such a thing be possible? And if you *could* go back, then could you change what had happened previously? She heard another guest nearby express the same thought, but the footman positioned beside the sign shook his head.

'Nothing can be changed,' he said. 'Whatever memory you choose, everything will be exactly as it was.'

'H-H-How—' Beatrice tried to force out a question, but the words stuck in her throat.

'How does it work?' a gentleman said over her.

'When you take your seat on the horse, you think of the memory you'd most like to revisit and the horse will take you there. If you haven't thought of anything before the music starts, then the horse will choose a moment for you. Whatever it believes will bring you joy.'

'Are the horses *alive* then?' a nearby woman asked. 'I thought they were clockwork?'

'You will have to judge that for yourself, madam.'

Beatrice looked at the size of the queue. There must have been a hundred people waiting, but there were at least twenty horses on the carousel and each ride seemed to last only two or three minutes. It would not take long to have a turn, although she sensed that people would have waited for hours on the frozen lake, if that was what it took. She felt her heart sink. If the Carousel of Icicles really did what Rosa claimed it could do, then Beatrice's plum trees must surely lose some of their wonder in comparison. What could the other lives you might have lived matter, when compared with the chance to return to a cherished memory from *this* life? One you had thought gone forever. Why, if it worked, then Beatrice would be able to see her mother again!

The yearning was so fierce that it seemed almost impossible to stand in the line and wait. When Beatrice joined the back of the queue, she felt the great urge to push her way to the front, quite certain that her wish to revisit the past must be far more urgent than anyone else's. But all around her she could hear the other guests discussing which moment they would return to. Their wedding day, or a precious childhood memory, or a meeting with a lost loved one – a parent, or a sibling, or a spouse. It seemed that everyone, no matter their age or position or how much unhappiness they had experienced, had had some past moment of joy that they longed to experience again.

And so as Beatrice got closer to the front of the queue, she felt a curious mixture of hope and dread. She wanted so desperately to see her mother, but she knew it would be very bad for her own chances of winning the competition if she was able to do so. In addition, she found it almost impossible to choose a particular moment to return to. There were so many good times before her mother became ill, and it seemed too hard to pick one at the expense of losing all the rest.

Soon enough it was Beatrice's turn to board the carousel. She sat down on the benches provided to swap her skates for riding boots made of ivory leather, and then climbed up onto the platform. Guests hurried towards their horses, jostling each other in their eagerness to claim their preferred steed. Beatrice quickly picked her own horse and climbed onto its back. Up close, it was even more impressive, and so very lifelike that she expected to feel it shift beneath her or let out its breath in a snort, as a real horse would.

The music began to play and the carousel slowly started to revolve. Beatrice gripped the white leather reins tightly through her gloves. She had not settled on a particular moment that she wished to relive and so had surrendered herself to the horse choosing one for her. She saw the frost fair spin and twirl around her: the guests in their fur-coated finery, the crackle and spit of the roasted-chestnut stand, the dazzle and sparkle of the clockwork pets, the jingle of frozen bells on sleighs pulled by clock-work reindeer. The carousel seemed to go much faster than it had looked from the ground. All the fire and light of the fair merged into one golden swirl. For a moment Beatrice thought it wasn't going to work, that it was just an ordinary carousel after all. Relief and dismay battled for first place inside her chest.

But then the fair melted away, and so did the horse, and the snow, and the ice and stars. It was gloriously warm and the air smelled of flowers and summer. Beatrice wore her favourite blue dress and held her mother's hand as she peered down into the depths of the wishing well.

'What did you wish for, Beatrice?'

She looked up at her mother, impossibly lovely and alive beside her. It was all just as it had been – every blade of grass underfoot, the moss on the crooked wishing well's weathered stones, the lazy drone of a passing bumblebee. And yet . . . without the patina of nostalgia, the real-life moment was different from the soft memory. The colours were brighter; the edges were sharper. There was a splinter wedged beneath Beatrice's nail that she had forgotten about. It was too hot to be comfortable, and sweat prickled her skin and made her dress stick to her. She felt that frustrated sense of restlessness that came with stifling summers. As an adult she had remembered only the idyllic parts, but the imperfections were somehow pleasant to her now too. They filled in the gaps of the picture and made this time real once again.

Beatrice felt like a passenger inside her own head. Her adult self wept with the joy of seeing her mother, but at the same time she was somehow still only a child, and this was just a day like any other; and she believed now, just as she had then, that this would go on forever. It would always be summer and her mother would always be right here with her, holding her hand. The alternative was unthinkable. And so the precious moment did not seem so very precious at the time. It was just the way things were.

Beatrice had fully intended to test what the footman had said and see if she could at least try to change what had happened, just to see if it was possible, but her child self leaned forward to peer into the cool darkness of the well, exactly as she had all those years ago.

'I w-w-w- . . .'

She trailed off, feeling that familiar sense of frustration as her tongue tangled and twisted in her mouth, refusing to let her speak the words she wanted to say. Her father became cross when this happened, but when Beatrice glanced up at her mother she saw only patience and love on her face.

'It is all right, dear,' she said quietly. 'Take a breath and start again.'

'I w-wished to d-discover a new f-f-flower. One that n-no one has ever s-seen b-before.'

Her mother tossed her own penny into the well. They heard the splash as it hit the cool water below them.

'Wh-What did you w-wish for, Mama?'

She smiled slightly. 'The same thing as always,' she replied. 'I wished for your wish to come true.'

Beatrice wrinkled her nose. It seemed to her a waste of a wish, but her mother only laughed.

'You'll see,' she said. 'When you're a mother yourself, you'll understand that your own wishes no longer matter so much any more.'

Beatrice promised herself right then and there that she would never have children. Her wishes were too important to her and she was not prepared to give them up for anyone.

'Oh, look, darling.' Her mother pointed at a web spun in the little roof above the well. 'A spider queen on her throne.'

Beatrice smiled and squeezed her mother's hand. She was the only other person Beatrice knew who liked spiders as much as she and James both did. When they saw one in the garden, her mother never squealed in distaste, like her nanny. And she never destroyed their webs, as the maids so callously did if they found one inside Half Moon House. Instead her mother saw that spider webs were one of nature's most fascinating, beautiful creations. Something to be marvelled at.

Her mother looked up at the sky now and said, 'It's getting late. We should go in for tea.'

They took the path out of the trees and began to walk across the lawn towards Half Moon House, but Beatrice could already tell that she wasn't going to arrive there. The house seemed to shimmer before her eyes, like a mirage. Soon it would be gone altogether. The blue summer sky darkened into a winter night. The scent of flowers vanished and ice crackled through the air instead.

Beatrice tightened her hold on her mother's hand, trying to keep her there through the force of her will, only to find that her mother was no longer beside her at all, but further ahead on the lawn.

'Aren't you coming in, darling?' she asked, shielding her eyes against the glare of a long-gone sun. 'Cook has made your favourite scones.'

*Yes,* Beatrice thought. *Oh yes, I want to go in with you and take tea together. More than anything in the world.*

'N-No,' her child self said with youthful carelessness. Back then she thought there would be endless scones, endless summer days and endless chances to sit beside her mother. 'I w-want to l-look for m-mushrooms.'

'Well, all right.' Her mother looked disappointed. 'But don't stay out too long . . .'

Her voice faded away, along with the rest of the memory. Beatrice's hands suddenly gripped reins instead. The frozen lake spilled out around her, along with the frost fair, and the other guests, and the dazzle and sparkle of the garden.

Beatrice let out a long breath. She could feel a wonderful glow of warmth deep inside her, and a quick glance at the other guests told her they all felt the same. She could see it glowing from their eyes and hear it in their laughter, so full of wonder. Any tears shining in the torchlight were of happiness. There was no regret or sadness. Not like with the plum trees.

Rosa was right, Beatrice thought numbly as she dismounted. The carousel was more joyful and the Spider Queen would surely prefer it. As she walked along the platform towards the steps, she went over every precious moment again in her mind, so clear and sharp where before it had been misted over by the long passing of the years. She had quite forgotten that she and her mother used to refer to the spiders as queens and their webs as thrones. She tried to recall who had started it and why, but the memory escaped her. It seemed a curious coincidence when the Winter Garden itself was looked after by just such a queen.

For the first time Beatrice wondered whether her mother had also seen the Winter Garden – had perhaps been there herself as a child. Maybe Beatrice had not been its first visitor after all. She longed to ask, but it was one of the cruellest parts of losing someone; you could never ask them a question again, never say anything to them that had not already been said. All those chances were gone forever.

Beatrice was the last person on the carousel and was just about to step down from the platform when she suddenly became aware that she was being watched. The back of her neck prickled, so she turned round, convinced there would be someone there. Instead she looked into the eyes of a clockwork horse. Like all the others, it was white from head to toe and had the same silver livery, but it was the only horse there that had a golden ribbon in its mane. Beatrice thought it was the most beautiful creature on the carousel but, more than that, she felt suddenly convinced that it was special in some way. There was something about its eyes as they looked at her. It was as if they really *saw* her; and not only that, but also that the horse knew things about her – things she did not even know herself yet.

'Wh-What makes the h-horse with the g-golden ribbon s-s-special?' Beatrice asked the footman as she climbed down into the snow.

'All the horses are special, madam.'

'B-But the horse with the g-golden r-ribbon is d-different s-somehow?' Beatrice persisted.

The footman shook his head. 'Not that I am aware of. I expect the duchess just thought it would be pretty to add a single gold ribbon.'

Beatrice frowned. She felt there must be more to it than that and would have liked to ask Rosa herself. But there was still a crowd of people around the duchess's sleigh and Beatrice cringed at the thought of trying to capture her friend's attention and stammer out her questions in front of all those people. Besides, time had run away from her and she needed to return to her own garden if she was to be there before it opened. So she changed back into her skates and made her way across the lake. And all the while, there was just one thought that seemed to resound over and over again in her mind:

*Rosa will win.*
    *Rosa will win.*
        *Rosa will win.*

But then her mind went to her plum trees and she considered that perhaps there was hope after all. For the plums held one final secret that she had not revealed to the public. The thought of doing so made her hands sweat slightly inside their gloves. She had only managed to eat one plum herself and the memory of it was still enough to make her gag. Sometimes it even woke her up in the middle of the night with a cry that sent Wilkie running to the corner of the room. Most people, she suspected, would not have the strength of character or the determination necessary to force down the entire plum. There were bound to be complaints. Probably tears and remonstrations. Perhaps a medical man might even need to be called for. But this was a time to be bold, to take chances and to give it all she'd got.

'It is hard to go on sometimes,' Rosa had said, more than a year ago at Half Moon House. 'You have to fight for it with every breath . . .'

Beatrice knew she must follow that advice now, that this was an opportunity that would not come again. She made her way back to the carriage, and as it rattled down the drive she saw fireworks lighting up the sky through the window. They must have been special ones designed by Rosa for they painted pictures on the clouds – dancing bears and tumbling acrobats and blooming flowers. Beatrice thought it like artwork in the stars.

When she arrived back at Half Moon House, she went up to the roof and thought again about the plums. They did not taste like any fruit she had ever had anywhere in the world. They tasted of regret. Until those trees, Beatrice had never known that regret had a taste, but she had sampled it now and it was so bitter it was almost impossible to eat an entire plum. But for those who battled through, the plums held a secret at their hearts – something that was worth fighting for, something wonderful and dreadful.

As she watched over her garden that evening she could not help thinking that it seemed too small, and quiet, and quaint compared to the large, fiery spectacle Rosa had put on. It was foolish to have the plums and not use them. From tomorrow, that would change.

# CHAPTER THIRTY-TWO

Rosa would never have seen the boy if it hadn't been for the fireworks. They shed so much light upon the ground that she glimpsed him disappearing into the dark walk at the edge of the garden. She could even see his withered arm because, inexplicably, he wore no coat. Her heart beat suddenly faster in her chest as the crowd oohed and aahed their admiration at the fiery display overhead. This was the first time she had seen the boy in months – the child whom everyone said did not exist. She glanced at the people around her, but they were all too interested in the sky to notice her, and Eustace had already returned to the house in a sulk.

Rosa was determined not to miss this chance and the snow crunched beneath her boots as she climbed down from the sleigh and hurried after the boy. She had not seen any guests venture into the dark walk – there was too much to capture their attention elsewhere. The snow muffled sound from the garden, and the fireworks filtered strangely through the branches, pulsing in red and orange and silver that made the trees stand out like the silhouettes in the pop-up book.

She hastened along the winding path, afraid she might already have lost the boy, but when she stumbled out into the glade where the carousel had first appeared, she found him. He sat alone on a tree stump, hunched over his knees, with his arms tucked in close to his body, as if he was trying to make himself disappear. Rosa strode towards him, determined to get to the bottom of who he was, once and for all.

'What on earth are you doing out here?' she demanded. 'You'll catch your death!'

The boy looked up as another firework blossomed in the air overheard, turning the snow pink. Rosa didn't think she'd ever seen a child with such joyless eyes and the sight made her shiver.

'Your mother would be furious if she knew you were outside on a night like this without a coat,' she said.

'No, she wouldn't,' the boy said. 'She doesn't want me.'

Rosa was shocked. 'I'm sure that isn't true,' she said. 'Why would you think such a thing?'

'She told me.'

There was something odd about him when he spoke, but Rosa couldn't place what it was.

'Well.' She searched her mind for words of comfort. 'We all say things we don't mean sometimes. A moment of stress or—'

'She tells me every day.' The boy shrugged. 'But I knew before she told me.'

All of a sudden, Rosa realised what was odd about his speech. Whenever she spoke, her words misted before her in the freezing air, but the boy's didn't. It was blisteringly, savagely cold, yet he did not shiver. And the only footprints in the snow were Rosa's.

*There are no children at Raven Hall . . .*

'Who are you?' she whispered. 'Where did you come from?'

'I told you,' he said. 'I live here.'

*You know full well what I want,* Eustace's voice spoke inside her head. *An heir.*

'I live here,' the boy said again.

*I'm going to be a duchess one day* . . . Rosa had told her parents.

'I live here,' the boy said. 'Not you.'

*Perhaps you saw the future, after all,* her ma had acknowledged on Rosa's wedding day.

*My mama doesn't want me. She tells me every day* . . .

Rosa closed her eyes briefly, horrified by the idea that had suddenly occurred to her. She looked right at the boy and forced herself to say the words aloud.

'You're not . . . you're not *my* son. Are you? The son I'm going to have – in the future?'

He looked at her like she was mad. 'My mama's name is Beatrice,' he said. 'The Duchess of Chalkley.'

Rosa stared at him. 'But . . . Beatrice didn't marry Eustace. I did.'

The boy hunched over a little further. 'Maybe,' he said. 'Maybe not. It depends who wins the competition.'

Another firework lit up the sky above and the red sparks were reflected in the boy's eyes when he looked at her. 'If my mother wins, then she's the one who lives at Raven Hall. Not you. And not Ada.'

Rosa's head began to ache. 'That can't be right. Beatrice doesn't want to marry Eustace. She would never use her wish for such a thing.'

'Wishes are complicated,' the boy replied. 'It's so easy to make the wrong one.'

*It is h-human n-nature to l-look in all the wrong p-places . . .*

'You need to win,' the boy went on. 'Please. I don't want to be here in this horrible house any more. It's always cold. And everything aches.'

He looked so small and alone that Rosa reached out a hand to comfort him, but her fingers passed right through him, like he was a ghost. She gasped and snatched her hand back.

'H-How?' She stared at him. 'You were solid before.'

She realised she had never actually touched him, but she had seen him pick up the *Winter Garden* book, hadn't she?

'You're closer to winning the competition than Mama is right now,' the boy replied.

A great bang echoed through the sky for the grand finale and everything around them glowed bright red for a moment. Although she had designed the fireworks herself, Rosa had not expected them to be so loud, and the sound startled her. Her eyes flicked to the sky through the trees. She could hear the delighted murmurs from the crowd beyond the pines. And when she looked back down, the boy was gone, as if he'd never been there to begin with.

# CHAPTER THIRTY-THREE

A week passed, and people continued to flock to the gardens at Raven Hall all throughout the run up to Christmas, but Rosa could not enjoy the success. Her thoughts returned over and over again to the boy. And at times it felt as if her entire body was on fire with the pain of missing Ada. This wasn't helped when they received a letter from Margaret saying they were enjoying their holiday – although she never mentioned where exactly they were. She went into some detail about what a fussy baby Ada was, and how excessively she cried.

*I fear you have been spoiling her, Rosa. But rest assured you will find you have a far more obedient child by the time I return her to you. I have noticed some improvement in her already. There is no need to thank me – I am more than happy to take on this duty. Spare the rod, you know.*

Rosa tried several times to argue with Eustace, and on one occasion completely lost control of herself and begged for her daughter to be returned to her.

'But, Rosa, you have only to say the word,' he said. 'And I will send for mother to bring Ada back home at once.'

'I will lock the ravens up in the aviary,' she offered, recalling how distressed the birds made him. 'All but one.' She had only ever intended them to be a deterrent, after all, but they seemed to have got inside Eustace's head, to the point where he sometimes complained of hearing them in the walls even when Rosa herself could hear nothing and was quite certain there were no birds there at all.

He went completely still at her suggestion and Rosa could see how he longed for the ravens to be gone from his house.

'That would be a start, certainly.' He nodded. 'Yes, confine the birds to the aviary and I will consider bringing Ada home. I am pleased to hear you finally begin to talk sense at last.'

And so Rosa locked up all but one of the birds, in heavy-hearted defeat. After that there was simply nothing more to be done. She threw herself back into the running of the garden with increased vigour.

Then word came that Beatrice had unveiled another spectacle in her garden, and that it was something to do with the plums themselves. Despite the signs Rosa had seen there earlier, Beatrice was now serving the plums at the supper booths and people all said they had the most extraordinary effect. Where the rain allowed you to glimpse another life, had you made different decisions in the past, it seemed the stone inside the plum would reveal to you a bad decision you had not yet made – and thus a chance to change it and avoid the mistake altogether.

If true, Rosa feared this would be a wonder to compete with her carousel. And despite her best attempts, she had never succeeded in turning the carousel into the one from the book – the magical ride that could allow you to put right a mistake from your past. More than that, from the moment she finished it, the horse with the golden ribbon had been strange. It was always hungry. Rosa had seen clockwork creatures like Cookie sometimes develop hungers once they'd been alive and out in the world for a while, but she had never known one to start out ravenous. The horse ate all food that it came into contact with, yet never seemed satisfied.

And if Beatrice's plums allowed someone to do the same thing for their future that Rosa had hoped her carousel would do for the past, then that was surely more impressive than merely visiting an old pleasant moment. And yet . . . Rosa had heard odd talk about the plums from those who'd been at the supper booths. Strange rumours quickly spread about the fruit and not all of it made sense, but it seemed that eating the plums was difficult and dreadful in some way that those who hadn't been there could not understand.

From the moment she heard of them, Rosa was determined to see the plums again for herself. To her great irritation, Eustace insisted on going too.

'Don't be foolish,' she said. 'Why would you wish to go? You hate Beatrice.'

'Hate her?' Eustace repeated. 'What nonsense. Lady Sitwell matters not one jot to me, either way. But why should I not see the garden and these plums that everyone is raving about?' He gave Rosa a close look and added, 'By all accounts, it is even more impressive than yours.'

Rosa clenched her teeth and said nothing. Eustace did not know about the competition, or why the two women had chosen to open such unusual winter gardens at the same time, but he sensed on some instinctive level how important the garden was to Rosa. He knew it was more than just a garden, and she dreaded that he might find some way to use that knowledge against her.

She lifted her shoulder in a shrug. 'Come if you must, but there is no guarantee that you will see the plums. The supper booths are invitation only.'

Eustace looked irritated by that, which pleased Rosa. He was used to having things his own way and she always enjoyed seeing him thwarted.

They arrived at the garden together that evening shortly before eleven. Rosa's clockwork raven accompanied her in the carriage and she was glad to see Eustace glance nervously at it more than once. His earlier comment about Beatrice's garden being better than hers had touched a nerve and she longed to make him suffer in return.

When they arrived at Half Moon House, Rosa went with the duke through the gate of roses and they set off down one of the many winding paths. After the flames, and fireworks, and floating music of her own garden, Beatrice's seemed even quieter and softer than before, full of twinkling lights and hidden delights.

As they walked past displays of magical flowers, and golden toads, and extraordinarily large butterflies, Rosa hoped that Eustace would forget himself and break one of the rules. There was nothing he hated more than being told what to do, and it would be so easy for him to stray from the path, or pluck a flower, or touch one of the animals. But he had heard what happened to rule-breakers and he behaved himself impeccably. And thus they found themselves on the outskirts of the garden, where they discovered two of the teacup rabbits.

They were hopping around one of the ice houses, a small, squat little building that hunkered down at the edge of the grounds, peeping out at them like a goblin from a tangle of overgrown ivy. It was built from red brick with a quaint thatched roof and looked rather like a woodcutter's cottage that had been stretched to double height.

The way ahead was partially blocked by the black apple trees on either side, their spindly, naked branches reaching out across the path like witch's fingers, ready to catch and snag on cloaks and hair, but the path meant they were allowed to go that way, and Rosa wasn't about to miss out on her chance to see the plums. She stepped forward, carefully ducking and twisting around the outstretched limbs. Ice glinted on the bark and a few late apples hung from the branches, their black skins shining in their glittering coats of frost.

Unfortunately Eustace had spotted the rabbits too and followed her. Almost immediately he accidentally snapped off a twig with his cane as he tried to pass through a gap, causing the apple tree to snarl menacingly at him. They had a brief impression of pale strings of saliva stretching between a monster's teeth, before the bark closed over once again and the tree resettled itself with the creak of grumbling wood.

'Would you be careful?' Rosa snapped. 'You'll get us both thrown out.'

'Horrifying things!' Eustace exclaimed, shuddering. 'I cannot think why Beatrice has them here.'

'They are her friends,' Rosa said. 'And they are fascinating.'

Beatrice had told her how the trees had kept her company during her lonely childhood, even creating swings and treehouses for her to play in. They were strange, certainly, but Rosa had always thought they were rather lovely too.

Finally they reached the little ice house, where the two china rabbits sat patiently, ears tall and straight and expectant, as if they were waiting for them. One was a creamy ivory with violet forget-me-nots entwined along its side and up one of its ears. The other was a glossy midnight-blue, the colour of frozen ice on a deep, dark lake. As soon as Rosa and Eustace emerged from the trees, the rabbits hopped right up to them.

The moment Eustace's fingers brushed the dark one, it transformed into a handsome teacup upon the path. He snatched it up and gave a self-satisfied smirk at the sight of his own name painted upon the bottom. The other rabbit stretched up on its back haunches, gazing at Rosa expectantly. She reached down and it became a teacup, as before, the bone china smooth and cold beneath her fingers. It was a shame that Eustace had to be there, but Rosa was pleased that she would get to see the supper booths even so. She must get to the bottom of whatever Beatrice was doing, for Eustace had been correct when he said that people were beginning to speak of Beatrice's garden as being better than hers.

As they continued to explore the grounds in the time remaining, Rosa noticed evidence of fairy life almost everywhere she looked. There were little doors in the trees, hung with tiny wreaths made from green holly and red berries. A mistletoe swing, too small for any human, was suspended from a branch. And a miniature pair of snow boots was tucked, almost hidden, within the crooked roots of a snow-capped pine.

Rosa had never seen a real fairy, and wondered whether these extra touches could have been added by Beatrice merely to give the impression there were fairies in the garden. It did not seem her style, though. Her garden was not about illusion. And Rosa had already heard the fairy music through the golden mushrooms.

Eustace did not appear to notice anything, and Rosa didn't bother to point these things out. But she looked for them herself, following them as best she could, and this took them once more to the edges of a dark walk. Whilst all the garden was softly lit, this path had no candles at all. It disappeared into a little grove of black apple trees and the only light came from a collection of large snails. They glowed a pale powdery blue, the colour of mountain snow and half-remembered dreams. Rosa recalled what James had said about his wife and realised these must be her snails.

They clung to the trunks of the trees and glided across the surface of the snow, leaving smooth, dark trails behind them. Rosa assumed they were simply random swirls and whirls to begin with, but then she looked closer and her breath caught in her throat. The snails were writing poetry – gilded words sparkled in the snow, whispering of opals and orchids, wishes and stars.

'Remarkable,' she breathed. Even though they were in competition, she could not help but feel a sense of wonder, along with the instinctive urge to share the enjoyment of the moment with someone else – but the only other person there was Eustace, and he was frowning up at the sky rather than looking down at the snails. Rosa turned back to the poems, already melting into the snow before her.

'Rosa.' Eustace's voice sounded strained. 'What is that up there in the trees?'

She straightened up and tipped her head back to look into the sky. It had started to snow again and large flakes fell into her eyes and gathered in her lashes. She saw only the skeletal branches of the trees to begin with, but then there was a flicker of something flitting from one branch to another and the unmistakeable rustle of wings as more dark shapes emerged from the darkness. Could they be birds, or perhaps bats? But then she picked out the billowing edge of a tiny fur-trimmed cloak, the flash of a buckle on a sparkling slipper, the flying tumble of long, dark curls.

'Oh my goodness,' she exclaimed. 'Those are—'

'You bitch! You said you locked them away.'

'What?' Rosa tore her eyes from the sky to glare at him. 'What are you talking about?'

The look on his pale face appalled her. There was a wildness there and his eyes darted about too fast. 'The ravens,' he breathed out the word fearfully, as if it was a curse that could bring the birds flocking down upon him.

'Those aren't ravens,' Rosa replied. 'Do you hear any clockwork? They're—'

But that was as far as she got before Eustace lunged towards her.

# CHAPTER
# THIRTY-FOUR

Rosa stumbled back, but Eustace wasn't aiming for her. With the end of his cane he smashed her clockwork raven against the tree, completely staving its head in. The bird tumbled into the snow and Eustace brought the heel of his boot down hard over and over again until the raven was ground into bits.

'Damn it, Rosa,' he said, breathing hard. 'What must I do? How can I make you understand that I am in earnest? I cannot and will not live with those infernal birds a moment longer! You must send them away.'

'They are not here!' Rosa gasped. 'They are only inside your head.'

'Don't you dare lie to me!'

'I'm not! Those were f-fairies in the trees. That's all.'

'I don't believe you. You're a filthy liar. You won't rest until I'm out of my mind.'

'You are *already* out of your mind!' Rosa hissed. The raven lay in pieces at her feet and its broken clockwork suddenly reminded her of Cookie, which, in turn, reminded her of the beloved dogs that she and James had owned together in that other life where she had been loved and happy. She tried to block the memories, but they swept in anyway.

She recalled lying in bed with James, her head resting upon his shoulder, basking in lazy contentment. And she remembered exploring the jungles of Malaysia, and drinking coffee in Venice, and celebrating their son's fourth birthday, and how they had both wept when the first dog they had owned together eventually grew old and died. But in this life she had only broken clockwork, and a useless title, and a husband who loathed her almost as much as she hated him. When she thought what she might have had in that other life, it was simply unbearable, and was only made worse by the fact that she had *chosen* this. What a fool she had been.

'You contemptible creature!' Rosa said, looking at Eustace. 'How I wish Beatrice had married you rather than leaving you for me to suffer.'

She was pleased that her words made him flinch, even as the look in his eyes appalled her.

'Sometimes,' he said in a quiet voice, 'I think you must want me to hurt you.'

He stepped forward with a sudden look of determination, and the cane twitched in his hand. Rosa stepped back, suddenly afraid. But whatever Eustace had been about to do, he broke off with a cry as one of the black apple trees struck him across the face, its thin branch lashing out as quick and vicious as a whip. The skin of his cheek opened up in a long gash as he reeled back, staggering to keep his footing in the snow.

'What is g-going on?' a sharp voice asked.

Rosa looked round and saw that Beatrice had appeared on the path, wrapped up in her winter cloak. For a strange moment, Rosa thought she saw the glittering outline of a big cat standing at her side, starlight stripes shining in the dark, but when she blinked it was gone. How long had Beatrice been there and how much had she seen? Rosa tried to summon up some quick explanation, but her tongue seemed frozen in her mouth, and her body fizzed with a sickening mix of adrenaline and shame. Had Eustace really been about to strike her with that cane? Surely he would not go so far as that? Even during the darkest nights at Raven Hall, he had never once hurt her in that way.

*It is all right,* Rosa thought. *I know Eustace and I'm in control. I am in control.*

Yet it no longer felt that way at all. Ada was gone. Beatrice's garden was providing too much competition. The wish seemed further away than it ever had before, and that feeling wasn't helped when she saw the boy with the withered arm peeping out from behind Beatrice's skirts, his eyes too big and sorrowful for a child. He was there and gone in a moment, and Rosa was the only one who seemed to have noticed him.

'One of those infernal trees attacked me,' Eustace said, breaking the taut silence at last.

'Are y-you all r-right?' Beatrice asked. Her grey eyes took in the clockwork raven in pieces in the snow.

'No, I am not all right!' Eustace snapped. 'This is what comes from keeping devilish trees in the garden.' He took a handkerchief from his pocket and pressed it to his bleeding cheek. 'I have half a mind to bring a lawsuit against you. The garden ought not to be open to the public if there are deranged and aggressive things lurking in it.'

*The only deranged and aggressive thing here is you,* Rosa longed to say.

'I w-was not t-talking to you,' Beatrice said. She barely glanced at Eustace before fixing her eyes on Rosa.

'The trees were . . . were startled by the raven.' She gestured at the sad pile of clockwork. 'That's all.'

Beatrice said nothing for a moment, but Rosa felt strongly that her friend did not believe her. Then her gaze dropped to Rosa's gloves and she said, 'Your h-hand. It's b-bleeding.'

Rosa looked down and realised she had broken her teacup. Eustace had dropped his and it had landed unharmed in the snow, but Rosa had tightened her grip on hers without realising it. Several shards of china lay by her feet, but the largest piece remained clenched in her hand, piercing her glove. A scarlet trail of blood ran over her palm and dripped dark, blooming spots upon the snow.

'Oh.' Rosa stared. 'Oh no, I'm so sorry! Have I . . . have I killed the rabbit?'

To her dismay, she could feel tears prickling the backs of her eyes, and the effort of keeping them in made it feel like there was a hand wrapped around her throat, squeezing tighter and tighter. Eustace tried to arrange his face into an expression of concern, but it only made him look as if he were chewing glass.

'It is n-not really a r-rabbit,' Beatrice said gently. 'Only a t-teacup that's b-been enchanted. G-Give me that p-piece. Take my h-handkerchief.'

Rosa tried to let go but her fingers were so tightly curled around the shard of porcelain that it was as if they'd become frozen there.

'I can't,' she said.

At that moment the chimes rang through the garden to signify closing time.

'For heaven's sake, Rosa, don't be obstinate,' Eustace exclaimed. 'I cannot miss the supper booths for this.'

'Why d-don't you g-go on?' Beatrice said, her gaze flicking briefly to Eustace. 'R-Rosa can c-clean her hand in the h-h-house. And then j-join you.'

'Very well.'

Beatrice glanced down at the clockwork pieces of the raven and then back at Rosa, 'W-Would you l-like me to—'

'Just leave her.' The words came out as a whisper. 'She is beyond repair.'

'At least, my dear, we can take solace from the fact that we have hundreds more of the wretched things at home,' Eustace said, a glint in his eye. For just a moment she caught a glimpse of the boar beneath and was surprised. Eustace was usually more in control of himself in company. She glanced at Beatrice and could almost sense the other woman's dislike for her husband coming off her in waves. But she said nothing and the three of them made their way back to the garden's entrance.

Beatrice told the footman to expect Rosa at the supper booths shortly. Eustace then went with the remaining guests to the plum gate, whilst the other two headed for the house. They walked in through the front entrance hall and Rosa gasped, unable at first to take in what she was seeing. Dark shapes hung from every available surface – the staircase and the doorframes and the chandelier itself. Initially she thought they were bats, but then she realised they were chrysalises.

'Beatrice!' she exclaimed. 'The house! What has happened?'

Beatrice paused. 'Oh. Y-Yes. The house. It has ch-changed. Since l-last you were h-here.'

She was not wrong. As they moved down the corridors, Rosa glimpsed rooms filled with strange, creeping vines that grew up the walls and hung down from the ceiling. Others had been entirely taken over by trees, whose roots ripped up the floorboards, or hanging moss that grew through the tapestries. The Summer Dining Room had been turned into a grotto filled with the glimmer of glow-worms that winked out of the gloom at them like golden eyes.

Through it all there was the rustle of different types of wings: leathery or soft, paper-thin or feathered. Rosa saw that there were not only birds inside the house, but bats, butterflies, moths and even a couple of pale owls as well. The wooden floor was splattered with their droppings, as were the elegant furniture, the priceless rugs and the antique carriage clocks. Toads, frogs and mice scattered before them like tiny shadows in the sputtering hiss of the gas lamps, and a host of bright, shining eyes seemed to watch from out of the dark. The smell of damp vegetation and animal waste filled the air.

'But I don't understand,' Rosa said. 'You love Half Moon House. How have you allowed this to happen?'

Beatrice glanced at her. 'Whatever h-happens with the c-competition,' she said. 'I w-will not be s-staying here. England is n-no p-place for m-me.' Her voice took on almost a defensive tone as she went on, 'I h-have protected the b-books.'

She opened the door to the library and waved Rosa through. The room looked almost the same as before, except for the dozens of white spiders busily spinning their webs from every surface. The chandelier above was so cocooned that it barely shed any light at all, and Beatrice was forced to light several candles that had been placed around the room. A fire still burned in the grate and she asked Rosa to sit in one of the armchairs beside it. She threw on a couple of logs and then left her for a moment to fetch a bowl of clean water and some bandages.

'The s-servants have g-gone,' she told Rosa as she set the bowl down. 'The house. Is not f-fit. For people. I s-see that.'

Beatrice gestured at Rosa's hand and she held it out wordlessly. This time she was able to unclench her fingers and let the other woman draw the shard gently from her skin. It was not a deep cut, and it did not take long to wipe away the blood and wrap it with a clean bandage.

'I am s-sorry about your c-clockwork p-pug,' Beatrice said as she tied off the end.

'What do you mean?' Rosa asked, her eyes fixed on the nearest spider, spinning its beautiful web from the arm of the opposite chair – an intricate portrait of a majestic raven.

'I expect Eu-Eustace is to b-blame for his absence.'

Rosa tore her eyes from the web and looked down at Beatrice.

'What makes you say that?'

Beatrice took a deep breath. 'I w-went into the p-plum rain,' she said. 'J-Just once.'

Her grey eyes met Rosa's and something wordless seemed to pass between them. Rosa saw that Beatrice understood – truly understood – what her life at Raven Hall was like.

'You saw the life where you had married Eustace,' she said.

Beatrice nodded. 'He is a b-beast.'

'He is a wild pig of a man. And yes, he destroyed Cookie. I think, if he could, he would destroy everything that I hold most dear.'

It was a strange, miserable sort of relief to say it to someone who would understand – the only other person in the world who truly could.

Beatrice nodded. 'He d-did the same to my b-black apple trees,' she said. 'In the other l-life. I am t-truly s-sorry.'

'That is kind of you,' Rosa replied. 'But it doesn't help me in any way. Oh, please. If you really know what life with Eustace is like, then won't you reconsider with-drawing from the competition?'

Beatrice did not reply, but stood up and began folding the bandages into neat, precise piles.

'I need that wish more than you do,' Rosa said. 'We both know that's the truth.'

Beatrice turned away from her. For a long moment she was silent.

'That is n-not f-fair,' she finally said. 'You ch-chose to m-marry him. I h-have my own r-regrets. That I w-wish to undo.'

'But your regrets don't matter as much as mine do.'

Beatrice glanced at her. 'They do to m-me. You do not kn-know what my w-wish would be. So you c-cannot say that y-yours has more w-worth. Than m-mine.'

'Tell me what it is then.'

Beatrice shook her head. 'It is n-not your b-business.' Her voice held no reproach. 'Just kn-know that my wish is as dear to my h-heart. As yours is to y-you. We all th-think our own p-problems are uniquely d-difficult,' she went on quietly. 'Because they are ours. But the t-truth is. Everyone struggles. With s-something. That is. Unbearable. To them.'

Rosa could feel her chance slipping through her fingers as she stood up to face the other woman.

'There's something I must tell you,' she said, her voice strained with the effort of keeping it level. 'It will sound strange. Unbelievable. But I need you to listen. Whatever it is you hope to wish for, it will have consequences you haven't foreseen. It will lead to your being married to Eustace rather than me.'

The words had the effect Rosa had hoped. Beatrice's face went grey and she physically recoiled.

'H-How can you p-possibly kn-know that?'

'The boy told me.'

'What b-boy?'

Rosa sighed. 'The one playing at your feet.'

He'd appeared slowly in the room during the last few moments. Just a faint outline at first, but rapidly becoming clearer and clearer until it looked as if he was really there. Beatrice had not reacted to him in any way, and Rosa realised she could not see him – that probably no one in the world could but her. When Beatrice looked down, she saw nothing but the rug, and a look of distrust crept over her features when she glanced back up at Rosa.

'You are t-trying to t-trick me.'

'There is another life,' Rosa whispered, 'trying to push through this one. It's the truth. I do not know why I can see the boy. Perhaps it is because I have a little second sight, like my mother always said. Or perhaps it's because I created the carousel. The child seems to be connected to that in some way that I can't work out. Oh, I know it sounds strange! But please believe that it is the truth.'

She could see it was no use, however. Beatrice didn't believe her. Perhaps Rosa wouldn't have done either, in her place.

'P-Perhaps you have l-lost your r-reason,' Beatrice suggested. 'Living th-there. In that dreadful h-house.'

'I am not mad,' Rosa replied, but even as she spoke, another Eustace appeared in the room with them.

It wasn't *her* Eustace. His face was unmarked by the gash from the black apple tree and he was looking at her with an expression of polite interest. There was no resent-ment, or bitterness, or hatred at all. Yet, now that she knew it was there, Rosa could still see the boar lurking beneath his features.

'Miss Warren,' Eustace said, putting his hand on Beatrice's shoulder. 'My wife didn't tell me you were here. To what do we owe the pleasure?'

Beatrice did not react to him at all.

'I am s-sorry for your l-lot in l-life,' she said. 'But I want that w-wish as much as you d-do.' Her eyes went to the spiders spinning around them. The gold webs glittered like ice in the dancing light from the fire. 'And I have the r-right to put my own h-happiness f-f-first. Just as. You do.'

Rosa closed her eyes and rubbed them hard. When she opened them, Eustace and the boy were both gone. It was only her and Beatrice left in the room, and the white spiders spinning their extraordinary webs around them. She felt her shoulders slump a little. She had needed to try, but Beatrice's response came as no surprise. A wish was such a wondrous thing to ask someone to give up. Perhaps there was no person alive in the world who would willingly give up a marvel like that.

She glanced through the window to where the pleasure garden sparkled beyond the glass. 'Is it true about the plums?' she asked. 'Can they really reveal to us a mistake we have yet to make?'

Beatrice nodded.

'How can we know it is not fated to happen anyway?'

'It c-can be ch-changed,' Beatrice said. 'I have s-seen it. With J-James.'

'James Sheppard?'

Beatrice nodded. 'His p-plum stone said he would r-regret not proposing to J-Jani.'

'Oh.' Rosa felt a fierce rush of envy and sorrow, like a bird spreading its wings inside her, desperate to take flight. She grabbed it and squeezed its feathers together, sleek and slippery between her fingers. She would not think about James right now. She would not.

'There is n-no such thing as f-fate,' Beatrice said. 'We always h-have the ch-chance to make things d-different.'

'Not if you're married,' Rosa said flatly. 'Then it's too late to change anything at all. I should go. I would hate to miss my chance to sample the plums.'

'B-Brace y-yourself,' Beatrice said. 'They t-taste of r-regret.'

Rosa paused at the door. 'Regret has a taste?'

'Y-Yes. But I c-cannot d-describe it.'

Rosa thought suddenly of the mourning orchid blooming for Esme back at the hothouse, its petals an entirely new colour that she had not known existed before. It would be an impossible task to describe it to anyone, and she supposed the plums must be the same. Some things in the world were so wondrous and extraordinary that you simply had to experience them for yourself.

'I w-will do everything I can to w-win,' Beatrice said quietly. She looked right at Rosa, but there was no challenge in her voice at all. Only a sort of sadness. Perhaps they both sensed, in that moment, that their friendship was over. 'Everything.'

Rosa nodded. 'And I shall do the same. Goodbye, Beatrice.'

She let herself out and quietly retraced her steps, back through the overgrown house and out to the sparkling world of snow and ice beyond.

# CHAPTER
# THIRTY-FIVE

Rosa passed beneath the plum gate and walked along the path she remembered to the supper booths. Eustace was seated at a table with a middle-aged, titled couple Rosa recognised – Lord and Lady Broderick. There was a spare seat for her and she took this, doing her best to look normal as the others politely enquired about her hand.

'It's such a shame about the poor little rabbit,' Lady Broderick said.

'Rosa can be terribly clumsy at times,' Eustace remarked.

At that moment the carriage clocks upon the tables began to ring out the chimes for midnight and the others' teacups transformed back into china rabbits, which presented them with the scrolls introducing the phenomenon of the plum rain.

'Good heavens, can it really offer a glimpse of another life, do you think?' Lady Broderick asked, staring down at her scroll.

'Everything in this garden is real,' Rosa replied. 'That is what makes it so wondrous.'

'I take it this is not your first visit to the gardens, your grace?' Lord Broderick enquired. He was a florid man with impressive jowls and a bushy moustache that no amount of wax seemed able to tame.

'I visited on opening night and experienced the plum rain then,' Rosa said.

Lord Broderick shook his head. 'I hope you will forgive my saying so, but it does not seem at all a fitting thing for a lady. My own sister, Vera, suffered a complete nervous breakdown after what she saw in the plum rain last week. I am on the board that grants the licences for the gardens, you know.' He gave them an important look. 'Some of us believe the one for this garden ought to be revoked. That's why I am here tonight, in fact – to write a report.'

Rosa felt a strange flutter of confused wings in her stomach. She knew she ought to feel pleased at this development if it meant Beatrice might be disqualified from the competition, but she found herself hating the pompous man across from her, even so.

'Quite right,' Eustace said at once. 'The garden is a dangerous place.' He gestured at his cheek. 'One of those black apple trees attacked me in the dark walk earlier. And just look at the mess that rabbit made of my dear wife's hand.'

'Disgraceful,' Lord Broderick said, shaking his head. 'I trust you have no objection to my including this in my report to the board?'

'None whatsoever.'

Before Rosa could say anything, the soft whisper of the plum rain began to fall in sheets around them. As before, there was a mixture of people wanting to experience it and others who stayed carefully shielded beneath the ceiling of parasols. Lady Broderick gazed at the rain for a moment before removing her hand from her muff and reaching out, only for her husband to catch her wrist and draw it back.

'Good God, Peony! Did you not hear what I said about Vera?' he demanded. 'It would be too bad to have your medical bills to pay, on top of hers.'

'How thoughtless of me. I apologise, Laurence,' she said in a meek tone.

She made no further move to touch the plum rain, but Rosa saw the wistful look in her eyes as she gazed out at it. Lady Broderick had had ten children in eleven years, three of whom had died in their infanthood. Surely that explained the quiet sadness in her brown eyes.

*There is another wasted life,* Rosa thought. She had no desire herself to experience the plum rain again. Once was more than enough.

She turned to Eustace. 'You are not going to partake?'

'I am not interested in other lives,' he replied. 'Only this one.'

For the first time Rosa wondered what Eustace's future mistake would be. It did not take a scholar to see that their marriage was a tinder box. Sooner or later, one of them was bound to go up in flames and no doubt take the other person with them.

The rain quickly came to an end. As before, there were some people who were badly affected by it and had to be revived in their seats with fans and smelling salts, or else helped from the garden altogether. But, unlike before, the evening was not yet over. Instead of inviting people to return to their carriages, the footmen instead came round the tables to enquire who would care to enjoy the greatest spectacle of all in the garden – the fortune plums themselves.

This time Eustace and Lord Broderick both accepted. Lady Broderick looked hopeful, but was immediately forbidden by his lordship, who claimed that the plums might be too dangerous. Eustace followed suit by making the same comment to Rosa, but she found herself laughing in his face.

'I am having one of those plums, Eustace,' she said. 'And there is simply nothing short of physical restraint that you can do to stop me.'

A silence fell over the table. Lord and Lady Broderick both looked shocked. That was not the way a well-bred woman spoke to her husband. As for Eustace, he and Rosa both knew he wouldn't have hesitated to restrain her in the privacy of their home, but there was no chance he would raise so much as a finger against her in front of others. His good name was too important to him. He stared across the table at her for a moment before giving a strained laugh and glancing at their companions.

'Americans,' he remarked, trying to make a joke of the unpleasant moment. 'So headstrong.' He looked back at Rosa. 'Very well, my dear, you may take part if it means that much to you.'

The footmen were inviting guests to pick their own plums directly from the trees. Almost everyone there rose from their seats to do so.

'Please be warned,' the footman went on. 'These plums taste of regret. Only those who manage to consume the entire fruit will find their fortune within.'

The guests hurried towards the trees, jostling each other to be the first to pick their plum. Each wanted to take the roundest, healthiest, ripest-looking fruit for their own, in the hope that this might have some impact on the fortune they found inside. When Rosa, Eustace and Lord Broderick returned to their seats, the frosted plums in their gloved hands sparkled with the forbidden lustre of Eve's apple in Eden.

Rosa looked right at Eustace as she raised the plum to her mouth and – relishing the moment of public defiance – bit into it.

Plum juice stained the cream fingers of her gloves.

The taste of regret flooded her mouth.

Her pupils dilated.

There was a strange animal-like groan, and it took Rosa a moment to realise it had come from her.

The plum fell from her hand and rolled over to her teacup. Everyone else at the table was staring at her. She could feel the purple juice sticky on her lips.

'Really, my dear.' Eustace sounded smug. 'Perhaps next time you will have the good sense to listen to your husband.'

He exchanged a knowing look with Lord Broderick, but Rosa had no attention left to resent him. All her thoughts were occupied with the lingering taste of regret upon her tongue. It was, as Beatrice had said, impossible to describe, much as she searched her mind for words to do so. It had some of the sweetness of fruit, but there was something horrid lurking beneath it too. The plum tasted of dark dreams, and starless nights, cold hands and rotten wedding cakes. It was, without a doubt, the most dreadful thing Rosa had ever eaten and her tongue seemed to burn with the echo of it.

Eustace smiled as he raised his own plum to his lips and took a bite. Purple juice stained the ends of the blond moustache that Rosa had once thought so dashing. There was a single moment of breathlessness, as when a child draws in air to scream. Then Eustace's pupils dilated and he leapt to his feet, staggering blindly backwards as the plum fell into the snow.

'Good God!' he gasped. 'What . . . what devilry is this?'

All around them other guests were having a similar reaction to the fruit. Rosa heard cries of dismay and voices raised in complaint. Several young women wept into their teacups. One gentleman used his knife to cut the stone from his plum, only to find that it was perfectly ordinary.

'It only works if you eat the entire plum, sir,' the footman said.

'But it isn't possible!' the guest exclaimed. 'No one could eat the whole thing. Nobody!'

Indeed, none of the guests returned for a second bite. Except for Rosa. She took a deep breath and reached out for her plum.

'My good woman, you cannot be serious?' Lord Broderick stared at her. His own plum lay discarded before him, without a single bite taken from it. One tentative lick of the purple skin had been enough to make him roar in protest.

Eustace turned his incredulous gaze on her too. 'Don't be a fool,' he said in a low voice.

'Just because you lack the strength,' she said, 'doesn't mean I do too.'

She raised the plum and bit into it – an even bigger mouthful than before. She was prepared for the taste this time, yet her eyes watered and, when she forced the fruit down, she thought it surely could not have been harder to swallow a lump of human flesh. It was dreadful. Unspeakable.

To her dismay, Eustace picked up his own fallen plum and resumed his seat opposite her. He took another bite, so Rosa did as well. They stared at each other across the table. It was now a battle of wills between them – the only two people in the supper booths who were attempting to persevere at all. Lord and Lady Broderick watched them in fascinated horror, and other guests soon gathered around their table too.

Eating that plum was one of the hardest things Rosa had ever had to do. Childbirth could hardly compare with it. If it weren't for Eustace, she probably would have given up, but if he was going to keep going, then by God, so was she.

*Keep fighting . . .*

Purple juice ran down their fingers, too sticky and too sweet. They both gagged more than once. Several times Rosa thought she could not go on. Yet the plum disappeared, bit by bit.

She finished hers a few seconds before Eustace. Some of the nearby guests even applauded, whilst everyone craned forward to see her stone. Rosa thought it was perfectly ordinary at first – that she had just gone through that ordeal for nothing. But then words appeared upon it in golden, flowing script: *You will regret leaving your ravens locked in the aviary.*

Rosa frowned down at the fortune for a moment before raising her gaze to Eustace. He looked ill as he scowled at his plum and the one mouthful of fruit remaining on it. Rosa sensed that he too would have given up, if he hadn't been trying to best her. Sweat had beaded at his hairline and trailed down his face. He fumbled for his handkerchief, wiped it over his brow and then glared at Rosa, as if holding her personally responsible for this ordeal. She thought for a moment that he was not going to manage that last mouthful. But then, still glaring at her, he raised the plum to his mouth.

There was a sucking noise as he ate the last of its flesh and dropped the stone onto the table. The next moment he lurched to his feet and was vomiting into the snow. The assembled guests cried out when they saw the words written on his stone, and those close to Eustace edged away from him until he was left quite alone. No one went to his aid or attempted to speak to him. Rosa saw the words and they echoed over and over again inside her head. She looked up at her husband and waited for the dark horror of it to sweep over her. Only it never came. She was not surprised, somehow, not really.

'What is it, in God's name?' Eustace demanded, straightening up. 'Why are you all staring at me like that?'

No one answered him. No one, it seemed, even wanted to look at him now.

Impatiently Eustace strode back to the table and snatched up the stone to read about the future mistake that everyone else had already seen: *You will regret killing your wife.*

Rosa expected Eustace to turn bright red, to roar and bluster. Instead the colour drained from his face so fast she thought he might actually faint. He stared down at the stone in silence for so long that the other guests around him started to fidget uncomfortably. No one knew what to say or do. Rosa felt everyone turning their gazes towards her, waiting for a hysterical outburst that never came. Finally Eustace put the stone down on the table, very carefully and precisely, as if it were made from glass.

When he spoke, it was in the same careful, precise way. 'It is not true.'

Rosa thought he would address the guests – the only people there whose opinion he valued – but instead he looked right at her.

'It is not true,' he repeated.

She could hear an edge of desperation beneath his quiet tone and could see it lurking behind his eyes. Eustace wanted her to believe him. But her mind went to the wild way he had looked at her in the quiet of the dark walk earlier, the bruises he had already bestowed upon her skin, the vicious hatred with which he had hissed that word: *bitch!* And she believed the fortune upon the plums, both his and hers. It had been a mistake to lock up the ravens, she saw that now, but it was a mistake that she would soon undo.

She stood up. It seemed like everyone was waiting to see what she would say. Perhaps they expected her to rage at Eustace, or to call for the police, or to seek sanctuary at someone else's house. Instead she ignored them all, looked right at her husband and said, 'Let's go home.'

'Home?' He stared at her for a moment, as if unable to believe what she had just said. 'You mean . . . you will return to Raven Hall?'

'Of course. I am its duchess, am I not?'

She headed towards the gate, leaving Eustace to hurry in her wake. When they reached their carriage, she ignored the hand he offered and climbed up on her own. She heard him tell their driver to take them home and then he joined her in the velvet interior and took the seat opposite. It was small enough inside that their knees lightly touched, but Rosa had learned to suppress her shudders long ago.

A strange heavy silence descended upon them as the carriage made its way down the drive. Rosa could tell that Eustace wanted to say something, but seemed to be struggling to find the right words.

'I am so glad,' he finally said, 'that you have the good sense to recognise those ridiculous plums for the parlour trick they are.'

Rosa shook her head. 'Nothing in Beatrice's garden is a parlour trick. It is real magic.'

Eustace frowned. 'But then—'

'I believe every word written upon that plum.'

Eustace's face was grey in the shaft of moonlight shining through their frozen window. 'But you cannot,' he finally said. 'I tell you it is not true. It isn't.'

Rosa said nothing. She had no interest in arguing with him about it. What was the point? As each moment went on, she felt colder and sadder as the words on the plum sank in.

Noticing her shiver, Eustace said, 'Here, have my cloak.'

His fingers fumbled to unbutton the clasp at his throat, but Rosa shook her head. 'Keep it, your grace,' she said, without heat. 'I want nothing from you.'

A little of Eustace's familiar bluster came back as he went on. 'Look, Rosa, you are far more intelligent than a woman has any right to be, so you ought to have more sense than to believe such hocus-pocus. I shall be instructing my solicitor to bring a slander suit against Lady Beatrice first thing in the morning.'

Rosa glanced at him. 'You're the fool, if you think I cannot see that haunted look in your eyes. You know the plums told the truth, just as I do.'

'For heaven's sake!' Eustace exclaimed as the carriage lurched over a pothole in the road. 'If you really believe that, then why would you get in this carriage with me? Why would you agree to come home at all?'

Rosa said nothing. She believed she was in a carriage with her would-be murderer and the knowledge was almost too sickening to comprehend, but she did not think he would lift a finger against her yet. It would not happen today. Nor would it happen tomorrow, or even next week or next month. But next year, or perhaps two, or five, or ten years from now, things might be different. She knew perfectly well what she must do to avoid it, and had known even before seeing the fortune in her plum.

They spent the rest of the ride back in silence. Eustace stared sightlessly out of the window at the icy swirls of mist that had descended to writhe and coil about the carriage as it passed along the dark country lanes. His face reminded Rosa of a wax mourning doll. He had the look of a man who had seen something that no one should ever have to see.

As with that endless carriage ride across the frozen Alps, Rosa had the strongest sense that she was being taken down a road that she had no wish to travel. Yet there was no point stopping the carriage and getting out, because there were no other roads available. They had all been closed off long ago.

It was almost two o'clock in the morning by the time they got back to Raven Hall, and Rosa's pleasure garden was still going strong. She saw the flickering light of fire dancing over the turrets, and heard music and laughter from the grounds beyond. When they climbed out, Rosa ignored the arm Eustace offered her and walked in the opposite direction.

'You are not going into the garden?' Eustace asked, surprised. He knew that she always remained until closing time.

Rosa paused and turned back. 'Soon. But I am going to the aviary first.'

She saw realisation dawn on Eustace's face. 'You are releasing the ravens,' he said in a flat tone.

'Certainly.'

'Please don't.'

Rosa gazed at him across the silver snow. It was so very cold. She wondered whether she would ever feel the warmth of summer on her skin again.

'Send for Ada,' she said. 'Write to your mother tonight and the ravens will stay in their cages, I give you my word.'

It was a reckless bargain, she knew, but her desire to get Ada back trumped all else. She saw Eustace hesitate. He seemed to consider it for a moment before clenching his jaw and shaking his head.

'You are trying to trick me,' he said bitterly. 'You think yourself so clever, Rosa, but I am no simpleton. Don't you think I know that you will flee with Ada the moment she is returned? That her absence is the only thing keeping you at Raven Hall?'

Rosa opened her mouth to try to protest, but they both knew there was truth in his words. If it were not for the garden competition, Rosa would have left with Ada months ago.

'Ada will stay with Mother until I have made you see sense,' Eustace said.

'Then the ravens are released tonight.'

Eustace scowled. 'So be it.'

Rosa felt the chance to bring them back from the brink slipping through her fingers as Eustace turned away from her and stalked into the house. She drew her cloak hood up over her head to protect her ears from the cold as she walked around the grounds to the aviary.

Her ravens cawed at her the moment she stepped inside, flapping their metal wings and pecking at the bars of their cages. She sensed their desperation to be set free. Even a clockwork raven was not happy inside a cage.

'I am sorry,' she said softly. 'I promise you'll never be locked up again.'

She set them free one by one and they swept past her with joyful, raucous calls. She expected them to head for the garden, but they soared to the roof of Raven Hall and poured down the chimneys instead. Their purpose was to watch Eustace – and watch him they would. Rosa knew that he had blocked up the chimney in his own bedroom, but that didn't prevent the birds pecking at his window or scratching at his door with their iron claws.

And if that meant he woke up screaming in the night once again, then he had only his own wickedness to blame.

# CHAPTER
# THIRTY-SIX

Rosa did not see Eustace for two whole days after the incident at Beatrice's garden. He did not emerge from his bedroom, and barely ate any of the food the servants left outside his locked door. Even his manservant was denied entry and came to Rosa to ask whether they should send for a doctor.

'I do not think that is necessary, Harrow,' she replied. 'The duke received a shock at Lady Beatrice's pleasure garden, that is all. I'm sure he will be himself again in another day or two.'

She had no idea whether this was true. In all likelihood it was the ravens keeping him to his room, although they had never prevented him from moving about the house before. At any rate, she was not going to send for a doctor unless it proved absolutely necessary. In the meantime she was pleased to have the pleasure garden to herself. It was harder for people to congratulate Eustace if he wasn't there. Yet there seemed to be excited talk of Beatrice's garden everywhere.

Rosa had hoped that the incident with Eustace at the supper booths might have put people off. After all, if even the Duke of Chalkley could be publicly disgraced in such a manner, then so could anyone. It was not as if the plums were even pleasant to eat. Yet she was forgetting that the only thing people loved more than something magical and beautiful was something cruel and monstrous.

And so guests flocked to Beatrice's garden in the hope of getting into the notorious supper booths. It did not matter that most people did not want to eat the plums themselves, or were even capable of doing so. There was always the possibility that someone else might, and that there would be a delicious scandal. Either way, there were clearly plenty of people who thought Beatrice's garden a wonder far more spectacular than Rosa's clockwork reindeer, or her carousel, or her frost fair. What if the Spider Queen agreed with them?

She racked her brain for how she could make her own garden more wondrous. There were still two days left before the competition ended. Still two more days to make any final improvements that might give her the edge she needed. She was sure that the answer lay with the carousel. She knew it could be so much *more* than it currently was.

She could feel its potential every time she looked at it, sparkling and beautiful in the middle of the frozen lake. Yet she could not quite work out what it was that needed to be different, or how she might turn it into the Carousel of Icicles from the book.

She had already spent many hours over the past months tinkering with its inner mechanisms, attempting to transform it from something that allowed one to merely relive the past into something that could actually change what had happened. That would surely be something to rival Beatrice's plums. She returned over and over again to the pop-up book, skimming through the pages looking for the carousel, but it remained stubbornly absent, as did the boy who sometimes haunted the mansion's corridors.

One day, after the guests had finally returned home and the garden was quiet and empty, Rosa made her way back across the lake to the carousel. It was so early in the morning that it was still dark, but the clockwork horses greeted her with enthusiasm, knowing that she would soon give them permission to venture onto the ice. The older the carousel got, the more the horses resembled real ones, longing for exercise. Rosa had taken to setting them loose each morning to stretch their legs and run.

They all seemed to enjoy this, but none more so than the horse with the golden ribbon. The creature was one of the most spectacular Rosa had ever made, and she felt a burst of pride now as she ran her hand down the horse's neck. The steed whickered softly and poked its metallic muzzle into Rosa's pockets, like a real horse searching for sugar lumps. It was still so hungry that Rosa was always catching it prodding at anything and everything in the garden, chewing on various plants expectantly before spitting them out. Whatever it was that it wanted to eat, it had not found it yet.

She ushered the horse from the carousel and it joined its siblings on the ice, painted silver by the ripe, fat moon above. After an hour or so, the horses returned to their carousel with an air of reluctance and Rosa said goodbye to them before returning to Raven Hall. It was still dark, so she lit a lamp and was making her way up the staircase when she suddenly became aware of a person standing before her about halfway up, deep in a pool of shadow, staring out of the window. She let out a yelp of surprise before realising it was Eustace.

'What are you doing?' she demanded. 'You gave me a fright.'

Eustace said nothing, and did not acknowledge her presence at all. There was something strange and unnatural about the way he just stood there, alone in the dark. He wore only his nightshirt and his feet were bare. Rosa had no intention of touching him, but it was as crypt-cold as ever inside the house and she was certain his skin must be like ice. There was a marbled look about the back of his hands that reminded her of raw meat.

Suddenly uneasy, she looked around for her ravens and was reassured to see them lined up like sentries on the walnut bannisters, their red eyes staring out of the shadows, their cogs whirring and clicking as they kept all their attention fixed on Eustace.

'How long have you been here?' Rosa asked quietly.

This time he jumped at the sound of her voice, finally seeming to realise she was there.

'It is still my house, is it not?' he asked in a hoarse voice. 'And I am allowed to wander it as I wish? The ravens have not made that much of a prisoner out of me yet.'

Rosa shook her head. 'Of course you are not a prisoner. That is not what I meant.'

'Yet I expect you would see me in prison, if you had your way. You would condemn me for something I have not yet done. Something that I swear to you I would never do.'

His eyes were bloodshot and sunken in his face as he stared at her.

'You have got it all wrong,' Rosa replied. 'I do not condemn you for what you may still do, but for what you have already done – not just once, but many times. I believe the fortune in the plum, because of what I already know to be true about you. You condemned yourself.'

'I am no murderer,' Eustace replied. 'But *if* such a hideous thing were to happen, then it would only be because you drove me to it. Your devilish birds would have me fear for my life.'

'I have told you before,' Rosa said, 'the ravens will not harm you if you do not touch me.'

'Are you quite certain?' Eustace asked sharply. 'I spend more time with the ravens than you do. I have seen the way they look at me. They long for my blood, just as the real birds feast on their blood-soaked biscuits in the aviary. You've said before that your clockwork creatures have souls.'

Rosa was surprised that he had taken this in.

'You've said that once they're created they develop in ways you do not always anticipate. Well, it seems to me that these ravens of yours will kill me one of these days, and yet if I lift a finger to defend myself, then I am the one who is somehow at fault.' He gave her a sullen look. 'I have only ever wanted you to care for me. Is that too much for a husband to ask of his wife?'

Rosa shook her head. 'That is one of the most frightening things about you, Eustace. I thought it was an act at first, but I realise now that you honestly have not the least comprehension as to how badly you have mistreated me.'

His eyes slid to her in the dark. 'I am sorry about Cookie,' he said.

Rosa was shocked, both by the apology itself and by the fact that he had used Cookie's name – the first time she could ever remember hearing him do so.

'I regret losing my temper that day,' Eustace went on. 'I will not say I am a perfect husband, but you cannot pretend to be the perfect wife. You tricked me into marrying you.'

'*Tricked* you?'

'Well, what else would you call it? You are fond of referring to our marriage as a business arrangement. You got the title. I was supposed to get an heir.'

'You got my millions—' Rosa began.

'Useless!' He cut her off. 'I am not one of these debauched noblemen up to his eyes in debt, and I did not marry you for your money. I have fortune enough of my own. I wanted a wife who would provide me with a son. That was the bargain we made at the altar. You said your vows that day knowing what marriage entailed, I suppose? If you had no intention of playing your part, then you had no right to accept my proposal.'

'But I *did* intend to play my part,' Rosa replied. To her fury, she felt sudden tears prickle the backs of her eyes. 'I was happy and excited and looking forward to being your wife. If you had only been kinder, and gentler—'

'So the blame is all mine. Of course. I tried to love you.' A thin, whiny note crept into his voice and he looked at her with an expression that was both beseeching and bitter. 'You cannot deny that.'

He reached out suddenly and Rosa flinched back.

'It is not enough,' she said. 'Whatever small kindnesses you might have shown me were only to get me to do what *you* want – to behave, and speak, and dress as *you* wish me to. You care nothing for whether I am happy, or fulfilled, or content with my life. And therefore all your so-called considerations are worthless, Eustace. Just dust and ash in a long-cold hearth.'

'What a wretched, unnatural female you are,' Eustace said.

But his words did not have the power to hurt her any longer, and Rosa did not bother to respond as she went past him and up the stairs.

'I heard from Mother today.'

His words made her stop instantly.

'And?' she said.

'Ada is unwell.'

Rosa spun round. 'What do you mean, "unwell"?'

'It sounds as if she is even more stubborn and bad-tempered than usual. She has been refusing to eat. She cries for you incessantly. She has made herself ill.'

Rosa took a deep breath and clenched her hands together. This was unbearable. She would surely go mad.

'Ada needs me,' she said. 'She is not a bad girl – simply spirited. I'm the only one who understands her.'

'You have turned her into the spoilt creature she is,' Eustace returned. 'You would have her be just like you – a coarse, common American who has no place in the English aristocracy. Mother is trying to help Ada. She even sent for a doctor to purge her bad blood with leeches. She needs to be thoroughly cleansed of all the toxic humours you have put in her. It is so bad that one blood-letting had no positive effect at all. The doctor told Mother the treatment may have to be repeated many times. I am only telling you because I thought you ought to know that Ada has been asking for you.'

'And what did your mother tell her?'

'The truth. That you do not love her enough to make any sacrifices at all to get her back.'

'Curse you!' Rosa said, each word like a lump of lead in her mouth. 'Curse this house and your entire family. I wish I had never set eyes on you.'

Something in her tone unsettled the ravens, who shuffled around on the bannisters, their metal claws clicking over the polished wood. She walked past Eustace and went up the stairs to bed. How she loathed this place and that witch, Margaret. The thought of her touching her daughter was unbearable. Rosa must get her back somehow, she simply must. As soon as Ada was returned to her, the two of them would slip away into the night and never come back.

She needed to win that competition. Her hopes of being reunited with Esme would have to be set aside after all. Esme was gone, but Ada was living, and breathing. And not just a baby any more, but a stubborn, funny, prickly, naughty, lovely little girl who needed her. Rosa had been so confident of winning the competition previously, but the cold chill of uncertainty had crept into her ever since she saw Beatrice's plums and what they could do. Unpleasant as the experience was, the chance to put right a mistake you had not actually made yet was precious indeed.

For the first time she allowed herself to think about what would happen if she didn't win and the wish slipped through her fingers. Would Margaret return Ada eventually or would the weeks quietly slide into months and then years? Perhaps, in the end, the only way to get Ada back would be for Rosa simply to give Eustace what he wanted – the dreaded heir? How her skin crawled at the thought of it. Something inside her would die forever if she was forced to such a thing.

She would not give up. There must be something else she could do. She had exhausted her ideas for making her own garden more spectacular, but what if she somehow made Beatrice's garden less so? The thought came into her mind so suddenly that she felt adrenaline shoot through her. Could she sabotage Beatrice somehow? And if so, *would* she? It would be such a wicked thing to do, especially to a woman who had once been her friend. Yet Rosa's first royalty was not to Beatrice, but to Ada.

*She cries for you incessantly . . .*

Eustace's words echoed inside her head and Rosa felt something harden inside her. She would trample over a hundred friends to get her daughter back safely. Her little girl was all that mattered now. An idea slowly began to form in her mind. She longed to put it into action that very night. But the pink blush of dawn was already starting to stain the sky, and she knew it was too late today. It would have to be tomorrow.

*Soon,* she promised herself. *Soon I will have Ada back with me and we will be gone from this dreadful house of wings and wickedness.*

# CHAPTER THIRTY-SEVEN

A heavy weight seemed to press down upon Rosa for the entire day that followed. She wished she did not have to do such a thing and that her garden had been glorious enough to win on its own merits. Perhaps, even now, it still was. Perhaps the Spider Queen would prefer Rosa's carousel to Beatrice's plums. But she wasn't going to take any chances.

And so that night, when her garden closed at 4 a.m. and all her guests had left, she did not return to the house as usual, but departed from Raven Hall on a horse of her own. She saddled the mare herself, collected a large sack and her clockwork dragon and slipped out quietly. It was a half-hour ride to Half Moon House, the dragon flying in her wake and, as expected, everything was quiet when she arrived. Beatrice's garden closed much earlier and her guests had all departed hours ago. There was no one to stop Rosa from passing through the plum gate, with the clockwork dragon slinking along at her heels.

Later she told herself that she had not picked the dragon because of his fire. She'd picked him because he was more frightening than a raven, but less conspicuous than her clockwork bear. He could also keep up with her horse better and provide her with protection, should anyone find her there and try to restrain her whilst the police were called for. Certainly she never meant for anything in Beatrice's garden to be damaged or hurt in any way. Her plan was simply to steal the plums. She would keep them at Raven Hall and see that they were returned to Beatrice once the competition was over.

As she walked through the garden it seemed even lovelier than usual. Rosa delighted in every plant and flower, every butterfly and frog. The snow and ice shone silver in the moonlight and she was just as enchanted by it all as the first time she'd seen it. A black apple tree soon noticed her and came sidling over on its tentacle-like roots to see what she was doing. Rosa feared it might try to prevent her from going further, but perhaps it remembered her from earlier visits, for it only reached a spindly branch out in a friendly sort of way.

Finally, Rosa arrived at the grove of plum trees, shining and beautiful in the dark, casting their violet glow upon the supper booths and the ruffles and lace of the canopy

ALEXANDRA BELL

of parasols. And here she paused, the sack trembling slightly in her hands. Would she regret this later? Now that the ravens were released from the aviary, would this moment be the destiny she would find, if she were to eat another plum? The thought made her feel suddenly exhausted. Even if you managed to avoid one mistake, there would always be a hundred more ready to take its place.

But she had come all this way and there was no further time for hesitation. Another two black apple trees had appeared at the edges of the grove and there seemed a more watchful air to them now. Time raced on, and Rosa couldn't risk being interrupted. She opened up the sack and reached up for a nearby plum, sparkling at her in the moonlight. Her gloved hand closed around it and she plucked it from the branch.

The effect was immediate. Everything seemed to happen at once. The nearest black apple tree whipped out a branch and wrapped it so tightly around her arm that its rough bark cut her skin and blood trailed down towards her elbow. Rosa cried out, but refused to let go of the plum. The clockwork dragon flew at once to her defence and a plume of white-hot flames blasted past so close that she felt the heat on her face.

'No!' she cried. 'Don't!'

But it was too late. The tree caught fire immediately, releasing its hold on Rosa and recoiling with a scream. It was a dreadful sound. Rosa had not known that a tree could make such a noise. It quickly brought the other black apple trees to them. They came scuttling from every corner of the garden, dragging their crooked bodies over to converge on the grove.

Rosa flew at the plum trees, stumbling through the snow, desperate to collect as many plums as possible. She would not be able to get them all, she realised that. Her hopes of quietly filling the sack with the fruit had vanished. But she could not have come all this way for just one single, solitary plum. She had to at least try to get more. Only the black apple trees fell upon her at once, and suddenly they were savage things, baring their teeth and hissing and drooling.

She suddenly felt that they would gobble her up if they could, tearing her apart with those monstrous teeth. Beatrice had told her once about how the trees could easily swallow a rabbit down whole. If the dragon had not been with her, then perhaps they would have done the same to her. But the clockwork beast roared out its fury and its white flames set the trees alight the moment they touched them.

One apple tree recoiled straight back into a plum tree and the fire spread to it instantly. After that, the other plum trees quickly caught alight too and the air became filled with purple fire and the smouldering smell of burning regret. The magical plums shrivelled upon the branches, their skins blackening and blistering.

Then, above the roar of the flames, a voice spoke her name and Rosa turned to see Beatrice standing behind her. She had pulled a cloak on over her nightgown, along with a pair of boots; her hair was long and loose down her back, and her mouth was twisted into a grimace of pain as she took in her burning trees and the clockwork dragon still blowing fire down upon them.

# CHAPTER
# THIRTY-EIGHT

Beatrice's opium dreams had been particularly unkind that day, and when she first emerged from the cruel cocoon of them, she could not quite tell what was real and what was a nightmare. She awoke to the smell of smoke and jerked upright in her bed to see the flicker and leap of dancing shadows across her bedroom wall. The crackle and spit of flames mixed with hideous, inhuman screams that surely must not be real, but part of some opium terror.

She leapt from her bed, staggered to the window and looked out upon a scene that filled her with a sickening horror. Her beloved black apple trees were all on fire, their dark branches bent and writhing beneath the flames like tortured, twisted limbs.

*Oh, please,* she thought as she threw on a cloak. *Please let this be an opium nightmare.*

There was simply no way that her garden could be on fire. After everyone had gone home for the night, she had ensured that all the lanterns and candles were extinguished, as always. It could not possibly be real. Certainly she could still taste the drug at the back of her throat, and even the house itself did not seem quite real to her as she made her way downstairs, past trees growing up walls, and flowers blooming through wallpaper, and spun chrysalises casting long shadows from the chandeliers. At one point she even thought she saw the tiger peering at her from the doorway of the library as she raced to the front door.

The moment she stepped outside, the cold hit her like a slap, and the shock of it helped clear her head. She saw at once that this was no dream. The garden really was on fire. As she ran round to the side of the house, her mind went to protesters. She received letters every day now from outraged people complaining about the garden. Letters filled with such heat. People did not like what they had seen in the plum rain, or they were devastated by some misfortune revealed by the stones, or else they felt it quite wrong that a woman should have opened such a garden in the first place. It would encourage impressionable young girls into the sciences, they said. Rosa's garden was not quite so bad because she was a married duchess, but Beatrice was a spinster, so what kind of example was she setting?

It had begun to seem as if there was no point to any of this. She had been so pleased and excited at the thought of sharing her discoveries, but it had been harder to delight and amaze people than she had anticipated. She was sure there were some who enjoyed what she had to offer, but plenty of others refused to find any wonder in the garden at all. And now someone had deliberately set out to try to damage it, and all her beautiful plants and flowers and animals were at risk. There was a purple light to the flames and the air smelled so strongly of regret that she almost gagged. She ran straight to the supper booths and there, in the middle of it all, was someone she had not expected to see.

'Rosa.'

Her heart lifted for a moment at the sight of her friend. It did not matter how or why she was there – here was someone who would help her put out the fire and would lend their support if whoever was responsible for the attack was still in the garden.

But then Beatrice saw the guilty look on Rosa's face as she turned round to look at her through the flames – one shining, perfect plum clasped in her gloved hand. She saw the clockwork dragon swoop overhead, heard the terrible whir and click of its clockwork as it roared more flames down upon her precious trees. And she realised there had never been anyone else in the garden but Rosa. The shock of the betrayal was like a punch to the gut. The violet flames, and black apples, and melting ice seemed to swirl around her as the world tilted from its rightful place.

'No!' Beatrice gasped under her breath. 'Oh, no! No!' Her eyes met Rosa's through the flames. 'H-H-How c-c-c-could y-y-you?'

In that moment she loathed the other woman, from the bottom of her soul. The words written on her plum stone back at the house played over and over again inside her mind and she wondered if this was the moment they spoke of.

'This . . . I didn't mean for this to happen,' Rosa said. There was real regret in her eyes, but she made no move to help, to try and put things right. Instead she called the dragon to her side and turned away. 'For what it's worth, I am sorry.'

And then she just walked away, her clockwork monster at her side, leaving Beatrice alone. The flames were no longer a fire, but an inferno – they did not nibble and lick at the trees, but tore along them ravenously, refusing to be extinguished even when the trees crumpled into the snow. There was no one to help and nothing that could be done, but that did not prevent Beatrice from running into the blaze.

The plum trees were already gone – nothing but piles of ash. The apple trees were stronger and had dragged themselves away from the rest of the garden so that the fire was contained, with no danger of it spreading to the delicate flowers, butterflies and other specimens on display. Beatrice ran to one of the nearby ice houses, grabbed a bucket and filled this with snow to hurl at the trees over and over again. Only it hardly seemed to do any good at all. Perhaps things would have been different if the servants had still been there, but Beatrice had made arrangements for them to stay in a nearby hotel after Half Moon House became largely uninhabitable. And one person alone was not enough.

She would never forget the sound that the trees made as they burned. She'd known that they had mouths and teeth and a tongue concealed beneath their bark, but she hadn't heard them make any kind of noise before. Those screams of pain seemed to brand themselves upon her soul as her dear childhood friends perished in the flames. Before her eyes flashed the image of the treehouses and swings they had built for her, the picnics they had shared, the games of hide-and-seek. The long summers that the trees had kept her company and had softened the sharp edges of her loneliness. All going up in smoke.

When all but one of the trees lay stretched out smouldering silently upon the snow like blackened corpses, Beatrice threw down her bucket and ran to the final tree, scooping up handfuls of snow and pressing it directly to the branches and bark. Sweat poured down her face and the skin of her hands blistered and burned, but she refused to give up.

As the pink light of sunrise kissed the winter sky, Beatrice finally slumped back against the apple tree. She was exhausted and her hands felt as if they were on fire, but there was still life in that final tree, although its bark was scorched and its roots were withered. She had no idea whether it would actually survive. She could hardly breathe through the agony of her burns, but far worse was the loss of her friends – the only ones she had ever known, apart from James and Rosa.

She could not bear to look at them twisted and charred upon the ground, but neither could she look away. Soot and ash felt gritty on her skin. Her lungs were full of smoke. Her heart was a gaping wound. A sob burst from her chest. But as she wept for the loss, she felt tendrils of guilt wrapping themselves around her – she had already shed more tears for the trees in five minutes than she had cried for her mother in almost twenty years.

The sweat beneath her nightdress seemed to freeze against her skin and her teeth chattered uncontrollably. Despite the heat of her burns, she was so cold that it was almost impossible to stagger to her feet. She wanted nothing more than to limp back to the house and climb into the clutching embrace of that opium fog – hopefully never to come out of it again. Had all the trees perished, then she certainly would have done so. But there was that one survivor and if it was going to live, then it would need all of her attention.

When Beatrice looked down at the tree her heart sank at the dreadful damage the flames had done. The bark had been stripped away entirely in places and its branches were stumps. It might already be that there was nothing she could do, but if it was at all possible to nurture it back to life, then Beatrice promised herself fiercely that she would.

She knelt by the side of the tree and rested her arm upon its side. 'I need to bandage my hands before I can help you, old friend,' she whispered. 'But I promise I won't be gone long.'

The tree twitched at her voice and feebly reached one of its charred branches towards her, rubbing it gently up and down her arm. She thought of the clockwork dragon and how she had first seen it in Rosa's garden, blowing a flame so hot that it even set ice on fire. She looked back at the dead trees and thought it was no wonder she had not been able to save them. They had never stood a chance.

Beatrice informed the police later that day, who visited her property and agreed to send someone to interview Rosa, but Beatrice had little confidence in them. Rosa would deny it, of course, and then it would be Rosa's word against Beatrice's. The last surviving apple tree required all her attention and so the rest of the day passed in a blur. She applied cooling poultices and remained by its side to whisper encouragement through the long hours.

Her rage was impotent and toothless, but all-consuming. It felt as if there was nothing else left inside her at all. Even the agony of her burnt hands made little impact. And she could not forget her own culpability in allowing the house to become so overrun that the live-in servants had left. Had they still been here, there would have been more people to help once the alarm was raised, and perhaps some of the other trees could have been saved.

She longed to go to Raven Hall and to . . . to . . . well, she hardly knew what. To hurt Rosa somehow, yes, and to take from her once-friend something she held dear so that she might know how it felt. Yet Beatrice knew well enough that this was a feeling Rosa was already familiar with. She felt the wounded-animal instinct to lash out, but she was at a disadvantage. There were no weapons to be found in her beautiful winter garden, nothing that could stand up against Rosa's ferocious clockwork beasts.

Beatrice slumped, feeling the great weight of defeat press down heavily upon her shoulders. Her servants had now cleared away most of the debris from the fire and closed up the plum gate. The garden could still open for its final night and guests could wander the candlelit paths, but the supper booths were gone for good and the smell of regret hung so heavily in the air that Beatrice felt sure no one would wish to stay for long. She fully intended to open one final time and at least try to limp over the finishing line, but she no longer had any confidence in her chances of winning. And the one certainty that burned clear and bright as a star within her was that Rosa was to blame. She had stolen the wish from her, and she must somehow be made to pay.

# CHAPTER
# THIRTY-NINE

*New Year's Eve morning, 1838*

Rosa had arrived back at Raven Hall in the darkness of early morning, her clothes and hair reeking of smoke and shame. The last few hours felt like a bad dream vividly recalled, and she shuddered as she remembered the screams of the trees that Beatrice loved so dearly. Oh, why had they lashed out at her like that? If they'd only let her take the plums, the dragon would never have attacked, and the fruit would all have been returned to Beatrice after the competition anyway.

Rosa felt a sudden sense of confused anger tangling with the guilt inside her. She knew, deep down, that she was to blame, but that only made her seek more desperately to put the blame elsewhere – with the apple trees for trying to stop her, with Eustace for driving her to such action in the first place, with the Spider Queen herself for offering the chance of a wish that Rosa must do dreadful things to try to win.

She was not cheered when she saw the boy with the withered arm disappearing before her on the staircase, ignoring her cry to stop and fleeing ahead of her into the Long Gallery. He had vanished by the time Rosa entered the room, and she was about to leave when she noticed the portrait of herself – the one Eustace had had commissioned when she became his wife. There was something not quite right about it, and for a moment she stared at the canvas, trying to work out what it was. It seemed that her eyes were a little too far apart in her face, and her hair was a shade darker than it should have been, and . . . and suddenly it was no longer her face at all, in fact, but Beatrice's.

Rosa felt herself start to tremble as she stared into the painted eyes of her old friend. The golden plaque at the bottom of the frame clearly read: *Beatrice Hamilton, the Twelfth Duchess of Chalkley.* That other life was still trying to push through this one, even after all Rosa had done. Her eyes stung from smoke and fatigue and she removed her soot-stained glove to rub at them with cold fingers. When she opened her eyes, the portrait was of her once again and her name was the one that appeared engraved upon the plaque. Yet as she stared at it, it seemed to Rosa that she could still see a trace of Beatrice hovering about her own painted mouth – another face on the canvas beneath her own, just waiting to come through.

Suddenly exhausted, she turned her back on the portrait and the painted eyes of the other unfortunate duchesses and went to her own bedroom. Once there, she went through to her dressing room, collapsed upon the chaise longue and stared at the plum in her hand. Was what she'd done worth it? Or had it achieved nothing at all? If sabotaging Beatrice's garden had been enough, then surely Beatrice's face would not be appearing in the gallery, and the other woman's son would not still be wandering the corridors? What more must she do? What *could* she do?

Rosa felt a sudden sense of despair that she would ever have Ada back in her arms again, warm and squirming and giggling, those small hands clasped about her neck. She wondered if her daughter would ever smile and laugh again, after whatever Margaret was doing to her – scolding, and beating, and bleeding; trying to force her into the same mould as Eustace. It was too much and a great sob racked her body.

For a wild moment she wondered whether she ought to walk down the corridor to Eustace's bedroom right now. Knock upon his door and tell him he could have his heir. She could feel in her soul that it would break something in her to willingly permit Eustace to lay a finger on her again and to lie beside him in those cold, clammy sheets. What kind of mother could she be, to Ada and any other children that resulted, if her own spirit was broken? Yet she must get Ada back, she simply must.

All of a sudden the bottom drawer of her dressing table started to rattle. Rosa frowned. The only thing in there was the pop-up book. She stood up and set the plum down on the table before opening the drawer. The book lay still and innocent inside and she could see nothing that could have made the drawer shake. She reached in for the book. The last time she had looked at it, the carousel had stubbornly refused to appear, but now when she opened the cover it was there immediately, springing up before her, resplendent in its coat of icicles sparkling like twists of barley sugar in a sweet shop's window.

She read the same words once again, looking for new meaning in them – some clue as to what she could do to make her own carousel more than it already was – but no insights revealed themselves. Finally she sighed and removed her hand. And that was when Rosa noticed that her thumb had been covering something, right at the top of the carousel's peaked roof. A single plum sparkled there.

She stared at the page. She had spent many hours examining every inch of this spread whenever it had appeared, and she knew without doubt that the plum hadn't been there before.

Rosa's eyes went to the plum at her elbow – possibly the last one of its type in the world. She thought of the horse with the golden ribbon and how, from the moment it was created, it had seemed hungry for something. Could she finally have found the thing it was waiting for? Might this be the link that had been missing in order to turn the carousel into the one from the book? A new type of hybrid, built from a carousel that could take someone back to a past moment and a plum that could allow one to correct a mistake.

She was so tired and every limb longed for rest, but she could not delay testing her idea. She snatched up the plum, threw on her cloak and boots and went out to the frozen lake. The pink light of winter dawn touched its surface and painted the carousel in honeyed hues of buttery rose and gold. As Rosa approached, the horse with the golden ribbon lifted its head. Its ears began to twitch and its tail swished until finally it could bear it no more and stepped down from the carousel platform. The ice beneath its hooves created a perfect mirror, so that it looked as if a water horse echoed its movements in the freezing aquatic world below.

Rosa met the horse halfway across. There was a sense of expectation in the frosted air as it gazed at the plum in her hand. She held the sparkling fruit up to the clockwork creature, who sniffed at it for a moment before gently taking a large single bite. Purple juice stained the animal's muzzle as it chewed and swallowed, one bite after another, until the entire plum was gone, stone and all.

The horse snorted its satisfaction in icy puffs of air and tossed its head, its golden ribbon shining in the winter sunlight. It looked unchanged and Rosa wondered whether she'd misplaced her hopes after all. The horse turned away and pranced back to the carousel, with Rosa following slowly behind. The only way to know for sure was to test it. She pushed the lever to operate the carousel and then climbed up onto the platform.

The horse with the golden ribbon whickered as she climbed up onto its back. She picked up the reins and concentrated hard on the moment to which she wished to return. The carousel picked up speed around her, its music filled the air and then the icicles, and the horses, and the ribbons faded away, and she was no longer on the ice at all, but back in the parlour of her family's London town house.

Rosa sat on a high-backed sofa and Eustace had just bent down on one knee before her. 'I hope,' he said, 'that you will do me the great honour of becoming my wife.'

The memory was all just as Rosa recalled it. Whenever she had visited this moment in the past, she had tried to give a different response, but had always been compelled to utter the same one over and over again. Her mother had impressed upon her the importance of being decorous and dignified when accepting a proposal, but the utter thrill of having won a duke had caused Rosa to forget all that. She had leapt to her feet and almost knocked Eustace down with her embrace.

'Oh!' she had cried. 'I thought you would never ask!'

Try as she might, she had never been able to get the scene to play out differently in any way at all. Until now.

'I am not sure,' she said. 'I would like some time to think about it.'

Eustace looked surprised, but not as shocked as Rosa was herself. She had done it! Spoken entirely different words and acted in an entirely different way.

'Of course,' Eustace said, rising to his feet. 'It is a momentous decision.'

Rosa looked at him. 'Might I say anything at all?' she said, for her own benefit rather than his. 'Perhaps I can reject your proposal altogether?'

She could hardly believe she was able to speak such words. That she was actually rewriting a moment from her past. One of the greatest mistakes she had ever made in her life.

'That would be your prerogative, Miss Warren,' Eustace said, 'but I sincerely hope you will not do so.'

Rosa took a deep breath. She could undo it all, right here and now. She need never know the pain of Eustace's fingers pinching her skin, or the agony of losing Esme. There would be no hideous frozen carriage ride through the Alps, a journey that did not seem to end. There would be no tormented night-time wandering of Raven Hall's endless corridors. So much pain and suffering that she would never have to live through. But there would be no Ada, either.

'I will leave you to think,' Eustace said. 'Perhaps I might call again in a week?'

He gave her a stiff bow and then turned for the door. His voice was perfectly courteous and his expression pleasant enough, but Rosa could tell from the set of his shoulders that her response had displeased him.

'Wait,' she said, so softly that Eustace did not hear, and she was forced to repeat herself to get him to stop and turn round. 'I do not need time to think about it, after all,' she said. 'I have my answer already. And, yes. I should be honoured to become your wife.'

Eustace's lips parted, exposing his white, even teeth. 'My dear,' he said, 'you have made me very happy.'

And thus the moment stitched itself back together again, returning to the path it had been on previously. Eustace walked forward to embrace her but, to Rosa's relief, the scene faded away before he could get there. The townhouse disappeared and the sparkling carousel rose up in its place. The tune came to an end and the horses stopped. Rosa realised her undergarments were damp with sweat and she dismounted on trembling legs.

'We did it,' she whispered to her horse. 'We finally did it.'

At long last here before her was the Carousel of Icicles that she had first read about in the pop-up book. The one that must surely win her the competition.

'It had to happen,' she told the horse. 'Why else would you appear in the pop-up book?'

The horse had no answer, but quietly licked the last of the plum juice from its muzzle. The scent of smoke was still strong upon Rosa's clothes, and the sound of the trees screaming echoed inside her head in a way that would surely haunt her for years to come. Yet she no longer regretted taking that plum, or damaging the garden, or setting fire to the trees. She would burn down the entire world if it meant being reunited with her daughter. And now, just in time for the end of the contest, she had something truly wondrous to offer the Spider Queen.

# CHAPTER FORTY

Beatrice opened her garden that night as usual, but her hopes for the competition seemed to have settled into dust in her chest. She felt anxious for the safety of her animals and specimens without the black apple trees there to monitor the paths and protect them. Most people had behaved decently up until now, but as soon as the garden opened that evening she could sense that something had shifted in the atmosphere. She had said publicly that this would be the final night, and people were watchful and eager. Many of them wanted to take a piece of the garden home with them.

When Beatrice ventured out, she found herself inundated with requests to buy the various plants and animals. She gave the same answer every time – that the garden was not for sale. Some guests accepted this graciously, but others were disgruntled. Beatrice saw the resentment in their eyes and did not trust them not to slip flowers into their pockets, or usher teacup rabbits into the folds of their cloaks when no one was watching, especially as the supper booths were closed.

Frustration tangled her insides up into knots. Why could it not be enough for people to visit the garden and bask in its magic? Why must they insist on possessing a piece of it as well? She was glad the garden was only going to be open for one final night. She was tired of it all. What was the point? The only thing that held any interest for her now was finding some way to punish Rosa for what she had done. It was a relief when one o'clock came and the guests finally went home, leaving the garden quiet and peaceful once more.

Beatrice was just about to return to the house when she saw the white frog upon the path and froze. There were frogs in her garden, of course, but none like this. It wore a golden crown and stared up at Beatrice, taking her right back to that dark, lonely night as a child when she had seen the frog upon her pillow. This time the creature only paused for a moment before hopping off down one of the lesser-used paths.

Beatrice followed. Although this was her garden and she'd walked through it many times, it felt strange without the black apple trees. She thought at first perhaps that was why this path seemed oddly unfamiliar to her. It twisted right when she expected it to twist left, and wound past mushrooms and snails when she had anticipated flowers and fountains.

She had thought they were heading towards one of the garden's dead ends, but then the path turned a corner and the white frog paused beneath an archway. Only it was not an arch Beatrice recognised. Her garden had two gates – the one covered in ice roses that formed the main entrance into the garden, and the one decorated in ordinary sugared plums that led to the supper booths. This gate was something entirely different. It was hung all over with keys.

They were a variety of sizes, from those tiny enough to fit into a lady's jewellery box, to heavy ones large enough to open a castle's door. The lantern light sparkled over their colours – gold and silver and white and black, cast in steel, and iron, and marble, and brass. Some were extraordinarily ornate, royal keys to unlock royal treasures, whilst others were plain and humble. Together they made up a beautiful array that took Beatrice straight back to playing with her mother's key chest. And as she walked closer, she realised that these keys were in fact the exact same ones.

She stared at the key with a gargoyle's head on the top that had always so fascinated her, and the tiny white one with the snowflakes etched into it, and the wooden one onto which she had carved her own name. There it was, her name looking back at her. How could this be? These were not just any keys. They were *her* keys. The ones she had thrown into the wishing well the day her mother died. So how could they also be here?

Beatrice looked at the frog, which had stopped and seemed to be waiting for her on the path just up ahead. She glanced back the way she'd come and it seemed even more unfamiliar than before. She saw the path was made from white marble rather than gravel. Had that been the case before? How had she failed to notice that the path beneath her feet was smooth and that her boots did not crunch over it? Either way, she knew there were no white marble paths in her garden. They were something from that other garden, the magical one that belonged to the Spider Queen.

She turned back towards the frog and passed beneath the gate hung with keys. Lanterns flickered from pines that she did not recognise, and gold spider webs sparkled from the branches, along with pink sugar mice and glass angels. And, most delightfully of all, she could see black apple trees up ahead, quite unharmed and reaching out their branches towards her. She now knew for certain that she was no longer in her own garden at all. Somehow, somewhere along the way, she had slipped into another one altogether.

As she hurried along, she kept her eyes fixed upon the white frog, its golden crown gleaming brightly in the starlight. And, suddenly, soft music caught her ears. Music she recognised from the Fire Gardens at Raven Hall. Music from the Carousel of Icicles.

# CHAPTER
# FORTY-ONE

Rosa's garden had never been busier than it was that final night. The queue for the carousel went all the way round the lake. There was a separate queue – even longer – for the horse with the golden ribbon, the only one that could take its rider back to change something from their past. The air above the carousel shimmered with multicoloured lights as small moments from the past rewrote themselves.

Rosa's New Year's Eve gown was one of the most beautiful she had ever worn. Made from pale-blue satin, it was bordered in luxurious swansdown, with a low corsage and sleeves that fitted tightly to the elbow before opening into dramatic long folds that were edged with more swansdown and cascaded halfway down Rosa's skirts. A golden headdress flashed in the firelight, studded with rows of icy diamonds that matched the jewels at Rosa's throat.

Eustace did not appear in the garden for its last opening. Rosa had left the ravens behind with instructions to keep watch over him, but had not confined him to his room, or even the house. He had chosen to confine himself. He was the subject of much gossip now and she guessed he did not wish to suffer the curious, scandalised glances. He would probably keep his curtains firmly drawn and stay well away from the windows. But that did not prevent the guests glancing frequently up at the house, hoping to catch a shadowed glimpse of the disgraced duke.

The hours sped by in a swirl of champagne and starlight until, finally, midnight was upon them and the guests all quietened to bid goodbye to the old year and welcome in the new one. Rosa stood to one side, rigid with hope and dread. What if it wasn't enough? Surely Beatrice would not win the competition now, but what if, after all this, someone else triumphed instead? One of the other gardens in Paris or Venice perhaps? One with jars of moonlight or precious mermaid pearls . . .

The hush deepened as Rosa's garden clocks chimed out the hours. The new year rolled in and her guests cheered and celebrated, but there was nothing to suggest that Rosa had won. There was no hint of the competition coming to an end at all. That night her garden closed shortly after midnight and it was a relief to be alone in the grounds at last when everyone had finally left.

Rosa lingered alone outside, and the clocks had just chimed once for one o'clock when she spotted a white frog upon the path in front of her. It stood out, not only because there were no real animals in Rosa's garden, but also because of the fact that it wore a shining golden crown upon its head. It stared right up at her before turning and hopping away down the path, towards the dark walk.

Rosa hurried after it into the darkness of the Scots pines. As she followed the path, something began to change. The trees lengthened and became spindlier until they were no longer pines at all, but some other tree that Rosa didn't recognise. Certainly she could not recall ever having seen trees like this in the grounds of Raven Hall.

And then Rosa saw tracks in the snow up ahead and stopped. They were like cat's paw prints, only far larger than those of any cats that might live in England. These looked big enough to belong to a leopard or a panther – or perhaps a tiger. The trees around her were hung with sugar mice and glass angels and white spiders spinning golden webs. Rosa realised she was no longer in her own garden at all. Everything around her was painted powder-blue in the light from the fat moon overhead and there was a gate covered in dozens of keys emerging on the path before her.

Excitement thrummed in her chest. Could this mean . . . ? Might she actually have won . . . ? She hastened after the frog, through the gate and, gradually, a familiar tune drifted to her through the trees. It was, unmistakeably, the melody from her carousel. The next moment she followed the frog from the trees and there it was. The Carousel of Icicles stood before her in the middle of a clearing, revolving slowly as it sparkled in the moonlight. Rosa hurried towards it so quickly that she did not even see the little crooked well that she passed at the edge of the trees.

She had left her carousel in the grounds of Raven Hall, and yet somehow here it was. Her own sign stood in front of it, explaining what the carousel could do, with the updated information about the horse with the golden ribbon. And, immediately below, was a new plaque that read: *The Carousel of Icicles – Winner of First Place.*

Rosa stared until the words made her eyes ache. Had she really done it? She looked up and stared around the clearing, hoping to catch a glimpse of the Spider Queen in her cobwebbed gown, coming to present her with her prize. But there was no one. Even the frog had vanished. It was just Rosa and the carousel. She closed her eyes tightly for a moment. The magic garden was real. That surely must mean that wishes were too:

*I wish for Ada back.*
*I wish for Ada back.*
*I wish for Ada back.*

The carousel came to a stop and the music faded away into silence.

'Ma?'

Rosa jerked at the sound and opened her eyes to see her small daughter clinging to the back of the horse with the golden ribbon. She wore her bonnet and cloak and was staring right at her, tears filling her eyes.

'Ma!' she exclaimed again – the only word she knew how to say.

'Ada!'

Rosa ran across the snow, leapt onto the platform and scooped her straight from the horse.

'Oh, my darling!' She held the girl close. 'There you are. We will never be parted again, I promise.'

Ada looked smaller and thinner than the last time Rosa had seen her, and she worried that her daughter might shrink away from her, that all her patient work spent building the bond between them might have been picked apart by the dowager duchess's cruelty. But Ada immediately wrapped her arms around her mother's neck and held on tightly.

'Don't worry, honey,' Rosa said. 'We're together now and all will be well.'

An angry sense of triumph mixed with a proud delight in her veins. She had really done it. Ada was back with her and it no longer mattered what she had had to do to get here, or what would happen next. For now, she was right where she wanted to be.

But then someone spoke her name, and when she looked up she saw no Spider Queen at the edge of the clearing, but Beatrice Sitwell instead. And she was surrounded by black apple trees.

# CHAPTER
# FORTY-TWO

Beatrice gave the order to the trees unthinkingly, forgetting, for a moment, that they were not her old childhood friends. Yet for some reason they obeyed her instantly and swarmed across the clearing and onto the carousel. Their spindly branches wound like nooses about the horses' throats, their roots tangled up the icicle poles and the horses' hooves, and their teeth snapped at Rosa, who shrank back from them and held Ada close as she hurried to climb down from the platform.

In that moment Beatrice did not care why the child was there, and she didn't care if she was frightened by the trees. All she wanted was to tear Rosa's creation limb from limb. The horses gave tinny shrieks of fear as the trees wrapped themselves tighter around the carousel. The fact that it was here in the garden told Beatrice that her old friend had won, even without seeing the plaque proclaiming it so. But then her eyes took in the sign above it and she called out for the trees to stop. They froze upon the platform, branches poised and teeth bared, ready to bite and tear at a word from Beatrice.

'Is it t-true?' Beatrice whispered. 'C-Can the h-horse really ch-change a past m-moment?'

'Yes,' Rosa said. 'It is true. But, Beatrice, what is going on here? Those trees aren't yours. Why are they listening to you?'

Beatrice barely heard the question. All that mattered was the carousel in front of her. Suddenly she realised that perhaps it might be all right after all. She did not need the wish. She could use the carousel to put things right. She took a step towards it, her boots crunching over the deep snow, but then Rosa's voice cried out in a strange, shrill tone she had never heard her use before.

'Beatrice, you mustn't! I know you don't believe me, but you must not! Whatever it is you wish to change, it will lead to your being married to Eustace instead of me.'

Beatrice stopped and tore her eyes from the carousel to look at Rosa. She was vaguely surprised that the child in her arms wasn't crying, but was staring at the black apple trees with an expression of interest rather than fear. Rosa, however, looked frightened enough for both of them.

'I wish only to s-say g-goodbye to my m-mother. That would not ch-change my wedding d-day.'

'Somehow it does,' Rosa insisted. 'Perhaps your mother would say something to you during that final conversation that somehow ripples down the years and affects what you do later. We never know what the consequences of each action might be, or how far they will reach.'

*The world is a difficult place to be a woman . . .*

Her mother's words from years ago echoed inside Beatrice's head now.

*Do not allow yourself to be bullied into unhappiness . . .*

She shook her head. 'Mama w-would approve of h-how I acted.'

Indeed, it had been the memory of her mother that had given her the final push she needed that day, to defy expectation and reject that life. To finally take a stand, to protect her own happiness.

'He has a withered arm!' Rosa blurted out.

Beatrice froze as a feeling of dread crept slowly over her. 'Who?'

'The boy. Your son. Oh, if you saw yourself married to Eustace in the plum rain, then you must have seen him too! Why didn't I think of it before? He's here with us now – I can describe him to you! He's about eight years old and . . . and he said that you do not want him. He said that you told him so every day—'

*'Stop!'*

The word burst from Beatrice so forcefully that she did not even stutter. She could not bear Rosa to go on. Her head ached as she stared across the snow at her old friend.

How could this be? Rosa could not have guessed about the withered arm. She could not have guessed that Beatrice said such wicked things to her little boy – told him every day that she did not want or love him.

'Beatrice,' Rosa said softly. 'He is so very sad. And he doesn't want to be here. You will bring him to life if you ride the carousel.'

Beatrice gazed at the prancing horses and could no longer be completely sure that Rosa was lying. Perhaps she was correct, and putting things right with her mother would lead to her marrying Eustace somehow. But, in that moment, Beatrice didn't care.

'Surely you would *w-want* me to ch-change the past in that w-way,' she said. 'It would f-free you. You would m-marry someone else. H-Have other ch-children—'

'I don't want other children!' Rosa exclaimed. 'I want the one right here with me! The one I have loved and cherished for over a year! The children I loved in some other life aren't here. Ada is.'

'But y-you would not know the d-difference—'

'Not if you rip it all from me, but I know the difference *now*, and I can fight for Ada *now*! I know it's a mess of a life. I know I made all the wrong decisions. But it is my life even so, and the joy could not have come without the sorrow, so I will accept both, and gladly.' Her voice lowered. 'Please. I don't want to think any more about what might have been or should have been. We have only what is right in front of us now. Think of my daughter.

She has no one to cherish her but me. She was born into so much darkness, yet she is . . . the best thing ever to have happened . . .'

Rosa trailed off hopelessly. Words were not adequate and she despaired of being able to make Beatrice understand how much she loved this small person.

'I think perhaps the carousel was a mistake. You see, there would be no end to it,' she struggled on. 'Every life has its imperfections and mistakes. You change one decision and later on down the line there would be another one. For better or worse, this is *my* life, and these are my mistakes, and I want it all.'

'Th-that is because your g-greatest mistake l-led to your g-greatest h-happiness,' Beatrice replied. 'N-Not so f-for m-me.'

'Perhaps it will one day,' Rosa said. 'Perhaps it's simply that you haven't found your greatest happiness yet. It could be just around the corner.'

Beatrice was already shaking her head.

'Wonderful things can come out of our darkest times,' Rosa said in a hoarse tone. 'I truly believe that. And it doesn't mean that we invite misfortune, or want to make mistakes or be unhappy. It only means that we refuse to be beaten down by whatever life throws our way, and we don't stop until we find ourselves in the place where we can rest and be content. I haven't found it yet. But I will. I will.'

'You c-cannot know that,' Beatrice returned. 'S-Some people s-spend their whole lives l-looking and are s-still. Doomed. To misery.'

'Not me,' Rosa said fiercely. 'Surely if there's one thing your plum trees prove, it's that there is no way to live a perfect life free from suffering, but there are a hundred different ways to be happy. Take James.' She swallowed hard, trying to keep a grip on her yearning for a man who would never be hers and a life that was no longer possible. 'We were happy together – in that other life I saw in the plum rain. But he's happy in this life too, with her . . . with Jani.' Saying her name aloud seemed to break some kind of inner dam, and Rosa felt the waves of jealousy, and sorrow, and loss crash into her over and over again, so that she had to grit her teeth and focus all her willpower on not being taken down by them. 'There is no one perfect life,' she said quietly. 'And no one perfect soulmate. There must be hundreds . . . thousands of different people who happen to be on this earth at the same time as us and who we could find joy with. There's happiness waiting out there for me somewhere, I know it, and I won't rest until I find it. I want someone to share my life with, someone who will love Ada and me the way we deserve to be loved. I've learned the hard way that we look for happiness in all the wrong places and put importance on all the wrong things. And you were right. But your garden also taught me that good things can come from hardship, that a poinsettia needs periods of darkness for its leaves to turn that beautiful red—'

'P-people are not p-plants,' Beatrice replied sadly. 'If I r-ride the carousel I can f-fix all our p-problems. Both yours and m-mine.'

'But that isn't true!' Rosa exclaimed. 'How can you say such a thing? It would not fix your problems at all. You've seen what life with Eustace would be like. You've seen the misery you would live in.'

Beatrice shrugged and her tone was impatient. 'I l-live in m-misery now! At least this w-way I would have m-made my m-m-mother happy when it m-mattered. And I w-would h-help you t-too—'

'Surely you do not have such little regard for yourself that you will meekly surrender to unhappiness in such a cowardly manner?'

'C-C-C-Cowardly?' Beatrice could barely utter the word. The very suggestion of it infuriated her. It was so very unfair. 'I am p-prepared to m-make a g-great s-s-sacrifice—'

'For who, Beatrice? Certainly not for me. I tell you I don't want your sacrifice, and your mother wouldn't want it, either. She would want you to live the best life you can.'

Beatrice glared at Rosa. How dare she presume to understand anything at all about a woman she had never even met?

'Y-You c-cannot sp-speak for her—'

'But I *can*, because she was a mother who loved you, and that's all I need to know about her to tell you this one thing: that she wouldn't want you to do this. So if you go ahead anyway, don't delude yourself into thinking that you're doing it for me, or for her. You'd be doing it for yourself.'

Beatrice's head ached more than ever and she longed to clench her fists, but dreaded splitting her burned skin. She could feel the weight of the plum stone in her pocket, and the mistake engraved upon it: *You will regret not listening to Rosa when you know her words are true.*

'I am s-so angry,' she whispered. 'All the t-time.' The words were inadequate. She pressed a palm to her chest and she could feel the anger pulsing and throbbing in there, yearning to get out and destroy everything in sight. She could give the word to the black apple trees and they would tear the carousel apart. She didn't know why they should obey her commands – perhaps they remembered her from the previous garden – at any rate she could feel that she had only to give the order and they would break apart everything in sight. Yet suddenly she felt exhausted with anger, exhausted with her own bitterness and self-loathing. Perhaps Rosa was right. Perhaps her mother would not have wanted such a sacrifice from her. The other life she had glimpsed in the plum rain had already proved to Beatrice that she was not cut out to be a mother herself, nor had she ever experienced any desire to be one.

She felt, deep down, that Rosa spoke the truth and she could not deny the words written upon her own plum stone. She walked over to the carousel steps and sat down in sudden defeat.

'You w-won the c-competition,' she said, staring at the snow rather than at Rosa. 'You w-won the w-wish. And you have t-taken. Everything. From me.'

'But what has she taken?' a new voice asked.

It was a voice Beatrice recognised, and she looked up to see the Spider Queen emerging from the trees and walking towards them in her cobwebbed gown.

# CHAPTER FORTY-THREE

Beatrice rose slowly to her feet. The queen looked just the same as she remembered her. She clicked her long fingers and the black apple trees released the horses and climbed down from the carousel, shuffling away with a sheepish sort of air as they disappeared back into the forest.

'Rosa has not taken anything from you,' the Spider Queen said. 'The garden is yours. It has been from the start.'

'M-Mine?'

'Please,' the queen replied, taking a letter from the folds of her dress. 'Won't you read it now? Is it not finally time, after all these unhappy years?'

Beatrice glared at the letter. She recognised her own name upon the front, written in her mother's elegant handwriting, and her whole body trembled with both yearning and dread. It was a letter she had not thought to see again, and now she could not work out whether she wanted it or not. She recalled how the queen had tried to persuade her once before, as a girl, and the request had made her so angry that she had flown into a rage and destroyed things in the garden.

'The p-plums,' she said. 'Rosa s-stole—'

'The plums don't matter,' the queen said. 'The carousel would have won, either way. In fact I think I prefer it how it was before. It is a fine thing to be able to relive a precious moment from the past, but I don't believe it does anyone much good to spend time dwelling on old mistakes. If I were you, I'd remove the horse with the golden ribbon from the carousel when you take over the garden.'

Beatrice stared at her. 'T-Take over?'

'Why, yes. I just told you. The garden is yours.'

'That makes no s-sense,' Beatrice replied. 'If the garden is m-mine, then the w-wish should have b-been too.'

'But I already know what you would wish for,' the Spider Queen said. 'I felt it when you hurled this letter into the well all those years ago. You regret how things were left with your mother. You fear you hurt her.'

Beatrice felt sudden tears prickle her eyes. How unbearable it was to hear those words said aloud, each one a bell that rang with a dreadful truth. A deep flush crept over her skin and shame made her hot, despite the snow and ice.

'There were things your mother wanted to say to you,' the queen said. 'You would not hear them back then. But you should do so now. You owe it to her.'

The Spider Queen held out the envelope again and, this time, Beatrice took it, holding it awkwardly in her bandaged fingers.

'The words it contains are private.' The Spider Queen glanced at Rosa and said, 'Perhaps I could give you and your daughter a tour, Miss Warren? The garden's magic will be gone soon, and I should like to show it to someone one final time.'

Beatrice wanted to ask how the magic could possibly be running out, but her tongue was a lump of lead in her mouth and her priority was the envelope in her hand. Her name curled across it in her mother's familiar handwriting. The sight was so arresting to Beatrice that she barely registered the Spider Queen leaving the garden with Rosa and Ada.

She stared down at the letter. How many times had she wished to be reunited with it? And how earnestly had she desired to know what was inside? Here, at last, was her chance. Her fingers trembled inside the bandages and her movements were awkward as she ripped open the envelope and pulled out a sheet of creamy writing paper. The margins of the letter were filled with her mother's beautiful drawings, but it was to the words that Beatrice turned her attention first:

*My darling Beatrice,*

This is the hardest letter I have ever had to write. I wish so ardently that there was no need for it, but there are some wishes that simply do not come true, no matter how we might long for them to. Alas, a good life needs dark leaves in the wreath.

I had hoped to say some of this to you in person, but when you fled my room earlier today I realised you were not ready to hear such sentiments as these, and may not be for some while. And I can wait no longer. Even as I pen these words, I sense that time is almost gone. Perhaps it is better this way – better for the message to be set down more permanently, so that I might reach down through the years and speak to you as the young lady you will one day become. The young lady who, unhappily, I will never have the privilege to know.

Looking at those words on the page now, I'm struck again with the bitter unfairness of it all, as well as the impossibility of writing this letter properly. In a myriad of ways, it will be hopelessly inadequate and I hope you can forgive me for that. I shall do my best, and that is all anyone can ask, after all.

I wish that I could be here to see you grow up, to share in your joys and triumphs, and to offer what comfort I could in the heartaches and setbacks that will inevitably come your way. This is what every mother wants. This is the great tragedy of having to leave you so early.

I wish that we could have had more time together. I love you more than you will ever comprehend. I wish I could have seen you on your wedding day. I wish I could have been a large piece of your life and not present just for the start of it. I am sorry that I have to leave you. I am sorry for the confusion and loneliness that will follow in the days to come. I am sorry that I frightened you when you came into my sickroom. It was a mistake, perhaps, to try to say goodbye in person but, you see, adults make mistakes too sometimes, even mothers. Especially mothers, I suppose, as so much more is required of us.

As time passes, I fear you will look back on our final meeting with pain and regret, and that you will feel guilty about the way we parted. My darling, I beg that you will not do so. If there were things you later thought you would have liked to say to me, rest assured that I already knew them. I knew them all. Sometimes things do not need to be said out loud. When you think of me, do not dwell on those final moments between us. If anyone is to blame for those, it is me – and me alone. Think instead of our time in the gardens at our beloved Half Moon House. How I wish we could have created that garden together, just as we planned. I wish I could have left you with a special place that you could go to watch the fairies dance, and talk with the Spider Queen, and taste magic, and be truly yourself.

My dear, I know that sometimes you feel unseen and unheard. This world is not an easy place to be a girl, or indeed a woman. But my keenest hope is that you will one *day make a good match, marry well and have children of your own. You have been my greatest joy in this life and I long for you to experience such feelings too. There can be no greater pride on this earth than the one that comes from being a good wife and mother.*

*And now, my dearest, I fear I must lay down my pen and can only hope that this letter will bring you some comfort. Be kind to your father and forgive him his faults. He will do his best.*

*All my love, always,*
*Mama*

Beatrice's eyes were so full of tears that at first she couldn't understand why her vision began to sparkle. But then she looked up and saw the Tiger of Stars stretched out upon the carousel platform above her. She leapt to her feet and the next moment he padded down the steps, reared up onto his hind legs and placed his huge paws on Beatrice's shoulders. Her hood fell back as she looked up at the tiger. He stood a head taller than her, and there was such absolute wildness in his eyes that a person could be forgiven for fearing he might rip out their throat with a single swipe. But Beatrice wasn't afraid and raised her arms to wrap them tightly around the beast's body, hugging him close, delighting at the huff of his breath in her ear and the icy diamond-fire smell of him. He was as cold as space, but

Beatrice did not shiver as she blinked the tears from her eyes and ran her hands down his galaxy stripes.

'Hello, my old friend,' she whispered.

They stood like that for a few moments more before the tiger returned to all fours. Beatrice gazed at the letter in her hand and took in the pictures in the margin. She saw that her mother had sketched fairies in fur coats, and frogs in golden crowns, a tiger made of stars and a beautiful lady wearing a crown and a cobwebbed gown.

*I wish I could have left you with a special place that you could go to watch the fairies dance, and talk with the Spider Queen, and taste magic, and be truly yourself . . .*

'My mother's wish brought this place to life,' she said softly.

Finally she understood why she had been the first visitor, and why she was the only person the tiger would allow to touch him. It was wondrous and the letter made her so happy and yet, at the same time, so very sad. Her whole life she had believed that her mother was the only person who'd understood her completely, yet if she had thought marriage and children could ever make Beatrice happy, this letter proved that not to be so.

But perhaps it was not possible ever to truly understand another human being. You were forever looking at them through the prism of your own experience. And all that really mattered was that she had not wounded her mother as grievously as she had always believed. Her mama had died knowing she was loved.

Beatrice sat back down on the carousel steps and the tiger settled himself in the snow at her feet. She wasn't sure how long she sat there in the clearing. It seemed an endless, timeless moment, with only her, the tiger and the clockwork horses. But finally the Spider Queen returned with Rosa and Ada, both of whom wore the same expression of utter enchantment that Beatrice knew she had worn herself when she first visited the Winter Garden.

'You have read it?' the Spider Queen asked in a kindly tone, indicating the letter in Beatrice's hand.

She nodded.

'There did not seem much point in staying at Half Moon House before,' the queen said gently. 'I realised you were not ready to read the letter, so I decided to return when the time was right. I did not think you would mind sharing your garden with other lost souls in the meantime.'

Beatrice stood up and walked over to the others, the tiger following in her steps. 'What did you m-mean about the m-magic?' she asked.

'A garden must have a botanist if it is to thrive,' the Spider Queen said. 'The garden has lived in your mother's vision for this long, but the magic has been slowly draining out of it. Many of the plants and animals have already gone, and my own time here is almost over. It will soon be an empty space for you to fill as you wish.'

'F-For *me* to f-fill?' Beatrice asked, startled.

'Of course. It is your garden, after all. Why do you imagine I set the competition when I did? And invited you, even though the wish was not destined to be yours? You must have other items to replace those that will soon be lost. Rosa's creation was, I thought, the most wonderful, but there were plenty of other extraordinary offerings, and you must see them all for yourself. I have recorded all the details for you as to where in the world you might find them. You will need people to help you rebuild the garden, and I sent invitations to only the best in their fields. And then, of course, I expect you will take the garden and explore the world yourself. Assuming that is what you want.'

Beatrice could find no words. It was the only thing she had ever wanted – to make extraordinary discoveries and share them with those who would appreciate them.

'Th-Thank you,' she finally said.

'The wishing well will remain,' the Spider Queen said. 'Although there is no magic left in it now. If you go down that path,' she pointed at one winding into the trees, 'it will return you to the Key Gate, and thus anywhere you wish to go. You have only to think of the place and the garden will take you there.'

'Anywhere?' Rosa asked eagerly. 'You mean . . . Ada and I need not return to Raven Hall?'

'Not if you do not wish to.'

'B-But all your p-possessions and c-clockwork are there,' Beatrice said. 'Do you m-mean s-simply to l-leave it all?'

'I have everything that I need right here,' Rosa said, tightening her grip on Ada. 'We will start again somewhere else. Somewhere Eustace won't ever find us.'

'What about y-your f-family?' Beatrice asked. 'In America?'

Rosa shook her head. 'My mother would not accept me back,' she said.

'Then wh-where will you g-go?'

'I don't know.' Rosa laughed, a strange mixture of relief and a sort of hopeless dread. How would they manage? She had no money and nowhere to live. Perhaps the sensible thing would be to return to Raven Hall after all, yet something told Rosa that if she returned to that house now, she would never come out of it again. She would not take Ada back there and risk Eustace snatching her away a second time. Nor would she risk being murdered at his hand.

She straightened her shoulders and turned to face Beatrice. 'I did you a great wrong,' she said. 'I know that, and I hope you can forgive me. For what it's worth, I did not mean for your apple trees to be hurt and I am truly sorry. I know I have destroyed our friendship and that you do not owe me anything.'

'And yet you w-will ask for s-something anyway?' Beatrice guessed.

Rosa's eyes went to the nearby wishing well. 'Might I make one final wish? I know the magic is gone, but I would dearly like to wish for one last thing, here in this special place.'

Beatrice hesitated, wondering if she ought to refuse out of spite. But the hatred had become too heavy a burden to bear and she found she was suddenly glad to put it down. She nodded and the Spider Queen took a coin from her pocket to hand to her.

Rosa carried Ada over to the well and handed the coin to her. 'Would you like to throw it in, darling?'

With a solemn expression, the little girl did so, and Rosa whispered the wish aloud.

'I wish to be a good mother.'

'Then you will be,' the Spider Queen said behind her. 'Even without the wishing well.'

Rosa laughed, but it was an unhappy sound. She turned round. 'It's as easy as that?'

'Easy? Why, whoever said anything about it being easy? I have no doubt there will be bleak moments when you give in to despair, and when you will feel out of your depth and just exhaustingly, achingly bone-tired. That is the way of motherhood.'

'But then . . . how can wishing to be a good mother ever be enough?'

The Spider Queen lifted a shoulder in an elegant shrug. 'You did not wish to be a *perfect* mother. Such a thing is, I fear, not possible, even with all the magic from all the wishing wells in all the world. For mothers are human beings too and thus destined to be imperfect.'

'What a pity,' Rosa said.

'Is it?' The Spider Queen looked quite shocked. 'If I had ever had a child, I would wish for them to see me work on my flaws and recover from my mistakes. How else are they to learn? My goodness, what a hard thing it would be to grow up beneath the shadow of a perfect mother. No, no, my dear, do not ever wish for that. Wish instead to be a good mother. Perfection has no place in such things. And, now, I must leave you. It was a great pleasure to make your acquaintance, Miss Warren, and congratulations again. Your carousel is astonishing. I think it will bring much happiness to many people.' She turned to Beatrice and took both her hands in her own. 'Good luck. I hope you will find some joy in this life. If you would like to continue to share a little of the garden's magic with those who need it most in the world, then you can find the names of all those people who are lost and lonely, hurting and heartsore, in the *Book of Lost Souls*.'

'Where will y-you go?' Beatrice asked, but the queen was already fading before her eyes like a ghost.

She smiled. 'Back where I came from, of course.'

The last word was a whisper and then she was gone, leaving only a few threads of sparkling web drifting behind her in the starlight. Beatrice looked up at Rosa.

'I wish you h-had not h-hurt my trees,' she said. 'But I understand that – to m-most people – a ch-child is more important than a p-plant. And you were r-right to stop me r-riding the carousel. It w-would have led to us s-swapping lives. And I c-could not l-love my s-son. I d-do not think I c-could ever be a g-good m-mother, but especially not married to Eu-Eustace . . .'

'I understand,' Rosa said, and Beatrice saw that she did. 'I understand what it would have been like for you.'

Beatrice nodded and glanced around the clearing. 'The b-boy,' she said, and Rosa wondered why she did not use his name, then realised that she did not even know it herself. 'Is he . . . ?'

'He's gone,' Rosa said. 'I don't think he will be coming back.'

Beatrice released her breath in a sigh. 'Good. That is. Best.'

The tiger padded through the snow to her now and brushed his starlight stripes against her skirt. Beatrice rested her hand upon his head, and Rosa thought it was the first time she had ever seen her friend look at ease in the world.

'Well,' Rosa said. 'We should leave. Thank you again. I hope you fill the garden with magic once more.'

'I w-will,' Beatrice said. She looked thoughtful as she drew a silver flask from her pocket and walked forward to throw it into the well. They heard the splash as it hit the water below, and then Beatrice turned back to Rosa.

'Would you. Help me?'

Rosa looked startled. 'Me?'

'You s-said you would s-start again. And I know you will n-not be here l-long. Your p-place is the r-real w-world – to find that h-happiness you spoke of. But p-perhaps the g-garden might sh-shelter you both f-for a while? Perhaps we m-might be f-friends. As we w-were. Before.'

Rosa smiled slowly. 'Oh, Beatrice. I should like that more than anything.'

# CHAPTER
# FORTY-FOUR

*Six months later*

James Sheppard sat on the veranda of his home in India and scanned eagerly through the newspaper. It was the first thing he did every time a new English one was delivered, in the hope that it might contain some news about Rosa or Beatrice. Britain had been agog with the scandal of their disappearance for weeks, but the information had since dwindled away to nothing.

All that was known was that both women had vanished on New Year's Eve, as had Rosa's young daughter, Ada, despite the fact that she'd been in an entirely different country, staying with her grandmother in France. Many of the plants and animals of Half Moon House had also gone, along with Raven Hall's famous carousel.

It was common knowledge that the duke had consumed a fortune plum in Beatrice's garden a couple of weeks before and everyone knew the shocking thing it had revealed. Speculation was rife as a result, with many people believing that he had killed Rosa and hidden her body somewhere.

The duke had denied it and, given the lack of evidence, no arrest had been made, but it appeared that Eustace was not at all stable these days. He lived in such dread of the clockwork ravens his wife had left behind that he finally admitted himself to an asylum. Rumour had it that he insisted he could still hear the metallic whir of wings and scrabbling of claws even from the isolation of his padded cell.

That morning, as usual, there had been no fresh news in the paper.

'We might never find out what happened,' Jani said gently, and James knew she was right.

Yet still . . . The not knowing was a torment to him and he often woke from nightmares in which Rosa called to him from beyond the grave.

But that evening Jani came in from the orange groves and said she had something to show him.

'What is it?' James asked, reaching out to draw her closer to him. They were expecting their first child within the month and whenever he looked at Jani he felt a surge of excitement mixed with fear. What mistakes would he make? Would he be a good father, in the end? Would his efforts be enough?

'It's a snail.' Jani opened her hands for him to see the clockwork snail nestled within her palms. Its golden shell was studded with sparkling jewels and its tiny metal antennae waved in the breeze. 'Do you remember?' Jani asked. 'Miss Warren said she would make me one.'

'Where did you find it?'

'It was on my favourite seat in the grove.'

'Was there a note with it?'

'Just this.'

She held out a thick white piece of card. The words on it read simply: *For Jani. Love him well. R.*

'So, you see, she must be alive,' Jani said, squeezing his shoulder. 'And if she is, then perhaps Lady Beatrice is also.'

'Yes.' James stared at the snail. It was unmistakeably Rosa's work. No one else could possibly create such beautiful, intricate clockwork. He felt a great weight lift away from him as he looked at it.

Later that evening he stood smoking a final cheroot on the veranda, looking out over the view that he would never tire of. He did not hear Jani step out behind him as he put out his cigarette and said quietly, 'Good luck, Cogs.'

'Who's Cogs?'

'Oh.' He looked round at his wife, then shook his head. 'Just someone I knew once. I don't imagine I'll see them again.' He held out his hand to her. 'Come on, my darling. Let's go for a walk, whilst there's still some daylight left.'

# ACKNOWLEDGEMENTS

Many thanks to the following people:

My agent Thérèse Coen and everyone at the Hardman and Swainson Literary Agency for being such great champions of my books.

Gillian Green for encouraging the idea for the Winter Garden and working with me to flesh out the concept and characters.

My editor, Sam Bradbury, for helping me to refine and improve the finished book. And to Mandy Greenfield for copyediting.

Designer, Emma Grey Gelder, and illustrator, Charlotte Day, for the beautiful cover art.

I've always appreciated a lovely garden, but never more so than during 2020 when it seemed like visiting one was one of the few remaining pleasures that was permitted and safe. Many thanks to the following for the solace their gardens offered during the pandemic: Hinton Ampner House, West Dean Gardens, Sir Harold Hillier Gardens and – best of all – the magical winter wonderland at West Green House Gardens.

I wrote part of this book whilst pregnant with my first baby and continued working on it in the months after my son was born. Motherhood forms such an important part of this novel, and the events of 2020 meant I was even more grateful to all the mothers who helped and supported me during that time:

Most importantly, my own mum, Shirley Bell, whose example I aspire to live up to every day. In addition, many thanks to:

My mother-in-law, Shirley Dayus.

My good friend, Fozia Cheychi.

My author mums, Sophie Cameron, K. L. Kettle, Amy McCaw, Ali Standish, Laura Steven.

My Frenglish yoga mums, Amy Lunn and Gaëlle Jolly.

And, finally, many thanks to my husband, Neil Dayus, for taking over various chores and responsibilities whilst I was busy writing this book. And to my son, Cassidy, for teaching me what it is to be a mum.

# ABOUT THE AUTHOR

Alexandra Bell was born in 1986. She studied Law at university and signed her first book deal at nineteen. Since then, she has written books for both adults and young people, including the Polar Bear Explorers' Club series and *Frozen Charlotte*, which was a Zoella bookclub pick, under the name Alex Bell.

She lives in Hampshire in a house ruled by Siamese cats.

Website: alex-bell.co.uk
Twitter: @Alex_Bell86
Instagram: @Alex_bell86